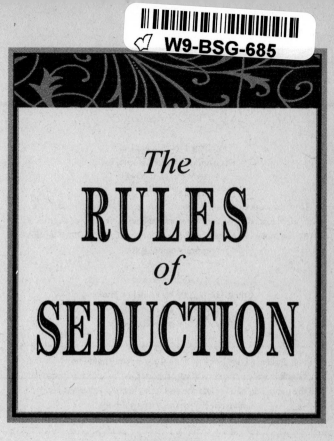

The
RULES
of
SEDUCTION

Madeline Hunter

A DELL BOOK

THE RULES OF SEDUCTION

A Dell Book / November 2006

Published by Bantam Dell
A Division of Random House, Inc.
New York, New York

This is a work of fiction. Names, characters, places, and incidents
either are the product of the author's imagination or are used fictitiously.
Any resemblance to actual persons, living or dead, events, or locales
is entirely coincidental.

Dell is a registered trademark of Random House, Inc., and
the colophon is a trademark of Random House, Inc.

ISBN-13: 978-0-553-58732-6
ISBN-10: 0-553-58732-3

Printed in the United States of America
Published simultaneously in Canada

www.bantamdell.com

OPM 10 9 8 7 6 5 4 3 2 1

"In yet another excellent offering from Hunter, her intriguing characters elicit both fascination and sympathy."—*Booklist*

THE SAINT

"[An] amusing, witty, and intriguing account of how love helps, not hinders, the achievement of dreams."—*Booklist*

THE SEDUCER

"Hunter . . . sweeps both her readers and her characters up in the embrace of history. Lush in detail and thrumming with sensuality, this offering will thrill those looking for a tale as rich and satisfying as a multi-course gourmet meal."
—*Publishers Weekly*

"*The Seducer* is a well-crafted novel. . . . characteristically intense and frankly sexual."—*Contra Costa Times*

"[An] intriguing and redemptive tale."—*Booklist*

"Angst and passion battle it out in this very sensual story."
—*Oakland Press*

LORD OF A THOUSAND NIGHTS

"Hunter's fresh, singular voice and firm grasp of history set this lively 14th-century romance apart. An electrifying blend of history, romance, and intrigue, this fast-paced tale is a testament to Hunter's considerable narrative prowess."
—*Publishers Weekly*

"I have enjoyed every novel Ms. Hunter has penned to date, and it's difficult to say, but each one seems better than the one before. *Lord of a Thousand Nights* is no exception; it's a masterpiece of storytelling, one that stands alone as a superb read, and one I very highly recommend."
—*Romance Reviews Today*

THE PROTECTOR

"Hunter is at home with this medieval setting, and her talent for portraying intelligent, compelling characters seems to develop with each book. This feisty tale is likely to win her the broader readership she deserves."—*Publishers Weekly*

"Madeline Hunter has restored my faith in historicals and in the medieval romance especially. *The Protector* is definitely a wonderful read."—*All About Romance*

BY DESIGN

"Realistic details that make the reader feel they are truly living in the 13th century enhance a story of love that knows no bounds; not social, political, or economic barriers, Ms. Hunter's knowledge of the period and her ability to create three-dimensional characters who interact with history makes her an author medievalists will adore."—*Romantic Times*

"I'd heard a lot about the previous two books in this trilogy, *By Arrangement* and *By Possession,* but little did that prepare me for the experience that was reading this book. Whether you've already enjoyed Ms. Hunter's books or she is a new-to-you author, this is a wonderful, sensual, masterfully written tale of love overcoming odds, and one I heartily recommend."—*All About Romance*

"With each of the books in this series, Ms. Hunter's skill shines like a beacon."—*Rendezvous*

"Ms. Hunter has raised the bar, adding depth and texture to the medieval setting. With well-crafted characters and a delightful love story, *By Design* is well-plotted and well-timed without the contrived plot twists so often used in romances. I highly recommend *By Design* to not only lovers of medieval romance but to all readers."

—*Romance Reviews Today*

BY POSSESSION

"With the release of this new volume . . . [Madeline Hunter] cements her position as one of the brightest new writers in the genre. Brimming with intelligent writing, historical detail, and passionate, complex protagonists . . . Hunter makes 14th-century England come alive—from the details of its sights, sounds, and smells to the political context of this rebellious and dangerous time, when alliances and treason went hand in hand. For all the historical richness of the story, the romantic aspect is never lost, and the poignancy of the characters' seemingly untenable love is truly touching."
—*Publishers Weekly*

"Madeline Hunter's tale is a pleasant read with scenes that show the writer's brilliance. *By Possession* is . . . rich in description and details that readers of romance will savor."
—*Oakland Press*

"Ms. Hunter skillfully weaves historical details into a captivating love story that resounds with the sights, sounds, and mores of the Middle Ages. This is another breathtaking romance from a talented storyteller."—*Romantic Times*

"With elegance and intelligence, Ms. Hunter consolidates her position as one of the best new voices in romantic fiction. I'm waiting on tenterhooks to see what is in store for readers in her next book, *By Design*."—*Romance Journal*

BY ARRANGEMENT

"Debut author Hunter begins this new series with a thoroughly satisfying launch that leaves the reader eager for the next episode in the lives of her engaging characters."
—*Publishers Weekly*

For my son Joseph,
whose inner strength
impresses me every day

The
RULES
of
SEDUCTION

CHAPTER
ONE

$\int$

A shadow entered the house with the early visitor. Alexia sensed trouble even before she saw who had called.

The low voices in the reception hall caused her to pause on the steps as she descended with her workbasket. She heard the tone of firm demand, even if she could not make out the words. She heard the servant's deferential resistance have no effect. Falkner, the butler, was called. Faced with determined, quiet power, the house's forces retreated.

Foreboding entered Alexia much as it had when the men arrived to tell the family about Benjamin. She had too much experience with the sensation to ignore its warning. Bad news alters the world at once. It changes the air. A human heart knows grief is coming as surely as a horse senses an approaching storm.

She could not move. Carrying her workbasket out to the garden to join her cousins in the early afternoon sun flew from her mind.

Legs appeared, heading her way. Long legs, sheathed

in black trousers and fine boots. They followed the butler toward the staircase. Falkner wore the expression of a servant who had been commanded by a king.

The visitor's torso appeared, then his shoulders and dark crown. As if sensing someone observed him, he looked up to her spot on the landing.

Alexia immediately understood Falkner's submission. This visitor's stature, face, and demeanor could intimidate even if one did not know his exalted station. Dark hair, unruly as if the brushes had been forgotten this morning, framed a handsome face composed of strong, chiseled planes. Signs of fatigue dulled his deeply set, midnight-blue eyes. Strained forbearance tightened his square jaw and firmly set mouth. Lord Hayden Rothwell, brother of the fourth Marquess of Easterbrook, presented the image of a weary man determined to see through an unpleasant task. It went without saying that he had not come in response to the many calling cards Timothy had left at Easterbrook's home over the last year.

As they approached her, Falkner caught her eye and communicated his dismay. The butler also sniffed the storm.

Lord Hayden paused on her landing and made the slightest bow. She had been introduced to him once, but he did not address her. As his head rose, his gaze scanned her from toe to head. The assessment was so complete, so oddly interested, that she felt her face warming.

The planes of his face vaguely rearranged themselves. As if a statue had come to life, warmth entered

his eyes and his mouth relaxed. Sympathy subtly softened him.

In a blink, his stern demeanor returned and abol-
ished the kindness, but she had seen enough to make her
heart sick. She recognized pity in the look he had given
her. Oh, yes, this man's arrival heralded nothing good.

"Are you bringing Lord Hayden to the drawing room
or the library, Falkner?" She was being too bold, but she
did not care. Over the years she had learned that anticipating bad news was much worse than actually hearing
it. She had no intention of submissively waiting and
worrying.

"The drawing room, Miss Welbourne."

Lord Hayden guessed her intentions. "Please do not
disturb Miss Longworth on my behalf. This is not a social call."

"We will not send for her, if that is your request.
However, it may be some time before Mr. Longworth
can attend on you. We can at least see to your comfort."

She did not wait for approval but turned on her heel
and led the way up to the second level.

She set aside her workbasket in the drawing room
and saw to the comfort she promised. She played the
hostess even though he did not want one.

"It is uncommonly fair for January, don't you
think?" she asked after he agreed to sit on the new, blue-
patterned divan. "The day thus far has been glorious."

His eyebrows rose a fraction at the unfortunate em-
phasis she put on "thus far."

"Yes, unseasonably warm these last days," he said.

"I think such days are cruel, much as I relish them."

"Cruel?"

"They tease one into believing spring is coming, when there are months of cold and damp ahead."

For a second a mischievous light sparked in his eyes. "It may be no more than a tease, but I prefer to enjoy the pleasure and worry about the cold when it comes."

It almost sounded improper when he phrased it that way. She changed the topic with an observation about the recent holidays. He agreed with whatever she said. With fits and starts, she cobbled together an awkward conversation.

His mind was not with her, she could tell. It was on his meeting with Timothy. The air in the drawing room grew thick from the impending doom this man exuded.

She could not bear it any longer. "My cousin is ill, Lord Hayden. Composing himself enough to meet with you may be impossible. Could this not wait for another day?"

"No."

That was all she got. That one word, spoken flatly, simply, and firmly.

He turned his attention away, to nothing. He kept doing that, just as he had on the stairs. She wondered if he found her company presumptuous. She was not the mistress of the house but merely a cousin. Since he had refused to have Roselyn informed of his visit, it was not her fault he was stuck with a poor second-best.

"Perhaps, sir, if I brought a message to my cousin on the purpose of your visit, he would . . ."

Her voice trailed off as he stared her down much like a vicar does when silencing a whispering child in church.

She did not care for the expression in his eyes that

said he knew what she was doing either. Hayden Rothwell was reputed to be brilliant and brusque and arrogant. She could not disagree with that assessment thus far.

Then again, she had not approached this inquiry very artfully. She tried a different tack. Since he was renowned for his financial acumen, she turned the conversation to that in order to make him amenable to other questions. "Have you heard any news from the City today, Lord Hayden? Does the bank crisis continue?"

"I fear it will continue for some time, Miss Welbourne. Such panics usually do."

"You have some dealings with my cousin's bank, I believe. All is well there, I trust."

"As of an hour ago when I left the City, Darfield and Longworth was still solvent."

"Thank goodness. There has been no run, then. With so many other banks suffering them, I have been concerned."

A dark, hard amusement entered his eyes. "No, there has been no run on the bank."

That relieved her. Several large London banks had failed in the last month. The newspapers were full of stories of the ripples of insolvency hitting smaller county banks. Everywhere one went, there was talk of failure, ruin, and bankruptcy. She suspected that Timothy's current illness came from worry over his bank's future.

"Do you have funds there?" He seemed actually interested.

"A mere pittance. My concern is for my cousins."

She had succeeded in garnering his attention with

her financial questions. Rather too well. He looked her over again, longer this time, with a casual arrogance that implied he was entitled to such forwardness while lesser men were not. It was the examination of a man who knew his worth too well and who assumed a dispensation from etiquette as a result.

His attention lingered intensely on her eyes, absorbing her so completely that she had to blink to find her thoughts again. Slowly and deliberately, he took in the rest of her. Her face warmed, and an uncomfortable liveliness prickled all her skin. He flustered her badly, in ways that echoed other flusters caused years ago by another man's gaze.

Her reaction embarrassed her. She did not think of herself as someone susceptible to a handsome man. She wasn't a silly girl like young Irene. She silently scolded herself for acting like a foolish spinster grateful for any man's attention.

There was nothing in his expression to indicate he noticed her ill ease. Nor did she suffer any illusion that his interest was of *that* nature. She knew what he was thinking. With her brown hair and ordinary face, she was not very impressive. No doubt he saw the ways in which pinching pennies affected her appearance too. This old dress not only was out of style but had discreet bits of mending. She suspected that he saw every secret stitch.

"Miss Welbourne, I think that you and I were introduced at Benjamin's service," he said. "You are the cousin from Yorkshire, am I right?"

A pang of horror sounded in her pride. He had not known who she was when he entered this drawing room. Her attendance on him must have seemed very peculiar, and her conversation exceedingly bold, if he did not remember they had been introduced.

A touch of vexation followed her momentary shock. The anger was not with him, although it managed to encompass him anyway. It came from the situation that made her so thoroughly forgettable.

"Yes, we met at Benjamin's service." The name and reference summoned an echo of old grief. A service, but not a funeral. Benjamin's body was not in England but lost at sea. It had been four years since he left England, and she still missed him terribly.

Suddenly Lord Hayden did not appear so stern. A more social countenance softened his beautifully sculpted face.

"I counted him as a friend," he said. "We met as boys. Their property is not far from Easterbrook's estate in Oxfordshire."

Timothy had always alluded to a special connection to Easterbrook and his family, one born of their being neighbors in the country. It was not so close a connection that Timothy's calling cards were ever returned, of course. If the friendship had been between Benjamin and Hayden Rothwell, however, that explained a few things, such as why Lord Hayden had been at that service.

"You also fought in Greece, did you not?" she asked, glad to explore this topic that made him less severe and that touched on dear Benjamin.

"Yes, I was one of the idealistic philhellenes who have joined the Greek cause against Turkey. I was there early in the war, at the same time as your cousin. Unlike him and Byron, I was fortunate enough to survive the adventure."

She pictured Benjamin, ever the optimist, a man so full of life and joy that it made him reckless, fighting like a hero for a people's freedom with an ancient temple on the hill behind him. She treasured that image of him. Since Lord Hayden had been there too, she supposed she did not mind too much that he had inventoried her unimpressive appearance.

He was doing it again, only it was not her dress that he scrutinized. It was her face and . . . *her.*

"Forgive me, Miss Welbourne. I do not mean to be forward, but your eyes are an unusual color. Like violets. Is it the light here, or has this been noted before?"

"It is not the light. That color is my one distinctive feature."

He did not disagree, which she thought ungallant. He weighed her response, then his own. "He spoke of you with respect and affection. Benjamin did, in Greece. Not by name. Violet eyes, however—I remember that reference. I did not notice at the service that yours had that color or I would have told you then, for what comfort it might have offered."

Her heart flooded with an emotion sweet and perfect, despite the painful nostalgia that provoked it. She barely contained her reaction, and her eyes misted. Benjamin had spoken of her in the days before he died. He had confided in this man sitting with her in the drawing room. Lord Hayden knew of their love and plans. She was sure he did.

She no longer cared about his purpose in coming. Her gratitude for this small indication that Benjamin had truly cared for her, had sincerely meant to marry her, was so intense that she could forgive him anything right now.

She looked on him much more kindly. He was a very handsome man, now that she let herself notice. Not entirely severe either, it seemed. The hardness around his mouth was the fault of breeding, after all. He could not help it if his bones made a portrait of angles and planes instead of happy hills.

"Thank you for telling me that. I miss my cousin badly still. It touches me that he thought of me while he was gone."

She yearned for him to repeat exactly what Ben had said. If he had such inclinations, they were thwarted. Timothy chose that moment to make his entrance into the drawing room.

Timothy looked quite ill, with florid color and glassy eyes. She wondered if he carried a fever. His valet had turned him out properly, however, so his sandy hair and flushed face topped coats and neckwear that spoke of his tendency to sartorial excess.

"Rothwell."

"Thank you for making time for me, Longworth."

Alexia rose at once and took her leave. Her heart still sang with happiness at learning that Benjamin spoke of her eyes to his bachelor friends while in Greece. She could not ignore that the mood of impending bad news had reclaimed the house, however.

Clutching her workbasket, Alexia entered the garden to join her cousins. The ivy and boxwood could not approximate the garden's summer glory, but the sun burned away the worst of the chill, and the lack of wind made the garden hospitable.

Roselyn and Irene waited at an iron table, with two bonnets and bags of ribbons and notions. Alexia decided not to mention the visitor inside. Maybe the foreboding still throbbing beneath her new joy was ill-founded.

"You were gone a long time," Irene complained. She held up one of the bonnets. "I still say it cannot be saved and I should get a new one. Timothy said I could."

"Our brother is too fast to spend," Roselyn said. "Unless we want your season to ruin us, we must be frugal when we can."

"Timothy does not speak of frugality. Only you do. Nor will it be a proper season, no matter how many hats and bonnets I have." A petulant note entered Irene's tone. "I will not be invited to the best balls. All my friends have said so."

"At least *you* will have a season," Roselyn said. "Would you rather be the sister of an important banker, or the sister of an impoverished country gentleman? You should thank God our brothers invested in this endeavor. If we were back in Oxfordshire, you would be happy to see one new hat a year, and would choose it most carefully instead of buying three that do not become you."

Alexia sat between them, hoping to end the argument by making a barrier. As the youngest of the Longworth siblings, Irene did not appreciate the good fortune that had come with Benjamin's decision eight years ago to invest in the bank. She saw only what she had lost in status and did not weigh that against the luxury that had been gained.

Roselyn at twenty-five remembered the bad years when debt caused the sale of their lands in Oxfordshire. Her own season had been impossible when she was of age for it, and her chances for marriage dim. When the bank's more recent success produced a long line of suitors, she had proven skeptical and discriminating. Alexia suspected that Roselyn resented that all these doting young men had managed to fall in love with her only after her family became rich.

"We can replace the pink satin ribbon with this yellow," Alexia said. "And look here, I can trim the straw on the sides, so it brings the bow closer to your face."

"I will hate it. I do not care for remade bonnets, even ones remade with your skill. Take it for yourself, if you want. You can have the dress that goes with it too, so you will not have to wear that high-waisted one anymore. I will tell my maid that it is to be yours, so she will not claim it first."

Alexia stared at the ribbons' mix of shine and color gleaming in the sunlight. Irene was not cruel by nature, just young and, due to the free-spending ways of her brother, spoiled.

A heavy silence claimed the table. Irene picked up the bonnet, fretted over it, then threw it down.

"Apologize," Roselyn said in a dangerous voice. "I have half a mind to send you down to the country. London is turning your head, and it is most unattractive. You forget who you are."

"She forgets nothing," Alexia snapped. She immediately wished she had not spoken, but it was out in all its pique and resentment.

She took a deep, calming breath. "Nor do I forget

who I am. Only you do because you are so good. Everyone else knows that I am dependent on this family, a poor relative who should be grateful for my young cousin's castoffs. Every bite I eat is out of the charity of your brother."

"Oh, Alexia, I did not mean . . ." Irene's face crumbled with regret.

"That is not true," Roselyn said. "You are one of us."

"It *is* true. I accommodated myself to my situation years ago. I do not mind."

Except she did mind. She tried not to, but it chafed. The humility and gratitude required of her situation sometimes escaped her, especially since she had not felt obligated to don that retiring demeanor at first.

Her slide had been inevitable when her family's property went to a second cousin. There had been no invitation to live with that heir, the way her father had assumed, however. Barely eighteen, she had been forced to write to the Longworths, cousins on her mother's side, asking for a place with them. She had brought nothing to them but twenty pounds a year and a talent for remaking hats.

Benjamin, the eldest, had never let her feel beholden, even though her arrival had coincided with the launch of his new venture and for the first year there would not be much to spare. His quick smile and good humor had refused to permit a pose of demure subservience on her part. Only after he died did the reality of her dependence become clear. Where Ben had assumed he should provide for her as he did for his sisters, Timothy did not. She only advised while on visits to the

London modistes now. Timothy saw her as the burden she was, while Benjamin had seen her as . . .

A carefully preserved memory of love, an echo of an emotion deep and poignant, made her heart ache. He had seen her as a dear cousin and a dear friend, and that last year had alluded to so much more. If what Lord Hayden had said was true, she had not misunderstood. If Ben had returned from Greece, he would have married her.

She picked up the bonnet. "Thank you, Irene. I will be glad to have it. Blue ribbon, I think now. Neither pink nor yellow has ever complemented my hair or complexion."

Roselyn caught Alexia's eyes with an apologetic look. Alexia returned one with her own message. *I was born the daughter of a gentleman, but here I am now, almost twenty-six, with no fortune and no future. Such is the way of the world. Do not pity me, I beg you.*

"Who is that?" Irene asked, interrupting the silent conversation. "Up there, at the drawing-room window."

Roselyn turned in time to see the dark hair and broad shoulders before the man retreated from the glass. "We have a visitor? Falkner should have sent for me."

Alexia began removing the pink ribbon. "He asked only to speak with Timothy and begged that you not be disturbed."

"But Timothy is ill."

"He rose from his bed all the same."

Alexia felt Roselyn's attention on her as she busied herself with the hat.

"Who is it?" Roselyn asked.

"Rothwell."

"Lord Elliot Rothwell? The historian? What business—"

"His brother Lord Hayden Rothwell."

Irene's eyes widened. She bounced and clapped her hands. "He came *here*? I may faint. He is sooo handsome."

Roselyn frowned. She looked at the window. "Oh, dear."

"You have been drinking, Longworth," Hayden said. "Are you sober enough to hear and remember what I say?"

Longworth slouched comfortably on the blue divan. "Too damned sober."

Hayden examined Timothy Longworth. Yes, he was sober enough, which was good since this could not wait. The plan's chance for success diminished with each hour.

"I spent the last two days with Darfield while you hid in your bed drinking," he said. "The bank should survive this current crisis, if you do as I say."

"I told Darfield it would. He is an old woman and feared the reserves were too low, but I said we were solid."

"It will survive only because I made the decision yesterday to keep the family deposits with you. Word of that alone stopped a run that began this morning."

"There was a run?" Longworth had the decency to look chagrined. "I should have been there, I know."

"Hell, yes, you should have been there."

"The worst has passed, however? The danger is averted, you said."

"Hardly. Despite pulling through today, the bank still is in serious danger. Furthermore, I am reconsidering my position with you. The choice is a hard one, because if I remove the family's money, the bank will fail. If it does, you will surely hang."

Longworth stilled. He became a sprawled statue of indifference.

Hayden resented like hell being entangled with Timothy Longworth. He had ensured the bank's growth with family funds and deposits in order to help a good friend. He had not signed on to save the neck of this younger brother.

Longworth smiled broadly. That made him look more like Benjamin, despite his light coloring, which was in contrast to Ben's dark hair and eyes. It was a resemblance that Hayden would rather not see right now.

"Of course you are speaking metaphorically when you say 'hang.' Although ruined is a bare improvement, it is not death."

"When I say hang, I mean hang. Gallows. Noose. Dead."

"Banks fail all the time. Five have during the last fortnight in London alone, and dozens in the counties. It is no crime. That is what happens during financial crises."

"It is not the bank's failure that will send you to the gallows but what the accounting afterward would reveal."

"Nothing to endanger me, I assure you."

Hayden's patience ebbed fast. He had not slept last

night as he and Darfield sorted through the mess hidden within the bank's accounts. The fury that he had barely contained upon learning the worst now threatened to break the frayed leash that held it in check.

"I decided to leave the family money with you, Longworth, but I worried about my aunt and her daughter. Their three percent funds are all they have, and they are dependent on the income. As their trustee I could not risk it. So that part, that small part, I decided to remove."

Longworth cocked his head as if this preamble confused him, but the first signs of panic sparked in his eyes.

"Imagine my shock when I saw that their consols had been sold and that my name, as trustee for my aunt, had been forged to do it."

Tiny pearls of sweat rose on Longworth's brow. "See here, are you insinuating that *I* forged—"

"I have proof that you repeatedly committed the crime of utterance. You forged other names in order to sell other securities as well. You continued paying out the income so no one would suspect, but you stole tens of thousands of pounds."

"The hell I did! I am shocked and grieved by this news. Darfield must have done it."

Hayden strode over, grabbed Longworth by the collar, and lifted him from the divan. "Do not dare impugn that good man's name. I swear that if you lie to me now, I will wash my hands of you and let you swing."

Longworth threw up his arms to cover his face, cringing away from the anticipated blow. His fear both checked and disgusted Hayden. He threw Longworth back down on the divan.

Timothy folded forward, his face in his hands. A sickening silence claimed the drawing room, one throbbing with Hayden's anger and Longworth's palpable desperation.

"Have you told anyone yet?" Longworth's voice cracked with emotion.

"Only Darfield knows, and he fears the implications for all the banks if such a scheme comes to light in the current mood abroad in the City." Hayden had envisioned that horror too often during the last two days. The "funds"—the solid government securities sitting in trusts and paying out income to untold women and retainers and younger sons and daughters—were assumed to be secure. Banks only maintained them for clients. The money was not supposed to be vulnerable at all.

Timothy Longworth had broken a sacred trust in forging those names and taking that capital. If it became known, the current panic would increase tenfold.

"What the hell were you thinking, Longworth?"

"I did it for the bank. We were vulnerable; reserves got low. I did it to protect the deposits—"

"No, *damn it*." Only when Longworth jolted did Hayden realize he had yelled. "You did it to buy this house and that coat and the coaches you ride in with your expensive mistress."

Timothy began to weep. Embarrassed for him, Hayden turned away and looked out the window.

Down in the garden, a pair of violet eyes glanced his way, then turned back to some ribbons and straw. *Eyes like violets in the cool shade, and a fetching form that*

hints of hidden glories. That was how Benjamin had
spoken of Miss Welbourne when in his cups one night
in Greece. Not entirely respectfully, but affection had
been in his voice, so Hayden had not really lied to her.
When he saw her reaction—the tears threatening and
the way her face softened so sweetly—he wished he had
not said a word, however.

Not a beautiful face, but those eyes made that irrelevant. Their unusual color captivated first, then one noticed how they reflected an intense spirit and intelligent
mind. Worldliness showed too, as if this woman understood the realities of life too well. While sitting under
the unrelenting gaze of those eyes, he had forgotten for
a few moments the horrible mission that had brought
him to this house today.

A mouth like a rose, with nectar as sweet. Apparently
Ben had trifled with more than Miss Welbourne's emotions. Nothing surprising about that. A man bursting
with life the way Benjamin Longworth was managed to
trifle with a lot of women.

Roselyn and Irene Longworth, Benjamin's sisters,
sat in the sun with Miss Welbourne. The elder was a
handsome woman with fair skin and dark golden hair
and a sweet face. She was distinctive in her beauty but
proud by all accounts. The younger one's hair was long
and pale, her form slight and still childish.

He felt a presence by his side. Longworth had risen
from the divan. He also gazed down at the three women
in the garden.

"Oh, God, when they learn of it—"

"I swear that they will never learn the truth from me.
If we can save your neck, you can tell them whatever

lies you want. A forger and thief should be able to devise good ones."

"Save my—there is a way? Oh, mercy, whatever . . . however . . ."

Hayden waited while Longworth again collected his composure.

"How much, Longworth?"

He shrugged. "Twenty thousand maybe. I did not mean to. Not really. The first time it was to be a loan of sorts, to pay off an unexpected debt—"

"Not how much did you take. How much do you have?"

"Have?"

"Your only chance is if we make them whole, every one of them. With what you have and with notes you sign."

"That will mean telling them!"

"If they suffer no loss, however—"

"It would take only one to speak of it for me to . . ."

"To hang. Yes. One forgery was enough to do it. You will have to hope that repayment will satisfy them and that they understand that only silence will ensure that repayment. I will speak for you, and that may help."

"Pay them all? I will be ruined. Totally ruined!"

"You will be *alive*."

Longworth gripped the sill of the window and steadied himself. He gazed out again and his eyes moistened. "What will I tell them? And Alexia—if we are reduced to the income from the country rents, if I must pay off debts with it too, I cannot support her." As if a new horror occurred to him, his face fell.

Hayden guessed why. "Did you steal her meager funds too? I did not check the small accounts."

Longworth's face reddened.

"You are a scoundrel, Longworth. Thank God on your knees tonight that I owe your dead brother a debt of duty and honor."

Timothy was not listening. His eyes glazed as he looked into the future. "Irene was to come out this season, and—"

Hayden closed his ears to the litany of grief that was coming. He had devised a way to save Longworth's life and to avoid revelations that would make the current panic burn out of control. He could not spare Longworth the ruin this solution would entail.

A profound weariness saturated him, one born of a long night full of calculations and anger and moral deliberations. "Sit. I will tell you how much is needed, and we will determine how you will repay it."

CHAPTER
TWO

R*uined*.
The word hung in the air. The room went silent.

Alexia's blood chilled. Tim appeared very ill now. He had retreated to his chamber after Lord Hayden left today but had risen from his bed this evening. He had just summoned her and his sisters to the library and informed them of this disaster.

"How, Tim?" Roselyn asked. "A man does not go from this"—she gestured to the house around them—"to ruin in one day."

His eyes narrowed and bitterness hardened his voice. "He does if Lord Hayden Rothwell decides he does."

"Lord Hayden? What has he to do with this?" Alexia asked.

Timothy stared at the floor. He appeared limp from lack of strength. "He has removed his family deposits from the bank. Our reserves were not sufficient to pay it out, and I had to pledge all I have to supplement the reserves. Darfield too, but his pockets are deeper. He paid part of my obligation and took my share of the bank in return. Still, it was not enough."

Alexia battled a mind-scathing fury. What did it matter to Rothwell where all that money rested? He had to have realized what this would do to Timothy, to all of them. He entered this house knowing that he intended to destroy the Longworths' futures.

"We will manage," Roselyn said firmly. "We know how to live more simply. We will release a few servants and eat meat only twice a week. We will—"

"You did not hear me," Timothy snarled. "I said I am *ruined*. There will be no servants and no meat at all. I have *nothing*. We have *nothing*."

Roselyn gaped at him. Irene, who had been listening with a confused frown, startled as if someone had slapped her. "Does this mean I don't get my season?"

Timothy laughed cruelly. "Sweet, you can't have a London season if you aren't in London. The scoundrel is taking this house. It is Rothwell's now. We are going back to what little we still have in Oxfordshire to starve there."

Irene began to cry. Roselyn stared in mute shock. Timothy's laughter dissolved into a sound between a cackle and weeping.

Fear crept through Alexia. Timothy had not once looked at her since she entered the room. He avoided her eyes now. A quiet panic pattered in her chest, wanting to become something bigger.

Roselyn found her voice. "Timothy, we can live in the country again. We still have the house and some land. It will not be so bad. It was not starvation."

"It will be worse than before, Rose. I will have debts from this to pay. A good part of the rents will go to that."

The beat quickened and spread to Alexia's blood. She flashed hot and cold. The fate she had feared since her father died had finally found her. She held on to her composure by a hair.

She would not make Timothy say it. That would be unfair, and poor repayment to the family that had given her a home.

She stood. "If your situation will change so drastically, you will not need the burden of one more mouth to feed. I have a small amount saved and it should keep me until I find employment. Now I will go to my room so you can freely discuss your plans."

Roselyn's eyes misted. "Do not be silly, Alexia. You belong with us."

"I am not being silly. I am being practical. Nor will I force Timothy to say the words that put me out."

"Tell her she does not have to go, Tim. She is so sensible that she will help, not be a burden. He does not want you to leave us, Alexia."

Timothy did not respond. He still would not look at her.

"Timothy," Roselyn cried in admonishment.

"It will be all I can do to keep the two of you, Rose." He finally turned to Alexia. "I am very sorry."

Alexia forced a trembling smile and left the library. She closed the door on Irene's and Roselyn's weeping and Timothy's embarrassment. She hurried up to her bedchamber, cursing with every step the man responsible for this tragedy.

Hayden Rothwell was a scoundrel. A monster. He

was one of those men who lived in luxury and destroyed lives on a whim. He did not have to remove those deposits all at once. He had no heart and no soul and trampled people under his boot if it suited him. He was as hard and cold as he looked, and she hated him.

She threw herself on her bed and buried her face in her pillow. She poured venom on Rothwell while she wept into the feathers. The panic coursed all through her now.

Ruined. She could not believe she was enduring this again. Her father had been ruined two years before he died. His legacy had been much diminished as a result. Most likely that was why she had not been taken in by his heir. Fate had now played a cruel joke on her, making her relive the worry and fear.

She groped for control. She had wondered sometimes what she would do if she found herself in this situation. She had always known it could happen. She poked through her misery to the calculations she made on those terrible nights when her precarious existence loomed in the dark.

She could possibly become a governess, if she could get references. She had the breeding and education for it, although the life was a dreadful one.

She could also seek work in a milliner's shop. She possessed a knack with hats and enjoyed making them. Working in such a shop would be the final humiliation, however. She was not born to such things, even if the idea held more appeal than being shut in night and day caring for another woman's child.

She might also marry, although at present there were no suitors. She had never even hoped for one after

Benjamin. He lived in her heart and always would. The girl who survived, hidden in her soul, loathed the notion of a loveless match made only to ensure security. Having tasted great love, such a marriage would be horrible. However, with neither beauty nor a fortune to entice a man, marriage was one practical compromise that she did not expect to face.

Enumerating her options gave her some heart, even if it was a sickening sort of confidence. She had twenty pounds a year and would not starve. She could make a future for herself if she ate her pride. As it happened, she had a lot of practice in doing that.

She gazed around her room at the furniture showing dimly in the lamp's light. It was not a big room. It lacked the luxurious fabrics of Irene's and Roselyn's and the new chairs and beds they had purchased last year too. But it was her room and had been her home since Tim moved them here from Cheapside right after Ben sailed to Greece four years ago.

She closed her eyes and wondered how long it would be before Hayden Rothwell threw her out onto the street.

Three mornings later Alexia sat in the breakfast room, reading the advertisements in the *Times*. The house quaked with silence. Servants barely made any noise, but their absence was noticeable. Only Falkner remained while he sought another appropriate situation. She could hear him in the dining room, packing the china that Timothy had sold yesterday.

Very little of the luxuries purchased over the last few

years would return to Oxfordshire with her cousins.
Rothwell would get the furnishings, and everything else
would be sold. Right now men were in the carriage
house, dickering over the equipage.

Roselyn entered the breakfast room and sat beside
Alexia. She poured them both some coffee. "What are
you studying there?"

"Rooms to let."

"Piccadilly would not be too bad, if you are not too
far east."

"I don't think I can avoid going east, Rose."

Rose looked like a woman who had cried for a
month. Red puffs swelled beneath her eyes. "I should
have married one of those men who were after my fortune. It would have served him right when my brother
was so ruined that he had to sell the pewter. The *pewter,*
for heaven's sake."

Alexia bit back a laugh. Roselyn caught her at it and
giggled too. They both laughed while tears streamed
down their faces.

"Oh, heavens, that felt good," Rose gasped. "This is
all so drastic it is almost ridiculous. I half-expect Tim to
sell my nightdress off my body while I sleep."

"Let us hope a bailiff isn't with him when he does.
That would give the town even more to gossip about."

Roselyn laughed again, sadly. "I will miss you,
Alexia. What are you going to do?"

"I asked Mrs. Harper for a reference, since she
knows me best of all your friends. I have applied to an
agency to seek placement as a governess. I am hoping it
can be here in town."

"You must let us know where you are, always. You must promise to visit."

"Of course."

Rose's eyes brimmed. She embraced Alexia firmly. As Alexia accepted the warmth that would soon be denied, she saw Falkner arrive at the doorway.

"What is it?" she asked.

Falkner gave her the same look he had three days ago. The one that said a storm was brewing. "He is here. Lord Hayden Rothwell. He has asked to see the house."

From the way Falkner's pointed nose twitched, Alexia suspected Rothwell had not "asked" for anything.

"I will not receive him," Roselyn said. "Send him away."

"He did not ask for you, Miss Longworth, but for your brother, who is not here. He then commanded me to accommodate him."

"Tell him you will not. I forbid it. He will have this house soon enough," Roselyn cried.

How soon had not been determined, a matter of some worry to Alexia.

"You are not being practical, Rose. It does no good to anger the man now. Nor should Falkner serve when he is no longer obligated. I will see to our visitor so you do not have to."

Lord Hayden waited in the reception hall, surrounded by walls that had already been stripped of paintings. As Alexia entered, he was bent, examining a marquetry table in the corner, no doubt calculating its worth.

She did not wait for his attention or greeting. "Sir, my cousin Timothy is not on the premises. I believe he is selling the horses. Miss Longworth is indisposed. Will I do for whatever your purpose in coming might be?"

He straightened and swung his gaze to her. She grudgingly admitted that he appeared quite magnificent today, dressed for riding as he was in blue coat and gray patterned-silk waistcoat. His expression, bearing, and garments announced to the world that he knew he was handsome and intelligent and rich as sin. It was rude to look like that in a house being deprived of its possessions and dignity.

"I expected a servant to—"

"There are no servants. The family cannot afford them now. Falkner remains only until he finds another situation, but he no longer serves. I fear you are stuck with me."

She heard her own voice sound crisp and barely civil. His lids lowered enough to indicate he noted the lack of respect.

"If I am stuck with you, and you with me, so be it, Miss Welbourne. My purpose in intruding is very simple. I have an aunt who has an interest in this house. She asked that I determine if it would be suitable for her and her daughter this season."

"You want a tour of the property so you can describe it to potential occupants?"

"If Miss Longworth would be so kind, yes."

"Kindness is in her heart in most situations. However, she is far too busy to honor your request. Being ruined and made destitute is very time-consuming."

His jaw tightened enough to give her a small satisfaction. The victory was brief. He set down his hat on the marquetry table. "Then I will find my own way. When I said my aunt had an interest, I did not mean a casual curiosity but rather that of ownership. This property is already my aunt's, Miss Welbourne. Timothy Longworth signed the papers yesterday. I presented my requirements as a request out of courtesy to his family, not out of any obligation."

The news stunned her. The house had already been sold. So fast! She quickly calculated what that might mean to her plans and to Roselyn and Irene.

"My apologies, sir. The new ownership of the house had not been communicated to either Miss Longworth or me. I will show you the house, if that will do."

He nodded agreement and she began the ordeal. She led him into the dining room, where his sharp gaze did not miss a thing. She heard him mentally counting chairs and measuring space.

The rest of the first level went quickly. He did not open drawers and cabinets in the butler's pantry. Alexia guessed he knew they were already empty.

"The breakfast room is through that door," she said as they returned to the corridor. "My cousin Roselyn is there, and I must beg you to accept my description instead of entering yourself. I fear that seeing you will greatly distress her."

"Why would my presence be so distressing?"

"Timothy told us everything. Roselyn knows that you brought the bank to the brink of failure and forced this ruin on us."

A hard smile played at the corners of his mouth. The man's cruelty was not to be borne. He noticed her glaring at him. He did not seem embarrassed that she had seen that cynical smile.

"Miss Welbourne, I do not need to see the breakfast room. I am sorry for your cousin, but matters of high finance exist on a different plane from everyday experiences. Timothy Longworth's explanations were somewhat simplified, no doubt because he was giving them to ladies."

"They may have been simple, but they were clear, as were the consequences. A week ago my cousins lived in style in London, and soon they will live in poverty in the country. Timothy is ruined, the partnership is sold, and he will have debts despite his fall. Is any of that incorrect, sir?"

He shook his head. "It is all correct."

She could not believe his indifference. He could at least appear a little embarrassed. Instead, he acted as if this were normal.

"Shall we go above?" he asked.

She led him up the stairs and into the library. He took his time browsing the volumes on the shelves while she waited.

"Will you be going with them to Oxfordshire?" he asked.

"I would never allow myself to be a burden on this family now."

His attention remained on the books. "What will you do?"

"I have my future well in hand. I have drawn up a plan and listed my expectations and opportunities."

He replaced a book on its shelf, quickly surveyed the

carpet and desk and sofas, then walked toward her. "What opportunities do you see?"

She led him through the other rooms on the floor. "My first choice is to be a governess in town. My second is to be a governess anywhere else."

"Most sensible."

"Well, when facing starvation it behooves one to be so, don't you think?"

The third level was not as spaciously arranged as the public rooms. He cramped her in the corridor. She became too aware of the large, masculine presence by her side as she showed the bedrooms. It seemed very wrong for this stranger to be intruding up here.

"And if you do not find a position as a governess?" The casual query came some time after their last exchange.

"My next choice is to become a milliner."

"A hatmaker?"

"I am very talented at it. Years hence, if you should see an impoverished woman wearing a magnificent hat artfully devised of nothing more than an old basket, sparrow feathers, and withered apples, that will be me."

His curiosity raised her pique to a reckless pitch. It was unseemly for the man who caused this grief to want the details. She threw open the door of Irene's bedroom. "My fourth choice is to become a soiled dove. There are those who say a woman should starve to death first, but I suspect they have not faced the choice in reality, as I might."

She received a sharp glance for that. Beneath his annoyance at how she mocked his lack of guilt, she also saw bold, masculine consideration, as if he calculated her value at the occupation fourth on her list.

Her face warmed. That stupid liveliness woke her skin and sank right through to churn in her core, affecting her in a shocking way. It created an insidious, uncontrollable awareness of her body's many details. The sensation appalled her even as she acknowledged its lush stimulation.

She had to step back, out of the chamber and out of his sight, to escape the way his proximity caused a rapid drumbeat in her pulse. In the few seconds before he joined her, she called up her anger to defeat the shocking burst of sensuality.

She continued her goads so he would know she did not care what he thought. She wanted this man to appreciate how his whims had created misery.

"My fifth choice is to become a thief. I debated which should come first, soiled dove or thief. I decided that while the former was harder work, it was a form of honest trade, while being a thief is just plain evil." She paused, and could not resist adding, "No matter how it is done or even how legal it may be."

He stopped and turned into her path, forcing her to stop walking too. "You speak very frankly."

He hovered over her in the narrow corridor. His gaze demanded her total attention. A power flowed, one masculine and dominating and challenging. An intuitive caution shouted retreat. The liveliness purred low and deep. She ignored both reactions and stood her ground.

"You are the one who asked about my future, even though it does not matter to you what becomes of any of us." Her anger had been building since leaving the reception hall. His cool self-possession on this tour had only added fuel to the fire.

She peered up at him. "These are decent, good people, and you have destroyed their lives. You did not have to remove all your business from Timothy's bank. You deliberately ruined him, and I do not know how you can bear to live with yourself."

His dark blue eyes turned black in the corridor's dim lights. His jaw squared. He was angry. Well, good. So was she.

"I live with myself very well, thank you. Until you have more experience in financial matters, you can only view these developments from a position of ignorance. I am sincerely sorry for Miss Longworth and her sister, and for you, but I will not apologize for doing my duty as I saw fit."

His tone startled her. Quiet but firm, it commanded that no further argument be given. She retreated, but not because of that. She was wasting her breath. This man did not care about other people. If he did, they would not be taking this tour.

She guided him toward the stairs rising to the higher chambers, but he stopped outside a door near the landing. "What is this room?"

"It is a small bedroom, undistinguished. It was once the dressing room to the chamber next door. Now, up above—"

He turned the latch and pushed the door open. He paced into the small space and noted every detail. The two books beside the bed, the small, sparsely populated wardrobe, the neat stack of letters on the writing table—

all of it garnered his attention. He lifted a bonnet from a chair by the window.

"This is your room."

It was, and his presence in it, his perusal of her private belongings, created an intimacy that made her uncomfortable. Him touching her belongings felt too much like him touching her. It created a physical connection that made the simmering liveliness more shocking and embarrassing.

"*For now* it is my room."

He ignored the barb. He examined the bonnet, turning it this way and that. It was the one she had begun remaking in the garden three days ago. No one would recognize it now. She had reshaped the brim, covered it all in finely worked cream muslin, and trimmed it with azure ribbons. She still debated whether to add some small muslin puffing near the crown.

"You do have a talent at it."

"As I said, being a milliner is only choice number three. If a lady works in such a shop, she can no longer claim to be a lady at all, can she?"

He set the hat down carefully. "No, she cannot. However, it is more respectable than being a soiled dove or thief, although far less lucrative. Your list is in the correct order if respectability is your goal."

She still hated him by the time they were finished with the tour. She could not deny he was less a stranger, however. Entering the private rooms together, seeing the artifacts of the family's everyday lives, being so close— *too* close—on the upper levels had created an unwelcome familiarity.

Her susceptibility to his presence had placed her at a

disadvantage. She wanted to believe she was above such reactions, especially with this man, who probably thought it his due from all women. She resented the entire, irritating hour with him.

They returned to the reception hall, and he retrieved his hat. She broached the reason she had agreed to receive him at all. "Lord Hayden, Timothy is distracted. He is not conveying the details to his sisters. If I may be so bold—"

"You have been plenty bold without asking permission, Miss Welbourne. There is no need to stand on ceremony now."

She *had* been bold and outspoken. She had allowed her vexation to get the better of her good sense. In truth, she had not been very practical in a situation where she badly needed that virtue.

"What is your question?"

"Have you told Timothy when the Longworths must vacate the house?"

"I have not said yet." He leveled a disconcertingly frank gaze at her. "When do you think is reasonable?"

"Never."

"That is not reasonable."

"A fortnight. Please give them two weeks more."

"A fortnight it is. The Longworths may remain until then." He narrowed his eyes on her. "You, however . . ."

Oh, dear heavens. She had raised the devil with her free tongue. He was going to throw her out at once.

"My aunt has a passion for hats."

She blinked. "Hats? Your aunt?"

"She loves them. She buys far too many, at exorbitant prices. As her trustee, I pay the bills, so I know."

It was an odd topic to start on the way out the door. He sounded a little stupid.

"Well, they often are very expensive."

"The ones she buys are also very ugly."

She smiled and nodded and wished he would leave. She wanted to tell Roselyn about the fortnight's reprieve.

"A governess, you said. Your first choice. Do you have the education to be a finishing governess?"

"I have been helping prepare my young cousin for her season. I have the requisite skills and abilities."

"Music? Do you play?"

"I am well suited to be a governess for young ladies. My own education was superior. I was not always as you see me now."

"That is clear. If you had always been as you are now, you would have never dared be as rude and outspoken with me as you have been today."

Her face warmed furiously. Not because she had been rude and he knew it but because his attention started that foolish excitement again.

"Miss Welbourne, my aunt, Lady Wallingford, will be taking possession of this house because she is launching her daughter in society this season. My cousin Caroline will require a governess, and my aunt a companion. Aunt Henrietta is . . . well, a sobering influence in the household is advisable."

"One that would keep her from buying too many ugly hats?"

"Exactly. Since the situation matches your first choice in opportunities, would you be interested in it? If you are so honest with me, I think that you would also tell my aunt when a hat is ridiculous."

He was asking her to stay in this house where she had lived as a family member, only now she would continue as a servant. He was asking her to serve the man who had ruined the Longworths and destroyed her tenuous hold on security. He was asking her to help give his young cousin the season that Irene would now be denied.

Of course, Lord Hayden did not see any of that. She was merely a convenient solution to staffing his aunt's household. She provided a unique combination of skills that were perfect for the position. Even if he saw the insult, this man would not care.

She wanted to refuse outright. She itched to say something far more outspoken and rude than she had ventured thus far.

She bit her tongue. She could not afford insulted pride these days.

"I will consider your offer, sir."

CHAPTER
THREE

I heard a rumor about you last night at White's."
The unexpected statement carried through the cavernous hall. It caused Hayden to miss the ball flying back at him.

"You are the marker, Suttonly. You are not supposed to help Chalgrove win by distracting me."

"Being marker is very boring. If I distract you, you will lose and then I can play."

The Viscount Suttonly's selfishness had been a characteristic of his nature since he and Hayden became friends at university. There was more to him, however, and Hayden took the bad with the good. The same slender, foppish man who languidly stood at center court, interfering with serves and play, could display great generosity if it suited him.

Chalgrove walked forward to take the serve position. "You knew there was no fourth today and we would have to take turns."

"You mean Rothwell and I would take turns. You always win, so you always go forward." Suttonly tipped up his long, fine-featured face and tried in vain to look down his nose at Chalgrove, who was a head taller. Suttonly's golden hair had suffered the torture of hot irons this morning. The perfectly careless curls would not survive his match when it came.

"He is the one with permission to use this court," Hayden said.

If not for Chalgrove's passion for tennis, and if not for a fortuitous win at the tables against the king three years ago, they would not be here. For payment of that gambling debt, Chalgrove had asked only to be allowed to use the ancient tennis building at Hampton Court when he chose. Since the game was no longer fashionable and no one else wanted to be here, the king had been delighted to extend the royal favor.

They left Suttonly to express his boredom on the sidelines. Chalgrove went on the offensive. Hayden knew he would lose soon.

The Earl of Chalgrove was all rugged and dark, compared to Suttonly's lithe golden appearance. His muscular body displayed more grace at this game than one would expect. A natural athlete, his powerful serves matched his ability to send the leather ball careening into the penthouses and other chase points.

Hayden watched the ball ricochet above his head and drop in front of the net.

"Off the court, Rothwell." Suttonly marched forward, patting his teardrop-shaped racket on his head.

Hayden took his place as marker. While a fraction of his mind kept track of the points and chases, the rest of it turned to the business with Timothy Longworth. His family would be leaving London soon, but no letter had come from Miss Welbourne regarding the situation he had offered her. He did not like picturing the price of her pride. She would end up in some sorry apartment on some rough street, eking out a miserable existence.

Her lack of practicality now meant he had to find another governess and companion. Aunt Henrietta would be arriving in London in a few days. He could not wait on Miss Welbourne any longer.

It took Chalgrove even less time to dispatch Suttonly. Afterward they retired to the club rooms above the court. Chalgrove had brought servants and refreshments. While they ate, Suttonly broached the subject of town gossip again.

"It is said—"

"I am not interested," Hayden said.

"I am," Chalgrove said. "It is rare to hear good gossip about you, Rothwell. Normally it is about how much money you made in this or that investment. Speaking of which, is there anything you want to tell two old school friends? Or are you waiting out the storm before launching the next ship?"

Suttonly never liked having the attention turned from himself. *"It is said,"* he repeated firmly, "that you ruined Timothy Longworth."

That impressed even Chalgrove. "Did you, now? I was not aware he was ruined, let alone that you did it."

"If you ever came to town, you would be aware of what is happening in the world," Suttonly scolded with lazy superiority. "What happened with Longworth, Rothwell? He is selling everything so fast that the bloods joke he would take a cheap offer on his sisters.

You were a good friend to his brother. He must have angered you very much for you to ruin him."

"I did not ruin him. The man's change in fortune is his private business. As for my own plans, there is a syndicate being formed regarding a venture in South America. It is very risky, but I will send you both the documents. I assume you will guarantee the usual discretion."

"I am in," Suttonly said. He speared a slice of ham from the cold platter. "Have the papers drawn up and let me know when they are ready to be signed."

"The Americas? This would not be like that McGregor scheme several years ago, now, would it?" Chalgrove teased. "You won't be issuing any bonds for a country that doesn't even exist, like he did, will you?"

"If he did, he'd probably find a way to pay them off with no one the wiser," Suttonly said. "My dead father and unborn son thank me, Rothwell, that I had the foresight to befriend you when we were in school."

"McGregor's scheme was doomed to fail. One cannot forever bring in more money to pay off the victims defrauded earlier. Eventually the pile of cards will tumble," Hayden said. He wished the world—Suttonly, in particular—would learn to be skeptical of investments. If Hayden had been McGregor, Suttonly would have signed over his fortune to buy those bonds from the fictional nation of Poyais in the Americas. Like all the others, he would not have even bothered consulting a map to find the country's location first.

"I suspect that swindle is at the heart of the current crisis," Chalgrove said.

His frown made Hayden concerned. Chalgrove did

not come up to town anymore, because last year he had inherited an estate in desperate need of attention.

"Have you lost big?"

"Not big, but enough. I had some minor dealings with a county bank that was a correspondent to Pole, Thornton, and Company in London. When they failed in December, so did our local establishment." He shrugged, but not with indifference. "Many good, solid tradesmen are in bankruptcy as a result. There will be a lot of misery before this panic ends."

Suttonly sighed deeply. "There is naught we can do about that, is there? Let us not mourn what we cannot change. For all the worry, the town is still busy and fun, and the season approaches. Chalgrove, promise you will stay in town this year. I was a little bored last season and hope to avoid that this time around. You can look for a rich bride to solve your problems. If she is pretty, you may even fall in love."

"Chalgrove is not a romantic fool like you," Hayden said. "You were bored because you are getting older and are less likely to be a romantic fool yourself now."

"You are bored too easily in any case," Chalgrove said. "Your life would be more satisfying if you practiced some constancy in your interests."

"You mean study mathematics as he does? Muck in the dirt of my estate as you do? I pray that I am never that old. As for being a romantic fool, I intend never to cease. Falling in love makes life exciting for the few months it lasts." He pulled out his pocket watch. "You have me for one more match, Chalgrove. I will serve first this time."

———

"I heard a rumor about you last night at my club."

Hayden looked up from the book he was reading the next afternoon. Very few pages of the tome had been turned. His mind had been preoccupied by other things. Now his brother Christian's unexpected arrival in the library distracted him further.

Christian rarely spent the afternoon in the library. His quiet comment as he settled into an upholstered chair near Hayden explained why this afternoon was different. It was annoying to have two rumors reported in less than two days. Hayden possessed the sort of regular habits and dispassionate character that rarely interested the gossips.

"I am not pursuing Mrs. Jameson, despite what she is telling her friends," Hayden said.

"It was not that rumor, which never interested me. Should you ever marry, it will not be to a woman like that."

The "should," spoken so knowingly, suggested that his brother had confidently laid odds one way or the other on the likelihood of Hayden ever marrying. The "woman like that" did not contain a criticism of the widow in question. Rather, it implied Christian possessed a precise understanding of Hayden's tastes, an understanding that exceeded Hayden's own.

They got along well enough for Hayden to remain a resident in Easterbrook's house on Grosvenor Square. However, Christian's assumptions that he saw his younger brothers more clearly than they saw themselves, and Hayden's suspicions that perhaps Christian really did, were damned irritating.

"It had to do with money, this rumor. Also with our relationship to the bank of Darfield and Longworth."

Hayden set aside his book. "Do you object to my decision to leave our accounts there?"

Christian's interference violated an understanding they had made when Christian returned to Britain after two years of traveling God knew where. Although just out of university, Hayden had dealt with the family finances during that time out of necessity. Christian could have taken over on his return but instead had asked Hayden to continue.

"I do not object to the decision to leave the money there. I am curious if you are truly confident that the bank will not fail, however."

"If it does, I will replace any funds lost by you or the others with my own. If necessary, I will return to the tables to raise it."

Christian's dark eyes glinted with cold lights. The aura of authority that he could exude suddenly poured off him. It was a presence that derived from more than his title and his status as older brother. Something had happened during those two years abroad. That was the source of this layered, restrained power.

Christian had never said much about his time away and the adventures he had seen. Hayden had sensed at once how the experiences changed him, however. His older brother had left England a dutiful, well-trained, newly invested marquess. He had returned too experienced, too seasoned, and a little *outré*.

"I do not expect you to wager your own fortune

against your decisions. I only want to know if you made this particular decision with your normal financial brilliance or if you were ruled by sentiment."

"I would have never left the accounts there if I thought the bank would not survive." Hayden considered the conversation finished and picked up his book again.

"It was not the fact you left the accounts there," Christian said after a long silence. "That was not the rumor."

"Then what rumor did you hear?"

"That you had somehow ruined Longworth and forced him to sell his share in the bank. Manipulated things so he fell."

"Since you have checked whether I removed our deposits and learned I did not, you already know that this rumor is not true."

"No one told me you had ruined him by removing the money. It was said that you *manipulated things so Longworth would fall,* which can be something else entirely. I find it hard to fathom why. The Longworths are an old family from our county. You also made them wealthy in the first place and were Benjamin's friend."

Hayden instinctively rested a hand against his chest. He could not feel the scar beneath his garments, but thinking of Ben always made him remember the pain that produced it. Whatever hand up he had given Benjamin Longworth had been more than repaid in Greece. That meant the balance had been skewed again, the other way, the night that Ben died.

He had failed a friend that night on the ship, by not forcing Ben to come below when he was so obviously drunk. Worse, it had been a friend to whom he owed his life.

"Are you concerned about my honor, big brother?"

"Should I be?"

Hayden glared at him.

Christian gazed back placidly, patiently. They looked much alike, but anyone entering the library might not notice that at first. Christian's dark hair was long, even for the current fashion. Its waves hit the shoulders of the black silk robe he had donned on rising today. Not a normal robe either. It flaunted an exotic, almost oriental pattern and cut and had much less structure than the ones normally made for men. Christian's typical lack of formality in the house meant he wore no shirt under it either, and the gap at the top showed no neckpiece but only skin.

Hayden thought about how stiff and proper his older brother had looked while their father was alive. He had been so damned *good* all those years. Then, within months of assuming the title, he had disappeared, only to return with this disconcerting worldliness.

"Men fail in business all the time. It is like a joust. A man enters the tournament knowing he might forfeit his horse. Ruin is always a danger."

"Not for you. Not with the mind and instincts you bring to the lists. If young Longworth had been another knight and not a mere squire, your analogy might hold. However—"

"Since you choose not to enter the competition at all, stay the hell out of my way." Hayden swallowed his building rancor. It was not really aimed at Christian but instead at his brother's irritating tendency to scrape the raw side of one's soul. "Longworth's ruin was due solely to his own lack of judgment. My honor is intact."

Christian appeared to accept that. "You have a ruthless side to you. In this we are too much alike. Controlling that requires some vigilance, as I am sure you know."

"See to your own soul. I do not need your help with mine."

"We all need help. However, if you say you have not indulged those inclinations, I will accept that Longworth's ruin was of his own making."

It had definitely been that, but in order to avoid bigger consequences than mere ruin, Hayden had been forced to walk the scoundrel through too many meetings and confessions and promises the last few days. No doubt one of the men listening to those promises had alluded to Hayden's role last night at that club.

Christian rose to leave. "Pity about the sisters. I see them around town. The older one is stunning. If not for your friendship to the dead brother, I would be tempted to offer to keep her."

"Taking advantage of her reversal in fortune, and ensuring a complete fall, would be highly dishonorable, don't you think?"

Christian shrugged. "In England, yes. Well, as I said, vigilance is required."

The salver glinted in the afternoon light coming through the window. The card on it surprised Hayden.

Miss Welbourne had called.

He slid his thumb over the card's high-quality stock

and engraving. He pictured her ordering it out of her meager income and deciding the card that bore her name should be a gentlewoman's, no matter what the sacrifice.

"I will see her."

Her visit pricked his conscience. Innocents had been hurt by his discoveries of Longworth's theft.

Of course, Miss Welbourne had been hurt long before the discoveries. Among his deliberations while he did not read in the library this afternoon, there had been some regarding her. He needed to devise a strategy for restoring her funds to her without her learning the funds had been sold off by Longworth in the first place.

Just as well his word of honor prevented him from explaining to her what had happened. He doubted she would thank him for the truth, even if he could reveal it. It would destroy her connection to the only family she had. There was also the chance she would feel so betrayed that she would be the one to send Longworth to the gallows.

He opened the drawing-room doors and saw his guest and her companion. Miss Welbourne had brought her young cousin with her. Irene Longworth's eyes were fixed on a bejeweled medieval reliquary that Christian had set on a table near one window.

The young girl's gaze snapped to Hayden on his entry and stayed there during his greeting. He recognized her mute, awed expression. He had seen it on ingenues often enough.

He much preferred the mature, self-possessed gaze that Miss Welbourne leveled at him.

"Irene, why don't you look at the paintings," Miss

Welbourne suggested. "She has an interest in art, Lord Hayden, and I thought to give her the chance to see part of Easterbrook's collection today."

With Hayden's approval, the girl strolled along the wall, examining the works.

"It was kind of you to bring her, if she is curious about art," he said. "I thought perhaps you had done so to remind me of what she has lost."

"That was one reason, but the opportunity to see part of Easterbrook's esteemed collection was another. Also, when she goes to Oxfordshire, it will make a difference if she can speak of having visited this house. Others with much more than she will possess will not have that connection."

Miss Welbourne spoke with the frankness that had marked their conversations from the start. It occurred to him he would have been treated to the same manner if he had never ruined Longworth.

He liked that. Something about him made most women retreat into irritating frivolity. Her lack of fear and fluster was refreshing. It created charming little challenges. Her manner on the house tour had provoked him at several levels and charged the air between them with much more than mutual annoyance.

She had felt that, he was sure. She did not welcome it, however. Perhaps she did not even understand it.

"I also had to bring someone with me, didn't I?" she said. "There are no maids now, nor even a footman. Since Irene had always dreamed of attending a ball here, a dream Roselyn and I tried to quash in the best of times, I thought she could at least see the art."

The girl had obviously been told to make herself

distant and scarce. She lingered over a Poussin at the other end of the room.

Hayden called for a footman. "Take Miss Irene Longworth to the housekeeper," he instructed the man when he arrived. "Tell her to give the young lady a tour of the ballroom and the gallery."

Barely containing her glee, Irene followed the servant out. Miss Welbourne watched her departure. "That was generous of you."

"If seeing this drawing room will be of help in Oxfordshire, describing the ballroom can only improve her stature more." He settled into a chair angled so he could see Miss Welbourne's face directly. "Since you had to bring someone, that means the purpose of this call is really yours, however, and not hers."

A subtle fire entered her eyes. This woman did not like him much, that was clear enough.

A lavender bow on her hat enhanced the color of those eyes. It was a simple hat, but it looked very expensive with its celestial silk brim and crown and full roses clustered around the bow. Perhaps she had made it herself. Like the calling card, it declared her station even as that station slipped from her grasp.

"I have considered the offer you made at my cousin's residence when last you were there," she said. "I would like to talk about that and see if we can reach an agreement."

It had been twelve days since he made that offer. With a move from that house imminent, it appeared she had finally chosen to be practical.

He decided to make it easier on her pride by being

brief. "The wages would be the normal ones for the situation, and—"

She raised her pointing finger, stopping him. His tutor used to do that when he was a boy.

"I accept the normal wages. However, since I will be filling two roles, those of governess and companion, I think I should receive both wages, especially since you will be spared the keep of a second person. Also, I would like the wages to be paid monthly. I will be wanting to send some to Rose and Irene. I do not want them to have to wait for the normal term to end in order to have some relief."

She was two days from being homeless, but she was boldly haggling as if she could provide the best references in England instead of none at all. From her repeated mention of the Longworths' predicament, she expected his guilt to give her an advantage in her negotiations.

Fascinated, he set his elbow on his chair's arm and rested his chin on his fist. "I expect the monthly payment can be arranged. As to the wages, you will not spend all your time on each role. That is impossible, so full payment for each is not warranted."

"One and a half, then. You must admit that is fair."

He almost laughed. "Fair enough for *you*. Fine, one and a half."

She made a little smoothing gesture over her skirt's fine pomona wool. It was a nervous movement that revealed she was not nearly as composed as she appeared. The dress was far nicer than what he had seen her wear before. Very elegant, it displayed a broad panel of blue embroidery around the bottom, and her midnight-blue pelisse sported a thin edging of fur. He guessed these were not her own garments. Miss Longworth had probably lent them for this call at the home of the Marquess of Easterbrook.

"Regarding my relationship to your aunt and cousin," she continued. "I have lived in that house as a family member, and it will be difficult for me to think of myself as a . . . well, otherwise. I should prefer if my primary position is understood to be that of a companion to your aunt, and my governess duties be secondary. I would educate your cousin the same either way."

Her tone, her manner, the way she kept dropping reminders of her changed circumstances, which she assumed he had caused, should anger him. None of it did.

She had come here dressed as the lady she was born to be, but she would leave a servant. She knew that even if she choked on the word. She was not yet a woman who did not know her place, however. She was just a woman fighting to retain a few shreds of her dignity when she walked out the door a different person than when she had entered.

He would feel sorry for her, but that would be an insult to a woman like this.

"My aunt has a good heart, Miss Welbourne. The danger is not that you will be treated as a servant, but rather that she will be too quick to treat you as a sister. However, I will explain the subtle shift in how you want the position considered. I am sure she will be agreeable. Now, if that is all settled—"

The finger lifted again.

"There is more, Miss Welbourne?"

"A small matter."

"I cannot imagine what it would be."

Her lips pursed at his sardonic tone. Nice lips. Rather full. Her nose turned up just a bit, which drew attention to her mouth.

Mouth like a rose. Not a rosebud, however. Not small and bowed, even when that little purse narrowed it. Rather, it was a rose in full bloom, promising the nectar Ben had described.

"As we both know, my situation will be much changed even if I still dwell in the same house," she said.

Her voice barely penetrated a wandering speculation about that nectar and its taste. The path aimed toward the kind of ruthless calculations that Christian had just warned about.

A fetching form that hints at hidden glories. He saw her again in the boring dress she had worn while she conducted the house tour. Its ivory color had yellowed from age and it had been stripped of decorations, probably to adorn other garments. The styles had changed a lot in the last few years, and its high waist announced her poor fortune. It had fit her breasts snugly, however, and revealed a lushness in shape and curves.

His mind latched on to the memory of her standing close to him in the upper corridor in that ivory dress. The sparks of anger in her eyes as she upbraided him jumped into his blood again and began a slow burn. His imagination began peeling that dress off to see what lay beneath—

"Are you agreeable, sir?"

Her question jolted him out of his erotic fantasy.

"Do you accept this last term?" she asked.

Hell if he knew whether he did or not. He had no idea what the term had been.

He fell back to the position he took in investment negotiations when something unexpected was proposed. "I want to think about this for a while before agreeing."

Her eyebrows rose just enough to communicate what she thought of *that*. "I do not see why it requires long contemplation."

"I am a very deliberate man."

"How admirable. Do you expect your deliberations to last long? Will they be completed in two days, so I know whether to stay in the house?"

She used the careful, kind voice one might employ with an old uncle who was addle-brained. He was not accustomed to anyone—let alone a woman—implying he was stupid. "Why don't you explain this request in more detail, and I can deliberate while you do."

"I cannot think of any other way to explain it. It is simplicity itself. What part did you not understand?"

Did she guess where his mind had been? See it in his eyes? Was she letting him twist in the wind as punishment?

How bad could it be? She had hardly requested that she be allowed to sell all the household silver. "I think my aunt can be convinced to accommodate this, yes."

"Then I would say we have reached an agreement." Immensely satisfied with their conversation, suspiciously so, she slid the handle of her reticule over her arm. "I will take my leave now. I will be in the house when Lady Wallingford and your cousin arrive, to greet them."

He escorted her in search of the girl. They found

Irene in the gallery with the housekeeper. Christian was there too, pointing something out in the painting they faced. He had dressed for the day, finally, and aside from his primitive-looking long hair was turned out like a proper British lord.

"Christian, this is Miss Welbourne. This is my brother Christian, Marquess of Easterbrook."

"I was explaining to your cousin that this is not an original Correggio but a copy of a painting in Parma, Miss Welbourne," Christian said.

Miss Welbourne peered at the painting. It depicted a softly curved and sensually painted Io being borne aloft by Jupiter, who had transformed himself into a cloud. Since Io was nude, it was probably not a painting that Christian should have encouraged young Irene to study.

"It is lovely, even if it is a copy," Miss Welbourne said, too self-possessed to reveal embarrassment at the subject.

Hayden thought it lovely too. Io's body looked quite a bit like he had just imagined Miss Welbourne's, now that he noticed it. Vaguely plump in the best way. Curves and softness waited.

Hayden sent the women off with the housekeeper. Irene began peppering Miss Welbourne with questions immediately, oblivious to the way her whispers carried through the gallery.

"Are you taking the situation?"

"Yes."

"He accepted all your terms?"

"Yes. Now hush."

"*All* of them? Even the free day and use of the carriage?"

Hayden wondered if he had heard correctly.

"Situation?" a low voice at his shoulder said.

He glanced over to see Christian also watching the two women retreat.

"She will be Aunt Henrietta's companion and Caroline's finishing governess."

"Ah, I misunderstood. The only women who negotiate terms with me are my mistresses. Hence my confusion. She has lovely eyes. Unusual color."

Hayden watched her hat's ribbons bob and her hem sway and her slender ankles move. "She wanted to be sure she understood what was required of her in the household. Our conversation concerned the normal sorts of things."

"Such as a free day and use of the carriage, you mean."

Hayden ignored the goad. Miss Welbourne turned to whisper something in Irene's ear. Her profile showed beyond the edge of the hat. A violet eye and a little upturned nose and an expressive full mouth formed a colored silhouette against the housekeeper's brown dress.

The door opened and the women disappeared.

Hayden glanced over to see Christian observing him.

Christian turned to go.

"Vigilance, Hayden. Vigilance."

CHAPTER
FOUR

Alexia strolled beside Roselyn in a funereal march. They made a silent procession from room to room while Rose made sure nothing had been forgotten.

A hired carriage waited in the street. It would take the Longworths only as far as a coaching inn right outside London. There they would transfer to the sad wagon that had left under cover of darkness before dawn, hauling the meager property that they still owned.

Rose peered around the drawing room. "I daresay Rothwell's aunt will find everything in order. I hope she and her daughter are happy here."

The sentiment would have sounded generous if not for the bitter tone.

Alexia did not offer any comforting words. She had already poured out every reassurance she could muster. She had even promised Irene to do her best to give her a season next year, which was as close to bold-faced lying as she had ever come. Her heart was breaking for all of them. Rose and Irene, Timothy, and herself.

Rose turned on her. Eyes glistening, she allowed her anger to show. "You must promise not to love them. I do not care how good they are. You must promise not—"

Alexia embraced her. Rose's body shook as she broke down and wept. It passed quickly. Rose swallowed her tears and found her composure, all with one long inhale.

"Oxfordshire is not far away," Alexia said. That had been repeated by all of them so many times the last week. "We will see each other often, I am sure."

She was not really sure, but perhaps it was possible. She had use of a carriage, didn't she? She had a free day.

"Let us go above and collect Timothy," Roselyn said.

They found Tim in his chamber, sprawled on his bed, ill. No, not ill, Alexia realized. She spied a chipped decanter beneath his washstand.

"The carriage waits, Timothy," Rose said.

"To hell with the carriage." Tim did not even move the arm draped over his forehead. "To hell with the bastards waiting to see it too. To hell with life."

Rose looked stricken. She had effected most of the plans the last few days. Once he had sold what could be sold, Timothy had become worthless.

Alexia went over to the bed. "You have indulged your unhappiness too long, cousin. Your sisters need you to find yourself now. Allow them to walk out the door with dignity, not carrying their broken brother between them."

He neither responded nor moved. She touched his arm. "Come, Tim. This was not of your making. Stand tall for Irene's sake at least."

After a long pause, he pushed himself up. Rose

smoothed his coat and did her best to make his cravat presentable. Timothy looked so sad and helpless that Alexia wanted to weep.

"Did you get his things from the attic, Rose?" He spoke in a muttered slur. "Ben's trunks and such?"

Rose's face fell. "We were so rushed . . . How could I have been so remiss? There is no room now on the carriage and—"

"I will take care of whatever you left behind," Alexia said. "I will be sure the trunks remain here while I do and take them with me when I leave. Eventually I will find a way to return everything to you."

"You are so good, Alexia," Rose said with visible relief.

Alexia did not mind taking responsibility for Ben's property. Part of him would remain with her in this house this way. She might find some fortitude about the life she faced if she remembered those trunks in the attic.

"I hate leaving you here," Tim said to the floor. "I hate that you will be beholden to him. That is the cruelest turn. That he should be able to see and enjoy your diminishment."

Alexia did not think Lord Hayden would enjoy seeing it, since he apparently did not think twice about his actions. In a few days she would be the convenient servant and nothing more. He probably would forget her name.

"I do not care what he sees or thinks, Tim. It is of no consequence to me." That statement at least was a truth. She already knew that if one took a step down, it did not matter why. The blow to one's pride was the same no matter what the cause. One either handled it with grace or with bitterness. She was struggling to do the former this time, as she had in the past.

Tim proved a little unsteady, but she and Roselyn got him down to the door. Irene waited glumly for their grand exit. No one doubted that the neighbors would watch from their windows to see the final curtain fall on the drama of ruin that had played on Hill Street the last two weeks.

"I hate him," Irene said. "I don't care if he is handsome and let me see the ballroom. I am sure his brother would be shocked to learn what has happened. I should have told Easterbrook everything while we were in the gallery."

Alexia gave Irene a farewell kiss. "Do not waste your heart on hate, Irene."

"No, do not," Roselyn said. "I will hate Hayden Rothwell enough for all of us, darling." Her face tightened into a mask of pride. She took her sister's hand. "Let us go now."

Timothy opened the door. He did not appreciate his sisters' poise as they filed past. He was not really seeing them.

He turned to the open door and stood there slackly for a long count. His face reddened with emotion.

Alexia rested her hand on his arm. "You are the son of a gentleman, Timothy. Not even this can change that."

His expression found composure and his posture some steel.

"Damn him," he snarled. He stepped forward and followed Roselyn and Irene into obscurity.

Alexia closed the door before the carriage rolled. She wiped stinging tears from her eyes. She dared not succumb to the impulse to rave at the unfairness of life. She had to ready the house for the arrival of Lord Hayden's aunt and cousin.

She also needed to prepare her pride for the moment those two women walked through the door.

"It was so good of you to escort us, Hayden, even if it is only a few streets from Easterbrook's house that we travel. I am quite helpless at arranging such complicated changes."

"I am glad to help. The situation requires a steady hand at the reins."

"As always, your command of the ribbons gives me confidence and tranquillity. I do not know how we would manage without you."

The reins in question were not those on the horses pulling Easterbrook's coach through Mayfair. Nor were they the ones leashed to the myriad of details that Aunt Henrietta's move to London created. Hayden had all of that well in hand.

Rather it was Henrietta, widow of Sir Nigel Wallingford, who needed firm guidance. She required more of his attention than his most complicated financial investments.

Upon learning after her husband's death that her income would be much curtailed, she had nodded with understanding but had not altered her spending one bit. As trustee, Hayden dreaded the ritual of riding down to Surrey to scold her about the bills, scoldings that she always accepted with chagrin but then happily ignored.

He eyed her now as she sat with her daughter across from him in the coach. A gargantuan hat covered most of her very fair hair. Its broad, steeply angled brim kept hitting Caroline's cheek. The largest red bow in the history of millinery dwarfed the high crown. An extravagant plume swept in a broad arch to brush Hen's delicate jaw. With Henrietta's slight figure, small face, and fine features, the hat looked like a weight about to bend her over.

No doubt Hen thought the hat just grand and worth every penny of its cost. She did not see how it aged her. As the much younger sister of his dead mother, Aunt Henrietta, at thirty-six, still possessed a youthful countenance, but in that hat she could have been fifty.

"You are very sure this governess speaks impeccable French?" she asked. "Caroline requires a firm hand there."

"Miss Welbourne is accomplished in all subjects required of her." Actually, he did not know for certain Miss Welbourne knew her French. If she claimed to have the education for her new role, however, he did not doubt she would produce it. He suspected she could teach herself French in a fortnight if she still needed to learn it.

"I hope she is not like Mrs. Braxton," Caroline muttered. A quiet, pale girl, Caroline rarely spoke. Hayden suspected the child he saw was not the real Caroline but one bleached and stifled by the presence of her mother.

"I am sure Miss Welbourne will be very different from your last governess," Henrietta said. "Hayden had to promise her some unusual concessions to cajole her to aid us." Her pale green eyes sparkled with a happy optimism that made her look dreamy and distracted all the time. "We are in town now, dear. It is a whole different world here. Mrs. Braxton would never do. That is why Hayden found us this house and the estimable Miss Welbourne."

She bestowed on Hayden one of *those* smiles. One of the grateful, affectionate ones that said he was the strong anchor to her rudderless ship. She trusted him completely, depended on him too much, and expected his attendance at her whim. She created one disaster after another that she regretfully handed him to fix because he was so damned competent at doing so.

He did not doubt that his aunt dealt with him much as she had her late husband. Her adoring looks, her circular explanations, her attempts to soften him with flattery—they were the hallmarks of a woman handling a man. He was fond of Henrietta and even found her amusing. However, being her trustee for six years had taught him much about the kind of day-to-day dealings with a woman that came with marriage. None of it had encouraged him to seek a wife.

"There it is," Henrietta announced when the carriage stopped on Hill Street. "I had the coachman drive me past yesterday. It is handsome enough, and of good size, don't you agree, Caroline? Of course, it is not on a square. I had hoped—well, I daresay if Hayden thinks this will suit us, it undoubtedly will."

Hayden knew what she had hoped. His brother Christian had known too.

Aunt Hen had neglected the details about moving to

London until finding a suitable place to let became difficult. Christian had surmised their aunt had an ulterior motive to her incompetence. He was sure she had counted on being left without a residence, at which time she would petition to launch her daughter out of Easterbrook's home.

Three weeks ago Christian had summarily decreed that would not, under any circumstance, happen. He would accommodate Caroline's debut ball but would not live with their flighty and intrusive aunt under his roof.

The Longworth house therefore solved a pressing problem. It had also provided a way for Timothy Longworth to reimburse Henrietta for the stolen securities without her awareness. Aunt Hen assumed Hayden had sold off her funds to purchase the house.

As he stepped out of the carriage, Hayden considered the rest of the plan. With luck, Caroline would be matched up this first go-round, and Henrietta would return to her home in Surrey. The house would be sold and the stolen funds replaced with new ones. If Providence really smiled on him, after Caroline was married, his aunt would look for a husband for herself, and Hayden could soon pass her reins to someone else.

Hayden handed his aunt and cousin down. By the time they entered, all the servants were lined in the reception hall to greet their new mistress.

Henrietta examined her household. Hayden had retained Falkner, but the rest of the staff was new.

He stepped forward when his aunt arrived at Miss Welbourne's. He introduced the two women, as he had not the butler or housekeeper. It was in his interest for them to get on well. With luck Miss Welbourne would reduce Henrietta's demands on him.

Aunt Hen gave her new companion a good inspection. Miss Welbourne suffered it with grace.

"This is my daughter, Caroline," Hen said, drawing her daughter forward. "Our delay in coming to town means her last finishing requires attention. I trust you are fit for it."

"I am, Lady Wallingford."

"I hear that you are recently come to such duties. That you are cousin to the family that last lived here."

Hayden was not aware that Hen had heard that. She had been in town only two days.

Miss Welbourne's eyes deepened in color, but she displayed no other reaction. "Yes, madam."

"We will have some conversation about that. I have no reason to question my nephew's confidence in you, however."

"Thank you, madam."

Hen moved on, to the maids and footmen and cook. Hayden watched the ritual from the side of the room. Mostly he watched Miss Welbourne.

Her gaze had not wavered since they entered the house. He realized it was locked on a spot on the wall behind him. Even when Hen spoke with her, those violet eyes had not moved. She was enduring this, but she was not seeing it.

He admired her composure and the slight hauteur she projected. She might stand with servants, but only a fool would miss the difference. No doubt his aunt had sensed it at once. Hence that little challenge.

Miss Welbourne's gaze subtly moved to him. Anger

and pride flexed over her face. *Do not dare pity me,* that quick glance said. *You of all men have no right.*

Her resentment of him looked ready to defeat her poise. He walked over and gestured her forward, away from her spot of subservience.

"You appear to have everything in hand here. It is admirable." He meant herself, not the household. She seemed to understand. Her expression returned to one of passivity. Her gaze found its spot again, past him on the far wall.

"Falkner saw that the others were prepared," she said quietly.

"Do you think you can manage her?" He looked at his young cousin.

Miss Welbourne glanced down the line too, only her gaze flitted to Henrietta, not Caroline. More specifically, it flitted to Henrietta's hat.

"I am thinking I was worth both wages to you," she said.

"I have been thinking that you might prove to be worth far more to me, Miss Welbourne." It sounded a little risqué once he said it. She did not react as if she noticed. That was probably because the potential entendre lived in his head alone, a reflection of calculations that did him no credit.

"I am thinking you are correct. However, I left our last meeting satisfied and will not expect more now."

"I am relieved. There will only be one carriage, you see, and my aunt will want to use it on occasion. If you had secured several free days instead of only one, that would have seriously inconvenienced her."

She could not resist smiling at the memory of having

bested him. Her rose mouth softened and revealed its sensual, welcoming potential. Her lips parted just enough to send inappropriate thoughts romping through his head.

Her gaze finally turned up to him, to share their little joke. He gazed deeply, commanding her reluctant attention.

He let the moment stretch too long. Shutters rapidly closed, as if she saw danger in his eyes. She stiffened perceptibly.

Suddenly bodies milled around them as the servants were dismissed. Henrietta's hat intruded between him and Miss Welbourne. "Hayden, I have informed the cook that you will dine with us tomorrow night. Easterbrook and Elliot too."

"Elliot is in Cambridge, and Christian is engaged tomorrow." He began to add his own regrets, but a view of violets and roses stopped the words. Miss Welbourne was speaking with Caroline, calmly taking her charge in hand.

"I will be glad to accept, however, if my presence alone will not be too boring."

"Never boring. I have not been in London in years and will be at a loss without your help easing me back into polite society. I have quite forgotten what Caroline should see and do. We depend on you to draw up lists of sites for us all to visit and diversions for us to enjoy."

He suspected she included him in "us all." Before tomorrow's dinner was over, Hen would have his diary filled with ways he would "help."

It was all Miss Welbourne's fault. She had distracted him and he had dropped his guard. If she left him at

Hen's mercy with one small smile, it was just as well she hated him and would not smile often.

He took his leave and received Miss Welbourne's cool farewell amid Henrietta's effusive ones. As he left the house, Hen was following the housekeeper up to see the other chambers, and Caroline was skipping ahead to find the music room.

Which meant that Miss Welbourne was the only one to actually watch him go.

Patience, Alexia said to herself. *Remember your place. Swallow the words that would express what you think.*

She sat at the dining-room table with Lady Wallingford, Caroline, and Lord Hayden. Keeping silent during these dinners proved fairly easy, because Lady Wallingford kept talking to her nephew. At the last two meals he attended, she had cajoled him to tell her all the current town gossip, complete with descriptions of important characters. Tonight she was cornering him into taking her to the British Museum.

Lord Hayden frequently looked Alexia's way, as if he expected her to interrupt and save him from his aunt's designs. Alexia had no inclination to do so. She was a servant, after all. It wasn't her place, was it? He was being too obvious too. It appeared he ignored his aunt when he turned his attention away like that.

He handled his aunt with an affectionate firmness that implied he thought her too mentally scattered to be blamed for her excesses. He apparently did not fully appreciate her character. In one short week, Alexia had discovered that Lady Wallingford's helpless, frivolous manner masked a very feminine type of mental brilliance.

"It would be more educational for Caroline if you brought us, Hayden," Lady Wallingford said. "I am ignorant of ancient history and could never explain the significance of the artifacts." She gave him a smile designed to melt iron. "And Caroline really does not know you and your brothers very well. Nor you her, now that she is no longer a child."

Caroline blushed to her ears. Her mother's sly glance shot her a cue. Caroline forced a hopeful smile. "It would be so wonderful to visit the museum with you, Hayden. If you can spare us the time, that is."

Within several minutes Lady Wallingford had her nephew hooked on her fishing line. Next week he would accompany them all to the museum.

Alexia rather enjoyed watching her new mistress manage this stern, proud man. Nor did he appear to suspect his aunt's grandest design, which was to hook him thoroughly and permanently.

"Now, we must decide on the modiste for Caroline's presentation gown," Lady Wallingford said. "I have heard that there is a Madame Tissot who is a wonder, and also that Mrs. Waterman would do. Can you can advise on this, Hayden?"

"Not at all. Miss Welbourne could help you, I expect."

All eyes turned to her, defeating her intentions to remain a mere shadow at the corner of the table.

"If I had to make the choice, it would definitely be Madame Tissot," she said. Mrs. Waterman had been the modiste chosen to make Irene Longworth's wardrobe this season. Caroline now lived in Irene's house and even slept in Irene's bed. By Lucifer, she would not have Irene's new gowns too if Alexia could help it.

The sharpness of her reaction warned her that she had not accommodated her situation yet. The resentments stabbed on occasions like this. Having to share a table with Lord Hayden left part of her soul seething too. Accepting his arrogant attention, fighting off his dominating aura, seemed a cruel expectation. She hoped he would show more fortitude and find a way to decline his aunt's dinner invitations in the future.

"Before you commission any gowns, you and I must have a little talk, Aunt Hen."

"Of course." Lady Wallingford's expression became one of dutiful obedience. "Caroline herself has insisted on strict limitations on the cost. She is much more sensible than I am in that area, aren't you, dear? The man who marries her will find her much easier on the purse than most other girls."

Caroline blushed again. Her cousin did not see the bait bobbing above him. He vaguely smiled his approval.

The meal finished and Lord Hayden's diary suitably full, they all went up to the drawing room. At the doorway, however, Lady Wallingford announced a new plan.

"Hayden, will you excuse Caroline and me for a short while? She has a surprise for you, and I need to help her. Miss Welbourne will entertain you while we prepare the diversion."

And so Alexia found herself sitting across from Lord Hayden in the drawing room, much as they had during their first conversation.

"Can you give me a hint about this diversion?" he asked. He stretched out his legs too informally. She was not really a member of the family and could do without poses of familiarity.

"It is a mystery to me."

"You are her governess."

"I think this was planned prior to their arrival here. There have been no rehearsals this last week, to my knowledge."

He regarded her in that direct, disconcerting way he had adopted. "Then there must not have been any at all. I doubt you miss much, Miss Welbourne. For example, you have probably realized that dear Aunt Hen has plans for Caroline and me that go beyond visits to museums."

"Indeed? How fortunate for you." His awareness of Henrietta's intentions ruined her fantasy. She had counted on watching him swim along in his arrogant way only to suddenly land on the beach at Henrietta's feet, wiggling helplessly.

"It would be helpful if you would discourage these plans."

"I cannot imagine how I can. Besides, I think it would be a splendid match."

"You intend to be Aunt Hen's ally against me, don't you?"

"We women are all sisters in this, sir. And we do *so* enjoy watching the mighty fall."

He laughed. "You speak as if you do not think I stand a chance."

"I expect you to be gutted, scaled, and in the pan by June."

Humor brightened his eyes. Amusement transformed him. He no longer appeared stern. Strong, yes, but not stern. "A fish? You liken me to a *fish*? Leave me some dignity, Miss Welbourne. A fox run to ground, a bull defeated by a matador—there are numerous analogies available, but a fish is too cruel."

She smiled in spite of herself. "I found the images very compelling."

Although still smiling, still . . . *appealing,* his demeanor turned more serious. "If you refuse to discourage my aunt, so be it. However, do what you can to keep the girl from accepting her mother's assumptions. I would not like to see her hurt or discouraging suitors on account of this scheme. There is no way I will marry my cousin."

"Why not?"

His smile firmed enough to imply she had crossed a line. There was nothing new in that, and she let the question stand.

"She is a child," he said.

"They are all children. If a woman at twenty-two is on the shelf, by necessity the churches are full of child brides."

"I have no interest in marrying in the near future, least of all a child. These girls have very frivolous, romantic notions that obligate a man to feign weakness and sentimentality. Also, she is my cousin. I know such matches are common enough, but it is an unhealthy practice and I do not approve of it."

Unhealthy? "Benjamin Longworth was *my* cousin. I would not want to think that my love for him is unhealthy."

His face went blank. "Of course. My apologies, Miss Welbourne. I am at times too forceful in expressing opinions."

A tight little silence ensued.

"Of course, we did not know each other as cousins when we were younger," she said. "He had never known me as a young girl, and—"

"Yes, exactly. You understand why a match with Caroline is . . . impossible." He ended the topic by rising and strolling rather aimlessly around the chamber.

"When did you meet Benjamin?" His query came casually, while he examined a domestic scene painted by Chardin. It had arrived along with several others soon after the Longworths left, a loan from Easterbrook's collection to fill the empty walls.

"When I joined them here in London. They lived in Cheapside then. I had written about my situation after father's death, and Ben wrote back and said I must come. He was very kind." Kind and joyful. The whole world became brighter when Ben was near. He inspired a lightness of the spirit, unlike the man with her now, who made her angry and always on her guard. "You said that you knew him when you were boys. Was the youth much like the man?"

"Maturity did not change his basic character. He was as impulsive and as carefree when he was a lad. He caused a lot of mischief back then."

"He was a naughty child, you mean."

"In the best way. Although . . . the boy, like the man, often did not calculate the consequences of his actions."

"That is because Ben lived for the moment. He was

not calculating at all. He counted on everything always working out in the end."

She loved that about him. She loved the way she felt free and almost reckless in Ben's presence. Life had forced her to become so boring and sensible before his smiles for her warmed during their last year together.

He had returned her youth to her for a short while, and she still hid that reborn, wistful girl in the same place where she guarded Benjamin's memory.

Rothwell had turned and was looking at her. He appeared hard again, and his dark blue eyes reflected deep calculation. Ben had never looked at people like that.

She met his gaze. That was a mistake. The connection put her at a disadvantage, just as it had in the reception hall last week when he brought his aunt here. He looked too deeply and saw too much. She felt he was reading her heart.

She reacted as she had too often to this man. It resembled the way Ben had made her feel, only it possessed darker tones. Danger tinged his attention, and fear shivered within the stimulation he provoked.

She suffered it. She told herself she was standing her ground. The truth whispered in her heart, however. She was powerless to look away, to reject the excitement.

"I expect life was never dull while you lived in this house," he said.

She felt herself flushing. It was as though he had seen those stolen kisses in her memory and now referred to them.

He appeared about to speak again but was interrupted. A footman arrived to say that their attendance was requested in the library.

"It appears the diversion is ready," Lord Hayden said.

He escorted her to the other room. His proximity reminded her of their tour of this house. That did not help her thwart the odd power he cast.

"I enjoy speaking with you about Benjamin," she said as they entered the library. "I hope that someday you will favor me with some stories about his time in Greece or from his youth."

"Certainly, Miss Welbourne."

A little stage setting waited for them in the library. Two low columns flanked a blue cloth strewn on the floor. A white cloth hung behind it, tied to the bookcases. The backdrop showed a painted hill and columned temple.

Lady Wallingford stood to the side. She bade them sit on two chairs that had been arranged in front of the blue cloth.

She clapped for attention. Another clap and the diversion began.

Caroline emerged from behind the backdrop. She wore a costume with an ancient Greek flavor. It left her arms bare and her ankles visible and showed too much skin at her neck and chest. Mama had done up her hair in a very mature style and even dabbed a bit of paint here and there on her young face.

Caroline appeared very pretty, very grown up, and close to scandalous.

Alexia slid Lord Hayden a sidelong look, to see his reaction. She caught him sliding one to her at the same time.

"And here I thought you had them well in hand, Miss

Welbourne," he whispered. "It appears my aunt does not intend to wait until June before frying me."

Lady Wallingford's pretty bait took her position between the two columns and began to recite a passage from the *Iliad*.

CHAPTER FIVE

~

Garbed in an old dress and wrapped in a long wool shawl, Alexia retreated to the library. She built up the fire, laid on the nearby sofa, and propped an open book on her stomach.

Silence. Freedom. A toasty fire and hours of privacy. She closed her eyes and savored the sensation of returning to a world she knew well. The rain gently pattering on the windows only made it better.

It had been brilliant to ask Lord Hayden for the free day every week. Bold too. She never expected to get it and was amazed when he capitulated. Perhaps he did feel a little guilty about the Longworths. There was no other explanation.

That was a mark in his favor, but she did not waste time examining his character. She planned to thoroughly enjoy these hours without Lady Wallingford and Caroline and especially Lord Hayden himself. He always seemed underfoot, visiting by day or dining by night. The man was young, unmarried, and rich. Surely he had better things to do than attend on his aunt.

She smiled to herself. Undoubtedly he did. However, his aunt possessed an uncanny ability to require his attendance, and he lacked the skill to escape her machinations. Alexia suspected the fish analogy had been inappropriate. Rothwell was not being lured. Henrietta had fixed a ring through his nose and was slowly, inexorably, leading him to the slaughter.

She giggled at the image. As a Minotaur plodded at the end of Henrietta's tether, however, the fantasy transformed. She suddenly saw him standing beside young Caroline in a church.

Her mirth died away and she examined the picture in her head. It would not be a love match. She doubted he had any romance in him. Caroline would think it one, however, because she was young and awed. By the time that illusion faded, they would have accommodated each other enough. Caroline would have what most women sought—security and support and hopefully kindness.

The picture changed again, and Rothwell no longer stood in that church. Benjamin did. She no longer watched from above but stood at his side. For an instant, joy filled her as if it were real.

She pushed the image from her head with wistful regret. Life did not always work out as one wanted. Sometimes one had to make do with less than one's dreams.

The book beckoned. Normally she would read Scott in her room, where no one could see. It was not the sort of serious literature that a governess would enjoy. It had not been included in the list she had given Caroline as part of her lessons.

Wrapped and cozy, she allowed herself the temporary liberation of living in a world of dashing men and
exquisite women, of passions too strong for reality and
of romance too dramatic to be real.

"Ewwww."

Caroline's face screwed up in disgust, but she shoul-
dered her way closer to the vulture's head preserved in
spirits. For all of the erudite artifacts crammed into the
museum's collection at Montagu House, this grotesque
specimen was surpassed in popularity only by the pick-
led cyclops pig and the Egyptian mummy.

Hayden smiled at her childish fascination and repul-
sion. That she would probably be married in a year was
criminal. He did not approve of these young girls being
matched off, and not only because his own mother's
early marriage had been so tragic.

"Now we really *must* see the marbles," Henrietta
cooed, pulling her daughter out of the crowd of vulture-
gawkers.

Hayden had distracted their party from visiting the
Elgin marbles twice already. He did not forget how Hen
had dressed Caroline up for that diversion. He suspected he knew why his aunt was so adamant about
seeing the marbles, and it had little to do with their reputation as superior examples of Greek art.

"I do not think Miss Welbourne would approve of
Caroline viewing the marbles," he said.

"I am the mother, and the decision is mine. However,
Miss Welbourne instructed that they be viewed. She

spoke so highly of them that I am compelled to see them again myself."

"If she was so adamant, she should have accompanied us and seen to the matter herself."

He had arrived to fetch all the ladies, only to discover that Miss Welbourne had chosen this as her free day. She had left him to Hen's mercy while she enjoyed herself going about the town doing heaven knew what. He had come very close to sending word that Miss Welbourne was to come down forthwith and get into his carriage and choose another damned free day.

His aunt herded him in the direction she wanted him to go. "Miss Welbourne said they were in a separate little building. They are this way, are they not?"

They left Montagu House, dodged the rain, and entered the annex that held the sculptures Lord Elgin had removed from the great Parthenon in Athens.

"Now, you must not be shocked, Caroline," Henrietta instructed. "Great artists take liberties that may appear scandalous, but since it is art it exists on a higher plane of experience. Also, these are very old, from before the Christians even existed."

Hayden suspected it was the shock that his aunt actually wanted Caroline to experience, and higher plane be damned. The male figures in this chamber were mostly unclothed. His aunt was conducting a sly form of initiation today, and his presence with them was inappropriate.

Aunt Hen wanted that too. She wanted her daughter to see these statues and begin wondering what existed beneath the garments of the future husband by her side.

If Miss Welbourne had come, she could have given

an art lesson to Caroline while he made himself scarce. He wondered if Hen had decreed the governess stay home so he would not have that option. More likely, Miss Welbourne had surmised the plan and helped out on her own.

He intended to have some conversation with her about that. Very soon.

They stood in front of the metopes showing the battle of the Lapiths and the Centaurs. Hayden told the story being shown. Hen exclaimed over the artistry.

Caroline gazed at those naked male bodies curiously. An awkward little silence ensued. Hayden tried to look very garbed.

Caroline's brow furrowed. "They are all broken. It is as if swords have hacked off heads and arms. I cannot imagine why these are even on display, let alone famous."

He almost blurted that bodies never look like this when limbs have been hacked off. The image of what they did look like invaded his head, and his soul sickened. He fought the reaction into submission by giving the ladies his concentrated attention.

"It is the sculpting of the forms, darling—that is why they are esteemed," Hen said. "The torsos and thighs and hips—"

"I do not like them at all."

"Others share your criticism, Caroline," Hayden said. "Greek art is an acquired taste for many. I am told that women appreciate these marbles more as they mature." He did the herding this time, out of the annex. "It is a pity Miss Welbourne did not accompany us instead of going to visit friends. I am sure she could explain the artistry in ways that fail my level of sensitivity."

"Oh, she did not leave to call on friends," Caroline said. "She intended to remain in the house, to take care of personal things. Letters and such."

That did not improve his mood. He faced another few hours of this outing while Miss Welbourne evaded her duties and wrote letters. Love letters, most likely, to the dead Benjamin Longworth.

She brightened only when Ben's name was mentioned. She became a different woman. The memory of that old love rejuvenated her for a spell. That was unhealthy. It was also a love built on lies. Once again Ben had acted impulsively, without calculating the costs, this time to the lady in question.

Ben never intended to marry Alexia Welbourne, no matter what she was led to believe. His sight had been set on a young lady of good fortune and aristocratic family long before that trip to Greece. Fighting in Greece itself had been intended as a path to the kind of heroics that would impress the wealthy, unattainable young woman being pursued.

Henrietta interrupted his thoughts by suggesting they visit the museum's library. Hayden braced himself for another hour of playing the teacher.

When he opened the door to the library, he spied a familiar face. His brother Elliot sat at a table, poring over a large manuscript. Elliot had returned to town from the Cambridge libraries only last night, but here he was, at it again.

"Wait here, Aunt Hen."

Hayden left the ladies at the door and walked over to

his brother. He had to touch Elliot's shoulder to get his attention.

The mane of thick dark hair tipped back. Elliot gazed up through his spectacles. The mind groped its way back to the present from wherever that manuscript had sent it.

"Hayden. This is a surprise."

"It will be. Come with me. If you object I will thrash you."

Befuddled but accepting, Elliot got up and followed him.

"Look whom I found ruining his eyes over a dense Latin tome," Hayden announced.

Reunion greetings flowed. Elliot could get lost in history, but he could also be very charming. Caroline brightened under his flattery at how grown up and pretty she was and how she would be besieged by suitors this season.

"The ladies wish to see the library and learn of its holdings, Elliot."

"I would be happy to show you the collection. There are many rarities that are both beautiful and instructive. There are also Smirke's drawings of the new museum building being constructed."

"What a splendid idea," Hayden said. "I leave them in your capable hands."

Henrietta's face fell. "But, Hayden, I thought that you—"

"I have appointments this afternoon and would have had to curtail this outing soon anyway. Now you can enjoy the library at your leisure. Elliot is far more qualified to give the lesson than I am. Show them everything, Elliot. They have all day."

He made good his escape. It was unlikely his aunt and cousin would emerge until close to dinner. He left the carriage to wait for them and went to find a hansom cab.

He had not lied. There really were appointments waiting this afternoon. Not for a few hours, however. He had somewhere else to go before he went to the City for his business affairs.

She emerged out of a dream, aware even as she floated toward consciousness that she had dozed off unexpectedly. Something pulled her to the surface. Not a sound. A sensation of intuitive caution stirred her awake.

She opened her eyes. The first thing she saw were other eyes, so darkly blue they startled. The sight of them caused an echo in her soul, of having just seen those eyes in the dream now fading into the mists of deepest memory.

The sights and scents of the real world burned away sleep's remnants, leaving her gazing up at the face of Lord Hayden Rothwell.

He appeared very tall standing there. Very serious too, with a little frown creasing his brow. Probably he disapproved of servants sleeping on the library sofa.

She pushed herself up so she sat. "Your aunt has returned?"

"I left her with my brother Elliot at the library." He hovered over her. His proximity unnerved her.

She resented that. Even on the occasions when they

spoke casually, even when she allowed him to lure her into forgetting why she should hate him, that discomforting disturbance remained.

She should not have to tolerate it today. "I gave Falkner instructions that no one was to intrude in this chamber."

"The servants would never think that you included me. To their minds I am the master of this house and all in it." He still did not move, as if to emphasize with his dominance that "all in it" meant he was master of her too. "Is this how you intend to use the free days that you cajoled me to give you? Reading by the fire?"

"It is my day to do as I choose. If you expected an accounting, you should have said so." She wished he would leave. He was ruining everything.

"So for a few hours you will live here as you once did and treat this house as your home again. I did not appreciate the symbolic meaning of the word *free* when you used it."

His words traveled to her heart, where they resonated with their truth. He understood her better than she did herself. He comprehended why these hours had been so delicious.

She had another reason to hate this man now.

She glared up at him. "Why are you here?"

"To see you."

His gaze shifted, taking in her plain cap and old green dress and thick, simple woolen shawl. She should be embarrassed by her poor appearance, but right now it seemed convenient and . . . safe.

"I also came to speak with you and make certain you understand what I require of you."

"I know my duties."

"It appears you do not. I expected you to be with my cousin today."

"Since she would be accompanied by you and her mother, there was no need for me. Your aunt agreed."

"We both know why my aunt did not want you with us. She could throw the girl at me more easily this way."

"Your aunt's designs on you are not my concern. I chose this free day carefully, so it would not interfere with Caroline's lessons."

"I think you chose this day so you could avoid me."

Again his words resonated. "Perhaps I did. You have been more present in this house than I expected. It is a strain for me to muster the grace that requires."

His expression hardened in a way she knew well. She was being too bold again. She did not care. This was her free day, and that meant first and foremost that she should be free of *him*.

"In the future, when I escort my cousin and aunt, you will join us."

"I do not need instructions in my duties from you. It is your aunt's decision, anyway, not yours."

"You will be there," he said firmly.

She gritted her teeth and looked to the fire, ignoring him as best she could. She trusted he would leave now. Having decreed the new law, there was no reason for the lord to remain.

He did not leave, but at least he strolled away. Unfortunately, he moved over to the fireplace, taking a position that demanded she see him. Tall, strong, and dark, he intruded in every way possible, visually and viscerally.

"You were smiling in your sleep," he said. "Were you dreaming about him? Ben?"

"I do not know." Eyes gazed out of her memory's deepest shadows. "I do not think so, but perhaps I was."

"He was my friend and I owe him a debt, but—"

"I hope you never owe me one, having seen how you repay them."

She hit her mark with that. His reaction made her nape prickle. The caution carried too many overtones of the other stimulations that he always evoked, however.

"He has been dead three years," he said. "Perhaps you should stop pining."

Anger surged in her head. It pushed her beyond prudence in a blink. She rose to her feet. "I treasure my memories, but I am not pining."

"You spoke of your love in the present tense the night of Caroline's recitation."

"I am sure I did not."

"You did, and you are wasting yourself in it."

"You are being too familiar. This conversation would be extraordinary even if you were a dear friend, which you most certainly are not. I would not tolerate such intrusive speculations from a relative, let alone *you*."

He walked up to her. She almost stepped back, but her anger knew no sense.

"You will have no future unless you let go of him."

She had to bend her neck to look up at him. He was doing it again, trying to command with his presence and will. He liked doing that, and she wanted to hit him for what it did to her. Her pulse sped even as her temper seethed.

"How dare you speak of my future? You of all men?

It was poor enough a month ago. I had neither fortune nor beauty, but I at least had a home and a family. It is outrageous for you to broach that topic with me."

He accepted her accusations without comment. She saw heat in his eyes to match her own. The caution rose to a high pitch, but she threw it to the winds.

"There are men who look beyond a fortune, and you have beauty enough." Considering his intense, hard expression, his voice sounded very calm.

"Now you are being cruel."

"Your eyes are wonders. Mesmerizing. And they reflect your indomitable spirit."

The flattery stunned her speechless. Her anger scurried around her mind, trying to collect thoughts that scattered from the shock, desperate to regroup itself.

He stood closer now. She had not noticed him move, but he was very close. Too close. He looked into her eyes, and she was the one mesmerized.

A velvet warmth, on her cheek. *He was touching her.* A tremor pulsed beneath his fingertips and slid down to her chest. She should—

"Your complexion is lovely too," he said, subtly caressing. The soft touch, so startling and intimate, took her breath away. His gaze lowered. "And your mouth, Miss Welbourne. Well, your mouth is beautiful in ways I doubt you will ever understand."

He looked into her eyes again and stunned her anew. His gaze burned hot and fiery, full of the danger she had sensed in him from the start.

Wide-eyed with astonishment, she saw the decision flash through him. It was so preposterous that she did not believe her instincts.

His mouth pressed hers. Warm, firm, commanding, the kiss produced shock after wondrous shock. Confusion reigned in her head. Somewhere within her chaotic reactions, the practical Alexia issued sensible orders on what to do, but she was too amazed to obey.

She reacted shamelessly. Flushing warmth cascaded through her whole body, pooling and tingling in her breasts and belly and lower. The excitement turned physical, threatening to rule her completely. Streams of pleasure seduced her toward abandon.

The sensations enchanted her. He embraced her, and she lost herself. She capitulated to an intimacy so delicious that she silently moaned with gratitude. The strength holding her, the firm body pressing her, the unbearable heat of the mouth kissing her lips, her neck, her chest—an Alexia who was not at all practical reveled in the sensual stimulation and welcomed the rain of passion.

The kisses stopped. Masculine, firm fingers held her face. She opened her eyes to see him gazing down at her. Desire transformed his severity. The hardness itself became seductive.

He kissed her again, and a battle began in her essence. She had seen too much in his eyes. Calculations burned in them. She had also glimpsed how she appeared to him—a woman submitting to a man she did not like or trust. A lonely spinster accepting any man's attentions.

A corner of her mind found its balance, but she did not want to give up the bliss of feeling so alive. She did not want to surrender the human connection. Even as she pressed her hands against his chest, demanding release, too much of her ached to melt into him no matter who he was and what shame awaited.

She saw and felt every instant of disconnection. The relaxation of his hold, the slow falling away of his arms, the withdrawal of his touch—her body reacted to every loss.

She walked away quickly to the window. She gazed out, unable to look at him. She tried to steady herself so she would look normal when she left the library. As good sense returned, raw humiliation came with it.

She hoped he would have the courtesy to leave. He did not. She thought he would at least apologize. No words came. She felt him watching her. That only made it worse. If he left she could curse her own weakness and his ruthlessness. As long as he stayed, she remained shaky and embarrassed, too flustered to compose herself.

"That was not very honorable of you, Lord Hayden."

"No."

He did not sound contrite. His tone all but said, *Perhaps not, but I do as I please.*

"I know why you did that," she said. "I know what you must think about me."

"You know a lot, then."

His voice sounded closer. She realized he had walked over to her. He stood no more than an arm's span away. To her horror, the excitement, the danger, began bewitching her again. Her heart began a slow, heavy beat.

"How do I think of you, Miss Welbourne? Since I am not sure myself, your explanation would be helpful."

A decent man would apologize and be gone. "Ben and I were not *that* close. You have misunderstood."

"I was not thinking about that at all. My only thought was that you needed kissing."

She turned, determined to end the way he toyed with her. Her heart lurched at the sight of him, but she smacked that girlish excitement into its place.

"Not by you, sir. I am not the servant for the lord's taking, and I ask you to remember that in the future."

He looked at her as directly as ever, only now his gaze reflected those kisses. It always would in the future too. Granting a man liberties created a palpable familiarity that forever undermined social formalities.

"I did not try to take you. I only kissed you, and not nearly as boldly as you would have permitted."

Her face scalded. "Now your speech is insulting."

"No, it is honest. I will leave you to pretend otherwise, however." With a vague bow, he headed toward the door.

"Lord Hayden, I trust that in the future you will show me the respect that my position with your cousin requires."

He stopped at the door and turned back to her.

"I haven't decided yet."

"Then allow me to help you decide. I did not like your kiss and you must not do this again."

He opened the door. "You liked it. Do you think a man cannot tell?"

CHAPTER
SIX

Hayden approached the columned portico of Darfield and Longworth. He barely remembered riding to the City from Mayfair. His thoughts had been so preoccupied by what had occurred in Henrietta's library that he hardly noticed the fine rain that dampened his clothes.

He had not behaved honorably. Women in Miss Welbourne's situation were vulnerable and too often misused. Men who took advantage of them were scoundrels. Nor was he a man who importuned ladies. The understandings he forged with his lovers and mistresses were clearly articulated and mutually beneficial.

Perhaps with time he would feel appropriately apologetic about Miss Welbourne. Right now nothing could compete with memories of those kisses and her passionate compliance. He was not an impulsive man, so the fact those kisses had happened at all fascinated him as much as her sensual reaction.

It was the kind of thing he might have done right after his father died. Mourning had been followed by a euphoria of freedom, similar to that experienced by a prisoner released from an underground cell. For a couple of years he had careened through life like a drunk, wallowing in extreme emotions and impetuous acts, indulging in the reckless joys denied for too many years.

He had been an actor on London's stage, trying on costumes, hoping one fit better than his own skin. He had been desperate to disprove the truth that hounded him—that he was very much his father's son and had too much of the old man in him.

Eventually he accommodated the legacy and tamed its darkness while exploiting its strengths. As he passed through the portico, however, the balance tipped anew. The speculations gathering around the memories of those kisses were more dishonorable than the kisses themselves. The ruthless side of him weighed the complete seduction of Miss Welbourne and the lures required to convince her that one of those mutually beneficial arrangements was in her interest.

The scene inside the bank wiped those calculations from his mind. A thick knot of about thirty men had gathered, forming a disorganized line in front of the offices.

Several other men arrived, too much in a hurry. He read the concern on their faces and in their quick steps. He saw the signs of a run beginning.

No one had noticed him yet. He heard Longworth's name mentioned. The door to the office opened. Darfield allowed one man to enter, then closed the door again.

Hayden approached the crowd. A ripple of panic spread.

A man blocked his path. "You'll not be going in first, Rothwell. We'll not be eating crumbs after your family is fed."

"My family has no intention of dining here today."

"So you said a month ago, but there's word of strange doings here, what with Longworth—"

"Mr. Longworth sold his partnership to Darfield for personal reasons. His private finances do not reflect on this bank's solvency."

"Then why are you here?" another man demanded.

"Not to remove any money, I assure you."

He received some skeptical looks for that. Too many banks were failing for anyone to trust overmuch.

"I have no cause to doubt this bank's strength." He spoke loud enough for all to hear. "I have no intention of removing funds or accounts now, nor reason to consider it in the near future. If you gentlemen want yours, Mr. Darfield will comply. The reserves are more than enough to cover all of your demands."

His bluntness checked their panic. He might have proven his capacity to be a scoundrel in his physical desires today, but his success in investments did not carry the stain of deceptive strategies.

The knot loosened. A few men bled away. Others regrouped to debate their course. The path to the office cleared.

He asked the clerk to announce him, even though Darfield already had a visitor. Darfield appeared in the doorway at once, crisp and serious in his dark coats and high collar, avuncular in his soft face and silvery hair. He slipped out and closed the door behind him.

Darfield shooed his clerk away. While he smiled

confidently at the men circling and watching, he spoke in a low voice. "I regret to say that our examination of the accounts was not thorough enough in ferreting out our friend's sins."

"What do you mean?"

He pushed the door ajar to reveal the visitor waiting inside. Hayden recognized him as Sir Matthew Rolland, a baronet from Cumbria.

Darfield closed the door again. "He wants to remove the funds that we hold for him. When I checked and explained they had been sold, he insisted he never sold them and had been receiving the income from us all along."

"We looked into all the sold securities from the last few years. I suppose we might have missed some. Were the income payments made?"

"I was on my way to ascertain that."

"I will wait with him while you do. It would not be a good moment for him to leave this office, angry and full of accusations."

Darfield glanced to the knots of men. "No, indeed." He aimed for another office, where clerks kept the accounts.

Hayden pushed open the door. Sir Matthew did not appear worried. A blond, round-faced man given to country pursuits, he looked to be calmly biding his time while a bookkeeping mistake was rectified.

"Rothwell," he greeted, adding a broad grin. "Come to save Easterbrook's legacy, have you?"

"I am not here for that purpose. I am a friend of Mr. Darfield."

"Then you can see that he fixes this misunderstanding. Says I sold those consols. Never did."

"I am sure he will find the error in his records quickly. How much were they for?"

"Five thousand."

Hayden occupied Sir Matthew with talk of hunts and sport. Darfield did not rejoin them for almost half an hour. When he did, he wore a mask of sobriety.

"Sir Matthew, I am embarrassed to say that sorting through the situation with your funds is complicated. Rather than keep you waiting, however, we will give you the money now and work out the particulars in the future."

Sir Matthew did not appreciate how extraordinary the offer was. Darfield sat at the desk and wrote a draft. Hayden noticed it was from Darfield's own account.

With smiles and good wishes, they saw a satisfied Sir Matthew out. As soon as the door closed, Darfield allowed his dismay to show.

"There is no record of payments to him," he said. "We show the funds sold, period. It is as with the others. Longworth must have been paying him off, and I am now five thousand the poorer. How many more did we miss, that is my question."

"I would not have said we missed any." A memory of a sensual mouth beckoned Hayden to distraction, but it would be a long while before he could indulge in speculations about that again. "It appears we will have to go through it all once more."

"Could it be that someone has revealed Longworth's game, and Sir Matthew is—no, that is too shocking to consider."

"Let us see if Timothy Longworth made income payments to him from his own accounts, as he did with the others. And let us be sure this is the last of it. When do the records say he sold the funds?"

Darfield sat down and opened a thick ledger. "1822. No, wait." He peered closely. "The ink is a bit smeared. It could be—but that date is impossible—"

"What date could it be?"

Darfield looked up, stunned. "1820."

Hayden shared Darfield's surprise. Timothy Longworth was not yet a partner in this bank back then.

Benjamin Longworth was, however.

A penetrating sadness drenched Hayden. It was not only evoked by what this day might reveal about his friend. A repressed suspicion regarding Benjamin's death suddenly became more plausible.

"We will need to examine all the records regarding the funds you held. All the way back to when Benjamin Longworth first bought his partnership. If you still have the information from Benjamin's private accounts, you had better bring that here too."

Darfield nodded, his sorrow visible. "I appreciate your aid and discretion. Will you require anything else?"

"Strong spirits. Whiskey might do it."

All three brothers dined at home that evening. Hayden would have welcomed the camaraderie on any other day. Tonight, however, even Elliot's dry wit could not pull him out of his thoughts. His distraction created long silences at the table. It also sent Christian's gaze in his direction too often.

"We are a sober group," Christian said. "If I had known you would be so boring, Hayden, I would have accepted the invitation to Lady Falrith's party. At least there the boredom would have had a variety of sources."

"I am contemplating a new proof that I am testing." Normally he did not lie so boldly, but what he truly contemplated could not be revealed.

He had left the bank today with too many questions. He had also carried away a horrible secret. Timothy Longworth had not invented the scheme of forging names and selling the securities. He had learned the trick from Benjamin, who had been doing it almost since he bought the partnership in Darfield's bank. After Ben's death, Timothy had continued sending the income payments to Ben's victims while he created new victims of his own.

Memories had filled his head in the hours since. Those of Benjamin as a boy, so reckless and spirited compared to the Rothwell sons. Their father had been a stern man, severe in his honor and dominating in his personality.

The rational mind is what makes us human. The Greeks knew that, and it is a lesson that a man forgets to his peril. Passion has its place, but the mind must always rule. Emotions lead to impulses that destroy honor, fortune, and happiness.

He had heard that lesson in one form or another every day of his youth. Worse, he had lived with the evidence of its truth in the misery that emotion and passion had brought to his parents. In the country, however, he could escape both the man and the lesson for hours on end. The boy down the road named Benjamin Longworth became a tonic against the way the lesson made joy and high spirits suspect and shameful.

"I thought you put strict limits on those mathematical investigations now," Christian said. "You must learn to do as Elliot does. When you are among the living, breathing world, you must live and breathe too. *He* is not being boring tonight."

Having just thought of their father, Hayden did not like hearing Christian sound too much like him. "It is not my obligation to entertain you, damn it."

Christian found the snarling response too interesting.

Elliot did too. "I do not think it is numbers that distract you, Hayden."

"Think whatever you like." He did not want to talk about it. His brothers knew nothing and could explain nothing. Only one person in London might possess information that bore on Ben and that bank. A woman who hated him but responded with passion to his kisses. A woman who had been in love with Ben and still was.

"Perhaps he is thinking about a woman," Christian said to Elliot. It was damned unnerving to have Christian guess correctly. "Although he never is much distracted by them. This would have to be a very special lady, only none of them is ever special to him either. There is no logic to romantic love, no mathematical equation for it, so he knows it does not exist."

Elliot shot him a quick glance. They had been allies back in the days when Christian was so damned *good*. Elliot could sense his moods in ways no one else could. "I do not think it is a woman."

He was both right and wrong. A woman strolled through all of his thoughts about Ben. What did she know? How would she react to discovering Ben's crimes? Would she blame Hayden Rothwell if it all came out and Ben's good name was ruined?

Darfield had promised silence again, to protect his own fortune and reputation. Hayden had pledged his own funds to cover any loss to the bank's clients. His debt to his old friend had just gotten very expensive.

With ruthless clarity, he saw it all unfold. Ben fit his role in the drama too well. Even the drunkenness on the ship home, his resistance to returning to the staid life of a banker—all that was the Ben he knew. What else besides boredom might have been waiting in London, however, and how had that affected his soul?

Was he despondent because he anticipated the discovery of his crimes? He had built a house of cards with those thefts. He had to know that eventually it would fall. Had he jumped off that ship? It had always been a possibility, considering Ben's mood those last days. A possibility Hayden had avoided contemplating, because if Ben had jumped, Hayden had permitted it.

A sick hollow had opened in his gut today and refused to leave. He had always harbored guilt about that night. Now he wondered if his own pride had made him blind to the depths of his friend's despair.

"Well, it should be a woman that distracts him. One of you needs to marry soon," Christian said. "I would like to have a nephew."

Elliot laughed. "We never have to marry, Christian. We do not have to curtail our eccentricities to please a wife. You are the one with that duty." He lounged back and examined Christian. "You might start by cutting your hair. I have heard the ladies use the word 'barbaric' to describe it."

Christian ignored the comment. He did not like others meddling in his life. Being intrusive and incisive was a right he reserved for himself.

"In the least you could both use mistresses," Christian muttered. "Hayden has become irritable of late, and that is why. And you rarely leave those libraries, Elliot."

"And you rarely leave this house," Hayden said. On the best of days his brother's presumptions annoyed him, and he was not in the mood to tolerate them tonight. "You shirk your duties to the title and have the brass to say we have to give you an heir. See to your own obligations and your own woman and your own habits, Easterbrook. When all that is in order, you can turn your attention to me."

Elliot sipped his wine with a little smile. Christian's eyes turned cold.

"I know exactly what I owe to my title and family," he said. "I know because I made clear choices regarding what it will be. It is possible to do it that way, Hayden. One need not accept the world's or a religion's or a father's dictates on these things. We can choose what we owe to an idea or to a person."

Benjamin's ghost loomed then, smiling and happy, as if Christian had called him forth. The image changed quickly, though. Hayden saw Benjamin on that ship's deck, cradling a bottle, refusing to come below.

Why had Ben really left Britain, and why did returning make him despondent? And if he had stolen over forty thousand pounds, where the hell was it?

Alexia eyed the hat perched on Lady Wallingford's head. One could not find serious fault with its design. It would look more elegant if the ribbons were a tad narrower and the satin flowers a bit smaller, but Mrs. Bramble, the milliner, knew her craft.

"The colors are a little too strong for you," Alexia said.

"But I adore the trocadero, and it looks rich with the blue." She pouted.

"Miss Welbourne's advice is not without merit, madam. You are so fair, and those particular hues draw attention from your own beauty." Mrs. Bramble glanced to Alexia for approval.

Alexia nodded subtly. The milliner and she had formed a truce.

Since arriving at this shop, Alexia had succeeded in discouraging Lady Wallingford from purchasing three very expensive hats. Without saying a word on the matter, she had let Mrs. Bramble know that if she wanted to write any bills of sale, she had better cooperate.

Mrs. Bramble brought over a basket of ribbon. Alexia plucked out a pure, intense yellow. She draped it in front of Henrietta's face and the green of Hen's eyes instantly darkened. She swathed the yellow over the flaming trocadero and pinned it expertly in place, so Hen could judge the effect for herself in the looking glass.

While Henrietta peered at her own reflection, Mrs. Bramble peered at Alexia. "You have an eye for it, I will not deny that," she said quietly. "Your own bonnet is very handsome and superbly crafted. May I ask where you bought it?"

"From a small shop in the City. Most of the wares are very ordinary, but there is one woman there whose artistry surpasses the others."

"Should you ever hear that this woman seeks another situation, I hope that you will send her to me."

Henrietta decreed that the yellow, while not nearly as dramatic as the trocadero, would be the better choice. She gave Mrs. Bramble an order for the hat and several caps for herself and Caroline. Alexia accompanied her out to the carriage, hoping Lord Hayden would appreciate that this visit had been a mere fraction as expensive as his aunt had intended.

The footman handed Henrietta into the carriage, but Alexia declined his help. "I should have ordered a cornette for myself," she said. "May I go back, madam? I will not be long."

"You may tend to it. Since Hayden will be bringing Caroline to meet us, Madame Tissot can begin taking measurements if they arrive there first."

The impending presence of Lord Hayden was one reason Alexia wanted to return to the shop. There was no generous way to view those kisses in the library. He had been a scoundrel and she had been wanton. It was as simple as that.

If she could believe that such a lapse would never happen again, she might try to pretend it had never occurred. Unfortunately, nothing was settled that neatly. He had visited twice in the last few days, and his awareness of what she had permitted affected the air between them. He did not say anything about it, however. He certainly had not apologized.

His expressions and gazes might not reveal the shocking truth, but his mere presence made the atmosphere turn so thick that breathing normally became a chore. Worse, a foolish excitement would pulse silently in her head and blood no matter how much she tried to scold it into disappearing.

"Did Lady Wallingford forget something?" Mrs. Bramble asked when Alexia reentered the shop. The milliner glanced around for a neglected shawl or reticule.

"I wanted to speak with you about the woman who made my bonnet. I have cause to believe that she fashions hats on her own, aside from the work she does for her employer. Her best designs are available privately because the owner of the shop has taste that is too inferior to appreciate them."

"It is all too common," Mrs. Bramble said. "I would not want my own people to do this, of course. However, if the shop owner does not want the hats . . . well, that is different."

"I expect that your shop would do much better for her than any in the City and far better than she could do on her own."

Mrs. Bramble's lids lowered while she considered the overture. "Would this woman bring these hats to me personally?"

"I would be happy to do so for her."

"If I use the hat you bring as a model, would she complete orders in a timely way? Execute the alterations requested?"

"I am very sure she would."

Mrs. Bramble's eyes turned shrewd. "You appear to know her well."

"We have had some conversation, and I know her to be honest and diligent."

"Then I encourage you to tell her to send me one or two, if they are the quality of the one you now wear."

Alexia hurried out to join Henrietta. Mrs. Bramble suspected there was no woman in the City. It had been kind of her to allow the deception for the sake of pride.

She had returned to the shop on an impulse, but it was also a decision born of years of debate about her future. Her first plan for her new employment had not developed quite as she had intended. If she remained Caroline's governess, she would be vulnerable to Hayden Rothwell's inexplicable, dishonorable attentions.

She could not lie to herself about that attention either. Those kisses had not been at all like Ben's. She could not pretend that love had inspired them. They had shared a raw passion that did not even need the slightest affection. The excitement he offered contained too much dominance, too much danger, and no romance.

Now, however, she might have found a way to be a milliner without ever working in a shop. That was far preferable to being a servant, no matter what name the position was given. It was also much better than becoming a soiled dove, no matter how pleasurable the seduction that led to it.

She would make those hats and see what she received from Mrs. Bramble for them. It might be enough to allow her to begin forging an independent life where she would never be vulnerable to Rothwell's dangerous addresses.

Hayden cursed himself. He would curse Alexia Welbourne too, but that would not be fair.

It wasn't really her fault that he was in this feminine cave, being shown colored plates and listening to Henrietta's incessant critiques. God help him, he had *offered* to bring Caroline here to meet her mother and governess.

He had waited until the ladies arrived, even though he could have left his cousin in Madame Tissot's capable hands. Now he was being punished for the sly desire that kept him attending on Hen too much in order to see Miss Welbourne.

The woman he pursued tried to act as if he were not in the room. The seducer in him noted every little flush and stammer, however. And the gentleman—well, he continued weighing honor against desire, and agreed to boring afternoons like this so he could enjoy the latter while pretending to practice the former.

He welcomed the insidious stimulation of the silent battles taking place in his head and in this chamber. For one thing, it obscured his relentless questions regarding Benjamin Longworth.

They occupied his mind, demanding attention. He wanted to know why Ben had stolen all that money and whether those crimes were connected to his death.

Alexia Welbourne might know the answer to some of his questions. When he was with her he managed to forget all about them, however. He told himself he sought her company so he could pry a few facts out of her, only to neglect even trying. None of that was good news for the honorable side of his internal argument.

"What do you think, Hayden?" Aunt Henrietta held up two plates of potential presentation gowns. "Which should we choose?"

"I am too ignorant to give advice. What does Miss Welbourne say?"

Alexia had retreated to a chair as far from him as possible. Henrietta called her over. Expression passive, posture dignified, she joined them. Her gaze did not light on him for even an instant. She possessed an uncanny ability to ignore him without appearing rudely deliberate in the cut.

The seducer did not mind that at all. She might avert her gaze, but her awareness could not be hidden. A velvet rope of sensuality bound them together now. He could not resist exerting little tugs through mere force of will.

She examined the two plates, then critically assessed young Caroline. She glanced at the hovering modiste. "Madame, we need a few minutes of privacy to make our choice."

Madame Tissot did not care for having her influence excluded, but she retreated.

Alexia held up one plate, angled so he could see it too. "This would be the most becoming gown. However, it will be the more expensive one. Its impression of restraint must not fool us. The embellishments include hundreds of pearls and yards of venetian lace. It will cost a good deal more than this other one and leave too little for the rest of the wardrobe."

It was an admirably practical speech, well-reasoned and compelling. Before the last words were spoken, he could see Caroline regretfully accept that the other gown would have to do.

Alexia did not look in his direction, but she kept the plate in his view.

"Aunt Hen, perhaps Caroline should choose some of her ball gowns before a decision is made on this one," he said.

Aunt Hen thought that a splendid idea. She and her daughter embarked on the long process of scrutinizing plates again.

He took the opportunity to address Miss Welbourne privately, something that had been denied since he kissed her.

"You favor that one, don't you?" He gestured to the plate still held by her fingers. Long, elegant fingers, perfectly tapered. He saw the gown with its thick border of pearl-studded rosettes on a woman. Not pale little Caroline but another woman, mature and confident, with chestnut hair and violet eyes.

"It is far more distinctive. It is a design that everyone will notice. It is too expensive for your aunt, however."

"You want Caroline to have this gown, don't you?"

"She will feel very special, very beautiful. Like a princess. It will affect how she bears herself. How she smiles and laughs." She glanced to where Caroline pored over pictures with her mother, then back to the plate. Not at him, however. Never at him now. "She is much cowed by your aunt. She is also very aware of their limited income. Unlike her mother, she has become quite practical as a result. Sometimes, however . . ."

"Sometimes one can be too practical?"

"She is very young. It is a virtue better worn in maturity."

He looked at the plate showing a gown that would make a girl feel like a princess. The woman holding it had never experienced that, but she evidently understood girlish dreams and insecurities very well. She took pride in her own good sense but did not want young Caroline to be imprisoned too soon by the same pragmatic considerations.

It mattered to her that Caroline have the gown. Enough that she had allowed this conversation when she would rather pretend he did not exist.

"My cousin will wear the gown you prefer, Miss Welbourne. I will tell Aunt Hen that it is a gift from Easterbrook, so she does not attribute it to intentions that I do not have."

He went to Hen and explained Easterbrook's generosity. Caroline's face lit with delight. She jumped up and ran to snatch the plate from Alexia's fingers. She giggled and danced around Alexia's chair and peppered Alexia with requests for advice on colors. Alexia laughed and joined in the celebration.

While he watched their excitement, he explained a few other things to Henrietta.

Hen called for her daughter's attention. "We should choose at least one of the ball gowns today, before other girls make claims on the best designs. You will have to come over here and attend to that. You too, Miss Welbourne."

"I daresay you do not need my advice on them," Alexia said.

"I do not require your advice but your own choice. As my companion you will attend some parties and diversions and need the appropriate wardrobe."

Alexia's expression fell with astonishment. "I cannot afford such things, nor will you require my attendance."

"I believe it is my decision what I require. Hayden's brother agrees that you will be needed and that you must be well turned out. Easterbrook has offered to provide the wardrobe." Hen turned her best adoring expression on Hayden. "You must tell him we are all grateful. I will express my thanks when I next see him, but he is so elusive that—"

"I will convey your appreciation."

"Please do not convey *mine,*" Alexia said. "I look forward to doing so myself. I will express my thanks in my own way to the man responsible for this unexpected generosity."

She glared at him, the first direct look in days. Her eyes spoke the furious words she dare not say in front of Henrietta and Caroline.

She suspected the wardrobe would come from him and not Easterbrook. She did not like that he had found a way to bestow expensive gifts without her agreeing to accept the arrangement.

The gentleman was losing the debate on what to do about Alexia Welbourne.

CHAPTER
SEVEN

Hayden passed over the documents for signing. Suttonly scribbled his name.

"You should read them," Hayden said.

"Does your brother read them?" Suttonly spoke in his typical bored tone. He handed the pages back to Hayden and lounged back in his chair.

"Easterbrook reads every one."

"My solicitor will see to it when the final papers are prepared. You have never steered me wrong thus far. My worth has doubled since I began riding your coattails."

"A less honorable man could have relieved you of more than you have gained these last years."

"If we faced each other in a gaming hell, I would have long ago left the table, Rothwell. In these chambers, however, you have proven less bloodthirsty."

Suttonly alluded to a past that, as Hayden's old friend, he knew too well. When he first stepped into manhood, Hayden's success at the gaming tables had been notorious. The thrill of victory drove him like a madness. It had all been part of his attempts to be a different man than breeding dictated.

He kept risking ruin at the tables, and instead became rich. It took a long time to realize that he played with an unfair advantage. Where other men saw random cards, he saw patterns. Even games of chance were governed by systems of likelihoods dependent upon recent cards played.

Then he discovered the work of Bayes and Lagrange and others. He read LaPlace's book on probabilities. The study of those likelihoods was becoming a science, one that fascinated him.

However, realizing the truth had taken the fun out of the games. He restricted himself to a fairer sort of gambling now. He still saw patterns, he still calculated the odds with instincts most did not possess, but the unknown variables leveled the field somewhat. Even better, there could be victories sometimes in which no one lost.

Suttonly rose and strolled around the City chambers where Hayden conducted his business affairs. It was part of a suite that contained both an office and a bedroom. He rarely used the latter but on occasion stayed late enough that it proved convenient.

"Still at it, I see." Suttonly poked at some die on a little table and scrutinized the ledger beside them. "Any luck?"

"I am making progress." The table contained the makings of an ongoing experiment. Laws governed the likelihoods behind what others considered chance and luck. Scientists thought the world worked like a well-designed clock, but he thought it might actually be ruled by fairly simple mathematical equations.

Suttonly kept moving, poking his nose into private things the way old friends tend to do. He focused his attention on a thick stack of pages lying atop a standing desk. "What is this?"

"A new mathematical proof recently presented at the Royal Society. I am seeing if it holds."

"You must be careful, Rothwell. Such interests have not made you boring yet, but ten years hence, if you are not vigilant, no one will want to know you except the dullards who frequent Somerset House."

"I restrict my play with abstract numbers to several hours a day," Hayden said. "As it happens, they are the hours passing now."

"I will leave you to it, then. By the way, that business with Longworth—I trust it was not a latent taste for blood on your part that caused his ruin. The rumors that you were behind it are still flying."

"I have not been at the tables in years."

"What an interesting response. It is ambiguous enough to raise my eyebrows, if I were the sort to care. Longworth is best gone, I say. Ben could be fun if one overlooked his exhausting enthusiasm, but Timothy proved too tediously grasping."

When Suttonly had gone, Hayden tucked the documents into a drawer. He then approached the standing desk.

Within minutes his mind traveled paths of formulas, winding through the awesome, wordless poetry symbolized by his notations. As a student he had considered mathematics a vaguely interesting chore at which he unaccountably excelled. Finally one master had introduced him to the profound beauty hidden in the more sophisticated calculations.

It was an abstract beauty, one present in nature but not physically visible. It had nothing to do with the world in which most people lived. There were no emotions or hungers or weaknesses in these numbers. No pain or guilt, no passions or impulses. This beauty was pure rationality, the most fundamental kind, and his visits to its power could be escapes, he knew. On those occasions when his soul was in turmoil for the most human of reasons, he always found peace here.

"Sir."

The voice jolted him back into the world. His clerk stood by his side. The man had instructions to interrupt at a specific hour so that the entire day did not get lost in these abstractions. Hayden could not say how long he had been at it, but he knew this day's intrusion had arrived too soon.

"A messenger came," his clerk explained. "He brought this and the instruction that you had said to see you received it at once. If I should have waited—"

"No, you acted correctly." He slid the seal while the clerk returned to the anteroom. He read the one sentence, written by an accommodating footman in Henrietta's household.

Miss Welbourne had a free day today and had gone to the shops on Albemarle Street.

If Phaedra Blair did not possess both style and beauty, the world would consider her merely strange. Since nature had blessed her with both qualities, society thought her almost interesting.

Phaedra was one of the few good friends Alexia could claim besides her cousin Roselyn. Theirs was not an especially public friendship, although they sometimes spent time together in town, as they did today. Phaedra was the friend Alexia normally called on for private conversation about books and ideas.

The illegitimate daughter of a reforming M.P. and a bluestocking, Phaedra lived alone in a small house on a poor street near Aldgate. She had inherited from her parents the ability to discard rules and beliefs if they seemed stupid to her. Since a good many did, Alexia and she engaged in some strong arguments on occasion. It was such an argument two years ago, one exchanged the day they met while both examining the same painting at a Royal Academy exhibition, that began their friendship.

"I think your plan to make hats is admirable. As you have finally learned, a dependent woman is a woman enslaved," Phaedra said. Since an uncle had left her an income of one hundred pounds a year, Phaedra was not enslaved by anyone or anything.

They strolled through Pope's warehouse on Albemarle Street while Alexia bought millinery materials. She had decided to make one hat and one bonnet. She chose some iron wire she would use to create the latter's brim.

"Do not let that milliner rob you. Your hats are worth a great deal," Phaedra said. "Design is everything in art."

"She will want to profit too. Even a few pounds a

month and I can support myself." Barely, but it could be done. If she was frugal, she might save some money too. In a few years she might open a school for girls. That was a common and respectable way for ladies to employ themselves.

"I am the last woman to preach against this course of action. Still, you care more about the world's opinion than I do, Alexia. Do not discount that as you make your choices. If it is learned that you engage in such piece-work for a shop, your attempts to maintain your station will be in vain."

Alexia sorely wished she did not care so much about that opinion or her station. Phaedra didn't, and her life was probably a lot more interesting than her own would ever be. Phaedra did not worry about propriety at all. She traveled alone if she wished. She entertained writers and artists in that small house. Alexia had reason to suspect that Phaedra had lovers too. Alexia did not approve of that, but she could not deny that her friend's indifference to social rules could be alluring.

Phaedra did not even wear caps or bonnets. Her long, rippling red hair just flowed too. She did not dress it.

As a result, they received a lot of looks from patrons in the warehouse. Once people looked at that hair, they noticed the garments and looked some more. Phaedra wore mostly black. She could be in mourning if not for the hair and the unusual, flowing cut of her dresses. The apollo-gold silk lining of her black cape further announced that black was her preference.

"I will confess that I am surprised by your decision to leave that house," Phaedra said as Alexia chose some

Dunstable straw for the hat. "You have this day to yourself and use of the carriage. You are not a prisoner. You are far more comfortable there than you will be on your own."

"I do not want the dependency, no matter what comfort it brings. Nor is it secure. I could be put out at any time, for any reason. Then where would I be?"

"How is that different from what you knew before?"

"Before it was family. Family do not put you out."

"That one did."

"Please do not criticize them, Phaedra. I received a letter from Rose today, and things are not going well. Tim is ill most of the time, and they ration fuel like peasants."

"Perhaps your cousin should improve his health quickly and find employment."

Alexia avoided the argument. Today was not really about the Longworths. They were not the reason she was buying materials to secretly do piecework.

She wished she could tell Phaedra about Lord Hayden and those kisses. If she did, however, her friend would bluntly name it as the base lust it had been. Phaedra would probably remind Alexia that she had not long ago written three long letters to Phaedra that heaped hatred on the man in question.

Her face burned at the thought of the carriage ensemble and dresses being made by Madame Tissot. She was sure Rothwell, not Easterbrook, was paying for them. Phaedra would scold her soundly about that. Phaedra might have lovers, but she opposed the practice of men paying for favors with gifts.

Alexia checked the supplies laid out on the counter

to make sure she had everything. She added up the long bill of sale and paid. The clerk wrapped her purchases in several bulky packages. Balancing them in a clumsy pile that reached her nose, she aimed for the street and the carriage.

"You will be wanting to start on the hats today," Phaedra said. "Otherwise you will have to wait until next week to make progress. Do not tell me that you will craft those hats by the light of a lamp after you are finished with your duties either. It will affect your health, and I will not countenance that."

"I suppose it would be best to get started if I am going to do this at all."

"I will go home in a hansom cab, so you do not waste an hour crossing town. It was kind of you to come for me, but I will not mind making my own way back."

Alexia turned her head to thank Phaedra for her consideration. From the corner of her eye she saw someone step in her path. She noticed just in time to avoid bumping into him.

Suddenly the top two packages on her stack disappeared.

She swung her attention to the thief and began to raise a cry before he ran away. Only it was not a thief.

"They were about to fall," Lord Hayden said. "I see that you are using your free day more actively this week, Miss Welbourne."

"Lord Hayden. What an unexpected surprise." He was the last person she wanted to see.

She had no choice but to introduce him to Phaedra. He did not even blink at her friend's appearance. He exuded an affable grace.

He looked at the packages. "The carriage is nearby? I will carry these and escort you ladies to it."

"I will be using a cab, thank you," Phaedra said.

"I will not have that." Alexia tried with a firm tone to communicate that Phaedra must now remain with her. "I will bring you back in the carriage."

"You have better use of the afternoon."

"Allow me to obtain the cab for you," Lord Hayden offered. He gestured to the man who stood sentry at the warehouse door. He fished some coin from his waistcoat pocket and gave instructions that a hansom cab should be hired for Miss Blair.

He then guided Alexia away from the door and toward the line of carriages waiting down the street.

"Your friend Miss Blair is distinctive."

"She is honest and true and incapable of dissembling."

"I meant no disrespect. She is an original. I should introduce her to Easterbrook. They can braid each other's hair."

"I suspect Phaedra would find Easterbrook rather boring. That is how distinctive and original she is, you see."

The slightly surly attitude with which her coachman had begun this outing disappeared when he saw Rothwell approach by her side. He rushed over to take her packages, then carefully tucked them inside the carriage.

"In the future, when Miss Welbourne uses the carriage to shop, a footman is to accompany her," he told the coachman. "My apologies, Miss Welbourne, for not making that clear to the household from the start."

He opened the door for her. She stepped inside. He did too.

"I do not need an escort. The coachman can protect me the short way back to Hill Street."

He ignored her pointed lack of welcome and settled across from her. "Was Miss Blair correct? Do you have another use for this afternoon?"

Yes, I do. I intend to take these packages to my chamber and begin making hats so I can earn the money that will permit me to never again have to suffer your presence.

"Some private matters," she said.

Apparently he thought that meant she had nothing important to do after all. He gave the coachman instructions to drive to Hyde Park.

"It is rather cold for a turn in the park," she said.

"Our stroll will be brief. I would like to speak with you about something."

Her heart filled with the heaviness that heralded bad news. "I doubt this conversation will include the apology you owe me. Nor do I anticipate receiving your reassurances of being spared such behavior in the future, since your intruding on this carriage would itself raise eyebrows."

Kindness softened his expression. A frank, knowing gaze added a sardonic touch, however, compromising the effect. "I am sorry that you are offended by my silence. I accept that you are due both the apology and the reassurances. I cannot say the necessary words yet, however."

"Why?"

"Because they would be lies."

The carriage grew very small then. He still appeared friendly. Nothing in his face or pose threatened her. Her entire being became too aware of him, however. Her body reacted as if he titillated her with a long, slow caress.

It was a mistake to be alone with him. She hated how this devil could so easily call forth such scandalous reactions.

"Lord Hayden, I will consider any further addresses of that nature as insults of the cruelest kind."

"I cannot decide if that is true. That you want it to be true matters, of course."

"How generous of you to consider my preferences."

"It is your true preferences that I contemplate. However, be content that I do not intend to discover what they are today. I wish to speak with you about something else entirely."

"What would that be?"

"A topic you will enjoy much more. Benjamin Longworth."

Dangling Benjamin's name silenced her objections. He suspected she would suffer all kinds of addresses if they included reminiscences about her beloved cousin.

If you become my mistress, I agree to hold two conversations a week about Benjamin Longworth. Only not in bed, if that is acceptable to you.

She ignored him as the carriage took them to the park. He spent his time wondering what was in the packages and noticing the careful mending along the cuff of her brown pelisse robe. The carriage ensemble being made by Madame Tissot would look lovely on her, and its cerulean hue would complement her eyes.

It was not yet the fashionable hour, but enough broad hats and nipped waists dotted the park to banish the sense of their being alone. She suffered his company beside her as they strolled. Her posture bespoke how she remained on her guard.

"We are in a public place, Miss Welbourne. I can hardly importune you here."

"You speak too boldly. One stolen kiss does not give you rights to such familiarity."

"Bold talk has marked our conversations from the start, and not by my initiative. Nor was it one kiss, and I stole very little. However, let us not argue today but instead speak of friendly things."

Her glance said he was no friend, but the allusion to the pending topic softened her. Her stride slowed and her ice melted. "Will you tell me how he decided to go to Greece?" she asked. "It was a shock to us, and so unexpected."

Reference to Ben brought a lovely flush to her cheeks and lively sparkles to her eyes. She appeared much as she had when he kissed her, and the memory caused the gentleman to disappear for a long count. In his mind he gazed into a field of violets while the breeze carried the rhythmic groans of a woman welcoming the pleasure as he stroked into her—

Vigilance. Vigilance.

"He learned I was going and decided to join our motley brigade," he said. "I believe it was one of those impulses for which he was famed."

"A generous one. He risked his life in a noble cause."

"Certainly."

Like hell. No one expected to really get hurt, let alone die. Nor had Ben gone on principle. He was motivated by an urge for adventure and the hopes of impressing an unattainable lady.

It was not his place to disillusion Miss Welbourne, however. Nor would she thank him if he did.

"I'm sure he was very brave," she said. "I imagine him there, like a hero in a painting."

He bit back the urge to tell her the truth. Ben had been very brave once, that was certain. Madly, impulsively so. The desire to confide in her confounded him.

"He fought as best he could, as did we all. The Greeks are not well commanded, however. They have no sound strategy, and their factions will not cooperate. I fear that the current siege of Missilonghi will end very badly."

"Ben said the Greeks must be freed. As a symbol, and to repay them for all that civilization owes their history."

Ben did not give a damn about that. He parroted the philhellenes to give you an excuse for leaving. He knew little about the politics or the history.

Those altruistic reasons had motivated the rest of them, however. They had been his own justification for doing something that, on hindsight, was irrational and impetuous and a mad grasp at the romantic heroics found in poems.

His principles had been noble, but the reality of that war had not been. He had seen unbearable atrocities committed by both sides. He had returned jaded and disenchanted, only to watch others go after him, all full of the same simplistic ideals.

"Do you think they will win?" she asked. "I would like to believe he did not waste the last year of his life."

"The Ottoman Empire is old and corrupt. It stands only with the help of countries like ours. The Turks will leave Greece someday, and the current war and its support in England will have helped that to happen."

They talked about that as they paced along, his boots crunching dried leaves that blew into their path. She peppered him with questions, forgetting that she was supposed to be angry with him or even that they were supposed to be talking about Benjamin. For twenty minutes the world stage occupied her inquisitive, intelligent mind.

He was the one who herded the conversation back to Ben. He did so regretfully, but this accidental meeting had a purpose.

"Was it difficult for the family while he was gone?" he asked.

The allusion to the Longworths produced a perceptible stiffening. "Timothy had begun at the bank by then, so it was not a strain that I could tell. We still lived in Cheapside at first too. It was soon after Ben left that their situation improved so significantly." A touch of resentment lifted the last words. *Only to be completely destroyed by you, of course.* She did not say it, but the accusation was there. It probably always would be.

"You saw no improvements the first years you were with them, while in Cheapside? It all came later?"

"Tim explained that the bank had been building itself those earlier years but now was established. We

could enjoy the fruits of his and Ben's careful steward-
ship. I will admit that I thought Tim enjoyed those fruits
rather too freely, but perhaps it was normal to indulge
too much."

He looked at her pelisse again. It was at least several
years old. He thought about her dull, high-waisted
dresses. Tim had indulged himself and his sisters but
not his cousin.

The bastard had been robbing people of their lega-
cies and had not even bothered to shower some ill-
gotten gains on the poor cousin in his house.

"Actually, the bank enjoyed steady growth all
along," he said. "The overnight change to extravagance
was not due to how it matured. Ben could have enjoyed
some of the fruits earlier. I would have expected there to
have been a slow but steady evidence of that. You say
there was not?"

"Not in ways I noticed. We lived very comfortably in
Cheapside. He had his club and a carriage the whole
time. There was no indication matters were changing
one way or another." She looked over with sharp curiosity. "Why do you ask about this?"

"I have been thinking about him of late, Miss
Welbourne. I am seeing him on that ship those last days.
He was in a deep melancholy. I wondered if he returned
to financial problems, but it appears not, from what you
say." He paused and assessed whether to go on. "I now
wonder where the increased income he received those
last years went, if not to his own household and habits."

"Back into the bank, I expect. Then Tim inherited
it all."

It was a good answer, just the wrong one. He had

seen the records of Ben's personal account at the bank. Little had been sitting there for Timothy to inherit.

Some money would have been used to pay the people who expected to receive the income from the funds that had been stolen, of course. That amount had grown with each theft. Much more than that had disappeared, however.

He would have to work it out, now that he knew Ben had not been spending a big portion of it on luxuries. And he should probably determine if Ben had other accounts at other banks, ones that held the fruits of his criminal labors.

Their walk had taken a circular path. The carriage waited ahead. Hayden put Benjamin out of his mind and just enjoyed strolling beside Miss Welbourne for the last hundred yards.

She kept forgetting to hate him. Their walk had been too *friendly,* and he was no friend to her or those she loved.

Now here they were in the carriage again, and that other lure, that damnable excitement, interfered even more. She found that very disconcerting. To sit across from a man whom your mind cursed but your body did not—the various vexations got all jumbled.

He regarded her the way he did too often now, with a lazy contemplation that created a subtle predatory mood. His drifting gaze paused and lingered on her hands. "My apologies are due. I have been inconsiderate of your comfort and health. I should have noticed that you wore half gloves and had no muff."

She looked down at her fingers, pink beyond the

gloves that ended just past her knuckles. She had worn half gloves so she could touch and assess the materials at the warehouse.

He flapped open a carriage blanket and wrapped her hands in it, swaddling them so the wool could warm her quickly. She suffered the attention, and her fingers tingled in the toasty cocoon. His closeness made her heart beat too hard. The sensation of his hands pressing hers through the wool stole her breath.

She possessed no control over that reaction. None at all. That frightened her. The part of her that forgot to hate him existed independently of good sense. The responses stirred so deeply she could not name their source. They emerged from a primitive essence that her rational mind could not subjugate.

Only absence from him would free her completely. Fortunately, she would arrange that soon. For now she sought refuge in the one place she knew she could find it.

"I have enjoyed our conversation about Benjamin. Your description of his melancholy surprises me, however. I never knew him to be like that." It did surprise her. A slight ill ease simmered, as if a question mark had joined all of her exclamation points about Benjamin.

"After the excitement in Greece, perhaps he mourned the loss of drama once he came home."

She did not care for that explanation. After all, he came home to *her*.

"Forgive me for being forward, Miss Welbourne, but . . . did Benjamin propose to you, either before he left or in a letter?"

She might never forgive him for being *that* forward.

His question resurrected one of her own. It whispered sometimes late at night when she gave herself over to memories. *Did I misunderstand?*

"He spoke of our being together forever."

"Then you had a fair understanding. Perhaps he worried that you would reject him when he formally proposed, however. That may have been the reason for his mood."

No, it had not been that. He had the advantage in their love. She was the one who had to worry about rejection.

That thought just sprang into her mind. She resented its honesty and the way this man had forced it on her.

"It is perhaps just as well that he is gone," she said. "If you were a friend, what you did to the Longworths— your duty, as you called it—would have been more difficult."

She searched for some signs of guilt in him at the reference. She saw none.

"I expect that you write to them," he said.

"Of course. And my cousin Roselyn writes to me. Timothy is a broken man. His health has been badly affected."

"Brandy does have a way of taking a physical toll."

"How dare—"

His full severity flashed as soon as she began the scold. Her instincts shouted a silent warning to hold her tongue. Their last heated argument had produced drastic results.

She swallowed her ire. "Roselyn writes that they barely have enough to eat, so I doubt he can afford brandy."

"Cheap gin will do the job just as well. I am sorry to hear of the ladies' distress, however. I will send Miss Longworth some money. If it goes to her, can we trust that it will remain in her hands and not be used for her brother's illness?"

"She will never accept it from you. Her pride will never permit it, nor will her anger. She will starve first."

"Then I will give it to you to give her. She need never learn its true source. Say, fifty pounds for now?"

The offer surprised her. She should grab it, she knew. However . . . she eyed him suspiciously. Would this be like that new wardrobe? Would it put her in his debt?

His slow smile showed that he read her thoughts. "Miss Welbourne, if I sought to make you my mistress, I would never be so subtle and indirect. You would know it, and I would never insult you with such a small sum."

The carriage arrived on Hill Street then, not a minute too soon. A footman hurried out and helped her step down. She walked away quickly while Rothwell stacked the packages into the servant's hands. She was halfway to the door before she made up her mind about the money. She turned and addressed him as he stepped out of the carriage.

"My pride should not interfere with my dear cousins having some relief. I will give it to her. Only ten, however, since I cannot explain having more. She will never know it came from you."

CHAPTER
EIGHT

〰

Alexia dragged Caroline through a stilted conversation in French. Her pupil's mastery of this graceful accomplishment still left much to be desired. Her own lack of attention to the finer points of grammar was not helping their progress.

Half of her mind remained occupied by her meeting with Lord Hayden three days ago. With distance from the man's unsettling presence, their conversation took center stage in her memories. Her confused reactions to him only formed a backdrop now to some serious speculations regarding what he had said about Benjamin. The new question mark kept getting bigger and bigger.

A footman found them in the schoolroom and deposited a package on the table. He announced that it had just arrived for Miss Welbourne.

"Did you buy a pillow while you were at the shops?" Caroline asked.

She had not, but this package looked to contain one. She broke the seal on the fine patterned paper. The wrappings dropped to reveal an ermine muff.

"Oh, my," Caroline cried. "It is beautiful."

The muff was made of the softest white fur. Ivory satin lined the little tunnel for her hands. Tiny pearls trimmed the seams on either side.

Alexia read the note that accompanied it.

I am told that you attend the theater tonight with my aunt. The nights are still too cold for a lady to be lacking suitable comforts. Please accept this with my gratitude for the aid you provide the family.——Easterbrook

Caroline's fingertip drew a little pattern in the fur's nap. "Mother thinks Easterbrook should have invited us to live at his house. She is also hurt that he has never visited us here, but I believe his heart is very good."

Alexia had no idea if Easterbrook's heart was good or not. She was fairly certain he knew nothing about the gifts showering down in his name, however.

The muff's luxury entranced her. Her hands ached to snuggle into its warmth. She remembered Rothwell wrapping the blanket, creating a crude version of this gift.

"What is that other note?" Caroline gestured to Alexia's lap. A second sealed page had fallen out when she opened the first.

She touched it and realized this should not be shown to Caroline. Her fingers sensed the size and shape of the paper enclosed within it. Evidently "Easterbrook" would be donating the ten pounds that were going to the Longworths.

She knew the truth. She incurred no debts yet,

however. The ruse of Easterbrook's largesse protected her pride. So did the odd reassurance given in the carriage. *If I sought to make you my mistress, I would never be so subtle and indirect.*

She set the muff and notes aside. All through the afternoon's lessons, the two gifts sat there, waiting to enclose her in illusions of security, seducing her to think kindly of the man who sent them.

Her dress was old but presentable and her long mantle elegant in its simplicity. Neither garment was fashionable, however, and Hayden assumed they had seen many years. Alexia had probably purchased them when Ben was head of the family. It was lack of use that left them free of the signs of wear.

She arrived at the box with Henrietta, content in her role of the subdued companion who formed a shadow to his aunt's flamboyance. A discreetly plumed turban announced her station as a lady no matter what her situation. Her fur muff rang a note of luxury in a quiet melody of outmoded restraint.

She kept the muff on her lap during the performance. The theater held a chill, and her hands remained hidden in its silken tunnel. Sitting on the other side of Henrietta, Hayden could easily see Alexia's gloved arm gently curve toward that hidden cave where her elegant hands dwelled. He imagined her tapered fingers, warm from their home in fur and satin, sliding down his naked chest in five velvety paths, glossing to the line of his hip and around his loins—

He rose and slipped to the rear wall of the box. He

could see only the back of Alexia's hat from here. And the nape of her neck. And the gentle slope of her shoulders. Her dress bared enough to send his imagination flying again, speculating about the taste as he kissed along that skin.

He laughed at himself, despite his clenched teeth. He was not a man to set his sights on women he could not have. His private life progressed as efficiently as his public one. This desire for Miss Welbourne made no sense and was proving damned inconvenient. And it was desire, plain and simple, the kind of hunger that had rarely focused so specifically on one woman, let alone one to be desired in vain.

The problem was that he did not really believe it was in vain. He *should* not have her, but the part of his mind that instinctively calculated odds said he could have her if he wanted to. She did not like him, she blamed him for great sins, but desire existed in a world apart from what *should* be.

The object of his attention moved. Her shoulders tilted toward the stage and the hat slowly rose. Turning, she set down the muff and walked in silent grace toward him.

He expected her to pass out of the box. Instead, she approached him, her eyes seeking him in the shadows along the back wall.

He battled the urge to grab her. "Are you enjoying the play, Miss Welbourne?"

"Yes. It was kind of your aunt to include me."

He had arranged that by being vague about his own plans. He had suggested Henrietta bring Miss Welbourne so there would be no chance she might sit in

Easterbrook's box alone. He scorned his impulse to sub-terfuge even as he surrendered to it.

"I wonder if I might have some conversation with you, Lord Hayden. It regards a matter that has weighed on my mind the last few days. It requires some privacy."

Not now, little wren. Stay close to Mother if you are wise.

"Certainly, Miss Welbourne." He guided her to the door.

The corridor was dimly lit, with mere pockets of deep yellow piercing the dark. Her skin appeared ethe-real and her eyes very dark and expressive. They re-grouped against the box's door.

"I have been thinking about what you said in the park, regarding Benjamin." Her brow puckered with concern. He wanted to kiss the frown away. "You spoke of his melancholy during his last days. I have been thinking how unlike him that was."

"We all have our moments. No doubt he did as well but at times the world did not see him."

"Possibly. Yet . . . may I ask, was he drinking that evening? When it happened?"

"A goodly amount." He rather wished they had not left the box now. She broached specifics he'd rather not give. He avoided dwelling on them.

"That was not like him either," she said. "Unlike his brother, Ben was not fond of spirits. I think, from what you described, that he was not merely melancholy but despondent."

"That may be too strong a word."

"Did you see him there, on the deck, before he fell?"

Now they were wading into bad waters. The urge

to grab her and kiss her had less to do with desire and more to do with an impulse to silence these questions.

"I saw him briefly."

Look at the stars, Hayden. They fill the entire sky all the way down to the sea. I feel as if I could walk across the water and touch them.

Those are not stars over there, but the lighthouse on Corsica. The drink has addled your senses. Come below with the others. The night carries a chill.

I will not be good company. I am better alone tonight.

You can be alone down below too.

Leave me in peace, will you? Don't you ever get in a mood, Hayden? Does that remote, calculating soul of yours never experience sadness or dread? The night sky can be soothing at such times.

You would be less sad if you were less drunk.

Now you sound like your father. All judgment and logical superiority. Will you lecture me now? Exhort me to moral correctness and honorable behavior? Hell, in twenty years you will even look like him. A damned good thing you don't have the sentiment to marry, because you would end up the ruthless hypocrite he was and—

Another word and I will thrash you, drunken bastard though you are tonight.

Leave me in peace and you will not hear any more words from this bastard.

I'll leave you in peace. Hell, I'll leave you to the devil if that is what you want.

"We had some brief conversation, but he did not want to come below." He shrugged.

She seemed to see the weight the gesture bore. He grew uncomfortable under her gaze.

"You blame yourself, don't you? You feel guilty that you did not make him leave the deck."

He slowly exhaled the rebellious fury that rose at her words. The accusation created a peculiar intimacy. She had just touched the raw side of his soul.

"I apologize for saying that. You are angry now. Even in this light it is evident. I did not intend—"

"You merely named one more sin in a long list. A man such as myself has many, as you have often indicated."

"I am sure you did not realize he was so inebriated as to fall overboard." She peered earnestly at him, trying to see deeply despite the dim light. She looked adorably worried. So much that he suddenly did not care what she saw or what she learned about Ben. He did not give a damn about any of that right now, because her full mouth pouted so sensually that he ceased noticing anything else.

"Lord Hayden, I must ask you—how difficult is it for one to fall overboard? I have been trying to picture it, and with the rails, if there is no storm, it just seems to me that—"

He laid his fingertips on her lips, silencing her. "Not so difficult, if one is careless. It happens too often—a game gone awry, a reckless dare. The rails are aids for the sober and sensible, not prison walls."

Her expression transformed with his touch. Astonishment eclipsed worry. Fear trembled beneath his light touch, and excitement shimmered in the pools of her soulful eyes.

The silence and shadows of the corridor wrapped them. Not a sound out here. They were alone.

He lowered his mouth to taste the cool satin of her bare shoulder.

Her sharp inhale expressed not shock but pleasure. That alone would have defeated his honorable inclinations, but they had already stopped fighting.

He pressed his lips along that alluring line of skin, feeling her warm to the gentle assault. She did not run away or object. She did not even step back. He slid his hand around her waist and pressed her closer, while his mouth followed a path up her neck. He parted his lips at her pulse and feathered his tongue over the quickly beating sign of arousal.

Desire did not obscure his senses. He still heard the silence and the gentle, frightened sighs that greeted each new kiss.

This was not the time or place, but he did not give a damn. He pulled her closer yet, pressing her against him while he held her face and took possession of her provocative mouth.

Her surprise seduced him further. Her melting capitulation sent flames to his mind. Tiny sounds of confusion lingered in her breathless sighs, as if she did not know what to do with this passion.

He broke the kiss and gazed down on her face. Eyes closed and lips parted, she presented an image of ecstasy. Her body felt slight and weak in his arms.

"Touch me," he said. "You know that you want to."

Her lids rose. Tentatively, her gloved hands rose and

touched his face, as if she sought proof that he was physically there.

Her hands came to rest on his shoulders with that same curious touch. Despite the layers of garments between them, her fingers seared his skin, sending a new heat blazing through him.

He kissed her harder. He barely reined in the ferocious hunger. His body burned. The persistent awareness of their location encouraged him but also heralded his ultimate frustration. Not everything, but . . . He would pay dearly, but . . .

He gently took her lower lip between his teeth. Her mouth parted more. He kissed her again, sweeping his tongue slowly, entering carefully. His embrace felt her new trembles of arousal.

Pleasure conquered the last shreds of his judgment. He turned her against the door and claimed her with kisses and caresses, pressing for her body beneath the dress, seeing her naked through his touch, listening to the melodic breaths and cries that spoke her surprise and helplessness.

Caressing down her arm, he slid the high glove low, exposing her skin. Turning his head, he kissed down the same path while his hands moved, cupping her bottom, grasping her hip, circling her waist, rising to the unbearable softness of her breast. He smoothed his palm over its fullness, glossing the hard nipple, urging her to abandon herself to him.

Her fingers dug into his shoulder. Her cries sounded clearly. He found enough sense to silence her with another kiss, but not enough to stop his hand. Soon. Later. Eventually . . .

The door thudded behind her. She stiffened and blinked, as if the low sound woke her from her sleep.

"Good heavens, is it stuck?" a woman's voice muttered on the other side of the wood.

Gritting his teeth, cursing his aunt, furious from the hunger, he quickly slid the glove back up and moved away from Alexia. In the dim light he could see her flush as she composed herself. She stayed in place for a five count and checked her garments with a quick, practical glance.

She gazed in his eyes with unfathomable thoughts, then turned and opened the door. Henrietta almost fell into their arms.

"My apologies, Aunt Hen," he said. "I should know better than to rest against the door of an occupied box."

"Indeed you should. Lost in thought, were you? Working out one of those theorems, I expect."

"I was also standing sentry, so Miss Welbourne would find the correct box upon returning."

"You can continue doing so for me. If I had known Alexia intended to go to the . . . well, just stand there, Hayden, so I do not get lost either."

Hen sailed down the corridor. Alexia watched in silence. Desire still howled inaudibly in the air between them.

He burned and his mind knew no sense. *I will come to you tonight, after the household is asleep. Open your door to me.*

He did not say it, but she heard it anyway. She sensed it in him, and maybe in herself.

She turned away and entered the box, closing the door between them.

He did not go to her that night.

As his body cooled, he admitted it would be both reckless and ridiculous to do so. The practical Miss Welbourne would never jeopardize her reputation, her situation, and her virtue, if she had the presence of mind to consider what she was doing.

Apologies were overdue. His behavior had become inexcusable. Although that continued to astonish him, he did not dwell on how unlikely the lapse at the theater had been. Further trifling with Alexia would be unforgivable.

It would take all the vigilance that Christian preached, however, because by dawn, lust still lacerated with its ragged knives. He lay abed past noon, debating his course, his honor dictating restraint but his body making primitive arguments with a louder voice. He finally found the discipline to rise and go to his City chambers, but he accomplished little there. Even his calculations could not distract him.

The next two days he did not bother being disciplined. He slept late, debated his course, concluded nothing, and haunted the house. Finally, on the fourth day he forced himself to the unwelcome task awaiting and sat down to compose a letter. Partway through he decided it would be cowardly to avoid a personal apology.

While he calculated how he could speak with Alexia alone, Elliot came into his chamber. He carried a letter.

"I see you are finally awake. This came for you this morning, Hayden. One of Aunt Hen's footmen brought it."

Hayden took the letter. In it, Henrietta managed to pout despite her flatteries and demurring words. She understood that he could not spend all his time with them, of course, and she did not want to impose or be a nuisance. However, he really needed to visit and have a good talk with Miss Welbourne, who was not making sufficient progress with teaching Caroline her French. She hoped he could make time this afternoon to do this.

"Whatever she wants, I could attend to it," Elliot said.

"You are a rare brother, Elliot. You sense I am preoccupied and offer to throw yourself in harm's way to protect me."

"The recent change in your habits says I sense correctly." He gestured to the letter. "You can just write and put her off if you think I'm not agile enough to dodge her snares."

Hayden read again his aunt's demands that he scold Miss Welbourne. He would have to see Alexia alone to do so. There was unfinished business between them that had nothing to do with French lessons.

"I will answer this summons on my own. The conversation that she demands I hold is long overdue."

Alexia fussed over the green ribbon's pleating on her first hat. It looked too even, too planned. She wanted a more careless and romantic effect, as if the sash had been tied with caprice, not calculation.

She carried the hat to the window to give it a good examination. Making it had been more difficult than she anticipated. Lacking a form, she had been forced to use her own kerchiefed head and a looking glass. Keeping it spotless meant she had applied the embellishments while wearing gloves.

Despite Phaedra's admonishments, she had indeed toiled on this hat by lamplight. She had turned to it upon returning from the theater four nights ago. In a daze of desperation she had stayed up until dawn primping at ribbons and sewing crepe, hoping to make a hat of such superiority that it would buy her way out of temptation's path.

She stilled with the hat in her hands as a presence entered her. His presence. Acknowledging their scandalous behavior could produce that in a blink. It horrified her that the sensation did not feel alien or intrusive, but warm and exciting.

Sounds in the street below drew her attention. She looked down to see Henrietta and Caroline entering the carriage. They went to fittings today at Madame Tissot's.

She should be going too, but she had begged off, claiming to be ill. Nor was that entirely a lie. Anticipating the humiliation of facing Hayden again made her slightly nauseous all the time. He had not been to this house since that night at the theater, but eventually he would return.

She set aside the hat and sat down to complete a letter she was composing to Roselyn. She had much more important things to accomplish today than going to Madame Tissot's. The wardrobe being made for her there would never be worn now anyway.

After sealing and posting the letter, Alexia hurried up the stairs to the servants' floor. Henrietta and

Caroline had already been gone an hour. She hoped she had time to conduct her little investigation. If she did not complete it now, she might not be able to for many days. She could not beg off on every outing.

The churning storm inside her had not only been caused by Rothwell's advances at the theater. Their conversation disturbed her too. She had sought him out for reassurance about Benjamin. She had wanted to hear that Ben's death was an accident and that her suspicions had no basis.

He had stepped away from the question, she realized now. Then he had swept her out of its path too, and into a river of passion.

It broke her heart to think Ben may have voluntarily left her forever. If love could not keep a man from killing himself, what good was it?

If he had, however, some indication of the reason might be among his belongings. If no such evidence existed, she would be more content about the peculiarities of that accident. She entered the attic space at the end of the corridor, hoping that nothing waited for her besides nostalgia.

She had to navigate past recent additions to the storage. Henrietta had sent up quite a few items, either brought from her own property or removed from rooms below. The marble columns from Caroline's recitation flanked the doorway, their polish gently reflecting the light seeping in one small window. Several rolled tapestries had been brought here, the walls given instead to Easterbrook's paintings.

She discovered Ben's trunks against one wall. A frock coat lay atop one, as if someone had found an extra item and thrown it here rather than storing it properly. She dusted off the coat and folded it neatly. She dragged the trunks closer to the window. Unable to find a convenient chair, she pulled over one of the tapestries and made herself a nest on the wooden floor.

The first trunk that she opened contained clothing. She knelt and lifted each edge to see what lay below. She recognized most items and could picture him in these garments. She spied a silk waistcoat deep in the pile, one with blue and red stripes. She pulled it out and held it up.

He had worn this the day he kissed her for the last time. She felt again this silk under her fingertips and the pulse of his heart beneath her touch. Their embrace had been secret and brief, like all the others. He had been excited about his coming adventure in Greece, but she experienced a terrible fear. And a disgraceful resentment too that he was leaving her.

He had seen her grief. He had understood. *I will return soon, you will see. We will be together forever.*

She replaced the waistcoat and closed the trunk. Would he have said that if he intended to get himself killed? Or, worse, if he had intended to kill himself?

Her little investigation suddenly seemed almost traitorous. Rothwell's questions had led her into inconstancy regarding Ben. He had planted seeds of suspicion about Ben's death that were not warranted.

No, he had not planted them. His questions had only provided a rain of worry that allowed dormant seeds to germinate and grow.

The memories uprooted them now. The image of Ben in that waistcoat, so alive and excited, full of the happy optimism that returned spring breezes to her life—she need not fear finding proof he had wanted to go away forever.

Her search now made pointless, she opened the other trunk with a different purpose. She had been feeling strange and alone in this house for weeks. Embracing Ben's memory, touching his possessions, warmed her. The glowing happiness was worth the ache of grief that flowed within it.

The second trunk held his personal items. She recognized the watch and its selection of fobs. Stacks of letters, his hairbrushes, a few books—the everyday possessions of a gentleman were piled within.

She lifted some letters to glimpse what lay beneath them. As she did, the ribbon holding them together loosened. The pile fanned and fell, covering the contents of the trunk. She smiled as she recognized her own writing on some. Those were the letters she had sent to him in Greece.

A scent wafted to her, one sweeter than that on his garments. She began gathering the letters into a new pile and realized the scent came from some of the letters themselves. Interspersed among the others were some of similar size, with a similar hand. A woman's hand, but not hers or one of his sisters'.

She lifted one and held it to her nose. She inhaled the remnants of rose water. A horrible stillness claimed her.

She looked at the letter for a long time, dazed with dread. She never really decided what to do. She still dwelled in a sickening limbo of indecision as her fingers unfolded the paper.

Benjamin, my love . . .

CHAPTER
NINE

〜

"Lady Wallingford is not at home, sir," the footman said.

It was just like Henrietta to send that letter, then leave the premises.

"Fittings," the servant confided.

"Then I can find them all at the modiste's."

"Not all. Miss Welbourne took ill and remained here."

Hayden reconsidered his aunt's absence, with new respect. She wanted him to address a governess's performance and had left so it could be done privately. He intended a different conversation, but Hen's delicacy would be convenient.

"Ask Miss Welbourne if she would kindly meet with me in the library. Unless she is so ill she cannot come down, of course."

The footman left on his errand. Hayden went up to the library and sorted his thoughts, preparing for the great apology.

He trusted she would accept it quickly and they

could be done with this. If she noticed he did not sound sincere, which in a large part he was not, perhaps she would not mention it. Then again, with Alexia's tendency to plain speech, he might leave this house today as the one soundly scolded.

It took the footman a long time to return. Instead of causing annoyance, the wait produced a rising anticipation. He had not seen her in days, a long stretch while he hid from his worst inclinations. Now this pending conversation lightened his mood despite its sorry purpose.

The footman returned alone. "I am sorry, sir. She is not in her chamber or the schoolroom."

"Has she left the house?"

"I do not think so."

"Then she has to be somewhere."

The footman hesitated. "I believe she is in the attic. A maid saw her going up to that level, and the door is a bit ajar. Someone is in there—a woman, I am sure. It is possibly she."

"Could you not have walked in to see?"

"I thought not to, sir. I believe the woman in there requires some privacy." He made a little face. "She was weeping, whoever it was."

Alexia weeping? His imagination tried to reject the image, but one formed all the same. The same strength and intensity that made it unlikely also made it dramatic should she ever break.

"I will call at another time," he said.

The footman wandered off to other duties. Hayden waited until he was gone, then climbed the staircases all the way to the top level. He passed the servants' chambers, aiming toward the attic door at the end of the narrow passageway. It was indeed ajar. He stepped closer to it. Muffled sounds of feminine sobs drifted out.

He entered and closed the door behind him. He spied her through the furniture and storage, sitting on the floor near the one small window.

Even at the distance, he saw floods. Her body shook. She clasped her hands over her mouth, pressing hard to smother the sounds.

He went to her, astonished by her emotion, wondering what could have caused it. He looked down into a trunk and recognized the watch lying atop some books. Anger spiked through his sympathy. She had come here to cry over Ben. Perhaps she did this every week or even every day.

She noticed him and turned her head away. Her valiant attempts to hold in her emotion racked her with spasms.

He knelt beside her to attempt some comfort. He pushed aside some papers strewn on the tapestry. The writing at the top of one caught his eye. *Benjamin, my love . . .*

He lifted the letter and read it. He looked at Alexia. Her eyes held so much sadness that he fumbled for a lie that would explain these letters away.

She covered her whole face with both her hands and lost her fight for composure. Her sobs filled the attic. Touched more than he had been in years, he sat beside her and gathered her into his arms.

His embrace both comforted and weakened her. Do not try to be brave, those arms said.

She collapsed against him and gave up the fight. Disappointment and humiliation wailed inside and poured out. Beneath it all, the practical side of her soul nodded knowingly like the worst kind of governess, the type who took satisfaction at being right even if it meant her charge was pained.

A few lucid thoughts broke through the black madness. *You always wondered. If he had been serious, he would have proposed before he left. You believed in him because your future was a blank if you did not.* She gritted her teeth and clawed at the coats beneath her fingers.

The embrace tightened. A kiss of comfort warmed her scalp. "Try to calm yourself."

The gentle command called forth the woman she presented to the world and not the fool who clutched at romantic dreams. Her heart calmed to a heavy pounding. The rivers dried to slow trickles.

A handkerchief materialized, held by a strong hand. She took it and dabbed her eyes and face. The blur of papers that surrounded them became crisp again. She brushed a few away from her skirt.

"She wrote to him in Greece, but there were others too, from before that," she said. "He never intended— he behaved dishonorably with me."

"Perhaps he behaved dishonorably with her, not you."

A tiny flame of hope sparked. It did not grow, but it flickered, desperately wanting fuel. It could have been that way. Ben might have lied to this other woman, not to her, regarding his affections and intentions.

She was too spent to weigh it all. Even if he had not lied to her, he had not been truthful either. "It is kind of you to say that," she said. "But the evidence is that I was a fool."

"I do not think so."

She should move away but could not find the strength. Once she left this embrace, she would be cold and alone and facing an empty past as well as a hard future.

"Did you know?"

"I knew there were women in his life, as there are in most men's."

"This one wrote love letters for years. This one wrote as if she also received love letters. Her name is Lucy."

"Then I did not know about this specific woman."

Another truth presented itself. One that her heart did not want to see. "When he spoke of me in Greece, it was not love or intentions that he revealed, was it? I was just another not too specific woman."

Stillness permeated his whole presence. That was answer enough.

She could not believe how empty she felt. The shock had cut her loose from herself. She dreaded the pending loneliness that would lack even silly memories. It loomed large, pressing on her. She laid her head against his shoulder to rest before she gathered her courage and walked forward again.

His embrace held her and filled her. His scent and warmth and human touch poured into the void. A sensual disturbance trembled through the connection too. She lacked the will to reject the perilous vitality he incited.

It entered her, stirring alive the parts that had just died in agony. She did not move but just absorbed it, not caring about the danger it carried. He did not move either. The silence of their embrace grew heavy. She became unnaturally alert to every part of her being touched by him. She sensed the same awareness in him.

She tilted her head and looked up. He gazed into the attic, not at her. His expression held the thoughtful sternness she had seen before, and his blue eyes had the hot lights that made him look angry.

She had misunderstood that face in the past, but she did not now. His hardness contained a fury, but not anger. He turned his head and looked down at her, and the source of those fires could not be mistaken.

He caressed her face, his fingertips lightly buffing away old tears. His attempt to soothe her made her heart rise. So did the desire in his hold and eyes. She could not piece together the reasons why she should reject that desire. All of that belonged in another world and life. She dreaded the end of this warmth he gave and did not want to face the lifelong chill waiting for the sensible Miss Welbourne beyond this dark attic's door.

She did not even think. Her battered spirit grabbed the chance to drown the truth and flood the hollow disappointment.

She reached up and touched his face too.

Except for the way the fires darkened, but for a new, sensual hardness to his mouth, he barely reacted at first.

Then his hand covered hers and held it flat against his skin so his warmth flowed into her. His strong fingers enclosed hers completely, then lifted her hand away. He turned his head and kissed her palm and her pulse.

Butterflies fluttered from her wrist to her heart, then

feathered their wings through her body. She closed her eyes to savor the lovely sensation. Its contrast to her numb emptiness awed her.

She opened her eyes to his direct gaze. She did not heed the warning that her heart whispered. She did nothing to help him win the battle she sensed in him. She wanted him to lose it. She wanted him to kiss her and fill her with the trembling liveliness.

He did, carefully at first, then less so. A leashed fervor called to her, demanding freedom in those kisses. With each response from her, it threw off another shackle.

The power of that kiss amazed her. The flutters entered her blood and gave rhythm to her breath. Their feathery titillation aroused her inside and out, and the excitement in her essence and on her skin merged, each thrill increasing the other.

His embrace moved, easing her down onto the tapestry. With one broad movement he swept the letters away, sending them beyond the trunks in a little gale of dismissal, removing the horrible discovery from sight and mind.

He shook off his frock coat while he kissed her again. She embraced him as he stretched beside her, taking him into her arms as best she could. The kisses quickly changed as they lay together in the small window's northern light. She submitted to the invasive, intimate ones he had used at the theater, only this time no shock inhibited her reaction. He did not have to lure her into an escalating passion. Unbearable pleasure cascaded through her, and she had already thrown off caution and concern.

She loved every moment. Loved the way his hands began moving, touching her through her garments, with firm, possessive, seeking holds. A delicious sensitivity awoke low in her body, its tingling itch creating a physical craving. Her breasts ached too, so much that his caress, when it came, was not enough. She clutched at his back, holding him tighter, vaguely aware that she kissed him back, dully alert to the ways this lovely madness made her move and sound.

Suddenly they were alone together in a chaotic, fevered daze, one that obliterated time and place. Pleasure ruled there, and a desperate aching need pushed her beyond modesty. She wanted more, and nothing else. Just more. The word chanted inside her as she urged and reached and cried.

He loosened her dress, but her stays defeated them. He muttered a curse at the garment and caressed her breast through it. His fingers found her nipple and pressed more effectively. A piercing shiver shot down her center, and sparkles of arousal burst at its mark, making her gasp.

He moved her arm from his body and laid it down. He pulled the stays' shoulder strap down her arm until one breast was exposed.

Her nakedness excited her more. The way he looked at her did too. His touch on the dark, protuberant tip undid her. The aching, impatient longing, deep and low, grew more intense. He caressed her breast and slowly palmed the nipple, titillating her more and more until she was so crazed she wanted to weep.

There was no relief, only more. The more of the chant in her head and of the demands of the man guiding her toward passion's edge. His head dipped and his tongue flicked at her nipple, and the sensations intensified yet again. A new caress, on her legs, moved the fabric of her skirt higher with each long stroke until the touch was flesh to flesh.

Her essence knew where that caress ventured. *Yes, more.* Even the luscious arousal at her breast aimed low now. Her anticipation turned frantic.

She was sure she could not be more excited, but the touch when it came proved her wrong. It incited a thrill so focused, so insistent, that she lost control. A completeness beckoned, and its denial made her insane.

More. He moved, spreading her legs, resting between them. *More.* He kissed her harder, silencing the sounds she had not heard until they returned to her head. *More.* She clawed at his shoulders, but he rose on his arms so she could not hold him to her. *More.* He reached between them and touched her again, stroking until she moaned.

A new touch, one that made her whole body tremble. A strong fullness suddenly relieved the desperation. Then it pressed and stretched, making her gasp. Pain sliced apart her euphoria.

Too much awareness intruded. Of the attic ceiling and the window's light. Of the man on top of her, his size and power dominating her. Of the fullness, so complete and astonishing. The burning stopped, but she pulsed there, alive and sensitive. New pleasures lightly trembled, but she was too shocked for them to grow.

He bent to kiss her. She glimpsed his face. Along with an expression that was male and hot and hard, she saw something else deep in his eyes. Surprise.

He moved. The fullness stroked, salving her soreness even as it prolonged it. The daze did not return. Instead of being lost in sensual oblivion, she was too aware, too alert, unnaturally so. To him and the sensation of him inside her. To her vulnerability. To an intimacy so invasive that it could not be escaped.

The starburst slowly dimmed. The transcendence of fulfillment gradually released him.

He looked down at the woman beneath him. She awkwardly embraced his hovering body with one arm. The other lay slackly by her side, imprisoned by the shoulder straps of her stays and chemise. He rose up on his arms, then dipped down to kiss her exposed breast. A beautiful breast, round and full, womanly and soft. A tremble shimmered through her, reminding him that she had not remained with him in the pleasure.

Her expression remained full of the vulnerability he had seen when he entered this attic.

"Did I hurt you badly?"

"Not badly. Enough, however. I am thinking that nature could have done better by women."

He almost laughed. Instead, he relinquished the feel of her. She considered his withdrawal with a little frown, as if trying to decide if he had made it better or worse.

He moved off completely and fixed his garments. With a final kiss on her lovely breast, he put the stays' strap back in place. "It is not always unfair. Only the first time."

She rolled away so he could close her dress. "You appeared surprised when you . . . You did not think it would be my first time, did you? Despite what I told you, you believed Ben and I were lovers."

He wished to hell he could say he had believed that. It would be an excuse of sorts. He could use one. The only thing he felt now was contentment, but guilt waited. Already an awkwardness insinuated itself between them.

"The surprise you saw was astonishment. It is one thing to desire a woman and another thing to live the fantasy."

She rose to her knees as soon as the dress was fixed, then froze. He looked over to see what distracted her. Her gaze rested on the letters covering the floor beyond the trunks.

"I will put them back," he said.

"Thank you, that is very kind. Your aunt will be returning soon and I should not remain here. I need to change and . . . As it is, this may be no secret from the household." Blushing, she began pushing herself up.

He grasped her arm, stopping her. "Alexia—"

She looked him right in the eyes. "No. Please. Do not say it. Do not say anything. *Please.*"

"There is much that needs to be said."

"Not really. Not now, certainly, and perhaps, if we are wise, not ever." She extricated her arm from his hold and stood. "Please allow me to make this the memory I want it to be." She glanced to the letters as she turned away. "I am very good at that, you see."

She lay in bed, listening to the silence of the night, trying to become familiar with herself.

She had left that attic a changed woman. She saw the world differently now. It was a truer view, she suspected. The disillusionment over Ben partly accounted for it, but the rest—the abandonment and intimacy and the startling pleasure—those experiences gave a woman a special wisdom.

She did not castigate herself or mourn her innocence. She was not really sorry she had done it. That was hard to admit, but doing so voided the need for dramatic recriminations. It also allowed her to face honestly the implications of what had happened. Pride, not fear, demanded that she leave this house now.

The hat's shadow darkened her writing desk. The night and the muslin obscured its details, but she saw it in her mind. She would not alter her intention to sell it, or any other plans either. What happened with Hayden would not waylay her from the path she had chosen. Her decisions were the right ones, and she should execute them more quickly if she wanted to control this memory.

She closed her eyes, hoping for sleep. Instead, her mind turned in on itself and on her body. She felt him. The soreness gently ached as if he still filled her down there. His presence still invaded her mind.

A wistful emotion kept sliding into her heart. She would allow that nostalgia to find its place and stay. It would be dishonest to build a memory full of sin and blame, after all. She had enjoyed herself too much for that.

CHAPTER TEN

What the hell was wrong with him?

Hayden pondered that question the next morning. There had been no sleepless night this time. Contented and sated, he had put off the reckoning until dawn. Now he examined his behavior hard while he dressed.

"Are you quite sure you want this waistcoat, sir? I thought you did not favor it with the blue frock coat."

His valet's question pulled Hayden out of his reverie. Nicholson was as methodical and organized, as rational and regular, as Hayden himself. Years ago they had fallen into a routine devoid of wasted time or movements. Hayden's distraction today had Nicholson sighing with strained forbearance.

"And the cravat, sir. That is the third one you have tied, and it won't do. Perhaps you would allow me to—"

"The hell you will. I am not a schoolboy." He whipped the miserably creased cloth off his neck, grabbed another, and began once more. He peered at his reflection in the looking glass while he manipulated the knot. He judged himself and showed no mercy.

The steady and rapid decline of his honor amazed him. Alexia's own passion did not excuse him, fondly though he remembered it. She had been distraught and vulnerable, and the man who first comforted her had then seduced her.

Nor did he regret it, scoundrel that he was becoming. Even while he acknowledged his sins, ruthless satisfaction glowed. Half his mind indulged in erotic fantasies of having her again.

A discreet cough interrupted. Nicholson waved the offending waistcoat beside the frock coat. They looked hideous together. Hayden could not recall choosing either.

"Whatever you think best, Nicholson."

"*Very* good, sir." With sublime confidence in his superior taste, Nicholson returned the waistcoat to its wardrobe and debated an alternative.

Hayden forced some order on his thoughts. He laid out the facts like so many entries in an accounting book. He had seduced Miss Welbourne. She had touched him and he lost all sense. He had intended to comfort her and instead had misused her. He had taken a good woman's virginity *on an attic floor*. His behavior had been inexcusable, dishonorable, irrational, and disgraceful.

And he wasn't nearly as sorry about it as he was supposed to be.

"Perhaps this one, sir?" Nicholson demanded attention and presented a different waistcoat.

"Yes, yes, *whatever*, man."

The most logical course was to ask Alexia to be his mistress. Passion never lasted, least of all the kind that had sane men doing insane things. He would make sure she was provided for afterward. She would establish some security. She would be better off in the end.

While that was the most sensible and predictable result of yesterday's impulses, he doubted she would agree to it. It would make her fall complete and explicit. Miss Welbourne would probably starve before she accepted a situation that so publicly denied her respectability.

He could make amends more directly, of course. He could simply settle an amount on her. If presented as a form of penance, she might not see it as payment for favors granted. Broaching the idea with her would require considerable diplomacy. It would also avoid the worst connotations only if he ceased any further pursuit of her. He had not yet convinced himself to accept that part.

Finally, he could do the right thing and marry her. He would have said he was the last man to make such a marriage, but he had not been himself of late. Would she even accept? She still blamed him for bigger sins than being a seducer.

He imagined the life they would have. Separate mostly, as was the way of most marriages he knew. Passionate at first, then later . . . He could not picture himself not wanting her. That was odd in itself. Normally he could imagine the end even before there was a beginning. *What the hell was wrong with him?*

However, *her* passion might cool quickly. Perhaps it already had. The reality of sexual congress might have chilled her forever. Nor did she care for him much. Accusations, not affection, usually warmed her eyes when she looked at him.

Passion has its place, but the mind must always rule. Emotions lead to impulses that destroy honor, fortune, and happiness.

He laughed at himself. Damnation, one false step now and he would prove his father right.

"Sir, I wish you would allow me to tie the cravat. That is the last of the fresh linen, and if you continue to massacre—"

"Hell, go ahead, then." He turned so Nicholson could get it right.

A knock on the dressing-room door interrupted them both. Nicholson stared down the footman who dared invade the valet's fief. The young man held his ground.

"The marquess requires your presence below, Lord Hayden."

The formality of the summons was peculiar, but the real mystery was that there had been a summons at all. His brother never played the nobleman so baldly.

"Where is Easterbrook waiting to give me this treasured audience?"

"The morning room, sir. He was having breakfast."

At nine in the morning? Hayden was almost curious to know what had caused his brother to rise so early.

He told Nicholson to take his time tying his cravat. He dallied while Nicholson gave his boots a final buff. With something approaching their normal routine, the valet helped turn him out presentably.

Finally, ready in his own good time and dressed for

his day's plans, he stuffed a small pouch in his pocket and went down to attend to his older brother's caprice of the day.

He opened the door to find Christian lazily eating a breakfast of fish and bread. As expected, the marquess was dressed informally, although he had eschewed the exotic robe for trousers and a morning coat. Still, the lack of a cravat, the open neck of his shirt, and the barbaric disorganization of all that hair left him appearing as inappropriate as if he wore nothing but a loincloth.

That impression probably had a lot to do with the fact that Christian was not alone in the morning room. He had a female visitor.

"Ah, here is Hayden," Christian said. "Look who turned up today, Hayden. Aunt Henrietta was good enough to visit. Before calling hours too, so it would not interfere with my day. This is such a treat, Aunt Hen. So often I am left to spend my mornings in isolation, sleeping too long, with nothing but peaceful silence to accompany me."

If Hen heard the sarcasm, she did not show it. "I am grateful you received me. I am far less unsettled now that we spoke."

"Aunt Henrietta is most distraught, Hayden. There has been a tragedy at her house."

"Not a tragedy, of course . . ."

"Now, now, don't try to be brave, Aunt Hen. The exact words sent up to me were, *We are facing a terrible tragedy. As head of the family, you must do something.*" He turned to Hayden placidly. "Informed of such a crisis, of course I rose from my bed to attend to the matter."

"Well, it *is* a tragedy," Aunt Hen said. "There will be no way to rectify the disaster that this inconstant woman has created."

"Woman?" Hayden asked, doubting he appeared as innocent as he tried to look.

"Miss Welbourne." Christian's lids lowered while he sipped some coffee. He allowed an eternity to pass before he spoke again. "It appears she is abandoning her duties."

"With no notice to speak of," Hen cried. "When she said last night that she would continue with Caroline, I assumed she was merely indicating she would leave after the season. I thought she was informing me of her plans so I could find another companion come summer. Today, however, before she left in the carriage, she explained that she would visit our house by day, but that she would remove herself from the house by week's end."

"She left in the carriage, you say?" Hayden asked.

"Yes, and that is another fine kettle of fish. She is leaving at week's end, but she still took this week's free day. Brazen, if you ask me. I am undone. Caroline's season will be ruined." She rose and began pacing around Easterbrook.

Christian ignored her hovering distress while he deboned his fish. "You must calm yourself. Hayden is here. He will fix everything. Won't you, Hayden?"

"Certainly." Damned if he knew how. He had not expected Alexia to bolt. "Why did you not come to me with this, Aunt Hen?"

Hen's face pursed into a haughty, wounded mask. "I thought it best to bring it to Easterbrook, *thank you*. He is head of the family, after all. You have not had much time for us of late. I did not want to *impose* on you more than I have."

"She is being delicate, Hayden." Christian kept most of his attention on his elegant, surgical manipulation of the fish. "She has alluded to concerns about this decision on Miss Welbourne's part. I think—forgive me if I am wrong, Aunt Hen—that she believes it has something to do with you."

Silence claimed the room. Christian ate some fish. Hen blushed to her brow and primly looked out the window.

"How so, Aunt Hen?" Hayden asked, knowing the answer might damn him.

"I think that perhaps you mishandled that little scolding yesterday. I am told you arrived while I was at Madame Tissot's."

"Scolding?" Christian looked over, too curious. "Have you been scolding the estimable Miss Welbourne, Hayden? The woman worth wages and a half, as well as use of the carriage?"

"Hen requested—"

"That you speak with her regarding Caroline's French, not that you drive her from the house," Hen cried. "You must have been most severe if she is leaving before she received the wardrobe that Easterbrook is buying for her."

Christian's fork paused halfway to his mouth.

Hen patted his shoulder. "You have been so kind to her, one would assume she would show her gratitude by treating the family more fairly. Why, the fur muff alone must have cost twenty pounds. Why would a woman in her poor situation abandon such generosity?"

"Why indeed?" Christian's half smile was for Hayden alone.

Hen began pacing again. "What are we to do? We can hardly have her continue as a day governess, as if we are some merchant family." She threw up her hands. "There is nothing else for it. Easterbrook, you will have to find Caroline another governess."

Easterbrook gave the fish a thin smile.

Hen became all business. "I daresay the only way to find a fit one now is if the household that employs her is of the highest reputation and station."

Easterbrook stared at his knife.

"We will have to live here, of course. Nothing less will quickly attract a governess of suitable accomplishment and references."

Easterbrook set down his breakfast implements. "Would it not be simpler to appease the governess you still have?"

"How can I appease her? I do not even know why she is throwing us over."

"I am very sure Hayden can discover why and speak reason with her." Those dark, all-knowing eyes locked on Hayden. "Can't you, Hayden?"

The carriage rolled to a stop in front of the handsome house in Oxfordshire. Alexia alighted and tucked her basket over her arm.

"The village is a mile down the road," she explained

to the coachman. "You can see to the horses there and refresh yourself. Come for me in three hours."

She walked up the stone path between strips of dormant garden plantings. The house was a good-size square of stone situated on twenty acres outside the village of Watlington. It appeared the property of a prosperous gentry family. Two generations ago that was exactly what it had been, and miles of the surrounding farmland had been attached to it.

The door opened. Roselyn rushed out, arms wide, laughing with excitement. They embraced closely.

Alexia had carried considerable guilt with her on this little journey, but it disappeared in Roselyn's warmth.

"I thank God you were able to come, but your letter spoke of next week," Rose said.

"I unexpectedly had a free day and decided not to delay the visit. I hope you do not mind the surprise."

"Do these tears look like I mind?" She tightened her hold in a final squeeze, then stepped back. She grinned at the carriage. "Whenever I think of how you managed to obtain use of it, I enjoy a deliciously naughty pleasure."

"You are looking well, Rose." She did look well. She wore a fashionable dress of Esterhazy wool, preserved when much of her wardrobe was sold. Her bright eyes and good color indicated that rationing fuel and food had not yet taken a toll on her health.

"Anticipating your visit gave me heart and good cheer, Alexia. For the first time in weeks I began feeling my old self again after I received your letter this morning."

They strolled arm in arm up to the house. "Tim is above, and I regret to say that he is too indisposed to see you. He is unwell." Rose's voice flattened on the last word. "Irene is visiting the Mortensons at Burberry Grange. The family has been generous to her, despite our situation, which, of course, everyone knows."

Alexia was sorry she would not see Irene, but she did not regret she would miss the unwell Timothy. "Your brother's persistent illness is unbecoming. I expected him to show more fortitude."

"He does nothing but mourn his past and curse his fate. Perhaps with time he will address the present and the future."

Rose had handled the present with a shrewd eye and practicality. Alexia had visited this property frequently with the family while they all lived in town, and now she noticed the furniture that was missing. Rose had selected carefully, selling off a few pieces of good quality that would not leave the chambers stripped.

They retreated to the library. Many books were missing but not enough to make the shelves appear stark. Alexia wondered how long the sale of bits and pieces could be sustained before the house was reduced to bare necessities.

She set her basket beside her on the sofa. "I have brought you a few things. I stopped at the shops before coming here." She pulled aside the cloth atop the basket. The gifts inside now seemed silly to her. Impractical things, bought on an impulse to bring joy to her cousins. Better she should have brought meat.

Rose plucked out the little gifts, unwrapping each with great care. "Tea! I was distressed I would have none to offer you. And scented soap." She held it to her nose and closed her eyes dreamily. "Such a luxury now." She poked more, discovering the new ribbons and pretty hairpins, exclaiming over each one.

"I have something else for you. I must give it now, lest Tim decide to grace us with his presence." She opened her reticule and produced the ten-pound note.

Rose's face fell. "You cannot afford that. I dare not accept."

"You can and must. It does not come from my wages or from my income. I have found a way to earn some money." She described her overture to Mrs. Bramble and the hat she had crafted in her room. "This morning I brought it to her. She paid me well for it." Not ten pounds, but Rose did not need to know that.

"You are making hats for a shop?" An unpleasant reaction shimmered over Rose's face.

"Secretly." Alexia laid the banknote on Rose's lap. "We must be selective in our pride, Rose."

"That is true. Every week I select more things over which to no longer be prideful." A serious expression replaced her mirth. "You are fortunate to have such a skill with hats, Alexia. I regret I do not possess any practical abilities, besides knowing which chest or chair might be sold without much notice."

Sounds above their heads indicated someone moved in the chamber there. "Let us walk. It is not too cold, and if he is about, I would rather— We argue too much, and today—"

"A walk would be delightful."

Rose left to get a wrap. She took the basket and money—to hide, no doubt. Once outside, they strolled down the lane that led to the village. Alexia asked after Irene.

"She chafes at our diminished circumstances," Rose said. "Such injustice cannot be countenanced by youth. She complains about helping clean the house and runs to the Mortensons' whenever they invite her. She builds castles in the air over their son, who will never have her now, of course." She pulled her cloak a bit tighter against the damp.

Rose glanced back at the house, now just a dot down the lane. "Tim speaks of selling it. He has lost all hope, all fight. Our family's home, he would sell. When things were bad the last time, Benjamin found a way to make them better, but Tim can only contemplate selling and selling until there is nothing more to sell. Where will that leave us when all is gone?"

"I will continue sending you some money. With the hats—I can always send a little. Enough so that Tim does not sell. If he does, most will go to debts anyway."

"So I tell him. At least we have a roof."

A nice roof. A nice home, and a place in their old world. The property was the last anchor to who and what they were supposed to be. Alexia knew all about that, all about hanging on to one's place and dignity with one's fingernails.

She linked her arm through Rose's. Her cousin had just opened a door that led to the past with Benjamin. Alexia had thought about him a lot last night. As the hours stretched toward dawn, her mind had swung between accommodating what had happened with Hayden and the shock that had led to her abandon. Discovering those letters had put Ben's memory in a new light, and she had studied the altered image with curiosity. Not with hate, though. Perhaps with time the hurt would encourage that much distance, but it had not yet.

"Rose, I have been thinking of late about our happy time in Cheapside."

"I wish we had never left that cozy home. The fall would not have been so far from there. Tim spent money as if the well would never go dry."

"But Benjamin did not. Yet that bank was doing very well earlier. For years, I expect. If all that money was available for Tim, much the same would have been there for Ben."

"We had those debts. The ones inherited from Father. I thought all was clear right after the war. However, Ben said there was one more debt, a big one, that he still had to repay. It was one reason I could not have a season."

That made sense, but then again it did not. It would be very coincidental if a big debt suddenly was paid at the same time Ben died. Tim had begun spending freely almost at once.

Alexia took some comfort in the bare facts, however. Hayden's allusions to Ben's melancholy and to the Longworths' finances had nudged at her for days now. She hated thinking that some dire predicament had waited for Ben in England. She resisted the notion that perhaps, due to that, he had become so drunk he fell off that ship. Or maybe did not fall at all.

Rose's story relieved her of that nagging suspicion. The debt had been an old one, not new. It would not cause a sudden despondency. They did not live in luxury in Cheapside, but it had been comfortable. The hard times had been conquered, even if a good deal of Ben's success was still going to pay for his father's bad judgments.

"I expect there might be something in his trunks about all of it," Rose said.

A chill shivered through Alexia at mention of the trunks. If they contained information regarding this debt, she did not see it. She had ceased looking once she found those letters.

The image of those letters invaded her head. The hand, the love, the scent—glimpses assaulted her, bringing back a taste of her shock. The memories poked and poked, demanding her attention and misery.

"I will be earning enough from the hats to pay my own keep, Rose. I will be leaving my situation soon." The brick buildings of the village could be seen through trees and brush, waiting ahead around a bend in the road.

"You have sold one hat, Alexia. Do not be rash. I hate the idea of your being in service at all, and for that man's family even more, but it is a home and some security and—"

"I am confident I can maintain myself. However, this may be the last time I have use of a carriage."

Rose's face fell. "Then it may be a long time before we see each other again."

"It will not be this convenient, but I will find a way."

"Maybe I will be the one to find a way."

Alexia stopped walking. "What do you mean?"

Rose faced her. "I cannot live like this forever. With Tim's behavior, it will only get worse. The house may eventually have to be sold after all. Perhaps it is time that I make some hats too, so to speak."

"You said you had no skill to sell."

"Nature gave every woman something to sell, Alexia."

They looked at each other. Rose adopted a solemn, determined expression, one that dared Alexia to scold and lecture.

There would be no admonishments. She had lost all rights to preach yesterday, when she gave herself to a man on an attic floor. Rose merely speculated anyway. It was nothing more than a calculation by a woman facing a bleak future. Alexia knew all about that, and where it sometimes led one's thoughts.

They began walking toward the village again. After a few footfalls the silence broke. A thunder of horses poured toward them, growing louder like a fast-approaching storm.

A large equipage rounded the bend and aimed right at them. They moved off the lane and the coach blurred past. Alexia noticed the crest on its door.

Rose's expression hardened. "It appears that Easterbrook is finally gracing the county with his presence. I should not blame the man for his brother's failings, but my respect for the entire family has been compromised, and I wish he had stayed in town. Thank heavens he never entertains, or Irene would be unbearable."

Alexia made the most of her few hours with Rose. They strolled the village and visited shops, then returned home for some tea and confidences.

Not the biggest confidence, of course. Rose must

never learn about what had transpired with Hayden. The memory of that spoiled the visit somewhat. Being back with the family he had wronged, noticing the details of precarious finances, added to Alexia's embarrassment at her weakness. How could she have forgotten what Hayden had done to this family? How could she have treated him as anything other than the enemy?

She took her leave in early afternoon, soon after the carriage returned.

"I will see you again soon, Rose." She kissed her cousin. "I will visit again as soon as I can."

"Once you are resettled, write and tell me where. Perhaps I will visit *you* and see what I am worth."

Alexia wished Rose did not allude again to the chance she might come to town to sell herself. It made the suggestion more than a groundless threat spoken in a fit of pique. She should not have let the last reference pass but received some reassurance that Rose did not truly consider such a thing.

As the carriage began its journey back to town, she debated the ways that she could help her cousins. Mrs. Bramble had paid two pounds for the hat and indicated she would charge five on any orders. If they could be made by day and not only by night, if the designs she invented drew enough orders, if she obtained this year's income and bought enough supplies . . . would it be sufficient when all was done to support herself and also the Longworths?

Not in style, but they were all past that. She had forgone such dreams long ago, and surely Rose would see that virtuous frugality was preferable to luxurious sin.

She gazed at the countryside winding past her

window. Her heart thickened with quiet dread. She saw again the hard lights in Rose's eyes as they faced each other on the lane.

There was an alternative. For reasons she could not fathom, she suspected that Hayden would offer her a special situation if she gave him the slightest encouragement. He had come close in the attic, but she had not wanted to hear the proposition that would damn forever what had just occurred.

She was already soiled, however. Ruined, if any of the servants had heard them. The security provided by a brief liaison with Hayden would far exceed any she could ever provide herself. She possessed neither Rose's exquisite beauty nor Phaedra's dramatic style. She was the most ordinary of women, yet Lord Hayden Rothwell had fixed his attention on her.

She weighed the choice. If she became his mistress, Rose and Irene might still salvage some kind of life. She would not be able to stand beside them in society, but she could obtain enough money to return them there for a while. They were both lovely, and perhaps that alone would bring marriage offers.

If one wanted to be practical, if one set sentiment aside and assessed who had the better chances to make an honorable and virtuous future, of the three she was the least likely to do so.

Nor would it be horrible to become Hayden's mistress. He had already proven that. If she allowed the pleasure to have its way, she might be able to ignore that she bartered her body with a man she would never love.

The carriage turned, rocking her out of her thoughts. She noted the crossroads through her window. It was the one where the lane met the road to London. The carriage had not turned south, however. They were heading north.

She opened the trapdoor and called for the coachman's attention. He stopped the equipage and turned to face her through the opening.

"The road is clearly marked, good sir. We are now going the wrong way," she said.

"M'lord said to bring you to Aylesbury Abbey once you were done with your cousin."

"You misunderstood, I am sure."

He shook his head. "They made a stop in Watlington and he saw the carriage. Told me to bring you along."

"I do not choose to visit with Easterbrook today. Turn this carriage around and—"

"Not the marquess who spoke with me. Lord Hayden, it was."

She saw the coach speed past and the blur of a profile within. Of all the days for Hayden to decide to come down from London, she could have done without his choosing this one.

"I refuse to accommodate Lord Hayden's whims. Take me back to London or it will be nothing less than an abduction."

"Well, now, you can explain all that to whoever wants to listen. You serve his family and eat at their board. You stepped into their carriage and sit there now. For a woman abducted, you have been most accepting."

He turned away and cracked the reins. All thoughts of the Longworths left Alexia's mind. It filled instead with the strong words she intended to shower on Hayden's head very soon.

Beneath her indignation, a quiet voice whispered. It was a sad voice, from the soul that understood the world all too well. *Why not?* it said. *You have nothing of value left to lose.*

CHAPTER
ELEVEN

Alexia judged Aylesbury Abbey to have over a hundred chambers. The ancient monastery was long gone from the property, replaced by a massive stone building.

Her eyes took in the Palladian raised portico and sprawling wings. She refused to be awed.

One of Aylesbury's servants handed her down. She addressed her coachman. "Do not go to the stable. I will be back very soon, and we will return to town in good time."

She and the servant marched up the stairs, entered, and began winding through the public rooms. Restrained luxury and saturated hues enclosed her like so many tastefully embellished jewel boxes. Perfect proportions marked each chamber, and superb craftsmanship enhanced every detail.

Hayden waited in the library, a chamber twice as long as it was wide and tall. Although furnished for comfort with sofas and reading chairs, the mahogany wainscot and carved moldings, the perfect bindings, the grand fireplace, the landscape oils—all of it identified the room as part of a great country house.

"You are delaying my return to town," she said. "It was an unfortunate coincidence that you decided to visit the family seat today and learned I was here."

"It was no coincidence. I followed you here. The coachman spoke of your plans to the groom, and—"

"And you inquired? And followed? What reason could compel you to make such a journey when I would be back tonight?"

"A conversation compelled me. One that is long overdue."

"Believe me, you do not want any conversation with me today. I have just come from my cousin."

He exhaled audibly. When he spoke again, his tone was almost gentle, but firmness sounded too. "I accept that you will never forgive me for their change in fortune. However, the Longworths are not part of the conversation I had in mind."

To be sure, this was going to be the conversation she anticipated.

"Will you not sit?"

"I prefer not to. Say what you have to say. Let us have this conversation, so I can be gone."

He strolled toward her. "Aunt Henrietta visited Easterbrook today. She woke him early this morning to complain about your plans to leave her house. She now believes she must move in with him in order to find another governess."

She was wrong. He was not going to ask her to be his mistress. His thirst no doubt had been slaked yesterday.

Now she was merely the servant with inconvenient plans, and he was just Easterbrook's lackey.

She strolled away, step for step. "Your aunt's design on Easterbrook's house is Easterbrook's problem, and perhaps yours. It is not mine."

They both stopped, newly positioned in the magnificent library, but just as distant. "My brother is most insistent that you be cajoled into staying."

"He sent the wrong knight on this errand. But then, he does not know why it would be hopeless if you spoke for him."

"Actually, I think he suspects."

"Then he is a little stupid to send you. However, if that is the reason for this abduction—"

"Hardly an abduction, Alexia. A slight detour."

"You may inform him you did your duty, but the lady, upon learning your mission, was unmoved, even if she was considerably relieved."

He walked again, but not in her direction. He strolled in front of the bookcases, thinking.

"You expected a proposition when you arrived here, didn't you?"

How had things become so muddled? She was insulted that he did not want her as his mistress, even though she knew the offer should be the bigger offense. "One is due. There are rules to seduction, aren't there? For gentlemen, at least. Or perhaps you only saw me as fit for a quick dalliance, such as men of your station enjoy with servants."

"I cannot blame you for thinking the worst of me, and you can upbraid me at length in due time. However, right now I only ask that you reconsider your decision to leave my aunt's house."

"I am sure you will see that she is not too inconvenienced."

"Her distress may be self-centered, but my concern is for you alone. Your decision is unwise."

"I weighed it most carefully."

"You will be vulnerable and alone."

"I am now. You of all men know that. You saw it at once."

He stopped pacing abruptly. "What do you mean by that?"

"If that had been my family's home, and my father had received you and my mother saw you at parties, if I had even still been the poor relative in the Longworths' house, would you have done it?"

Surprise and discomfort passed over his expression. Then he assumed the sternness that so often masked his thoughts.

It was enough of a reaction to release her dammed-up insulted pride. "There are rules to seduction, as I said. In going into service I lost the protection of the best rules, the ones reserved for daughters of good families. Here is the truth of it. If I had been a woman worthy of the best rules, I do not think you would have even noticed me. It was my fall that made me interesting, the fact I had tumbled outside the demands of strict honor. You are an intelligent man with efficient habits. I doubt you waste desire on ladies whom the rules make unattainable."

"Fine, I am a damned scoundrel. Right now we will

return to your decision to leave that house. Do you even have enough to buy a room in which to sleep?"

"Do you think I am so stupid as to make such a move if I did not?"

"When what you have is gone, who will provide for you?"

"I will provide for myself. I am turning to one of my other options. The first, being a governess, did not suit me."

Surprise cracked his mask. "Since you are incapable of theft, that leaves the hats. You are taking employment in a *shop*?"

"Perhaps it was the other option that I now contemplate. There was one more. Maybe you are not the only man who is pursuing me and I accepted someone else's protection."

She confounded him again. "I do not believe that."

"Of course you don't. I am not the sort of woman who would dazzle several men at once. Actually, I am not the sort to dazzle any at all, which puts an unpleasant light on recent events."

"I do not believe it because it is not in your nature."

"Perhaps it is. I always assumed it would be hideous to be kissed by a man whom I did not love, but I was wrong. I have discovered that love and passion are not the same thing."

She received a deep, direct gaze for that, the kind that would have flustered her not long ago. She was not nearly as afraid of this man today as she had been in the past, however. Yesterday had leveled the field between them quite a bit.

"You came here thinking I would proposition you,

but you entered the house," he said. "You feared hearing it, but you intended to listen. You are willing to consider it."

It took her a moment to get her response out of her throat. "Yes."

"Because of the pleasure?"

"Because of the *money*. A woman facing an uncertain future, a woman seeing her family in dire need, will consider anything."

"Would it not make more sense to marry? Most women consider that first."

"Then find me a man of substance who will marry a woman of my age, countenance, fortune, and stained virtue."

"You would marry out of practicality? I assumed you would not. It was not on your list."

No, it was not. It should have been, unlikely though that option would have been. She had always dismissed it as impossible, but in truth she had rebelled at settling for such a match after once believing she would have much more.

"I would seek such a man for you, but there is always the good chance you will not care for him," he said.

"Then I will have much in common with many other married women. But we speak nonsense, and my carriage awaits." She turned on her heel and headed toward the doorway.

With a few strides he blocked her path. "Actually, *my* carriage awaits, and it will wait a little longer."

"Easterbrook's carriage, if we are going to be particular."

"Not yours, however."

"Mine for the day."

"Only because I was undressing you in my mind while you negotiated."

"Then you should clear your thoughts before you negotiate in the future."

"That is excellent advice, Alexia. Considering the direction this conversation has taken, very timely advice as well."

"There is nothing to negotiate."

"You just invited a proposition."

For a large library, it suddenly felt very small. Even so, the door was far away. She attempted to maintain her plain-speaking stance, but the ground beneath her wobbled.

"Do not waste your time, unless you intend to offer carte blanche."

He laughed quietly and moved closer. "That would be reckless. I would never invite such ruin."

"No, probably not. I expect that before you negotiate, you calculate the accounting with precision."

"Always. Therefore, I am aware that your lack of affection for me requires some enhancements in the offer." He made a display of thinking it over. "A house of your own. An army of servants and a cook. A carriage with a matched pair, for your use alone, and, of course, a new wardrobe. How does that sound?"

She stared at him. Her shock amused him. He made a little gesture under her chin, to suggest she might close her gaping mouth.

"Oh, and jewelry, of course. This, to start." He removed a velvet pouch from his coat, lifted one of her hands, and emptied its contents into her palm.

A necklace of rubies and gold dripped around her fingers. The glitter mesmerized her. She could not move.

"Are they real?"

"There are rules, as you said. One is that a gentleman does not give a lady fake jewels."

"Do I get to keep it, no matter what?"

"Yes."

"The house and coach too?"

"The jewels and wardrobe are yours. The house and coach will be mine but at your command."

Being able to keep the house when he tired of her would be better, but she could see where that was expecting too much. And the jewels alone would go a long way to ensuring her future and seeing that Rose and Irene had a second chance.

"And in return for this generosity?"

"You are mine alone for as long as I say."

"I require a more complete answer. I have heard of things that would not be worth all the jewels in England to endure."

He took the necklace from her hand and stepped behind her to fasten it on her neck. "Are you implying that I might be a pervert, Alexia?"

"Goodness, no, but you have never married, and I just thought that perhaps—"

"We could call in the solicitors and draw up a contract. One that lists my preferences and your agreement or lack of it, act by act."

"I merely thought that you are being rather generous for such as me and that there may be a misunderst—"

"You discount your own worth too quickly. As for

what happens in bed, we will negotiate all of that as honestly as we have this."

She felt the jewels on her neck. She saw them sparkle beneath her face in a looking glass on the other side of the room. She looked much more sophisticated and pretty than she had just minutes ago. Hayden's dark form backed hers in the reflection, but he was looking down at her, not at their images.

"So in return I will be your lover."

His hands circled her waist. His head dipped. The warmth of his lips pressed her neck. "Yes. Oh, and you will also help with Caroline's finishing."

She giggled, because his kisses were tickling her. All of her. She had the shocking thought that a man's kiss felt more exciting when you were wearing jewels worth several hundred pounds. "Your aunt will hardly agree to that if I am your mistress."

He kissed her nape, and a thrill spiraled down to the soreness that still gently throbbed. "She certainly would not accept you then. However, this is not so much a proposition as a proposal. I am speaking of marriage."

More shocked than when she saw the necklace, she stared at his bent head in the looking glass. She stepped away and turned to face him.

"Marriage? *Why?*"

He laughed and began to embrace her. She slipped out of his reach.

"You were correct. If you had still been living with the Longworths, if you had a father or family, if you were not alone and vulnerable and poor, I would have never seduced you. I would have wanted to, but those protections would have checked me."

"So now you have concluded the best rules apply to me after all, and you make the obligatory proposal. I confess that I thought you had more . . . independence."

"It is not only the rules. Your forthright nature, which has probably put off most men, happens to suit me. We are much alike in our sensible ways. We will know what we have in each other and treat each other with more honesty too."

He was itemizing what she brought to this marriage. The list struck her as fairly dismal. "You gain little from this. You do not need any wife. If you have decided you want one, you should find a woman with a fortune or style or beauty."

"In your own way, you have all three."

The flattery disarmed her, as it had in the library the day of that first kiss. He said it to make the best of an awkward situation, but her heart smiled anyway.

It was the jump from mistress to wife that confounded her. She had all but agreed to the former. He did not need to offer the latter.

"Why did you not press your advantage?"

"I try not to be ruthless, even when a pretty lady is willing to allow it. I have behaved badly with you, but I will not be responsible for your final fall. I want you, however. In such cases a gentleman offers marriage."

"That want, peculiar as it is, will pass."

"If it does, I will have a wife who does not expect me to lie to her, any more than she misunderstands that want now."

She should be elated. A wealthy, handsome man from one of England's best families had just proposed.

A joy did want to take hold of her, but it could not find an anchor in her heart.

Being his mistress would be limited. It was not irrevocable. As she had said that day on the house tour, it was an honest form of trade.

Being his wife—that meant a lifetime. Forever. Even so, she should grab the security. She should not miss this chance. But deep in her heart, a girl who had once thrilled to love's exciting romance stared out, appalled. It was one thing to accept she would probably never know that again. It was another to take the step that would make it forever impossible.

Nor would this be just any practical marriage. He was Hayden Rothwell. She heard Timothy's slurred voice damning her. She saw Rose turning away. She would not be able to help them if she did this. Rose would not accept a penny from Rothwell's wife.

He watched her closely as she sorted her reactions. She suspected he knew her decision before she did. After one final, long gaze in the looking glass, she unfastened the necklace.

She was about to do the most impractical thing she had ever imagined.

She walked over and placed the necklace on the mantelpiece. "It is a wonderful offer for any woman, but I cannot accept. As I said when I entered, this was not the day for this conversation."

"But it was a day to proposition you, I take it."

"Perhaps so. I had begun justifying that temporary practicality after I left Rose today."

"You are an amazing woman, Alexia." Since an edge of anger tightened the statement, it did not sound like a compliment. "The Longworths will be far better off if you marry me."

"Ah, you do know how to press your advantage when you choose to. However, you are wrong. They will never forgive me if I marry you. They would never speak to me again."

"They will come around. But this is not about them. It is about you and me."

"They are all the family I have."

He allowed her to walk past him to the door. His voice followed her. "It is not only because they are your family. It is about him too. They are your bond to Benjamin. Despite what you learned yesterday, you still hold him in your heart."

His accusation made her throat burn. She could not deny that despite the new distance and new truths, Ben's memory still touched something deep inside her. "Is that so wrong?"

She braced herself for a blunt response, the same one that her own mind quietly spoke. Yes, it was wrong. She was stupid.

Instead, he smiled with a warm kindness that touched her. "No, it is not so wrong, Alexia. It is very . . . romantic."

A cleansing clarity entered her. She might have blinked away a latent drowsiness after waking from sleep.

It *was* romantic. Hopelessly, childishly so. A handsome man of significant wealth had just offered marriage, and there were not many good reasons for any woman to refuse. For a woman in her situation—poor,

homeless, adrift, and ruined—there wasn't a single one
that did not sound like a bad line of poetry.

"You are correct, Hayden. Sometimes I forget myself and indulge in sentimentality." She gestured to
the mantel. "You promise it is mine, to do with as I
choose?"

"Any jewels are yours. I expect there will be others."

If I am pleased. He did not say it, but she heard it.
The negotiations of becoming a wife were not much different from those of becoming a mistress, when you got
down to it.

"There will also be a settlement, of course," he said
simply, although his expression revealed sharp awareness that she had reopened negotiations.

"I bring nothing to a settlement."

"I will provide for you. Whether I live or die, you
will never count pennies again."

Never again. The lure of eternal security had the effect he intended. He offered a safety and peace she had
not known since she was too young to understand how
close she walked to poverty.

"Can I assume we will have the usual sort of marriage, such as I see in polite society?" she asked.

"I will not be around much, if that is what you fear."

Except at night. Oddly enough, that part of marriage
seemed the least onerous and dangerous. With time he
would go elsewhere for that too, as was normal in aristocratic marriages. She might, as well, if she ever fell in
love again.

"You will have your own friends and your own life."
He moved closer as he answered a question her racing
thoughts had not considered yet.

"Even Phaedra? I do not want you forbidding—"

"Even Miss Blair. I do not approve of men who interfere with their wives' interests and friends."

She tallied up the obligations and payments in this marriage. The balance tilted so much in her favor it could not be denied. If one had to accept a practical match, one could not do better than marrying Lord Hayden Rothwell. That was so obvious that even Rose would see it eventually.

She silenced the final, whispered objections of the silly girl inside her. She took a deep breath, walked back to the mantel, and picked up the necklace. "I accept your proposal, Hayden. I will marry you."

CHAPTER
TWELVE

They made good time back to town, but then a coach and four with a crest on the door usually did. Hayden had Alexia ride with him, although he guessed she would rather not. He spent the time contemplating what marriage to this woman would mean. Her expression suggested her thoughts dwelled on the future too.

He was doing the right thing, there was no denying it, but he could not evade the notion that he also tempted both history and fate. Sometimes the right thing was not the best thing. Even though he showed the honor his father preached, he wondered if he would also prove the old man correct about the impulse of passion and the misery it created.

Hayden's mother had not married a man she loved either but instead accepted the proposal of the peer who bedazzled her that first season with his power and wealth. Ten years later, after giving her husband three sons, she had asked him to let her go to the army officer whom she had always held in her heart. Whatever warmth there had been in their marriage died the day he refused.

She found a way to go anyway, of course. In response, her husband had arranged for her lover to be posted in a distant colony, where he died of fever. The chill in their marriage had turned to ice after that.

He could hear his father, intoning his lessons at the dinners his mother ceased to attend. *Romance is an invention of poets. It is a drama devised to make men's base needs more acceptable to women. Play the role if you must, but have no illusions such sentiments last or really matter.* He did not know his sons had guessed the whole of their parents' own drama very early, and even knew the name of the lover she pined for in her isolation.

Of course, Alexia was not a sixteen-year-old ingenue accepting a proposal with starry eyes. She possessed an honesty that should spare them the worst marital storms.

And if someday she fell in love again and reclaimed the illusion she had known with Ben . . . His reaction to the idea surprised him. Underneath the generosity he wanted to think he would have, beneath the understanding that could accept such an arrangement, a primitive instinct bared its teeth.

He tamed the beast by retreating into the most logical of deliberations. He turned his mind to numbers and how he would arrange the settlement. He was debating the size of her allowance when she turned her gaze from the passing countryside toward him.

"There was a big debt," she said. "You asked in the park why Ben did not enjoy his success. Rose told me today that there was a large final debt to repay, inherited from his father."

He looked across the coach, and a shadow veiled the future. She had just become engaged. She sat with her future husband. Her mind, however, had been thinking about the Longworths. Perhaps she had been rehearsing what she would say to bring her cousins around. Nothing he would want to hear, he was sure.

"Well, that explains it, then."

"It is a bit odd that the debt went away when Ben died. Would it not have in turn been inherited by Timothy?"

"The remaining amount could have been so little that the man whom they owed forgave the rest when Ben died. Or it may not have been a collectible debt at all, and Ben repaid it only out of honor, not legal necessity."

"That would be like Ben. He was the most honorable of men."

"A paragon of virtue." He managed to thwart the sardonic note that tried to color his agreement.

It was in his interest now to let her know the truth about Benjamin. He had only to picture her tears in the attic to know she would not learn it from him, however. His word of honor to Timothy would be compromised then, but another reason sat across from him. He did not want to see her that hurt again.

"Alexia, we should make some decisions about this marriage."

"A quick wedding, I think. Very private, with a simple announcement, if you do not mind. Everyone will know that you would marry a penniless governess only to do the honorable thing. It would be in bad taste to have a large, dramatic wedding."

"We will do it that way if you prefer. However, this season we will host a ball and you will order an exorbitantly expensive gown for it."

"To make up for the small wedding?"

Yes, and for the first season and all the feminine indulgences and joys she had been denied. "It will be a convenient way to introduce you to all of my friends."

She smiled weakly. The notion of facing his friends sent her back into her private contemplations. She did not emerge from them until they entered London. "We have been in this coach for hours, but you have not even tried to kiss me."

"Have you been waiting for a grand seduction all this time?" Temptation's arrows had prodded him the whole way, but he'd be damned before he admitted it. Passion might pass and not really matter, but for now it ruled him more than he thought possible. "I thought I would wait until we are married."

That amused her. "So now I am an innocent again, until the wedding? It is a charming hypocrisy, but I appreciate your care with my dignity."

"Since you requested a quick wedding, I need not wait long. I can afford to be magnanimous."

She laughed. The setting sun's light flooded her face. Its golden glow eliminated the shadows of caution that had darkened her eyes the whole day.

He did not bring her back to Hill Street. Instead, he took her to Easterbrook's. She did not ask why. This was not a man whom one challenged over small decisions.

He settled her in the drawing room, where she had negotiated for use of the carriage.

"I gave instructions for a late supper to be prepared," he said. "I have also sent for my brothers."

"Do you intend a dramatic announcement?"

"Absolutely."

"Would it not be more prudent to inform them privately?"

"Prudence has never marked my behavior with you, and I see no reason to dredge it up for my brothers' sake. Or do you mean so you will not see their astonishment? I promise you that any shock they reveal will have nothing to do with you."

He looked very relaxed. Almost lighthearted. The notion of surprising his brothers amused him.

A young man, perhaps twenty-five in age, wandered in a few minutes later. They had never been introduced, but she recognized him as Lord Elliot Rothwell, the precocious author of a renowned volume on the last years of the Roman army in Britain.

He did not appear much the scholar, although she could imagine his dark, brooding eyes taking the step toward total distraction that such endeavors might induce. Perhaps it was his attention to fashion that was incongruous with the source of his fame. The snug fit of his double-buttoned, knee-length dark gray frock coat showed the very latest style. The layered cut of his thick dark hair was that of a young man about town.

Hayden introduced her. Elliot's manner was more personable than his countenance promised. His smile put her at ease. He asked after his aunt, but Hayden interrupted.

"Elliot, Miss Welbourne has accepted my proposal of marriage."

Elliot's surprise was noticeable but brief. "That is wonderful. I look forward to the day I address you as sister, Miss Welbourne. Have you begun planning the particulars, Hayden?"

"We will be wed as soon as I procure the special license."

"Then I will be sure to remain in town for the next fortnight or so. Have you told Christian yet?"

"I have asked him to come down so I can."

"I do not think he will respond to the request. He has had one of *those* days."

"If he will not come down to us, I should go to him. It would not do for him to learn about my engagement from the servants' gossip. Will you stay with Miss Welbourne, Elliot?"

He left her to his younger brother's care. She tried to call up enough pleasantries to fill the time. Elliot examined her like a man who had just found a butterfly and tried to determine what specimen it might be.

"Did he seduce you?"

The question startled her. The poise she had donned as armor to survive this visit suddenly felt paper-thin.

"Considering the abruptness of our impending nuptials, and the fact you and I have never met before, I cannot blame you for wondering about that. I did not expect the question to be put so baldly, however."

"Remarkable." He suddenly found the specimen very interesting indeed.

"I realize that I am not what you expected, under these circumstances or any other."

"I had no expectations, other than expecting he might never marry at all. It is not his choice of woman that I find remarkable. It is the evidence that he did something impetuous. Four or five years ago, possibly, but now—it is amazing."

"You do not appear displeased."

"Not at all. Assuming, of course, that you do not make him forever regret his moment of madness."

This man had arrived at a request for reassurance by a peculiar path, but they stood at its crossroads all the same. He asked for something even Hayden had not broached, other than stating he expected her fidelity for as long as he wanted it, which implied he did not expect it forever.

And she had accepted the proposal without fully weighing the private obligations entailed. They loomed now. The naked truth of her decision pressed on her.

It would be a marriage. It would mean the forever she had initially rejected. She would owe him more than temporary fidelity and the right to her body. Being a wife meant more than that.

She contemplated her response to Elliot's overture. Her words would be important, to herself as well as to him. She looked in her heart to discover what she could honestly promise.

"I will try to be a good wife, if that is what you mean." It sounded very thin, but her heart beat heavily, as if she had committed to a momentous goal.

His smile of approval heartened her in a silly way, but her poise refused to reassemble itself. She remained too aware of the changes waiting in her life. Elliot's bluntness had forged a bond, however. She sensed that this brother might be an ally and a friend in the years ahead.

"Why did you say he might have acted impetuously in years past but not now?"

"He has lived several different lives. There is the one you see, sensible and efficient and a little stern, the one unlikely to seduce Miss Welbourne. Then there is the one he lives every morning. You will learn about that one soon enough." He laughed, then spoke very seriously. "It is not entirely of this world, that life, and you must make sure he does not get lost in it."

"You make him sound like someone for whom moments of madness are common rather than amazing things. Pray, do not frighten me."

"It is a type of madness, I suppose, but he controls it. Then there was the life he led as a youth. Dutiful and boring and correct. It was the same with Christian. They were two soldiers under command of a field marshal."

"That would be your father."

He nodded. "Our father brooked no arguments. He molded my brothers, but when he passed away, the molds suddenly crumbled. Faced with the freedom to be themselves, my brothers did not seem to know who those men were. Hayden tried being the blood on the town, then the political extremist, then other selves. Eventually he discovered the self you see now."

"Of all the ones to choose, why this one?"

"One's true nature may win out in the end, and this is his." He shrugged. "Going to Greece may have done it. The decision was foolhardy, full of romantic ideals and little practicality. Perhaps the reality of battle taught him the costs of sentiment too well. I would not know. He does not speak of it to anyone."

That was not true. He had spoken of it to her, a little. "You describe your brothers' journeys to find their true selves. Were you spared?"

"As youngest, it was easy to escape my father. I learned to hide in the library."

Where he hid still. She wondered if he had escaped as much as he thought.

"Enough about my brother. You will know him too well soon enough. Tell me about yourself, Miss Welbourne, and how you came to be my cousin's governess."

She did not care to have this observant man analyzing her life. She began her story. Considering all the details she intended to leave out, it would not be a long tale.

Christian's sitting room was dark, but a lamp glowed in the bedroom. As Hayden aimed for it, something moved near him in a corner. He stopped and peered into the deep shadows. Christian sat there on a wing chair, too upright for sleep. He might have been sitting there all day, for all Hayden knew.

"Are you drunk?" he asked.

"Cold sober, actually." Christian's tone reflected profound distraction and irritation that he had been disturbed.

Hayden never knew what to do when his brother got like this. Christian's total escapes from the world were brief but disturbingly intense. Nor did he work formulas or read documents while he was gone. He appeared to do absolutely nothing at all.

"I told the butler to have a supper prepared. Come down and join us."

"I think not."

"It is not healthy to indulge your melancholy like this."

"Is it melancholy that sends you to those numbers, Hayden? Or Elliot to his libraries? I have not been visiting any dark chambers in my mind, if that is what you fear."

The hell he hadn't. The darkness poured out of him, making the air thick. Hayden strode to the bedroom, fetched the light, and returned.

It revealed his brother. Christian was not in the robe, as Hayden expected, nor unkempt. Rather, he had been groomed impeccably and wore his finest coats. His expression showed no ill effects of his strange vigil. His countenance appeared more crisp, more alert, than Hayden had seen in months.

He gestured to the coats. "Do you intend to go out tonight?"

"No."

"I really wish you would not act so peculiar at times, Christian. You are too young to be boldly eccentric."

"And you are too young to be emotionally abstract."

What the hell did that mean? Hayden set the lamp down. "I would be grateful if you came down to supper. Or perhaps only for a few minutes now, if that is all you can grant. Miss Welbourne is here, and I would like you to welcome her into the family."

Attention rippled through the stillness. Christian did

not move, but he thoroughly returned to the world. "You are marrying this woman?"

"It appears so."

"Not vigilant enough, eh?"

"It appears not."

"Damned decent of you. The only thing to do, of course."

There had been other things to do, and they both knew it.

"I always knew you would marry a woman like her."

"Of course."

"Although I had hoped—well, let us go to her. As it happens, I am already dressed for it." He rose to his feet. "I anticipated some need to look civilized. I did not think it would be this, however."

They trailed toward the stairs together. "What did you hope?" Hayden asked.

Christian's expression darkened, as if he thought the question too bold. Then it cleared in an instant. "Ah, you meant my comment just now. It was a very small hope, and not important."

"I am curious all the same."

Christian shrugged. "I had hoped you would fall in love, Hayden. But it is better this way. Less dangerous."

She was not entirely on display in the drawing room. Once good wishes and a blessing of approval had been administered by Easterbrook, the brothers chatted among themselves while they waited the call to supper.

A quarter hour after Hayden's return with his brother, another guest arrived. Henrietta sailed in, wearing a formal dinner dress of blush tulle and *gros de Naples*. Her face glowed with delight beneath the bird of paradise plume that adorned a pink beret-turban that Alexia had allowed her to buy last week.

She targeted Easterbrook with her stride, not looking at anyone else. Halfway to him, her eye caught Alexia. Confusion flickered, but Henrietta was not to be waylaid.

"How generous of you to invite me, Easterbrook. After this morning, I worried that perhaps you—I was undone to receive your request to come, although surprised that you meant tonight. Such short— Well, I am here, grateful and relieved."

Easterbrook's welcome carried a formal edge. Alexia sensed the coolness was not for his aunt so much as for her unexpected addition to their group.

When Henrietta acknowledged Alexia, she spoke indulgently. "I am happy that my nephew could find you. I trust there will be no more talk of your leaving. How generous of Easterbrook to allow you to stay for our little party as well. You may take my carriage back once the meal is finished. I am sure that my nephews will see that I am returned."

Hayden took his aunt's hand between both of his. "Aunt Henrietta, this will not so much be a little party as a little celebration, and Miss Welbourne's attendance is essential. She and I became engaged this afternoon."

Henrietta smiled up at him in her dreamy way. Very slowly, her mouth tightened and her eyes turned to ice. A chilled silence claimed her for several slow moments.

"How wonderful, Hayden. I wish you both every happiness."

"It is wonderful, isn't it? I could not be more pleased," Easterbrook said. He offered his arm to his aunt. "Let us go down. I hope it is not a cold supper. I detest them."

Henrietta was not a happy woman. She never addressed Alexia during the meal. She shot little glares across the table, however. Hayden read the insults. *Scheming Jezebel. Wanton adventuress.* And, most often, *traitor.*

Hen's mouth pursed in disdain when he described the quick, private ceremony, but Christian and Elliot acted as if it were perfectly normal for the brother of a marquess to marry that way.

"Where will you make your home?" Elliot asked, raising a problem that quick weddings produced.

"In my happiness at Miss Welbourne's acceptance, I did not turn to that yet. I will visit estate agents tomorrow."

"With the season approaching, you will not find anything to let now that you want," Elliot said.

"You could always live here, of course," Christian said, emerging from a long period when he merely observed. He proceeded to drink some wine, oblivious to the astonished silence that greeted his quiet statement.

Henrietta looked ready to swoon from her shock at the injustice. "I would think Miss Welbourne would prefer her own home," she suggested, her voice strangling on her dismay.

"Is that so, Miss Welbourne?" Christian asked. "Would you prefer your own home right away? Say, one like the house on Hill Street where you now live?"

"I will be content wherever Hayden chooses. A house like the one on Hill Street would be more than adequate."

"The solution is clear, then. Hayden must take residence in that house rather than your coming here."

"What?" Henrietta cried. "Easterbrook, there is not enough room. If you had visited you would know that. Why, we barely manage as it is and—"

"It has over twenty chambers. My brother will soon find one better for his bride, but that one will be adequate for now. Miss Welbourne says so."

Hen's face reddened. "It is *my* house, may I remind you."

"But you will allow them to live there, won't you? Because of all the kindness Hayden has shown you. And as a special favor to me."

Hayden tilted his head toward Alexia and spoke quietly. "Do you want that? If not, speak now."

"It is my home," she whispered. "I would be happy to remain there."

Hen did not miss the danger in the silken tone Easterbrook used. She tried to swallow her dismay and looked miserable in the effort. "I suppose we can all manage together for a few months."

"I think you and Caroline had best leave," Christian said. "If my brother wanted relatives underfoot, he would have accepted my offer that he and his bride live here."

"Sir, that is not necessary," Alexia said. "I do not want to live there if it puts your aunt out in any way."

Christian called for more wine. He gazed at his full glass for a long minute. "My aunt will not be put out without also being accepted in. You and Caroline will live here, Aunt Hen."

He might have announced the French had invaded. Everyone stared at him.

"We will? Oh, my, now I am truly undone. You are too good, Easterbrook. Why, this will make Caroline's season an untold success. And she will have the chance to really know both you and Elliot. I cannot express my emotions—"

"Yes, yes. Well, I am glad it suits you."

Oh, it suited her. Hayden saw the triumph beneath Hen's tears of gratitude. No more glares went Alexia's way. The governess was no longer a fallen woman getting better than she deserved but an accomplice whose strategies had achieved the impossible.

Christian ignored Henrietta for the rest of the meal. He would get a lot of practice at that now.

CHAPTER THIRTEEN

⌒⌒

The ladies from Hill Street alighted from the coach in front of St. Martin's Church. Alexia looked up at the portico. This morning its columns looked dirty and the shadows behind them appeared menacing.

"Why don't you and Caroline go ahead," she said to Henrietta. "I will take some air for a minute, then follow."

Caroline grinned. "A little unsettled, are you? I have heard that some girls bolt, just run away. There was that one two years ago who—"

"That will be quite enough," Henrietta said. Her cheeks sucked in and her lids lowered. "I am very sure that Miss Welbourne is neither unsettled nor afraid and has no thoughts of running away. She merely wants some air. Come with me."

They walked up the stairs, getting ever smaller until the portico's shadows ate them.

Alexia's gaze darted from spot to spot on the steps and street, hoping to see what her heart knew would not be there.

She had written to Rose and Timothy a week ago, two days after the supper with Easterbrook. The letter had been difficult to compose. The logic for accepting this marriage seemed less rational when she tried to pen the words.

However, she had also denied the impulse to beseech their forgiveness. Hayden had wronged the Longworths most grievously, but her acceptance of his proposal had complicated her loyalties. If she was going to marry the man, she should not damn his character in a letter she wrote after her engagement.

Instead of the long outpouring of excuses, she wrote a brief letter that explained her decision in a few sentences. She asked them to attend the wedding and for Timothy to give her hand in marriage. She offered to send a carriage for them. She even promised to find them a place to stay in town for a few days.

No reply came. No request arrived for the carriage. By the fourth day she accepted they would not even acknowledge her marriage. All the same, as she prepared this morning she had listened for their familiar voices in the house, hoping they would surprise her at the last minute.

The vacant steps, the empty portico, showed that had been a childish fantasy. She would do this completely alone.

She tried to bury her sorrow beneath the other emotion overwhelming her. Unsettled did not do justice to describing her state today. Panic swelled whenever she thought about the step she was taking. Bolting was not out of the question.

A figure appeared between the columns above. A man walked down to her.

"Would you allow me the honor of escorting you, Miss Welbourne?" Elliot asked.

"Yes, I think so."

They began to mount the steps. Halfway up, another figure slid into place beside her. Elliot glanced over at the billowing black drapery and flowing red hair, then looked again, longer.

Alexia paused and accepted Phaedra Blair's embrace and kiss. Phaedra and Elliot examined each other while Alexia introduced them.

"Your cousins could not swallow their anger, I see," Phaedra said.

"No, and I am all the more grateful for your attendance."

"If I do not approve of such matches, that is my own view. I accept that my path is not suitable for most women. Well, let us do it, then." She took Alexia's hand and urged her forward.

"You intend to give her hand?" Elliot asked.

"What an interesting idea. The symbolism would be preferable to that of the usual practice. However, I will only walk with her, if that is acceptable to you. She comes to this church dependent on no man, so no man should presume to give her to another. She will relinquish her freedom by her own judgment, for good or ill, and it is a pity the church is not full of people to see the truth of it."

Elliot retreated into bemused silence. Phaedra marched alongside, her garments floating back in the breeze like a Nike of the night.

Easterbrook, Caroline, and Henrietta waited within the church with a small group of guests. Hayden stood near the altar, alongside a young man whom Alexia did not know.

"My, my," Phaedra whispered. "The Earl of Chalgrove has come up to town to stand by your fiancé's side. And that foppish, tired fellow with the gold hair is Viscount Suttonly. The guest list may be a short one, but the blood of your witnesses is very rich."

As she walked down the aisle between her escorts, Alexia's heart pounded. Her mind raced through a final reckoning.

She might be making a terrible mistake, one that all the security would never outweigh. What did she know about the man waiting there ahead? He had shown her some kindness and warmth, he could make her moan with pleasure, but she had also seen his coldest cruelty. The latter might be waiting for her in the future.

Phaedra and Elliot left her standing alone at the end of the aisle. The priest took his position. Hayden came to her and offered his arm. She grasped it too hard.

"You look frightened," he said.

"Not frightened," she lied. "Just too aware, too alive."

"When I was a boy, I would sometimes deliberately venture down an unknown road, not knowing where it would bring me. The sense of adventure was similar to what I experience today." He guided her toward the priest. "I think that we will be good companions on this journey, Alexia. I promise that you will be safe with me."

They departed from Easterbrook's house after the wedding breakfast. The coach did not carry them to Hill Street but to a property that Hayden owned in Kent.

"Your aunt was already packing yesterday," Alexia said as the coach rolled into the country. "Caroline is very excited by the change in residence and promised to work very hard at her French and dancing while I am gone."

"My brother expects Henrietta to effect the move in two days, now that she has her victory."

"Easterbrook was very kind to give it to her. I think he is an interesting person. One senses something within him. A silent center that watches and waits. Yes, that is it. He is waiting for something. It is palpable."

She looked charming, her expression serious as she picked through her memories and attempted to understand the cipher that Christian presented. In naming the source of Easterbrook's darkness, she had also succeeded where for years Hayden had failed. Christian's eternal distraction *was* much like that of someone who waits for news.

She wore the carriage ensemble ordered from Madame Tissot. Its cerulean blue complemented her fair complexion. Her dress for the wedding had come from that small wardrobe too. She would need to commission a much larger one when they returned to town.

She had appeared so fearful, so unsure as she came toward him in the church. Questions had shimmered on her much as the light had glossed over the silk she wore. Her vulnerability had touched him and also crystallized his own questions. He felt more the seducer in that church than he had in the attic, luring her with wealth and jewels away from a self-possession that had given her strength.

"I am glad that when we return to town it will be to that house," she said. "My life and my circles will probably change much in the months ahead. It will be reassuring to return at the end of the day to familiar chambers and passageways."

He was happy she would be comfortable, but he wondered if their choice of home was wise. There were ghosts in that house, and more memories than he knew about. It might have been better to let a hovel in a rookery.

"Did you inform your cousins of the wedding?" He poked a stick into the river to judge its depth and current.

The old tightness flexed through her. A false passivity claimed her expression. "I wrote. There was no response. It will be as I predicted, I think. Perhaps, with time . . ."

He took her hand and pulled her toward him. He grasped her waist and set her on his lap. The bonnet's brim poked his face, and he untied the ribbons and cast it aside.

He lightly traced the side of her face. Alexia Welbourne, cousin to the Longworths, remained distant from him, but his touch awoke a different woman, one who existed for him alone. The hunger to totally possess her simmered within his desire, but he would settle for less.

"We will help your cousins as they will permit," he said.

Little fires ignited in the eyes gazing up at him. A wise man would retreat, on this of all days.

She spoke no accusations, but they were there all the same.

"There is more to your cousin's ruin than you know," he said, responding to the impulse to douse those fires even though he never could.

She frowned. "What more?"

"It is not for me to tell you. I only say that it was not all as it appeared."

"That is conveniently vague, Hayden. I think if there is more to it, you would have told me by now."

He kissed her, silencing her skepticism, abandoning the futile urge to remove her inner anger. He prolonged the kiss, tasting and claiming, luxuriating in his building arousal, until he sensed her trembles submerge the old resentment.

"We will not speak of it now," he said. "I cannot command your forgiveness, but when I kiss you I do not want your bitterness between us. I want you to leave the Longworths outside the door when you and I meet in bed."

She appeared to ponder his demand. Her fingertips slowly skimmed his face. The small touch tantalized him to the point of senselessness.

"I think of nothing much at all when you kiss me, so I may be able to forget my cousins during the times that I do my duty as your wife." She paused. "All of my cousins."

He kissed her deeply to ensure that she did. He unfastened her pelisse and caressed her breast, determined to prove that in the pleasure she belonged to him alone.

She had not meant it as a challenge, but he reacted as if she had. The slow, long kisses, the devastating touch on her body, deliberately drove her to madness. Even the rocking of the coach became sensual, a rhythm that echoed the throb of arousal that built with each mile.

He did not try to undress her further, but she wished he would. Her breasts became so sensitive beneath the subtle play of his fingertips that she wanted to tear off the garments that shielded her skin. Her awareness constricted to the sensations. They slid down her body in titillating streams, pooling between her legs, awakening again the physical yearning for completeness.

He kissed her neck, her chest, her breast, his ardor restrained but its power palpable. Memories of the pain became insignificant.

His touch grew less gentle, reflecting the strain she sensed in him. His caress handled her breast possessively, demanding more from her. Arrows of fire shot to her vulva and her mind.

More. The relentless hunger intensified so badly she wanted to whimper. Her body ached from the exquisite torture, and her mind screamed from frustration.

He pressed his hand against her swaying hip, stopping both the rhythm and the vague relief it gave. "Are you feeling dutiful, Alexia?"

"If you would like."

His hand slid to her stomach, its firm pressure over her womb. "I did not ask if you are ready to do your duty in this coach, but if you felt merely dutiful." He turned his gaze to her. His expression made her breath catch. "It will not be duty you bring to me. That is one lie we will not live. You will accept me because of this." He pressed gently, and a wonderful warmth shuddered through her loins. "And this." He bent and kissed her breast.

He caressed lower, pressing down her thigh and leg, then up again, below her skirts. "And this."

The feel of his hand on her bare skin mesmerized her. The confident fires in his eyes, the sensual hardness in his face, left her breathless. Her body knew at once what he meant and began pulsing with anticipation. His slow, upward caress ruthlessly teased.

She bit back a moan when he touched her, but a cry shrieked through her whole body. The intense sensation repeated again and again, sending her into abandon.

He shifted her hips onto his thigh. "Spread your legs."

She did not obey. The need was almost painful. Her madness frightened her.

He pressed against her knee, in command and encouragement. "Do as I say."

Her legs parted without her choice. She felt his touch better then. Too well. Long slow strokes made her tremble. Short rapid ones teased at a spot of unbearable sensitivity. A darkness closed in on her, one that obscured him and herself and all of her body except where his caress focused. The chant for more turned into a rising, desperate demand.

Pleas entered her head. She lost control of body and

mind and did not care. She was going to die anyway, so she gave herself over to the wonderful anguish.

A warmth pressed her temple. His embrace tightened, supporting her. The caress changed, making it worse, better, frightening, excruciating. She plunged further into pleasure's insanity. Suddenly the sensation increased tenfold in an instant. It reached a crescendo of awesome perfection, then snapped and split and showered through her in a rain of beauty.

The release awed her. She accepted it in stillness, amazed by the unearthly rapture of such a physical experience. She kept her eyes closed and dwelled on its last remnants as they sparkled through her limbs.

She finally opened her eyes. Hayden held her closely, her head tucked to his shoulder. The sensual tautness had not left him. He appeared incredibly handsome, gazing nowhere with fiery eyes. His strength dominated her size and spirit all the more because her stupor left her weak.

He looked down in frank acknowledgment of what he had done to her. Her fluttering tremble responded. That had always been between them, from the start, even when she gave him the house tour.

She doubted she would ever be able to look at him again and not feel it.

She never fully recovered from that touch. He held her the rest of the way. Their conversation was casual, aimless, pointless. Sensuality drenched the air. He occasionally caressed her. The slow, languid path of his hand kept her aroused just enough that delicious anticipation licked at her. The chant for more only whispered now, but it did not disappear.

Their arrival at his home meant they had to part. As she composed herself on the opposite seat, she peered at the house they approached. She was not surprised by its classical derivations, but it displayed them with a purity not normally seen. The six columns arrayed in front of the entrance did not stand atop stairs but close to the ground. The height and breadth did not overwhelm. It did not appear to be an especially large house, yet its perfect proportions gave it a majesty that the biggest pile would lack.

"It was completed not long ago," he said.

"Then you built it." She could see him in the design. Every measurement had been carefully calculated. This structure possessed a clarity, a legibility in how it was put together, however. Hayden the man did not have that. At least, not to her. "Was it your design too?"

"No, but the architect was of similar mind and amenable to my suggestions."

The servants waited to meet the new wife. Hayden instructed Mrs. Drew, the housekeeper, that his bride should be settled into her chambers before receiving a tour of the property.

Her apartment was strung across the back of the house in a series of chambers full of light and air and decorated in saturated summer hues of yellow, blue, and green. She gazed out a window in her sitting room. It looked down on a large garden surrounded by other wings of the building. The house was deceptive in its size. The rest of it, forming a square around the central garden, made it very large indeed.

Joan, the girl assigned as her lady's maid, began unpacking in the dressing room. Alexia did her best to move them past the initial awkwardness. The trunk was almost empty when a side door opened and Hayden entered. Alexia spied a narrow passageway that she assumed led to his apartment.

He smiled kindly at Joan in wordless command. Swallowing a giggle, she abandoned the trunk and scurried away.

He did not say a word to Alexia either, but she understood why he intruded. The sensuality of the carriage ride returned with him, and desire deepened the blue of his eyes.

"It is a beautiful house," she said as they strolled into the bedroom.

"I am glad that you like it."

She stood near a window and looked down again. "I expect the garden will be magnificent in summer."

His hands circled her waist. "I will tell the gardener to make some changes and plant some new things this year. Roses, I think. And a large bed of violets."

"You have your own fortune, but it is not a middling sort, is it? It appears that for all my negotiations, I neglected to ask. I might have guessed if I had weighed it much. That necklace, for example—"

A kiss on her neck caused the last words to disappear into a long inhale. The heat of that kiss, the silk of his hair on her jaw, the power so close behind her—in an instant her body returned to the excitement that led to that wondrous release, and well along the path at that.

"The necklace was my mother's. My fortune is not of

a middling sort, and I am pleased that you forgot to ask."

"Do you not worry that I may not be up to managing households of this size?"

He caressed up her back. She felt the hooks of her dress begin to loosen. "I do not doubt that you will manage whatever you choose. Except me, of course. It would be a mistake to attempt that. If I had wanted to marry a woman with my aunt's tendencies, I would have chosen from among the hundreds I know and would have wed years ago."

He stepped away. She turned to see him shedding his coats. He threw them over a chair, then sat to deal with his boots. She watched, feeling awkward. Then she walked to another chair and began undressing too.

The expectation of pleasure teased her, but the daylight made her uncomfortable. She had anticipated his coming to her at night, in the dark, almost invisible. In the least she thought that today he would immerse her in pleasure until she found herself beneath him again, much as she had in the attic. Instead, they engaged in this deliberate ritual.

She propped a foot on the chair and rolled down a stocking, too aware of the man ten feet away. The truth, if she wanted to be honest, if she wanted to allow the silenced, hidden girl to speak, was that she found this a tad too calculated and domestic. Eventually matters might devolve to acts so relentlessly matter-of-fact, but this was her wedding day. She had counted on their feigning that there was more than marital rights and carnal pleasure today. It would have been easier, less unsettling, if he had just undressed her right there at the window while they kissed.

A spike of pique stabbed her. She did not slide the stocking over her foot carefully but yanked it too hard. The gossamer silk shredded beneath her clutching fingers.

She stared at the ruined stocking in her hand, astonished that she had been so careless. It was the finest stocking she had ever owned. Her brain calculated the cost of replacing it.

"We will send your maid for new ones in the nearby town," Hayden said.

She looked over at his chair. He had not progressed far with his garments. He sat comfortably in trousers and shirt, with his elbow propped on the chair's arm. His thumb and crooked forefinger held his chin in a pose of casual deliberation.

He had been watching her undress. She looked down at her naked leg, still propped on the cushion. Her chemise fluttered around her thighs, barely covering her private parts. She suspected he could see her dark nipples and the hair on her mound through the thin fabric.

Carrying on seemed scandalous now. He smiled slowly, acknowledging her sudden disadvantage. He appeared very charming and devastatingly handsome.

Feeling her face redden, she set aside the ruined hose. She set down her naked foot and propped the other on the cushion. Suddenly this disrobing was not so ordinary and matter-of-fact. It possessed a seductive power. The bed waited right there, and they both knew what else did too. The silence all but buzzed with what would occur.

She rolled down her hose. By the time she reached her foot, she had realized something important. It came to her as a brilliant insight, the kind of truth no one ever told you about.

This was what this man wanted, and little else. He had said so when he proposed. Being a good wife meant first and foremost being accepting and sensual in bed. If she pleased him there, she might have a good life. If she did not, she would be a barely tolerated intrusion on his world.

She bent to slip the silk off her foot. She realized with a start that the pose made her chemise hitch up too far in back, exposing her bottom. She snuck a glance in his direction.

His expression had become intense and hard.

She set down her foot and faced him.

"No one tells us that our husbands will want to watch."

"Actually, it is not a common custom between husbands and wives."

"So husbands do watch, just not their wives?"

"Something like that."

"It appears it will be different with us."

"It will be any way you want it to be, Alexia. We can draw the drapes if you prefer. You can hide in the dressing room and swaddle yourself in an undressing gown. You can be shy and delicate."

He would permit that, but he would prefer she not be shy. He had begun things differently this day for a reason. There was nothing between them but passion, after all. It was the only reason she was here.

"I will not be hiding, Hayden. Nor getting shy or delicate. I was prepared to be your mistress, and you made me your wife. It seems unfair that you should sacrifice your pleasure by doing the right thing."

"I do not intend to sacrifice much, even if you want to be shy at first. I have a lifetime to teach you about pleasure."

That certainly made his intentions clear. "It sounds as if you would like me to be your mistress as well as your wife. A courtesan in marriage, so to speak."

She received a charming smile for that. "I would not have put it that way, but it is a provocative suggestion."

His eyes contained enough heat to show he contemplated the possibilities. Her confidence ebbed fast. Saying such a thing had been rash.

"You did say we would negotiate the details. I assume that your promise about that still holds," she added.

"Certainly. Right now, for example, I want you to remove that chemise. You can negotiate, however."

Remove her— She looked down at her garment. If she removed it, she would be standing in the daylight totally naked!

"It would be a very small thing for a woman as bold as yourself," he said. "Insignificant for a woman who refuses to hide and be shy. As for a courtesan in marriage, such a woman would welcome the chance to display her beauty."

He was teasing her. Challenging her.

Exciting her.

Standing here almost naked made the flutters beat in her blood and her body tingle with anticipation.

It really *was* a small thing. There wasn't much that

wasn't visible already. Still, her face burned as she reached for the shoulders of her chemise. She felt very shy as she slid them down her arms. The fabric skimmed her body while it floated to the floor. She looked down in astonishment on her full nakedness.

"You are an amazing woman, Alexia. And very beautiful."

He got up and strode toward her. His expression made her heart jump. She began to cover herself with her arms, but it was too late. He pulled her into a tight embrace, stretched his fingers into her hair, held her head firmly, and kissed her furiously.

It was a stunning kiss, starkly passionate and frankly possessive. Just shy of violent, it was also a kiss confident of a response, and she could not control hers. While he commanded her mouth, his hands moved over her skin, over all of her, touching virgin flesh unused to exposure and caresses. He blazed new paths of excitement on her back and shoulders, down her hips and bottom, and to her damp inner thighs.

The spiraling desire entranced her. Her nakedness made it more erotic. Her body loved every titillation. The urge for more began its chant.

His palm closed on her breast, and the pleasure became more delicious. His arm arched her toward him, raising her so he could cover her neck and shoulders with firm, hot kisses. A delirium of want and relief vanquished her. She did not realize they moved until he gently pushed her shoulders and she floated down to the bed.

He stripped off the rest of his clothes, but there was no real separation and no pause in what was happening.

His eyes aroused as surely as his mouth and hands. She lay there under his visual caress, watching his body emerge from his shirt, fascinated by the way his muscles corded with his movements. She had seen male bodies only in art before and was surprised at how similar those sculptures and paintings were to reality in their depiction of a man's taut hardness.

Her gaze locked on a scar that marred the perfection. Very long but surprisingly thin, it drew a line from his right shoulder to left hip, like half of an X over his torso.

"It is a war wound. There is a another just like it on my back."

"It does not look like it was deep, at least."

"It was not meant to kill." He began to unfasten his trousers, but paused. "How bold are you feeling?"

"Bold enough." Very bold, actually. Desire made her a different person, reckless and free. Her body waited for his. She was sensitive all over. Her breasts rose high, and she could not wait for him to touch and suck them again. She was beyond embarrassment, she was very sure.

She was also very wrong. In one area of the male body, the artists had not been very accurate. Of course, she had never seen a statue where a man was hard and aroused before.

He knelt on the bed, hovering over her, and kissed her again. His tongue played at her teeth and lips, inviting her to participate. She gingerly touched his tongue with hers, then the sides of his mouth and his palate. The intimacy of doing that surprised her. It was so clear that a part of her was inside him.

His head dipped. His tongue flicked at her nipple.

She gritted her teeth and her back arched, offering, wanting. Shocking images entered her head, of his doing that all over her, of every inch of her skin being licked like this.

She gripped his shoulders to contain herself, but it did not help. Something had changed, and it left her helpless. The experience in the carriage had altered the hunger, deepened it. The *more* now made sense, and the climbing urges, the desperation, had a goal.

The way he teased her breasts with his mouth and hand left her whimpering. She thought the sensations could not increase, but they did, more and more until they owned her. She slid her palms down his skin, over his chest. She barely noted the thin ridge of the scar, but its feel penetrated her daze all the same. Like a little bump on the road to oblivion, it reminded her who she would see if she opened her eyes.

He was in her head then. His face and his scent shared the dark mystery transforming her. His voice spoke into the timeless fog while he reached down to caress the heat between her thighs to make her ready. *Tonight we will enjoy each other slowly, but I have to have you now.*

It did not hurt this time. Not really. The stretching satisfied a craving. His domination of her body excited more than frightened. When he moved it felt good, a rhythm of relief that salved the ache and filled the void and awoke a new desire, one ruthless and determined, which slowly claimed her so completely that she was crying out when his thrusts got harder.

It wasn't enough. A maddening desperation unhinged her, much like the one in the carriage, only worse because now she *knew* what she sought and her essence wept for it.

He shifted his position. He slid his hand between their bodies. His touch helped her to crest the summit and fall, fall, into the dark bliss.

Diamonds, he decided. Amethysts would be too predictable.

It was the first sane thought that came to him afterward, while he listened to her breath and his consciousness recentered itself.

He braced his weight on his forearms. She still drifted, her eyes closed and her lips slightly parted. Ecstasy softened her so much. He could see the girl in her now that the sensible Miss Welbourne had lost hold of her senses.

As if his gaze intruded, her lashes fluttered and her lids rose. A soulful acknowledgment of the power passed between them. Then the day began invading, creating little distances.

If this was evidence of how it would go, he was fortunate in his choice of wife. She was as honest in her passion as in her plain speaking. She may hold much against him, but she did not deny the desire. That was a rare thing.

"Do you ride?" he asked, moving off her so he could look at her body. His trailing caress over her breast made her blush. She was not so bold once the madness passed.

"I did when I was young. My father had a good stable before he was ruined."

Ruined. The word hung there. She said it calmly, without acrimony, but it was a word that wanted to throw up stone walls around her. She had experienced it before, it seemed. Timothy Longworth's fall must have seemed like a returning nightmare.

"Gambling?" he asked.

She shook her head, then glanced down her body. She blushed and closed her eyes. She withdrew within herself so her nakedness would not be scandalous to her. How interesting women could be, especially this one.

He pulled up a coverlet and draped it over them. "Drink?"

"Investments. The promise of wealth untold. The things you are renowned for, but he lacked the luck and judgment. Benjamin's father lured him in deeply, and they drowned together."

"There was nothing left for you when he passed?"

"The land was entailed to a second cousin, whose wife did not want me in their home. I wrote to Benjamin, hoping he would take me in out of guilt for his father's role in it all. I discovered that my cousins were better than that. They accepted me not out of guilt but goodness."

Her rose mouth, very dark from being soundly kissed for an hour, turned up at its ends. She still did not open her eyes. She did not reject the pleasure, but perhaps she wanted to deny the man who gave it to her.

"We have broken the rule," she said. "Talk of them is not supposed to enter our bed."

"That is true, and it was my questions that led to it." He would not make that mistake again. He was not sorry he had this time, however. He comprehended her devotion to them better now.

Sunlight and conversation had burned away the latent bliss. She merely suffered his presence beside her now. He threw off the bedclothes and got out of bed.

"Call for your maid. Have her prepare a bath if you want. I will show you the house before dinner. Tomorrow we will ride the estate."

He left his garments for his valet to collect later and strode to the dressing room and his own apartment. Her small revelations made him stop before he left.

"Alexia, your freedom in your passion pleases me. I am not a man who thinks a woman's timidity is virtuous. However, you are not obligated to agree to everything." He almost left it at that. "Nor should you think that you have to pay for your keep by agreeing to behave like a courtesan in marriage."

She sat up, clutching the sheet to her body. She looked at him in the direct, honest manner he admired. "You are not in love with me, nor I with you. But this . . ." She glanced to the bed. "This is a joy, and perhaps what we share is a good foundation for a marriage. While it lasts, I would be a fool to pretend it is not real."

CHAPTER
FOURTEEN

"I think it is safe to say that I am returning to London a changed woman," Alexia said as the coach entered town.

She referred to her body's discoveries, Hayden supposed. Whether he ravished her or took his time, she did not complain. Her happy compliance had provoked him to see just how bold she was prepared to be. Very bold, if the last few days had been any indication.

His courtesan in marriage appeared thoroughly sated but not so changed. She smiled impishly as she made her allusion, but he saw no private spark, no knowing glance that indicated she meant more than a sexual transformation had taken place.

How changed are you, dear wife? When the release came and he collapsed atop her, so spent he lost hold on his soul, did she also feel the contentment so vast, so binding, that it begged for a prayer to be said or a poem to be written? Had she experienced the yearning that had no name, that ached to penetrate thoughts and know her the ways their bodies and sweat quietly promised?

She looked lovely today. Very sweet. Very warm. Their passion had taught him a few things too, however. He had gazed deeply into those violet eyes as he moved in her. He had seen far into the distance, where private shadows tried to veil her thoughts. He had seen further than she wanted, feeding his yearning to know, until he went too far. Eventually a wall always appeared, thwarting him.

There were miles behind that wall.

"I expect your aunt has settled into Easterbrook's house by now," she said.

"I would not be surprised if my brother has refused to leave his apartment, however."

"He will regret this arrangement, you mean."

"He suspects that once ensconced in his home, Aunt Hen will be impossible to remove."

"Then it is odd that he invited her to come merely to accommodate us. He knows you made a bad bargain in this marriage."

"I think he sought to make this easier for you." He took her hand and kissed it. "As for a bad bargain, if gentlemen spoke of the carnal side of their marriages, my brother and friends would be envious of my choice of bride."

"I am glad you are pleased, Hayden."

He looked into her eyes. Only the nearest fields were visible now. This marriage would be companionable in the daylight. She would see to his comfort and give him children and, unless another man stole her heart, be faithful. Intimacy would be reserved for bed, when she forgot for a while that he was a man she did not love who had inconveniently seduced her.

Not a bad bargain. Not really. It was better than most men achieved. And yet . . . he could not deny that his fondness for the estimable Miss Welbourne had grown in the last weeks and that more than his body warmed in their embraces.

A conspiratorial spark of glee compromised Falkner's formal countenance. "Welcome home, madam."

Home. Merely entering the house comforted her, much like donning an old, well-worn shawl. The winds of life had buffeted her the last few weeks. The days in Kent almost frightened her, they were so full of new experiences and unexpected intimacy.

She returned to this house as mistress, however, not as poor cousin or governess. Even in the familiar there would be alterations. They were visible in the bows of the servants.

Hayden escorted her up to the library.

"We should call on Easterbrook soon," she said. "I must arrange to continue my duties with Caroline."

"No longer a duty. It is your choice whether to continue."

"I thought you came to Oxford that day first and foremost to ensure Caroline's finishing was completed."

"The necklace I carried had been removed from safekeeping the night before, Alexia. We would have had that conversation even if you had not told Hen you intended to leave this house."

He disarmed her when he said things like that. It was kind of him to leave out the rest of it and not mention that only the events in the attic brought that conversation about. She was not sure she wanted the truth to be obscured like this. She often lost hold of the facts in their marriage bed, but it would be foolish to allow that illusion to infect the days.

"I would like to continue with Caroline. It is late for her to learn the humors of a new governess."

"We will call this afternoon, then. You can see to Caroline, and I can see if my brothers are surviving Hen's invasion."

"It can wait until tomorrow."

"I should go with you on this first call, and I need to be in the City tomorrow. There are affairs that need my attention. I have neglected them too long."

Is that what occupied his mind when he turned so thoughtful in her arms? While his body melted into hers in satisfaction and his breath invaded her being, was his mind contemplating the affairs waiting his attention? Perhaps. The impression that their minds rested in unity along with their bodies might have only come from her own lack of separateness.

It would take some time before she sorted through the truths of this marriage and discovered just what was real and what was not. Right now, his reference to his affairs heralded one change. Henceforth they would live separate lives. The companionship they shared in Kent would not continue.

She had not expected it to. That was not how couples actually lived. She was glad to have had the chance to know him better, however. To learn something of the man within the man.

The inner man was not so different from the one the world saw, just more complicated. The inner man laughed at her jokes even if they were not very humorous. He treated her kindly even though he commanded her activities during the day and her passion during the night. He emerged most often in bed, with a warmth that in no way weakened him, that actually increased the power that made her tremble. He enfolded her in a security she had never known before. She had grown to believe the promise he made in the church, that she would be safe with him.

Falkner entered the library, bearing a large stack of mail neatly tied with ribbons.

"This was sent by Lord Easterbrook yesterday," he explained.

Hayden untied the ribbons and flipped through the letters.

"Falkner, did any mail arrive for me while I was gone?" Alexia asked.

"No, madam."

Her heart fell in a long, sad sigh. She understood that her cousins would be angry. She did not anticipate quick acceptance. However, she had not expected to be ignored. A letter full of accusations and fury would have been preferable to silence. They acted as if she were dead to them.

She had not dwelled on that loss while she was in Kent. Hayden had seen that she did not have much time to.

He sat near a table now. The light from a northern window gently washed his face. Her heart swelled at the sight of him, and sensual memories fluttered through her head.

"They will come around. Give them some time." His

gaze did not leave the letter he read. He had not even had to look at her to know what she was thinking.

"I think that I should write again."

"I would prefer you did not, Alexia. I do not care for the idea of your writing another letter to your cousins, begging their forgiveness for marrying the horrible Lord Hayden."

He did not actually command, but a husband had just directed a .wife on the behavior he expected of her. A good wife would obey, and she was committed to being one. However, she had not anticipated that he might interfere in such a private matter.

She did not argue, although she sensed he was poised to hear objections. She did not explain that she had not yet begged their forgiveness and did not intend to. His display of husbandly authority left her disinclined to soothe his ruffled pride.

He had promised when he proposed that he would not obstruct her friendships, and her cousins were her closest friends. She would hold him to his word.

Nor would she wait for her cousins to come around. If she did, maybe they never would.

They found Henrietta well ensconced in Easterbrook's house. The manner in which she greeted them indicated that to her mind she was not a guest but mistress now.

She received them in the drawing room. She gave Alexia a good look, then bestowed a woman-to-woman smile. "It appears that marriage *suits* you, dear."

Alexia felt her face warm at the insinuating tone. "It suits me well enough."

Hayden drifted away, leaving her to suffer Hen's examination alone. Caroline's arrival veiled her mother's curiosity but did not put off the inquisition.

"You found Kent *pleasant*?"

"It is a lovely property."

Hen's glance swept to Hayden, who strolled along the bank of windows. "He appears very *contented*."

Caroline looked over too. "He does, doesn't he? Not nearly as frightening as before."

"It is said that only Venus can tame Mars," Hen cooed.

Caroline frowned, confused by the allusion. Alexia lost her patience with Henrietta's smirks. "I am no Venus, and he is too intelligent to be cast as Mars. However, if you perceive contentment, I am heartened. I take my responsibilities as a wife very seriously, as did you, I am sure."

"I relished my *responsibilities,* Alexia, and miss the joy they gave me."

"I fully expect to enjoy them too," Caroline said. "I have been learning all about planning dinner parties while you were gone. It will be great fun to be a hostess." Her brow puckered again. "But you were on holiday. Did you host a party in Kent?"

"We speak of other duties, dear," Hen said.

"Your mother will explain in due time," Alexia said. "Now we must decide when I will join you for your lessons."

Caroline wrinkled her nose. Hen began suggesting schedules, only to throw out each one in turn as inconvenient. Hayden, no doubt sensing that the conversation had moved beyond how *contented* he looked, ambled closer.

The attempts at planning had begun to bear fruit when Easterbrook arrived. His appearance startled Alexia. He wore no waistcoat or cravat, and his frock coat was unbuttoned to reveal the expanse of his white shirt. He would have appeared very common in his lack of proper attire if not for the exquisite cut and fabric of the garments that he did wear.

Hayden did not react as if his brother's informality surprised him, but Hen rolled her eyes.

"Really, Easterbrook. I thought we agreed last night that you would not roam the house in dishabille," she said.

Easterbrook's countenance remained bland. "You voiced your opinion on the matter. That does not mean I agreed."

"I daresay you are shocking Alexia, receiving her like that."

"Are you shocked or insulted, Alexia? Are apologies due?"

"It is your home, sir. I would not be so bold as to be shocked or insulted."

"An admirable answer. Would that all women were as sensible and forgiving."

Hen expressed lack of sense and forgiveness by shaking her head in dismay. Easterbrook and Hayden strolled away for a private chat. Alexia drew Hen and Caroline back into their plans.

"Where is the reliquary, Henrietta, dear?" Easterbrook's ominously calm voice floated into their midst.

Hen turned to where he and Hayden stood near a

table. Alexia remembered the bejeweled reliquary that once held place of honor on it.

"This chamber is classical, and the reliquary is Gothic. It did not complement the decor at all, so I had it moved to the library."

A smarter woman would have squirmed under the gaze Easterbrook directed at Henrietta, but his aunt returned one of her dreamy smiles.

Hayden strode out of the drawing room. A short while later he returned, carrying the reliquary. He brought it to Hen. "May I suggest that you put it back? Christian has a particular fondness for it. I am sure that you did not know that when you demanded its removal."

Hen looked ready to argue, but Hayden's stern expression checked her. She glanced over to Easterbrook, who eyed her too much like a fox sizing up a chicken that has stupidly wandered into its path.

Alexia reached for the reliquary. "Allow me to—"

"No," Hayden said.

Henrietta glared at her two nephews. She rose and took the reliquary. Managing to look hurt, rebuffed, submissive, but not cowed, she quickly walked past Easterbrook and set it down on its table. Then she sailed toward the door, chin high. "Come along, Caroline. Alexia, we will see you when you visit tomorrow."

Perplexed at whatever had occurred, Caroline joined her mother. After the door closed on them, Easterbrook went to the table and nudged the reliquary to the center of the surface.

"You have bought me a week, no more, Hayden." He sighed with resignation. "Elliot is never about now.

He escapes into the libraries by day and into some woman's boudoir by night. It is just me. And *her.*"

"We will find another house," Hayden said. "I can see that she will make you miserable."

"I will survive. Your wife will be visiting her frequently in the days ahead, and I expect she will be further distracted from ruining my peace once the season starts."

"I promise to visit often," Alexia said.

"Good, good." He shed his interest in Hen's designs. "My brother looks smug, Alexia. I hope that he behaved well and that the satisfaction was mutual. We come from a family that has reason to think the initial joys of the marriage bed are all that recommends the wedded state to either man or woman."

Hayden sighed and shook his head. "You might let her test the water and get used to the temperature, Christian. Seeing you dressed like that was enough for one day. It was good of you not to enter in your robe."

Easterbrook looked down at his garments. "If looking proper would not have given Henrietta a victory, I would have gone through the trouble for your bride."

"I quite understand," Alexia said. "I have been known to deny some people a victory or two on occasion."

"I am sure that you have. It is why I favored you at once." He took Hen's place on a nearby chair. "Several more letters arrived for you today, Hayden. No doubt from those who missed the miserably discreet announcement that was published last week. Although I expect the word circulated among the women quickly, since the batch sent over earlier contained many invitations. Hen reports that there is much curiosity about the lady who succeeded where so many failed."

"They will all meet her soon. We will accept most of those invitations."

"Does the notion of being inspected frighten you, Alexia?"

"A little. It is best to be done with it quickly, however."

"How sensible. She really is very sane, Hayden. In a town full of feminine frivolity even among the men, she is refreshing."

They stayed a while longer. The men spoke of politics and sport. The conversation drifted over and around her. She sensed that Easterbrook prolonged the visit for her sake, so she would feel welcome. Or perhaps he did not mind her company because he thought her sensible.

It had been a compliment from a man who did not waste breath on false flattery. It had not been the sort of praise that most women would look for, however.

Sensible. Not beautiful or entrancing or clever. Sensible. What a dull word. *Yes, here I am, little sensible me. A paragon of practicality. A citadel of sobriety. Even the passion I experience with this new husband is a matter of accepting that which I cannot change. We are both making the best of a marriage decreed by foolish impulse and heartless pragmatism.*

She looked at Hayden. He appeared in no hurry to take his leave. He enjoyed conversing with his brother.

He felt her gaze and looked her way briefly. Warmth softened his countenance, and his eyes reflected memories of their intimacies.

For a few sweet moments, the life she lived at night

intruded on the day, and she did not feel very sensible at all.

Hayden did not retire with her that night. She left him in the library, writing a letter. Joan waited for her in her bedroom. Joan had arrived from Kent at midday to serve as her lady's maid. Alexia had decided it would be silly to look for another maid if she had found one who suited her. The girl was excited about her new duties and the chance to come to town.

Joan helped her change into a nightdress, then brushed out her hair. She dismissed Joan and laid in her bed.

This chamber had not been used in all her years in this house. Rose had not occupied the mistress's chamber, reserving it for the future wife of Benjamin, then Timothy. It connected to the master's suite of chambers that Hayden now used.

She gazed at the ivory drapery suspended above her. She had promised Hayden that thoughts of her cousins would not invade their nights, but Hayden was not here now. The events of the last week had kept reflection at bay, but now she was alone again. She had once expected to lie in this bed, waiting for a different man, and Ben's memory eddied through her in increasingly vivid ripples.

She owed that memory nothing besides the fond thoughts of a close cousin. Her emotions regarding Ben had been unsettled since she read those letters in the attic, however. It hurt her to think she had been only one of many dalliances to him. She had never suspected that his insistence on discretion was because he did not want his brother and sister to know that he behaved dishonorably toward her.

He had, however. Her pride wanted to believe she had been his true love, his future wife, and that those letters came from a woman who merely satisfied his needs until he married. Hayden had even suggested that was the case. The romantic girl in her heart would probably hold on to that explanation for years. Alexia Welbourne, the woman who had learned the world's harsh truths too well, was less inclined to be so generous.

That woman could not exorcise Ben's memory completely, however. He demanded attention of a different sort than that of wistful regret or longing. Walking through the door, she had also stepped back to her recent worries about him. His memory remained vaguely incomplete now, in certain essential ways.

She again saw him when he kissed her before leaving for Greece. Had it only been excitement she sensed in him? She had resented his eagerness to leave but had buried that perception. It loomed now in her mind, released from the lie that wanted to ignore it. She watched his smile and heard his reassurances. She also saw the other emotion deep in his eyes.

Relief. He was glad to be gone. From her? She doubted she mattered enough. He could be rid of her without going to Greece.

He had been relieved to leave England, and despondent about returning. Hayden believed the latter melancholy had made Ben careless on that ship. So careless that he ended in the sea.

She squeezed her eyes tight against the tears beginning to burn. Whether as lover, fiancée, or cousin, she
had loved him dearly. She did not want to think of him
so unhappy, so desperate, that he . . .

Because of her? It would be a terrible kind of significance, if his entanglement with her made him so unhappy. Surely it had been something else in his life.

She wished she had read those letters more carefully
and seen more than the evidence of another woman in
his life. She wished she had not ignored the other papers
in the trunk. She had gone to it only to find the answer to
the question that plagued her tonight. She had been too
quick to grab at the belief that he had never changed and
too distracted to remember her goal once she smelled
that perfume.

She rubbed her eyes, wiping the tears that had
brimmed through her clenched lids. She blinked hard
and looked again into the night.

Hayden stood a foot from the bed. The light of a
small, far lamp created a nimbus around the edges of his
body. She startled on seeing him. She had not even
heard him enter.

As the shadows came alive with russet glows, she
saw that he wore a loose robe, carelessly tied. The fabric
was dark and of a substance that flowed softly.

"You were crying."

"I wasn't. Truly." It was not really a lie. The tears had
not flowed enough to be called crying.

He shed the robe. Vague highlights played over the
hard angles of his body and face. Her awe at his beauty
obscured the thoughts that had filled the last hour.

He joined her in bed. He pulled her closer and

looked down. A sly shimmer of anticipation quivered through her.

He did not kiss her. His hand rested on her hip in the firm pressure that expressed so much about him. He did not clutch or grip. He did not have to. This more gentle hold spoke his assumptions of possession more eloquently.

"Why were you crying?"

He should not demand an answer like this. It did not really matter to him.

"You said there were some things we would not talk about at night, Hayden. I am thinking that was a good rule."

His head turned slightly. He gazed away, at nothing.

"I will let or buy another house. West of the park, if necessary. I guessed that living here would be a mistake."

"Please do not. Please. It is not this house. The nostalgia will come on occasion wherever I live."

His attention returned to her, as if she had said something profound. His hand caressed down her thigh and leg. With long strokes, he pushed her nightdress up. "Perhaps I should leave you to the nostalgia tonight, but I think not."

Did he believe he competed for her attention after that? Was that why his kiss was so long, so thorough, so designed to leave her breathless? She could not ignore the new, subtle hardness in the way he handled her. His kiss did not so much cajole as direct. He dominated much as he had in the carriage when he insisted her body admit that their passion was not mere duty.

She submitted easily. She wanted to. She had been

so alone in her thoughts. So adrift from the people and love that gave her existence some meaning. The intimacy waiting seduced her more than the pleasure.

His skin pressed hers as he stroked his face against her hair. His breath entered her, stirring her as much as his caresses did. He lifted her shoulders and pulled the nightdress off, then laid her back down, naked beside him.

She loved the way his hand moved on her. She closed her eyes to savor the sensation of those slow, confident paths along her body. Every inch of her waited to experience that warmth, to grow more alive under that touch.

He spread her legs and moved atop her, resting between her thighs. Her body instinctively positioned to accept him, but disappointment whispered within her arousal. It would be quick tonight. She had hoped . . .

He did not accept the offer her body made. He removed her hands from his shoulders and set them to either side of her head. The lack of embrace added a new note of vulnerability. Her breasts rose, utterly exposed, so sensitive the air titillated her.

He did not tell her to stay like that, but she knew he expected her to. He had seemed pleased in Kent when she participated, but tonight he wanted her only accepting. She felt much as she had in the carriage and sensed the same aura in him too. She did not think generosity moved him now any more than it had then.

A kiss on the side of her breast obliterated the vague resentment forming. The warm press of his lips, the fluttering touch of his hair as he dipped his head enchanted her. There was beauty in whatever he thought he proved by this. The way he kissed the fullness of her breast made her feel precious as well as owned.

Soon the impatient chant for more whispered in her head as her body knew what would come. He took his time letting her have it. Her anticipation grew excruciating before his fingers replaced his mouth and his caress slowly circled her nipple.

He brushed the tip. Her whole being groaned with relief and hunger. He teased until a chaos of pleasure and frustration filled her. His weight kept her lower body from moving, denying her even the small respite promised by the urge to shift her hips.

He flicked his tongue on the other nipple, creating a sensation that was too delicious to bear. He laved gently, multiplying the shuddering downward pulses until they flowed in a continuous stream of wonderful torture. His touch on her other breast added to her delirium. She arched her back shamelessly, begging him to continue forever.

She crossed to that place where only carnal hunger existed. Her mind clouded to everything except the way he aroused her and her need for it, for *more*. That chant entered her physically. It beat in her heart and pulsed in her blood and ached between her legs where her sex waited, hollow and incomplete, tingling and throbbing.

He shifted and she felt the dampness between them, the slickness weeping out of her. She tried to slide down, so he could enter her.

"Do not move."

He was the one who moved lower. He kissed a hot path as he did. She frowned when he passed her waist and kept going. He was not—surely he did not intend—

The heat of his mouth on her mound stunned her. Shocking kisses on her inner thighs made her gasp. She looked down her body at the scandalous way he lay so low, so near— She glanced to the small lamp. He could probably *see* her.

He touched her carefully, precisely. Heavenly spears of pleasure overwhelmed her shock.

"I intend to kiss you too. Do you want to negotiate, Alexia? You are allowed to refuse."

Kiss her? The instinct to stop him, to cover herself with her hands, was demolished by another caress. The sensation stunned her whole body. Her hips rose in offering.

He did not kiss her. Not really. But whatever he did with his mouth and tongue created pleasure so deep, so astonishing, that she moaned. Her release crested slow and long and shattered so violently that she screamed into the night.

He was with her before her cry ended, turning her so she hugged the mattress, covering her with his body. He did not ask if she accepted this part. He totally cloaked her so no part of her was not touched. There was no doubting his domination this time. His thrusts kept the trembles of her climax echoing where they joined. They were still pulsing when his finish came.

He did not move for a long time. She felt his hard breaths on her hair and shoulders and his weight on her hips. Subtly, the forearms bracing his strength above her back pressed closer in an embrace. She was too spent to care how submissive she felt beneath him. But not afraid. Never afraid. Nor did she feel badly used. There was nothing cold or indifferent in his desire.

He pressed a kiss on her back, between her shoulder blades. "We will remain in this house if you want." Then he was gone, the robe flowing around him as he left the bedchamber.

She rolled onto her back. She still had not recovered, but she realized more had happened than learning new pleasures.

Perhaps she was wrong about the warmth, the . . . caring she felt in him. Maybe tonight had been only a test, to see if her history in this house would interfere with what he expected.

CHAPTER
FIFTEEN

Vague scents of spring blew on the crisp breeze as Hayden rode through the City. He raised his face to the bright sun, noting its position. It had begun its hopeless annual attempt to tame London's eternal damp.

He stopped in front of the imposing sprawl of classical facades that compiled the Bank of England on Threadneedle Street. He had dealings here often enough, but today he had not come on normal business. Among the letters awaiting his return from Kent had been one from Hugh Lawson, an assistant cashier at the bank.

Lawson was an ambitious young man who curried favor with Hayden in the hope of being included in promising investment syndicates. Lawson's letter had been a response to Hayden's own inquiry. Yes, the gentleman in question had kept a private account at the Bank of England, he wrote. If Lord Hayden would call at the bank, Lawson would try to answer any other questions.

After he left Alexia last night, he had thought for a

brief while that he would not make this visit. Passion had a way of obscuring reality while it reigned.

She had been quietly weeping when he entered the room. Over her cousins' rejection? She had gained worldly wealth in marrying him, and status and security. She had discovered physical pleasure and appeared to revel in its power. But she had lost the love of the only family she knew.

Worse, he sensed another presence in the chamber and guessed she had also been crying over Ben. The letters in the attic had compromised that memory, but women had a habit of loving scoundrels even when they knew the truth.

He had resented the intrusions more than he should have. He had exploited the power that pleasure gave him in any competition with the past. He had carried her into a different world, one that the Longworths did not invade.

No ghosts had hovered around that bed when he left. If he had stayed much longer, however . . . would one specter have seeped in again, lading the air with nostalgia and sorrow?

If so, it would not have been entirely Alexia's fault. Not only her eternal love kept Ben ever present in their lives.

Questions that demanded answers loomed about Ben. An instinct warned that a wise man would leave it alone, but his negligence the night of Ben's death was a guilt that begged for more information.

He made his way through the high-vaulted chambers of the bank's offices and down some stairs. Lawson received him in a small, spartan chamber beneath the bank's public rooms.

Lawson appeared conspiratorial as he closed the door. Discussing one client's dealings with another was not accepted, even if one of those clients was dead. Hayden was glad for the exception, but he would never again trust Lawson overmuch.

"Benjamin Longworth indeed had an account here, as you inquired. In fact, it still exists, and a respectable amount remains in it. His heir must have been unaware of it."

That meant Ben's records of this account were not among his papers that Timothy received upon his death. "Was it a large one?"

"It varied. A good deal of money would come in, then a good deal would go out. It appeared much as one sees with active merchants, especially importers. Money is moved to an account, then removed to pay bills of sale and such."

"How large were these amounts that moved out?"

Lawson shrugged. "Anywhere from a hundred to thousands at a time."

"Bank drafts?"

"At first. Then notes exclusively."

"I would like to see the records."

Lawson had already crossed a line. Now his expression indicated he hesitated to take the next step.

"I have cause to think that Longworth was under financial stress. As his friend, I would like to put my mind at rest that he was not," Hayden said. "It would be a great favor, I realize. One impossible to repay, although I would do my best to try."

Lawson's expression cleared. If he made a loan against his honor and prospects, he only wanted assurance that the accounts would be balanced. He was a banker, after all.

He removed a thin account book from among a stack of similar ones on his desk. He placed the book atop the others, and left the chamber.

When the door closed, Hayden lifted the account book. Ben had first put money here years ago, about six months after he bought the partnership in Darfield's bank. First small sums, then larger ones.

He ran his finger down the deposit column, mentally adding. Over four years, Ben had hidden more than fifty thousand dollars in the Bank of England. This must be where the money came after he forged the signatures and sold out his victims' funds. It was much more than he and Darfield had thought. Darfield was still busy tracking down all the sales and determining which were frauds. If this account was any indication, the poor man would suffer apoplexy before he was done.

Six months into the account's life, a series of drafts began, creating a long list of dispersals. Some moved money back to his account at Darfield and Longworth, presumably so he could pay the ignorant clients their income and they would never guess the principle in their funds was gone. Some went to individuals, and others to accounts at county banks in Bristol and York.

He scanned the drafts. Halfway down the list, a new name appeared that arrested his attention and made the others insignificant. A series of drafts had been made to one individual. They occurred at regular intervals but too frequently for income payments. Then, a year prior to Ben's death, they stopped. However, at the exact same two-month intervals to the very day, money continued to be removed, only in notes.

The pattern jumped out at him, proceeding to the month when Ben left for Greece. The intuitive caution that had warned to leave it alone sneered viciously in his head.

It was worse than he thought. Ben had been blackmailed, and the demands had escalated his last year in England. And Hayden himself had introduced Ben to the man who bled him.

"It is a little late to be asking me about him," Phaedra said. "You are still tied to him no matter what I say."

You did not ask my advice before you agreed to marry him, so why do so now? her tone said.

Alexia wanted to know what Phaedra thought of him because her own thoughts were confused. Her vision kept clouding. At night, when their bodies joined and entwined, she experienced an intimacy so stark, so binding, it frightened her. Her nights had begun to seem more real than her days.

"I did not realize you knew him. The introduction outside the warehouse appeared to be the first. However, you just referred to him as cold, so I asked why you think so."

"I had never met him. One hears things, however. And you must admit that he does not appear very warm by nature."

They sat in Phaedra's rather odd sitting room. Alexia never knew what to think of the place. The divan showed quite a bit of wear on its sapphire upholstery, but a careless array of exotically patterned shawls gave the appearance of luxury all the same. The furniture was a mix of finishes and styles yet managed to please the eye with its eclectic disarray. Two cats roamed the chambers freely, one black and one pure white. The white one had a habit of jumping on Alexia's lap and now curled there, shedding long hair all over her brown pelisse.

Books tumbled over the two tables flanking the divan. Piranesi engravings of eerie staircases decorated the walls. Only a small watercolor to her left looked like the normal sort of art people owned. Crystalline washes of color depicted the view from a hill down on a lake.

"I would not put much faith in what one hears, nor in a countenance that is the result of breeding," she said.

"Then I assume you have not found him cold and have overcome the aversion that his behavior toward your cousins caused," Phaedra said. "I am heartened to hear it. A married woman has no choice about sexual congress, so it helps if she enjoys it."

How like Phaedra to just start talking about that, like it were perfectly acceptable to do so. Yet it relieved Alexia that the door had been nudged ajar. She had mourned the loss of Rose's easy friendship the last few days. A woman needed to have another woman to confide in sometimes.

"I enjoy it rather too much, I think," she said. *It overcomes my aversion too well. Too thoroughly, perhaps.*

"What an odd thing to say. I hope you do not hold with the stupid notion that pleasure is sinful."

"No." Not sinful. Just . . . dangerous. She could not

explain that to Phaedra. She did not begin to know the words to use. But sometimes, when she abandoned herself, she sensed that she offered him a part of her soul.

"I only wonder if it is quite normal to enjoy such things with a person whom one does not love."

"If men do, why shouldn't women?"

Why not, indeed? Alexia could not deny the soundness of the question. She doubted that Hayden worried whether *he* experienced too much pleasure.

Phaedra rearranged herself on the divan, turning her whole body and hitching one leg up. She presented the image of a woman settling in for a good gossip.

"Since you asked why I said he was cold, I will tell you it is not merely due to the somewhat severe humor he shows the world. I know one of his former mistresses."

"This mistress called him cold?"

"She said he was a good lover but he remained remote. She shared pleasure with the man the world sees, who is hardly warm, you must admit. Normally, in bed, another man will emerge."

Alexia understood that. She had sensed the inner man emerge. It flattered her that perhaps Hayden had been less reserved with her than with this mistress Phaedra knew.

"I expect he had a lot of lovers." No doubt he would have more mistresses in the future. He had all but said he would. There was no danger for *him* in their intimacy.

Phaedra shrugged. "It is common enough. My friend said he was a bit odd about it. He could have seduced merely with that face of his. Instead, he always made very sure his women understood what they would gain and what they would never have. The arrangement was comfortable but lacking even the slightest romantic illusion. Even courtesans like to pretend there is more, you see. We all do."

He had made the arrangements explicit with her too. So explicit she had assumed he was asking her to be his mistress, not his wife.

Even courtesans like to pretend there is more. Was that what she was doing? Pretending there was more? Maybe the warmth, the sense of a bond, was an illusion conjured up by her heart to spare her from the harsh truth that she really *was* a courtesan in marriage.

"The oddest condition of his protection," Phaedra continued, "was his insistence that his mistresses be examined by his physician first. He did not seduce first and negotiate later." She chose a little cake from a plate on her table and offered one to Alexia. "That does not speak of a man overwhelmed by emotion, does it? It is logical precaution but also coldly calculating."

Alexia accepted a cake because she knew Phaedra actually made them herself. She had no servants, not even to clean, even though her income would allow one.

"As you can tell, I have been asking about him, once I knew you would marry him," Phaedra said. "I heard about those oddities in his family history, of course."

"What oddities?"

Phaedra's eyes widened as she paused in biting the cake. Alexia laughed at her comical appearance. Phaedra laughed too, spewing a snow shower of cake crumbs down the front of her dress.

She brushed them off. "As I said, this was a conversation we should have had *before* you wed. You knew nothing about him."

"I knew enough," she muttered, studying her cake.

Phaedra's laugh had a bawdy note. "The effects of your awakening are delicious, Alexia. Who would have guessed that pleasure would conquer that practicality of yours? A man seduces you and you lose hold of your judgment? Next you will say that you fell in love and do not care who and what he is."

"Mock all you want, but do not accuse me of being a romantic fool. I did not quiz him on his relatives' past. There was no polite way to do so."

"It was a point of history worth knowing, perhaps. It is said that his mother would go for days, weeks, never leaving her chambers. Perhaps she suffered from deep melancholies. However, I have heard that she had a talent with the pen, and I think it more likely she lost herself in her art. The last years of her life, she retired completely to their country estate, however. Some think she went mad. That is often the reason a family member becomes reclusive."

"I do not believe Hayden's blood is tainted that way. He would have told me, warned me."

Phaedra brushed a few errant crumbs off her garment's skirt. "Perhaps it was not bad blood, so he did not believe he needed to tell you. It is a topic that has found new life now that Easterbrook is turning eccentric, however. Those who raise the speculations believe she was mad and that one day Easterbrook will be too. There are other explanations for how and when she disappeared, however, and I tend to favor one of them."

"What explanations would those be?"

"Devotion to her art, some say. The need to shut out the world and create became so intense she retired from society. Others with artistic temperaments favor that explanation."

"You do not offer that explanation with much conviction."

"A woman does not have to become a hermit to be a writer. Nor does she have to retire entirely from society. This absence was thorough and permanent."

"Which explanation do *you* favor, then?"

"Either of the ones that fits the few facts I know. It could have been an illness. Syphilis, for example."

Alexia stared at her. Phaedra misread the blankness. "That is—"

"I know what that is. I am not a child."

"It would explain Rothwell's requirement about the physicians. He would have a bigger fear than most men if he saw its effects firsthand. He might desire a woman, but he did not act until he knew the act would not kill him."

Except one time, on an attic floor, he *had* acted without knowing. He could not have been certain she was a virgin. He had not calculated the risks much at all that day.

She tried to sort it out in her head. "And his father?"

"I have heard nothing similar there. It might have taken its toll more slowly, of course, and not been evident prior to his death. But there is a flaw in that theory, which is why the last one is more plausible. She may have retired from society by her husband's command, not her own choice, and been sent to their country home as a form of imprisonment."

"Aylesbury Abbey is hardly a prison."

"Any place is a prison if you are confined there and lack the freedom to leave. With the power a husband has, if he wanted to separate her from the world, he could do it."

"I am sure you are wrong. There would have been no reason for such harshness."

Phaedra looked on her as if she were a child ignorant of the world. "There is a good reason. It happens all the time. A husband would do it to separate his wife from another man."

"I think it more likely she wanted to write. You should take up the pen yourself, Phaedra. You spin a good tale out of a poor woman's preference for privacy and country air."

Phaedra got up and retrieved a large portfolio from its place against the wall. "Perhaps you are right, but do not let pleasure blind you with that new husband. It is said the last marquess could be rigid, hard, and ruthless when it suited him. There are those who say Lord Hayden has much of the last marquess in his character." She sat down and opened the portfolio on her lap. "Now, look at these drawings with me. A new friend made them, and I think he shows great talent."

Upon Alexia's return home, Falkner informed her that Hayden would not be dining at the house. No explanation was given, nor did she ask for one. She wondered where her husband went tonight, however. Under the circumstances, she rather wished she had made her own plans, so her own right to a separate life would also have been articulated.

With hours to herself, she retired early, but not to her new bedchamber. Instead, she ventured back to her old room. Although her garments and toiletries had been moved, she had not instructed it to be stripped of all her belongings.

The room seemed strange at first. She might have been absent a year. As she moved around, touching the few books still stored here and the writing paper waiting for her pen, the space warmed to her presence.

A deep basket caught her eye. Tucked under the writing table, it held her notions. She had received an order from Mrs. Bramble right after she became engaged and had made the hat before her wedding out of obligation. The work had joyed her, however. Concentrating on its construction had settled her jumpy emotions that week.

She lifted the basket and pawed through the ribbons and threads. She went to the wardrobe and found some of the Dunstable straw she had bought at the warehouse. She no longer had to make her own hats, but perhaps on nights like this it would be good to have something to do. It would keep her from feeling so much like a woman waiting for something interesting to happen.

She lost herself in the work. Deciding the shape of the crown, daring an innovation in the brim, choosing the colors—all of it lightened her heart.

She forced herself to stop near midnight. When she returned to her bedchamber, she heard vague sounds that said Hayden was home. It had not been much of a night on the town.

Relief flooded her. The reaction was so marked, so *thorough,* that her breath caught. She closed her eyes and assessed her emotion honestly. The implications were not good news.

Her heart had been holding its breath, waiting to learn when he returned, wondering if he would at all. Phaedra said he'd had mistresses, and inevitably the day would come when he would have another one. She'd secretly feared he had already arranged that or had never broken with whomever he kept before they married.

The relief's sadness, the way it twisted her heart, indicated it would matter to her. She might know it would happen, but she did not want it to. It was not a practical reaction at all. She had long ago given up on resenting or resisting the truths of her life. If you could not change things, if you could not win, rebelling only led to more unhappiness.

She rebelled now, however. Her heart did. She could not quiet it. She did not want him taking his passion to another woman. Imagining him doing so made her stomach clench.

She undressed herself, since she had told Joan not to wait up. She slipped into bed and waited for the door to open.

The chamber fell silent. The whole house did. It occurred to her that Hayden might have come to her room earlier and found her gone. The hat had distracted her long into the night.

She rose and donned her dressing robe. She padded down the connecting corridor on bare feet. Easing the door open, she peered into Hayden's bedroom.

The smallest lamp glowed, barely adding to the dull illumination leaking through one half-closed window drape. It was enough light for her to see that he was in bed. She could not tell if he slept. He reclined on his back, with his hands behind his head and his bent arms splayed on the mound of pillows that propped his upper body. The position tensed his arms' muscles, defining their strength.

She glanced around the chamber. Nothing had been moved. The furniture remained exactly as it had been. And yet nothing of Timothy remained here. Her cousin might have never set foot in this room. Without changing a thing, Hayden had made it completely his own merely by occupying it.

He moved, startling her. He sat up and supported his weight on one arm braced behind him. She felt like an intruder.

"I am sorry. I did not mean to wake you."

"I was not sleeping. I was indulging a dark mood."

Definitely an intruder. She began easing back, out of the doorway.

"What did you want, Alexia?"

It was a question for which she had no answer.

"Come here."

She wished he would allow her to retreat gracefully. She walked over to the bed.

He reached out, took her arm, and guided her toward him. After some fussing with the bedclothes, he had her tucked in beside her. He laid with an arm around her, gazing at the drape above much as he had when she entered.

He did not intend to make love to her, she realized.

He had not come to her chamber earlier. He had not sought her out because he did not want her tonight. Perhaps he had gone to a mistress after all. One who had already made that required visit to a physician months ago.

The notion bothered her less now, although it still rankled. Perhaps her contentment in the familiar way his arm embraced her caused the difference. It was very pleasant being held like this, with no expectations in the air and no sated desire creating a selfless fog.

They had never done this before. There was always a point, a specific moment, when the aftermath of passion evaporated. He always left then, to seek his own bed. She wondered if he experienced the gentle comfort of this calm embrace as she did.

"You were not here when I left this afternoon," he said. "I would have explained my plans this time, since it was the first since we returned from Kent."

This time, but not in the future. His intentions had been kind, but he also instructed her on how this was done.

"It was thoughtful of you to want to explain this first time, but I know that we will often go our own ways at night as in the day."

He chuckled lowly. She liked the sound and the evidence that the dark mood was passing, but she had no idea what he found humorous.

"There is a man in from Bavaria. A dinner was held for him. Men only. We drank and talked hunting, but the real reason was business."

"You do not need to explain. I am very sophisticated. Really."

"I did not want you wondering if I had gone to a mistress so soon after our wedding. I should have remembered that you are too sensible to be jealous, especially when there is no evidence."

She was glad it was dark and he could not see her face warming. She wondered if she would be so sensible in the future, when there *was* evidence. She feared not, considering the way his description of his night lightened her spirits.

She turned and rose up on her elbow so she could see his face. "Today I ordered that exorbitantly expensive gown you commanded me to buy. Madame Tissot almost wept with happiness at the cost of it."

"What color is the gown?"

"An unusual one. Like ivory washed in firelight."

"It sounds like a color that would be complemented by diamonds."

"I do not know." She did not think she had ever seen any real diamonds.

"We will see."

He all but said he was going to buy her some. That delighted her, as it would any woman.

"You said you nursed a bad mood. Did that dinner not go well?"

He did not respond. She really did intrude now. She had pushed this cozy mood too far.

He pressed her shoulder, returning her to the pillows. "It was something else that provoked it. A duty calls that cannot be avoided. There is some danger my mood will be darker yet in the days ahead. If I do not come to you, it would be best to leave me alone with it." He began untying the ribbons on her dressing robe. "However, I am glad you did not tonight."

"Tell me about your family," she said.

His floating senses heard her quiet statement. They did not talk much in bed, but this time had started differently. That must be why her question flowed on the silence quite normally, summoning him out of the relaxed satisfaction. Almost half his mind remained suspended in the stillness of sensual contentment, however. He would not return to the world completely until he had to. Unpleasantness waited for him there. He would face it squarely when he had to, but not just yet.

He shifted enough so his weight did not crush her. There had been no experiments tonight. No initiations. He wondered if she had sensed that he took his time because the shadow hovered too long, even affecting the desire at first.

"There are an assortment of cousins. You will meet them all soon."

She subtly flexed along his body, reminding him of her physicality. In the aftermath, it was easy to forget about their bodies for a while.

"I meant your brothers and parents."

"You have met my brothers." He thought to leave it there, but perhaps she deserved some explanations. Very soon the ladies of society would be filling her ears. Perhaps some already had.

"I envy you them. I had a brother who died young, a year before my mother. I would have liked to grow up less alone."

"We formed alliances that were useful. Not against my mother, who was very gentle."

She did not pry, but he could imagine what she might have been told. He did not like the idea that she had formed an image of his mother that was untrue. If they had met, they would have probably taken to each other at once. "She was a bit eccentric and had the ability to retreat into her own mind for lengths of time. Her last years, she never came up to town."

"I hear she was a writer."

Yes, someone had shared those stories with her. "A good one. My father refused to allow her to publish, however. He did not consider it appropriate."

"Too revealing, perhaps? Whether prose or poetry, her pen would expose herself to the world."

And possibly expose him too. His cold rigidity and the cruel satisfaction he took in her unhappiness. That had been his real fear.

A memory beckoned, one his mind tried to avoid. Of a dark room and a woman sitting at a table, pen in hand, bent over paper. Her eyes were always sane when she wrote those pages. Sane and alive with the joy of visiting a better world.

Look at her, boy. Never forget what you see. That unhappiness is the result of the irrational impulses the emotions breed.

He read those pages after she died. He found poems of beauty and optimism that revealed her in ways her distance had denied him. For a long, unholy moment, he had hated the man who had silenced that voice.

"She retreated from the world, and from us, but she

did not go mad. Do not be concerned that the family blood has that taint."

Alexia did not protest and claim she had never wondered. She did not speak at all. Perhaps his rough tone silenced her.

She merely turned in his arms and placed a gentle kiss on his brow.

CHAPTER
SIXTEEN

Suttonly received Hayden in his large dressing room. He shared cigars and confidences with his closest circle here, beneath a ceiling festooned with gold moldings and painted tondos that depicted nymphs and satyrs.

"It is early, Rothwell. At this hour I assume you come on business."

"Yes."

"Has a problem developed with that new investment in the Americas?"

Hayden sat on a sofa of enormous size and comfort. The chamber reminded him of other visits here, years ago and before Suttonly inherited the title. This dressing room had been Suttonly's private lair where he brought friends for long nights of cards and drink.

"I have come to talk about Benjamin Longworth. I have had reason to look into Ben's finances at his death. In helping the bank assess Tim's fortune and debts, its source, from Benjamin, arose as well."

"Timothy Longworth claimed to be a banker. He should be able to assess all of this himself."

Hayden ignored the truth in that response. "Yesterday I learned that Ben had an account at the Bank of England."

"That is rich. He did not trust his own bank with his own money but expected all of us to do so."

"This was a special account, one for a special purpose. Money moved in for a short while and then moved out. In some cases he took notes, but he also wrote drafts early on to a number of people. Including you."

A languid smile expressed Suttonly's wry amusement. "Poke into Longworth's finances all you want, Rothwell, but do not presume to poke into mine."

Hayden rose from the comfortable sofa. He strolled along mahogany-shelved walls holding a collection of varied rocks and feathers. Suttonly had been something of a naturalist while at university, but those interests had been abandoned to the pleasures of London long ago.

He lifted a striated red rock brought back from a visit they had made to the Lake District one holiday. "Years ago you had Darfield and Longworth hold some funds for you, did you not?"

"A small amount. It was a mere gesture, to help the friend of a friend. It was not a significant sum."

"The records say you soon sold them out."

"I decided I had no obligation to help a friend of a friend if I found that man tedious. Yes, I sold them out."

"And yet, over the next years, Ben gave you money privately."

"It was private money to repay a private debt."

"Was it the drafts alone? Or did the banknotes go to you too?"

"Do you think it wise to go down this path, Rothwell? To pry into the dealings of two old friends?"

He was very sure it was unwise. He also knew he had to fill in the colors in the new portrait of Benjamin being painted in his mind. Right now it was a flat and primitive sketch, a caricature of criminal avarice and despair. He barely recognized the face.

"The funds you sold amounted to one thousand pounds. The bank drafts, combined, to five thousand. More was removed in notes, at similar intervals. Over fifteen thousand all told."

A deep sigh of boredom greeted this information. "I do not share your fascination with numbers. Who cares?"

"I have reasons for caring."

"How unfortunate for you that he is dead and cannot satisfy your curiosity."

A new note punctuated the lazy tone. Smug contentment. It caused Hayden to turn from the rock collection and look at his friend.

Suttonly's pose announced lack of concern. His face remained pallid. His eyes burned, however. Anger reflected in them, but so did caution and a disturbingly alert slyness.

He gazed ever so placidly with those revealing eyes, perhaps unaware that they contained all the answers Hayden sought. Or maybe he wanted someone to know how clever he had been after discovering the theft.

"I must excuse myself, Rothwell. I have a full day." He rose and strolled toward the door. "My man will see you out."

"How big was this debt?" Hayden asked. "How much did he owe you?"

Suttonly paused and half-turned. Pride defeated prudence after a brief contest. "In a manner of speaking, you could say he owed me his life."

Hayden rose from his bed in his City chambers and staggered, blurry-eyed, toward the washstand. He did not even glance in the looking glass above it.

He had arrived here three days ago after his meeting with Suttonly. Or had it been four now? Time had gotten away from him. Faced with the knowledge that Suttonly had discovered Ben's forgery and made him pay, seeing that Ben had good cause to dread returning to England, he had retreated into this private, silent home. His clerk saw he was fed, but he gave the man no other duties. Instead, he spent uncharted hours on his calculations and slept when complete fatigue overcame him.

Early dawn's silver light turned white as the risen sun's rays streaked in the window. The sudden brightness shocked him into an unwelcome state of alertness. The truth emerged from the shadows of his mind, no longer obscured by exhaustion or distraction. It ripped through him like a hot knife.

He had allowed Ben to die. The suspicion of that had haunted him for years. In hindsight, the details of that night had been blaring trumpets.

He should have heard them. Stopped it. He should have thrashed Ben if necessary and carried him off the deck. Instead, he had allowed his anger at Ben's goad to make him deaf and blind, and he had turned away.

That had been deliberate on Ben's part. He had already known what he was going to do. And Ben had not confided the truth. He did not believe he would find help if he confessed but instead only censure and a walk to the noose. *Now you sound like your father. All judgment and logical superiority.*

Anger wanted to split his mind apart. Anger at himself and at Benjamin, and also at the circumstances that made this all so pitifully ironic.

He stripped off his shirt, braced himself against the washstand, and splashed water on his face. It trickled down his chest, snaking over the long scar. A sickening memory flashed through him, one of pain and fear as a blade sliced this path. That farmhouse was not much larger than this bedroom, and just as dark. Being an English lord's brother had meant nothing to the Turkish soldiers using him for sport.

If not for Ben's impulsive, mad heroics, he would have died in that farmhouse. Slowly. They had already beaten his youth out of him by the time Ben crashed through the window.

He pulled his shirt back on and immediately went to the standing table in the next chamber. He escaped into the sublime purity of the calculations like an opium user seeking his drug. Grappling with the divine design of creation submerged him in a separate existence, one apart from the world of physical pain and chaotic emotions that made living all too profane.

Alexia tapped the edge of the letter against the surface of her secretaire's writing surface. Hayden's long absence from the house vexed her. She tried not to dwell on where he might be and with whom he might be dallying. She tried not to see this as abandonment or betrayal, even if it felt more hurtful having occurred after that quiet night together.

Her growing annoyance concerned the letter in her hand. Rose had written. *Finally.* The note bore the tone of a distant acquaintance. It spoke of commonplace things and never addressed their differences. The contact had come, however, and Alexia did not want the door to close before she had a chance to walk through it and attempt to reclaim her cousins.

The good wife wanted to tell her husband. It would not do to just take that carriage and leave town. She doubted Hayden thought *she* should just go off whenever *she* wanted for days on end without *his* knowledge or permission.

A discreet question to Falkner had elicited no information this morning. No one in this house had any idea where Hayden had gone. His valet indicated no baggage had been packed and he had taken his horse, not a carriage. He was somewhere in London, perhaps relieving that dark mood with someone more experienced at dispersing clouds than his wife had proven.

She opened the letter and read Rose's restrained sentences again. She could simply write back, she supposed. With enough polite correspondence she might achieve a rapprochement in a few months. She did not want to wait that long. She wanted to see Rose and know for certain that her cousins were not lost to her.

She left her chamber and called for her carriage. She would make an attempt to find Hayden and speak with him about this. If he proved elusive, she would make the journey to Oxfordshire without his permission.

She gave her card to the servant and asked to see either the marquess or Lord Elliot Rothwell. A short while later she was escorted to the latter, who waited in the library.

"Christian is not receiving today," Elliot explained. "It is always my pleasure when you visit, however."

"I have come to seek your help," she explained. "I would like to send a message to Hayden, and I thought you might know how to do that."

Elliot assumed an expression of bemused curiosity. "Forgive me, but I do not know my brother's daily appointments. Perhaps his valet . . ."

"He has been gone three days now. I am sure he is in London." She attempted to maintain a sophisticated tone. She hoped her face did not show her embarrassment. "It is important to me to at least attempt to inform him of a matter that requires I leave London for a day or two."

Elliot frowned. "Three days, you say." His attention retreated into his own thoughts. "I know what you are thinking." His brow smoothed, but his eyes remained concerned. "When my brother had mistresses, he did not stay with them. Ever. Nor was he involved in a liaison in the weeks prior to his marriage."

She appreciated his frankness. Relief swelled in her, but a spike of fear made it irrelevant. "I just assumed . . . Is it possible he was hurt, or—"

"Unlikely. Your carriage is outside? Let us go, then."

He walked toward the door decisively. "I will speak with his valet, and then I will take you to him."

She hurried after him. "Truly, I only wish to send him a message."

"If he has gone where I think, that will not be enough. Trust me on this."

"You look like a prisoner on a hull, Hayden."

Elliot's voice sounded like a cannon in the silence. It jolted Hayden out of a concentration so intense that his jaw ached. He glanced to the south-facing window that displayed the sun's position. It was past midday already.

Elliot carried coats and packages. He took them into the bedroom. "You are not even changing to sleep, I see. It hasn't been this extreme for a long time. Years. Not since that bad spell right after you returned to England."

Elliot's sudden arrival brought reality through the door. The world had to realign on its axis to accommodate the intrusion. While his brother tended to matters in the bedroom, Hayden adjusted to his reawakened senses. He felt like a man rising from bed after a long bout with a fever.

He looked down at his chest and noticed how soiled his shirt was. "Did Christian send you?"

"No." Elliot emerged from the bedroom. "Another person alerted me to your disappearance." He angled his head toward the door.

Hayden opened it. Alexia stood in the anteroom. He closed the door before she saw him.

"You could not even spare the time to send her a note?" Elliot asked. "You left her to wonder if your body was in the Thames or if you were holding a week-long debauch in some bordello."

"I do not hold debauches in bordellos."

"*She* does not know that." Displaying more anger than Hayden had seen in years, Elliot strode to the door. "I leave you to her. If I remain I might demand to know what caused this. Perhaps she will be too relieved or too ignorant to wonder."

"You would never demand to know. That is why I like you, Elliot. You do not exhort me or criticize. You bring me fresh shirts but are prepared to leave me to my unique form of inebriation."

"I do not criticize because I understand the drink that lures you too well. That does not mean I am not concerned when you drown in it, Hayden."

He strode out, leaving the door open. Alexia looked in. Her expression fell at his appearance. She swept past the clerk, entered, and closed the door.

She gave him a good look, head to toe. He became too aware of how disgusting he appeared.

"Your valet wanted to come, but Elliot forbade it. I thought the request peculiar. Little did I know that he guessed what we would find." She gestured to the bed-chamber. "He was good enough to collect the necessities for us, however. I trust you keep a razor here, or should I send your clerk for a barber?"

Hayden felt his face and the growth there. Alexia strolled around the office, taking in his private sanctuary.

"Would you like to hear news of the world, husband? Amazing things have happened while you played the hermit. Scandals and wars and great discoveries." Her tone edged toward a scold. "What is this, Hayden? What are you doing here?"

He retreated to the bedroom and stripped off the foul shirt. He began to wash and glimpsed the wild man in the looking glass. Elliot was right. It had not been this bad in years. And the last time, upon his return from Greece, had been for the same reason. He had found some peace during that earlier retreat. He had forged enough ambiguity and lies out of that night's memories to allow himself some forgiveness. Oddly enough, the honesty this time offered more relief.

Alexia followed and perched on the bed, waiting. She did not say a word while he washed his face and torso in the morning water long gone cold. Its frigid splashes brought him further into the world.

He found his razor in the washstand drawer and began to prepare to shave. He could see her quizzical expression in the looking glass.

She waited for an answer to her question. What was he doing here? He could hardly blame her for wondering, but that did not mean he had to like feeling an obligation to explain.

"My brothers and I all inherited my mother's ability to lose ourselves in our thoughts," he said while he tested the razor's edge. "We do so on occasion, each in his own way."

"For days on end?"

"Not usually. Several hours at most."

"This was not several hours."

"It happens sometimes. It is neither dangerous nor remarkable."

"That dark mood you spoke of caused this, didn't it?"

He paused in his preparations. He supposed this was inevitable. Married couples showed the world a formal alliance, but it was impossible to avoid the stark familiarity that emerged in the marriage bed. The physical intimacies exposed one to the other in spiritual ways, unless an effort was made to avoid it. Her curiosity was understandable, probably. He wondered what lay in those distant fields, after all.

"Yes, that mood did provoke this. My retreat dispelled that mood, however, so it was for the best."

"You warned me that I should leave you to it. Are you angry that your brother brought me here?"

"No." Nor was he. Not really. He could have done without her seeing him like this, however. He suspected he appeared very weak right now.

"Your mother wrote when she lost herself in her mind. What do you do?"

He picked up the razor. "There is a table and desk in the other chamber, near the window. My work is there."

She left to see what he meant. He dealt with his beard, then thoroughly washed and dressed. When he emerged from the bedroom, she was still examining the sheets of mathematical notations.

"I do not understand most of it, of course," she said. "It is like a language where one knows the words but cannot read the sentences."

"Like any language, there can be poetry in it."

"I have sensed as much at times." She set down the sheets. "If unending poetry awaits in these chambers, perhaps the wonder is that you ever leave them."

"I enjoy the world of the senses too much to give it up overlong."

He liked the way she nodded, as if he made perfect sense. He did not doubt that she also appreciated the discipline required to move from one realm to the other and how circumstances might defeat him for a while.

His day had begun in that rarefied consciousness, but now it was totally ordinary and physical. The only unique note was Alexia's presence in this office.

"Did you go to Elliot because you were concerned?"

"I only wanted to send a message to you. I thought he might know how to do so."

A small disappointment stabbed him. She had not speculated about the worst or worried over him. Nor would she have questioned him upon his return. She expected nothing from him, least of all explanations.

"What message?"

Her posture subtly straightened. Her eyes reflected the low, angry lights he had seen so often since they met. That always meant one thing.

"Rose wrote to me. I intend to make a small journey to see her. I thought I should inform you, so you would not think me devious."

"Did you write to her again, Alexia?"

"Yes. Twice."

"You directly disobeyed me. Your concern about being devious is a little late."

"I did not disobey you, if we are particular about the details of that command. I was not disloyal to you in my brief notes to them. In fact, you were not mentioned at all. You promised when you proposed that you would not interfere with my friendships, and I took you at your word."

Annoyance prodded at his temper, and not only because she had parsed his words to her convenience. He doubted she could see the Longworths, or even think about them, without hating him. Fifty years hence, the mere allusion to them would probably still cause that expression in her eyes.

"Has your cousin invited you to visit?"

"If I wait on that I may grow old first. She has at least admitted I am still alive, and I will go anyway. If she refuses to see me, so be it. I do not think she will."

This meeting was inevitable. Eventually, Alexia would reclaim them. He did not want to deny her that, but he would be damned before he gave them unfettered influence over her.

"I will not forbid this journey, Alexia. However, I will join you on it. We will go down to Aylesbury Abbey for several days, and you can meet with your cousin while we are there."

CHAPTER
SEVENTEEN

A damp haze hung over the town of Oxford, creating a watercolor of muted, misty tones. University scholars walked by the old stone buildings in little packs, their youthful faces displaying a joy and lightness that seemed inappropriate amid the formalities of the colleges' architecture.

Hayden's carriage rolled up St. Giles' Street, leaving the university's territory behind. Here shops and inns strung out as in other country towns, and the mood was less rarefied. They stopped across the lane from St. Giles' Church.

Alexia began to move. Hayden's hand firmly covered the door latch, stopping her. "We will wait here in the carriage until she arrives."

"I would prefer to wait in the church. I do not want her to leave if she sees you."

"If she requested you meet her here and not call at her house, if she is paying to hire the conveyance to get here, she will not leave. It is not my intrusion she fears but her brother's."

Alexia was not so sure. Rose had responded quickly to the letter suggesting they meet. Perhaps she guessed that if she did not comply, Alexia would turn up at her door anyway. That had been the plan. She had sent a note when she arrived at Aylesbury Abbey, asking to be received, but had fully intended to call and risk a door being slammed in her face.

She peered out the window, looking for the approach of a hired carriage that Rose could ill afford. "Will you at least allow me to greet her alone?"

"The coachman will hand you down. She may not even realize I am here."

They spoke in flat tones. Yesterday, when Rose's response had arrived at Aylesbury Abbey, they had argued about his accompanying her to Oxford. She had itemized the sensible reasons why he need not and should not. He had proven uncompromising.

Neither of them had raised a voice, but the air had been full of silent anger. The debate had centered on her safety and protection, but she suspected the argument was really about other things. Her cousins' situation remained an unhealed wound between them. He did not like that she was doing this.

He sat with her now, his expression the remote one that made the world think him cold. His distance caused a worry to tremble in her heart.

"If your brothers had cut you off because of your choice of wife, would you not attempt to build a bridge back to them?"

"That would depend on what they expected me to do to placate them and the cost of that compromise."

"There is no cost to me in attempting this rapprochement."

"Nor would there have been one to me in building the bridge you describe."

His meaning slowly unfolded in her mind. He was not anticipating that *she* would be made to pay a price as a condition of success with her cousins. He thought their expectations would have to do with him and would compromise her loyalty to the "horrible Lord Hayden."

A silence fell, one heavy with the anger he did not show. She feared if she said a word he would order the coachman to drive away.

A humble gig rolled to a stop in front of the church. Rose, wearing the fur-trimmed pelisse that Alexia had borrowed for her first visit to Easterbrook's house, alighted. She did not acknowledge the presence of the fine coach across the lane but walked to the church and disappeared through its portal.

The coachman opened the carriage door and set down the steps. Alexia looked through the opening. A clear path led to Rose. Her heart filled with joy at the promise the day held, but confusion shadowed her happiness.

She hesitated in taking the coachman's hand. Would there be a cost? A compromise? Would again embracing her cousins bring grief to her new life?

Hayden's distance and anger pained her. Physically pained her, in her heart. She felt chilled, as if a warmth that bathed her had been withdrawn. She had not noticed its importance, but now its absence frightened her.

She looked at him. When had that warmth spilled out of night's hours? When had she begun waiting for him so hard and found such comfort and peace in merely embracing him? He had not come to her last night, and her disappointment had been so intense, so sad, that she had not known what to do with it.

Nor did she know what to do with the jumble of emotions assaulting her now. She could not sort through it. She feared that leaving this carriage held the danger of losing something important.

A warmth covered her hand. Hayden's glove lay atop hers in a gesture of comfort and possession. She looked over to his profile. He also gazed through the open door.

He raised her hand to his mouth and kissed it. Then he passed it to the coachman.

Rose waited right inside the portal, veiled by the old church's shadows. She peered out at the carriage looming behind her gig.

"Is he in there?" Her question bit the quiet of the church's narthex.

"Does it matter? I am here now. Just me. No man stands beside me. You look lovely today, Rose. But then, you always do."

Rose's attention snapped to her. In the dim church light they faced each other. Alexia ached to move closer. She wanted terribly, desperately, to make things right with Rose at least.

"You are most lovely yourself, Alexia. For all my vexation at your escort, that is what I thought as you approached. He is taking care of her, at least. She is finding contentment with her situation."

"Would you have preferred if I did not find contentment, Rose? Would it soften your heart if I were miserable?"

"Yes." A long sigh followed the hard reply. "No, that is not true. Oh, I have had my moments when I cursed your betrayal." She laughed sadly. "Picturing you unhappy gives me no satisfaction, however. It would have grieved me if he had destroyed you too, and in such an irredeemable way."

She sounded more the dear friend now instead of the vengeful cousin. Alexia forgave her the insults to Hayden. Rose knew only the public man, the one who could be hard.

"Will you allow me to embrace you, Rose? I have badly missed you."

A moment passed during which the ache became physical. Perhaps Rose felt it too. Suddenly they were in each other's arms, laughing when their bonnets bumped, sniffing back tears.

Alexia closed her eyes and inhaled with deep contentment. Her whole being glowed from the contact and love.

They entered the church and sat in a back pew.

"I apologize for making you come to this cold, damp pile," Rose said. "However, Timothy . . ."

"He is still ill?"

"He is ill often enough to be useless. He is quite well other days. I prefer the sick ones, I confess."

"He is not cruel, I hope."

"Not cruel, just . . . sad. And angry. If you had arrived at our door, I do not know what would have happened. He was furious about the news of your marriage.

He said horrible things. If he knew I had come to meet you . . ."

"I am very grateful you came, Rose. I have been so alone since you left London. No friend can replace the woman I see as my sister."

Rose clasped her hand. "I came because we are like sisters but also for reassurance that this marriage was your will. Timothy says Rothwell must have . . . that the rogue importuned you. The sudden wedding, your dependence on him—well, Tim tells a lurid story."

Not a true story, however. She did not expect them to forgive Hayden, but she would not allow their imaginations to add to his crimes.

"Rose, I was careless with my virtue. However, he did not importune me. I will admit that I succumbed to passion's lure, probably because I had so little experience in its power."

"If there was a lure, someone held the line. I suppose I should give him some credit for doing the right thing after his seduction. He could have abandoned you, ruined. Too ruined to be his cousin's governess, so without income or protection as well."

Alexia said nothing. If Rose admitted Hayden had behaved honorably in the end, she did not want to disabuse her of that conclusion.

"But to marry such a man, Alexia. To be bound to a man with no mercy." She made a face of distaste. "To share a bed with a man when there is no love."

"It is less horrible than we think it will be. Love has never been a requirement for marriage, and I am understanding why."

"That is useful to know. I have wondered of late if intimacy on those terms is tolerable."

Alexia did not like the sound of that. Rose appeared to still be contemplating the scandalous notion of becoming a courtesan.

As if her allusion desecrated the church, Rose stood. "Let us take a turn in the churchyard. It is out this door over here."

The mist in the yard made little improvement over the damp in the church. They strolled side by side through spare plantings and rows of graves.

"How is Irene faring?" Alexia asked.

"I slapped her last week. She was pouting and acting childish, and I lost my temper and slapped her. I hated myself for days. She has only just begun speaking to me again."

"I daresay she acted less childish in the intervening days."

Rose chuckled. "Oh, yes. And one cannot whine if one is being silent out of pique. I try to remember that this is hardest on her. She knew little else but luxury in her life."

"I would like to be allowed to help her." She broached the subject with caution and waited for Rose's reaction.

"You have to know that Timothy will never allow it. To accept charity from Rothwell, on top of everything else—it would send him to his grave, and I fear he would take us with him."

"You speak as if he has gone mad. Surely he is not dangerous."

"Bitterness can turn a person's mind, and I fear it is

turning his. He has even begun to blame Ben for all of this. *Ben,* who is long dead. If that does not suggest a touch of madness, I do not know what it says."

"How can he blame Ben? I realize that Hayden might have stayed his hand if Ben lived, but—"

"He says we would have had enough to survive this if Ben had not sent all that money to Bristol. You can see how he is irrational. Ben paid one of our father's debts. He behaved with honor, but Tim now finds blame." She slid an arm around Alexia's waist. "Let us spend the time left on more pleasant conversation. Tell me about your new silks and jewels. I may hate the husband who bought them for you, but I am glad you are finally indulged. I will eat them with my imagination and try them on in my mind."

"I must go if I am to return home by nightfall," Rose said.

They sat on a bench in the yard. The cold had long ago numbed Alexia's fingers, but she did not want to end this interlude. This last hour had been much like old times, sharing casual talk of simple things.

They trailed back to the side church door. Hayden had been waiting in the carriage all this time. She did not think she would find him any softer upon rejoining him.

When they reentered the church, she tried again to offer help. "I understand that you cannot accept anything from my husband. I have a little of my own, however. Our settlement secured my old income to me. I have also been thinking that I will continue making hats, very discreetly. I would like you to accept a few pounds from me on occasion that would be my own money, not his."

Rose paused at the front portal. She leaned over and kissed Alexia's cheek. "It is all of a pot now, isn't it? Your money is his. Will you be so discreet that even he does not know? No, dear cousin, let us not rely on deceptions that might expose you to his anger. You and I will be friends as circumstances permit, but I will not accept money from you."

They opened the portal and walked outside. Rose halted at once, staring straight ahead.

Hayden's carriage had moved. It waited right at the end of the short stone path that led to the church. Hayden stood beside it, biding his time. Rose's gig was gone.

He walked toward them. "Miss Longworth, I perhaps have been too bold. Your driver grew impatient and was set to come find you. Rather than have you disturbed, I paid the man and let him depart."

Rose appeared fit to kill. She glared daggers at Hayden.

Alexia glared a few of her own. "Perhaps it would have been wiser to allow the man to seek my cousin out. Then she could have decided her own course of action."

"I knew how important this meeting was to you, my dear. I sought to give you both whatever time you wanted." He gestured to the carriage. "We will be staying at Aylesbury Abbey tonight, Miss Longworth. We will take you home."

"I must decline."

"It is on our way and no inconvenience."

"It is not your convenience that forces my refusal."

"Nothing forces your refusal but pride, Miss Longworth. I will sit with the coachman, if that will allow you to accept."

They waited for Rose to come around. Alexia could see her weighing the options, debating if she could hire another gig in town immediately, considering the compromise Hayden offered.

"He will not be *in* the carriage with you," Alexia whispered. "And we will have a little more time together."

Reluctantly, Rose allowed Alexia to coax her into the carriage. Hayden closed the door and climbed up beside the driver.

It was a long, quiet ride back to the Longworths' house. Rose refused to be drawn into conversation. She kept glancing to the carriage roof, as if she sensed the man whose weight hovered above them.

Alexia practiced the scolding she would give her husband, but halfway to the house she lost the heart for it. He had only tried to be kind. He wanted them to have as much time as possible. Surely Rose would see that, if she would just open her eyes to more than his injury of them.

It was too much to expect. A family pinching pennies could hardly think kindly of the man who had sent them into impoverishment.

When they approached the lane to the house, Rose opened the trapdoor and called for a stop. Without ceremony she opened the door, kicked down the stairs, and alighted. She was halfway down the lane before Hayden climbed down.

"She does not want Timothy to see the carriage," Alexia explained. "He would make her life hell if he knew she had ridden with us."

"I expect so." He watched her turn a slight bend in the lane and disappear. He closed the door. "Wait here. Find a blanket and keep warm. I should not be too long."

"Too long where?"

He pointed to the roof visible amid the trees. "There. I have business with Timothy Longworth."

He waited at the door. Eventually they would open it. If they did not, he would enter on his own.

The door finally cracked ajar. Rose's face appeared, ashen and worried. "Leave. Please leave. You have no right—"

"I have come to see your brother, Miss Longworth. It is in his interest and yours that he learn what I have to say."

"He will never speak to you. Now you must go."

She began to close the door. He grasped its edge with his hand. "Tell him that Benjamin left at least one bank account that was not among his papers. I know where it is."

Rose appeared skeptical, but she opened the door and allowed him to enter. She brought him to the drawing room, then left.

"You will roast in hell, you know."

He swung his attention toward the young voice that damned him. Irene stood in the threshold, wearing a petulant expression.

"You have ruined my life. Your cousin sleeps in my bed and will have my season, and I will never marry now since I have no fortune and . . . and . . ." Tears started to spill, interrupting her harangue. She wiped her eyes in vain and continued to charge blindly. "Rose says Alexia had her reasons to marry you, but I can't think of one good enough. It was hateful of her to do so. You of all men. Nor will she forgive you, not really, not ever. She loves *us,* not you. She—"

"That will be enough, Irene." Rose's scold caught Irene unaware of her sister's reappearance outside the drawing room. She pivoted around to face Rose's severe expression.

Irene began weeping in anger and frustration. "He . . . he . . ."

"It is not a child's place to upbraid him, and right now he is a guest in this house. Go to your chamber now."

Irene ran off. Rose entered the drawing room. She did not apologize for her sister. Hayden assumed she had agreed with every impertinent word.

"Timothy will be down soon. Can you occupy yourself until then?"

"Easily."

"Then I will leave you to do so."

He did so by wondering what Rose and Alexia had talked about during those hours in the church. He doubted his wife had defended him against all charges. There had been much truth in Irene's immature ravings. *Nor will she forgive you, not really. She loves us, not you.*

He had no obligation to make amends, but he would

mitigate the damage if he could. For Alexia's sake he would, and for Rose and Irene. The ladies did not know Timothy was a criminal, nor would they ever, most likely. They did not know how he had brought this suffering on his family and how close he had walked to the gallows.

When Longworth entered the drawing room, it did not appear his delay had been spent on grooming. Unlike his dashing appearance at their last formal meeting, he looked unkempt. Cravat askew and eyes shot with red, he walked in the slow, deliberate manner of a drunk trying not to stagger.

"Rothwell."

"It was good of you to make time for me, Longworth. Are you sober enough to understand what I have to say?"

Longworth laughed. "Same words, same man, same answer, Rothwell. I'm *too damned sober.*"

Hardly. But not too damned drunk, which was what mattered.

"Bit of a row down here a while ago. Was Irene yelling at you?"

"She blames me for your ruin. So does my wife. You lied to them."

"Told me to, didn't you? Said I should come up with whatever lies I wanted to keep them from knowing the truth." He grinned. "I figured it was better they hated you than me."

"I want you to tell Alexia the truth."

"Causing problems for you, is it? Sorry, I can't do that. She would find a way to let Rose know. You can't tell her either, can you? Gave your word of honor, as I recall. You will forgive me if I am not sympathetic to your quandary."

Hayden had not expected anything different from Longworth, but this blithe refusal made him want to thrash the man.

"Rose said you dangled a bank account to get me to receive you." Longworth threw himself on the divan and sprawled. "Is there money in it?"

"Some. Not enough."

"Of course not enough. There will never be enough. That is my punishment, isn't it? To never get out from under this."

"With industry, you could. If you did not succumb to your illness so willingly, you could."

"Do not preach. Rose does that enough for five men. Where is this account?"

"The Bank of England."

"It is odd the records were not with his other financial papers."

"Not so odd, considering the use to which this account was put. You learned your scheme from Ben, I have discovered. He had been at it a long time. This account was where he placed the money he stole."

Longworth scratched his ear. "I wondered where he put it. There should be a lot, though. More than enough."

"He spent some and also paid off the income due his victims, just as you did. There were other dispersals of a private nature. Three thousand remains, however. It should help."

Longworth nodded, closed his eyes, and drifted into a reverie. Hayden wondered if he was falling asleep. He opened his eyes, however. "Gin has my mind a bit fogged, but even so, this is not making sense."

"How so?"

"If you know he was doing it, then you know which funds he sold. Why would you let me have the three thousand? Why isn't it going to making those people whole?"

"The account is under Ben's name, and you are his heir. I cannot keep you from having it even if I want to. As for his victims, I will make them whole myself, to protect his name."

Longworth whistled. "A lot of money. So you will cover Ben's criminal debts but not mine."

"Since he is dead, Ben cannot cover his own. Also, he was my friend and you are not."

"Should still be a lot more than three thousand. I worked it out after he died and I was stuck covering that income from his earlier schemes. I had a good sense of how many he had done, so to speak. Seems odd there isn't more in that account."

Hayden knew too well where a lot of the money had gone. It had enhanced Suttonly's fortune. "I do not think you will find any other hidden treasures. There were transfers to banks in Bristol and York, a good amount over time, but the accounts were not in his name."

Tim's disappointment showed. "The money to Bristol repaid one of Father's debts, so that is no good. Who got the money in York?"

"A Mr. Keiller. Ben sold out his funds very early, the records show. He was one of his earliest victims, but it appears Ben paid the man back completely."

Longworth entered into another distraction, this time

while he stared at the carpet. He emerged with a shrug of resignation. "Then I am left with only the three thousand."

"For your sisters' sake, I am sorry it is not more." Hayden reached into his waistcoat pocket and retrieved a small piece of paper. "Here are the details on the Bank of England account. It will save you time if you have them."

He set it on a table and walked to the door.

"It is odd that you married Alexia," Longworth said lazily. "Doing the right thing, I assume, but that was odder still. She isn't a woman to turn a man's head, let alone yours. Someone like you doesn't need to seduce governesses. Ben thought her pretty, but I think she is very plain."

Hayden stopped and turned back to Longworth. The impulse to thrash the man spiked again. "I doubt you would recognize any person's worth beyond their financial wealth."

Longworth grinned slyly. "Wish I had thrown Rose at you. You'd have gotten a beautiful wife while you did the right thing, and I would have gotten a rich brother-in-law."

He chuckled at his own cleverness. Hayden left the drawing room in disgust. As he made his way to the door, he passed the library and spied Miss Longworth's golden head bent to a book. He retraced his steps and entered unannounced.

"Miss Longworth, I have just told your brother that three thousand pounds are sitting in the Bank of England under Benjamin's name. As his heir, your brother can claim the money. However, since he is so often ill, you may want to inform yourself as to his intentions for it."

Miss Longworth closed her book. She did not look at him. "Thank you for telling me, Lord Hayden. I will endeavor to help him use it wisely."

CHAPTER
EIGHTEEN

Alexia did not confront Hayden about the way he had forced his presence on her cousins. Instead, she wrote to Rose as soon as she returned to London, hoping she could just pick up the threads of their reunion. For four days she impatiently waited for Rose's response.

Hayden was with her in the morning room when the early post arrived on the fifth day. When it contained no letter from Rose, the annoyance she had been harboring spiked.

While she simmered with agitation, she fussed with the letters that had come. Invitations from the curious were pouring in as society returned to town for the season.

She noted the names of families that would have never received Rose, let alone Alexia Welbourne. She would never have real friends among his circle. They would always be whispering about her marriage, always assuming Hayden had said his vows at the point of a sword.

"You appear vexed, Alexia," Hayden said.

"You misinterpret my mood."

"I do not think so. What about the mail angers you?"

She wished he would go back to his own letters and papers. Actually, she wished he were not even here. When had he changed his morning habits like this? He used to be gone when she came down, but now he was often still in the morning room when she took her breakfast.

She held up the letters. "There are too many of them. Starting next week I will be onstage every night, performing for people who are not even your friends."

"Then we will accept fewer."

"You said we would accept most."

"Not if it makes you unhappy. Choose those that interest you, and decline the rest."

That should make her feel better, but it did not. She shuffled through the letters again.

"Is it the letters that have come that vex you or the ones that have not?"

How like him to sense the truth. How unlike him to force a conversation about the Longworths, however. By agreement the subject never invaded their nights, and it rarely touched their days.

He commanded the room even in his relaxed pose on the chair. He had dressed for his day in the City in dark coats, and his appearance stunned her a little, as it always did. The coolness that had claimed him since they argued in Aylesbury hung like crisp air around them. He did not command her, but he expected an answer.

She balanced for a moment between prudence and

plain-speaking. As too often in her life, the latter won out.

"Rose has not written since we left Oxford. I fear she will not and that my visit to her was ruined."

He reacted to the last word, badly. "By me?"

"Your arrangements with the carriages could be seen as a kindness, if not for the way you followed her into the house."

"It is a pity she has not written and told you what happened in that house. It is peculiar that you have not asked me about it."

"Some subjects are better left alone. You have indicated that my cousins and their situation are among them."

"I did not anticipate how you would not need words to communicate your resentments. I do not intend to have my home filled with unspoken recriminations. Let us clear the air now."

"On everything?"

The challenge hung there. The danger it contained shivered through her, and she wished she had not flung it out. She did not want to talk about all of it.

Nor did he, apparently. In subtle shifts in posture and expression, he retreated from the brink. "I went to that house to tell Timothy Longworth I had discovered that Ben had an account at the Bank of England, one unknown to Timothy. A good amount of money rests there."

"That is all you spoke of?"

"That is all that matters."

She did not know what to say. "Does Rose know this?"

"I told her myself, so she would be aware that he was coming into some money."

"You could have just written to Timothy."

"I chose not to."

She looked down at her letters. The absence of one from Rose had a different meaning now. Perhaps their reunion had not been as successful as she thought. Maybe she had misunderstood. It might have merely been the final visit before a death.

Hayden stood. His expression reflected thoughts of other things already.

"Thank you for finding the account. That must have taken some time."

Her words surprised him. "It was an accident of sorts."

"Then I thank Providence for allowing you to find the account. It was very kind of you to be sure Rose knew of it too." She looked up at him, and that physical pain stabbed her heart. "I wish we had not argued at Aylesbury. I want you to know that I am not disloyal to you when I speak to Rose. I do not compromise you in trying to build that bridge."

He cupped her chin in his hand. His gaze entered her, and his thumb lined along her jaw. Suddenly he was not distant and cool but so close and warm in body and spirit that it mesmerized her.

"Are you going to your City chambers this morning?" she asked.

"Eventually. I have some meetings first. Chalgrove and a few others . . ." He spoke in a random mutter, words that did not matter because all she noticed was how he prolonged the moment's delicious connection.

After the last days' distance, this sudden intimacy, so close she felt their thoughts melting together, awed her. He stood before her so real too. So of the world and time, not a visitor who touched her body and soul under the cloak of night's silence and mystery.

Did he experience the same thing? Did he deliberately make the connection last and intensify, or did time stretch only in her imagination?

He bent and kissed her. "I will not be able to return until tonight. Be here."

The servant found her in her old bedroom. She had retreated there to work on her new hat. Even though this activity would not earn the money to relieve her cousins' straits, she still enjoyed it. She would wear the hats herself. Not having to please Mrs. Bramble's customers freed her to design this one just the way she wanted.

She accepted the letter the servant brought and recognized Rose's hand. She carried the letter to the window as joy and dread battled in her. Would this missive be filled with the warmth they had shared again in Oxford or politely explain that Hayden's intrusion had made any further alliance unlikely?

Neither hope nor fear was warranted. Rose had written with a different purpose.

Timothy has left. I fear he has abandoned us.

She read the details with increasing alarm. Her impotence to stop this final injustice brought her to the brink of tears. The urge to do something, to somehow thwart Tim's irresponsible behavior, sent hopeless, disorganized plans streaking through her mind.

She sat on her old bed and read it again, trying to concentrate. Why had Tim done such a thing? Surely Rose was wrong and he would return.

She wished Hayden were home. She wanted to show this to him, to ask him if it heralded the disaster she feared. She wanted him to reassure her that he would never allow Rose and Irene to become truly destitute.

He was not here, however, nor would he return until night.

When had it happened?

The thought came to Hayden at the peak of his passion, when his consciousness split apart in an explosion of sensation.

Did she hear the question? Did he speak it? She was with him in the ecstasy, her legs wrapping his body and her scent and cries filling his head. The question echoed in the aftermath, while they slowly relinquished the unity.

When had it happened? When had the passions of the nights altered the realities of the days?

When had the desire to share her company changed his habits? When had her moods begun to determine his own? Her smile brought joy and her frowns brought worry. Either way she filled his thoughts, distracting him. No diversion appealed enough to keep him away long. He always came back early enough to slide into her bed, as he had tonight.

He floated in a peace so perfect it would be a sin to disturb it. He did not care right now that his affection put him at a disadvantage. It was during the day that he sometimes analyzed this unexpected emotion and how it made him a man he did not recognize.

He waited for his self-possession to reassemble itself, not much caring if it ever did. When that moment finally came, it jolted him awake. He realized he had drifted to sleep. He began to reach for Alexia and understood why the separateness had come so abruptly. She was not in the bed.

No sounds came from the dressing room. He rose and looked anyway, then checked his own chambers. Curious now, he put on a robe, lit a lamp, and made his way to her old bedroom.

A half-made hat perched atop a makeshift form. A scattering of notions indicated she had worked on this creation recently. Was that how she occupied herself while she waited to build a presence in his world? He examined the hat's careful stitching and wondered if she would always prefer this artistry to making calls on ladies.

A visit below to the library revealed only darkness. Concern began to simmer, then another possibility occurred to him. He mounted the stairs to the top floor and walked the length of the corridor that separated the servants' chambers. He eased open the door at the end and entered the attic.

A glow of light greeted him, swallowing that from his own lamp. Alexia sat on the floor near the window, much as she had the last time he found her here. Papers surrounded her again, and one of Ben's trunks stood open.

She did not cry this time. She sat straight, head high, her eyes closed, utterly self-contained. She seemed so separate from him that she might have been a stranger.

He tried to tame the anger that flared in him. Perhaps this was how she spent her afternoons, not making hats. How often after he left her bed did she slip up here to gain comfort from this last remaining connection to her old love?

She was his wife, damn it. *His* wife. She was turning him into a romantic fool, the kind of man he scorned, and she did not even know it. Nor would she care if he did know. He was only the man who had ruined her family, seduced her, then done the right thing.

The anger conquered him, stoked by the admission that she had made him ridiculous, prodded by the stupid weight in his chest that proved how much she mattered.

He strode toward her. His shoulder brushed some books stacked on a chest, knocking the top ones to the floor. The sound startled her. She opened her eyes and cocked her head, as if his presence made no sense.

He stared down at the open trunk. He recognized the personal effects of an old friend long dead. They were also the talismans of a rival whose presence was so strong that even the grave could not hold it.

Benjamin. Hale and happy Ben. So impulsive, so free. Logic did not decide Ben's path in life. Practicalities did not curb his impulses. Nor did laws and morals, it seemed.

He had tasted that freedom of spirit vicariously through Ben. Ben had been the direct opposite of

Hayden Rothwell, and that had been his appeal. To Alexia too, he did not doubt.

He understood. Right now it infuriated him anyway.

"These trunks do not belong in this house," he said.

"I know that I should have sent them to my cousins weeks ago. I am glad I did not, however."

That did it. "I am going to burn them come daylight."

She grabbed the edge protectively. "Burn them? Why?"

"Why?" She shrank as if he had yelled. Had he? "You leave my arms and sneak up here to wallow in sentimentality about a man who played you false, and you ask me why I want to burn the damned trunks that feed your unhealthy attachment to his memory?"

She angled away in shock. His satisfaction at her reaction was short-lived. Composing herself, she straightened and faced him down. She might have stood and donned armor, so confidently did she pull her dignity into a defense to meet his assault.

Hell, she was magnificent. Incomparable. No wonder he wanted her.

"First of all, I did not sneak here," she said, her eyes blazing. "Second, I did not come here to indulge in sentimentality. I received a letter from Rose today that greatly distressed me. Some details prodded my memory while you slept, and I came here to see if—well, I came to check a few things."

Her crisp, angry words punched the brittle silence that had engulfed them.

"Rose wrote to you? Why didn't you tell me?"

"I wanted to, but you were not home."

"I am home *now*. I have been home with you for hours. If you were distressed by her letter—"

"You made a rule that my cousins were not to be discussed at night. You made it clear that you did not want *your* pleasure disturbed by that which distresses *me*."

She said it factually, without bitterness. Her calm took him aback more than her assumptions. It was the voice of a dutiful wife accepting the limitations imposed by her husband. It was also the voice of a woman who had no expectations.

Of course she saw the banishment of her cousins from their bed that way. What else would she think? Not that he had vaguely sensed from the start that they might share more than mere pleasure, but only if that acrimony were put aside at night.

He sat beside her on the floor, just as he had the day he took her virginity. His loss of control had so astonished him that afternoon. It made much more sense now.

"It was a selfish rule, Alexia. Very selfish, if it leaves you alone at night with your worries when you are distraught."

"I was not alone for a while," she said softly. "I was not distraught for a while."

He was glad to hear he did not imagine the best of it.

"What did the letter say?"

"Tim has left them. Rose writes that after your visit he stopped drinking. He became *ruthlessly sober*— those were her exact words. He left three days ago."

"I expect he came to London to see about that bank account."

"That is what he told her. Off to find his fortune, he

said. He kept laughing when he said it, as if he harbored a private joke. As of last night, he had not returned."

He smoothed her hair with his hand. "He is probably enjoying a good debauch now that the money is his. There is no reason to think he is abandoning them."

"Rose says he took a goodly amount of clothing. Two trunks. When she asked why he packed so much, he said there is more money, and he thinks he knows where to find it."

"Once he looks where he thinks, he will return." He spoke with more conviction than he felt now. The bastard may well have left his sisters to their fates and taken off with the three thousand. He'd think it was his right to run through it while he ignored his debts back home.

The little pile of letters on the floor drew his attention. "Why were you reading these again, Alexia? They have nothing to do with Timothy."

She lifted one. "I was not reading them. I came here to check their dates and the location of this woman." She pointed to the letter's top, and the date and town. "It was sent shortly before he left for Greece. It was sent from Bristol."

"So it was."

"Rose said something odd when we met in Oxford. It nudged at me then, but I forgot it as soon as we left the church and you—well, you were there."

You interfered, she almost said. He *had* interfered. He had staked his claim on her, visibly and physically. He had made it clear to her cousin that whatever had been said as they spoke privately, he would not have his place compromised. He had announced his possession and authority and been as petty about the whole meeting as a green boy.

He had been an ass.

"What did she say that provokes you?"

She looked at him, checking whether he was really interested. Evidently convinced he meant well, she re-settled her rump so she faced him.

"When I visited their house before we married, I had asked Rose about Benjamin, just as you had asked me. I inquired about his finances when we lived in Cheapside and why he did not spend more then. Rose said he had still been paying one of his father's debts and that was where the fruits of his early success were spent."

"That was the honorable thing for him to do. It would not make him melancholy."

"In Oxford, Rose told me that when Tim was in his cups, he'd begun to blame Ben for their situation. He said they would not be in such dire straits if Ben had not sent all that money to *Bristol*. Rose and I thought it a little mad for Tim to blame his brother for paying off his father's debt. Tonight, however, I remembered Ben had another connection to Bristol."

She waved the letter. The town's name hung in the air. It loomed from the letter in her hand. Her sharp mind had latched on to this coincidence, and her expression showed how significant she thought it to be.

"Hayden, what if Ben was not paying off a debt but sending this woman money? A lot of it. Perhaps he owed her, or perhaps he loved her, or perhaps . . . perhaps he had even married her. She writes with great familiarity, as if he is most certainly hers forever. What if her demands, or his obligations, had become unbearable? What if—"

She stopped, biting her lower lip. *What if Ben found himself in a situation where he was bound to one woman through promises or fortune but actually wanted another?* Would it be enough to send him into the sea?

She was halfway to a plausible explanation of everything, even Ben's death. Only it was the wrong explanation. Money had indeed gone to a bank in Bristol, but to repay that old debt from his father. And much of the other fruits of Ben's success had gone to Suttonly.

There was no way to explain that without telling her about Ben's and Timothy's thievery. The temptation to do so grew as he watched her hopeful expression. Her story absolved Ben of playing her false. She could go back to believing he had loved her as she loved him. Hell, Ben's name would probably be the last word she spoke before she died then.

"I think the answers to a lot of questions can be found in Bristol," she said, tapping the letter against her palm. "I think that is where Timothy has gone too. I am thinking I will make a brief journey there, find Tim, and also meet this woman and find out about her relationship to Ben." She nodded as she laid it out to herself. *Here are the questions I have, there are the answers I seek. The most practical solution is to visit Bristol and this woman and learn if I am correct.*

"No."

His response pulled her out of a daze of planning. "It is the only way to learn the truth, Hayden."

"There is no truth in Bristol. Timothy Longworth is not there because there is no reason to go there."

"He is not in Oxford either," she reminded him.

"If he is chasing after visions of hidden treasure, let him. He will return home soon enough. Do not worry about Rose and Irene. With Timothy gone, they will allow us to help them, so they may be the better for his absence."

"If there are no hidden treasures, where is all of Ben's money? You wondered yourself, or have you forgotten that?"

If it were day, if she did not look so lovely in the lamplight, if he were not creating a knot of lies to spare her the truth, he would have been able to devise an answer for that question, he was sure.

"Alexia, we cannot make this journey. I have affairs that require my attention in London, and I cannot spare the time to take you to Bristol now. It would also be impractical for us to chase Timothy all over England on the mere coincidence of this town's name. Nor would it be appropriate for you to confront the woman who wrote those letters. They were private ones and not meant for your eyes."

She considered him at length. He noticed that the violet fields appeared very shallow right now. Did she deliberately block his view, or was it merely the low light doing that?

"I will admit there is some sense in what you advise," she said.

He stood and offered his hand. "I am glad you see the rightness of it."

He sensed no rancor in her as they left the attic. He was relieved that she accepted his authority on the matter.

In bed later that night, he did not sleep at once. His mind kept seeing Ben's account book and the transfers to the bank in Bristol. They were some of the earliest dispersals from the account and had continued down to the end. His interest in them had been cursory while he examined the account book and eclipsed once he saw Suttonly's name.

He rarely forgot numbers of any kind, and the columns in the account came to him with precision once he called them to his memory. The amounts sent to Bristol had not been regular in their timing, like the drafts sent to York. He added their sum in an instant.

A lot of money had gone to Bristol. Less as Suttonly's demands increased, but still a goodly amount. Possibly a lot of the later notes had gone there too. Maybe there was no old debt inherited from his father.

A secret treasure might wait in Bristol for Timothy Longworth after all. He hoped so. Then Longworth could buy his way out of his ruin, and that sorry episode would be over.

CHAPTER
NINETEEN

By night Alexia embraced her husband. She explored a sensuality so intense that her body responded when she heard him open the door. Nameless emotions infiltrated the pleasure too, ones born of the knowing that deepened with each night and each kiss, that lightened her heart and flowed in the warmth.

By day she lived her separate life. She patronized modistes but crafted her own hats. She continued with Caroline's lessons. She visited Phaedra and wrote encouraging letters to Rose.

She also planned her journey to Bristol.

Hayden had not forbidden her to go but only advised against it. Had he issued an order, she might not have obeyed anyway. Even a good wife was allowed an occasional disobedience, and this situation was important enough to warrant one. All the same, it was convenient that he had neglected to lay down any laws.

She did not intend to lie outright to him. She merely planned to omit her inclusion of Bristol in other plans. In order to effect those other arrangements, she visited the City later in the week and called on the bank of Mr. Darfield.

Mr. Darfield appeared suitably sober. He was just the sort of man one would trust as a banker, Alexia decided. Silver-haired and restrained in dress, he projected mature good sense and prosperity. If not for the moisture on his brow and the long pauses in their conversation, she would have been totally confident in the bank's solvency and abilities.

"You say that you wish to sell out your funds," he said.

"Yes." She had said so three times now. He did not look so old, but perhaps his concentration was not the best.

"It is not advisable to do so. With your cousin's departure from this bank, I became your trustee, and I do not think it wise."

"They do not amount to much, and with my marriage I no longer need the small income. My marriage settlement left this paltry income in my hands, as you can see from the copy I brought. You can also see the substantial new trust that my husband created for me."

He blanched at her mention of her marriage. He peered down at the settlement with pursed lips. Hayden had almost ruined this man and this bank, and she doubted Mr. Darfield thought kindly of him. Darfield had helped ruin Timothy in turn, so she did not think kindly of Darfield.

She had expected this to be an awkward conversation, but not such a long one. His astonishment at her arrival had been surpassed only by his mute confusion as he lengthily pondered her business.

"Madam, it is not much, but most married ladies are wise to hold whatever they can, for their children or—"

"The money would do better elsewhere."

"May I ask where?"

"No, Mr. Darfield, you may not. You have the evidence in front of you that I am now provided for one hundred times over. I request that you agree to the funds' sale."

He pawed at the settlement, squinting his eyes. "I want our solicitors to confirm that your husband has no claim on the income. I do not want trouble with him. I also want to confirm that this other trust was established."

"How long will that take?"

"A week, perhaps two. Then another at least to liquidate the funds."

"Mr. Darfield, I am beginning to understand why my husband removed his family's money from this bank, if it takes you so long to effect such a simple transaction."

His face fell. A peculiar, vacant expression entered his eyes. His weak smile looked a little stupid.

Then, with a jolt, he turned alert and officious. He rudely checked his pocket watch. His face flushed as he peered at it.

He stood. "Madam, I will write to you as soon as I ascertain if we will do as you request. Now I regret to say that I expect a visitor."

After wasting the better part of an hour, he was now throwing her out. "I will await your message, and I trust you will proceed quickly. I also hope that you will not allow any ill will toward my husband to create delays."

The meeting had not gone as she expected. She

wanted to bring that money to Rose, and now she would not be able to.

Her vexation occupied her enough that she barely noticed her surroundings as she left his office and walked to the bank's door. Therefore it took her mind several moments to accept what her eyes saw. Hayden entered the bank and aimed right toward her. When his gaze lit on her, he momentarily stopped in his tracks, then proceeded with a determined stride.

She waited for him to reach her. "The groomsman told you where I was going again, didn't he? I think the servants should not act as your spies, Hayden."

His attention shifted past her. She turned and realized Mr. Darfield watched from his doorway.

"He is expecting an important visitor," she explained to Hayden. "Having met the man, I half-understand why you did not trust him with all that money."

"Why did you meet with him, Alexia?"

Mr. Darfield hurried over and inserted himself between them. "Lord Hayden, a fortuitous coincidence that you are here."

Hayden acknowledged the banker. The banker beamed that stupid smile.

"I came to sell out my funds," she said. "I want to give the money to Rose, now that I do not need it. *He* does not believe the settlement and thinks I must hold on to this other amount too." A thought came to her. "Mr. Darfield, if my husband assures you he has more than provided for me, would that satisfy you?"

Darfield looked at Hayden beseechingly, as if hoping his fellow man could translate the strange woman's demands.

"Darfield, perhaps we can attend to this in your office, so all of London is not aware of it," Hayden said.

"He is expecting an important—"

"No trouble. No trouble. Settling this now with your husband present is a splendid idea." He swung out an arm in the direction of the office.

She retraced her steps and sat once more in the chair.

"Would you like some time alone together to discuss this decision?" Darfield asked Hayden.

"It is not necessary. I understand my wife requests that you sell out those funds, correct?"

"That is her request. She showed what she claims is the marriage settlement, and if it is, I would be hard-pressed as trustee of this small amount to refuse her. We are expected to be reasonable, after all. I said I would prefer if you knew of this intention to *sell,* however." His voice carried a new firmness. He peered at her. "That is what you want, correct? For us to *sell the funds*?"

"Yes, for the fourth time, I wish to *sell the funds.*"

He glared at Hayden as if the very notion were intolerable.

"I have more than provided for her future, Darfield, and that of her children. I would appreciate it if you would arrange the sale for her quickly."

"Quickly?"

"It is unusual, I know, but I am sure there is a way. Say, why don't you advance her the money and repay the bank upon the sale? That is done sometimes, is it not? I am sure you have made such arrangements before."

Darfield looked her way cautiously. "Would you be agreeable to that?"

"If I have the money in hand right away, why would I not be?" She wished Mr. Darfield had suggested it half an hour ago. Then Hayden would not have found her here.

Darfield removed a large leather book from his desk drawer. Glancing one final time at Hayden for agreement, he dipped his pen. After some scratching, blotting, and cutting, he handed her a bank draft for four hundred pounds.

"He does not inspire confidence," she said as Hayden walked her to her carriage. "I always assumed he was the real banker and that Timothy merely held his coattails. I do not think so now."

"He is not accustomed to ladies acting on their own. Why did you?"

"I did not think you would be welcomed there."

He opened the carriage door but did not hand her in. He looked down at her. "The truth is you did not want me to know you were doing it."

"I intended to explain it all tomorrow."

"Explain what?"

She opened her reticule and plucked out the draft. The sum appeared huge, written out like this. "I am going to bring this to Rose. This and Ben's trunks. You are correct, and his property no longer belongs in that house. As for this money, the income from it is not much, but the capital may carry them a few years. It will go to her, however, so it is not swallowed by Tim's debts."

He was not pleased. "Normally a wife asks her husband if he will allow her to make a visit out of town, even to relatives. Even *you* sought to do so the last time."

"I knew you would not mind my going. You yourself commented on the trunks, and this is far too much to send in a letter." She admired the amount again. "That is odd. Look, he signed his name, but there is no indication this is the bank's account or that he signs as its owner or officer. It could be his own money, for all this shows."

He gently coaxed the draft from her fingers, returned it to her reticule, and closed it away. "It is done that way sometimes."

"That is not very practical. There could be confusion then. Money could get all mixed up."

He handed her into her carriage. "How long do you think you will be gone visiting your cousins?"

She was delighted he had capitulated so quickly on the general idea, but wished he had not asked the length of her absence right now. She did not want to negotiate here on Threadneedle Street. "Three days, perhaps."

He lounged against the door frame, crossing his arms. That was not a good sign. "Two, Alexia. Two."

"Once the season starts, I will not have another chance to see them for months. I do not think four days is too much."

"Four now?" He quirked a smile. "I am not inclined to be without my new wife for four nights."

"I intend to see that you do not miss me too much. I thought we might dine at home together tomorrow night and retire very early."

Her allusion to a long night of pleasure distracted him from whatever scold he intended. The look he gave her caused glorious shivers in the most sensual spots of her body. She half-expected him to climb into the carriage and have her at once.

"Since you intend to make my agreement worth my while, perhaps it can be three or four days."

She would make it worth his while. He would agree to three or four days. He would get angry only when it turned into five or six.

"You cannot imagine my shock when she was announced," Darfield said. "Then to learn she wanted me to sell out the funds that her cousin had already sold—well, I was undone."

Hayden shared some port with Darfield behind the closed door of his office. The man was still beside himself, but the port was helping.

"In my dismay, I thought to stall her until you arrived for our meeting. When she said you had removed all your family's money from this bank, I knew that would be a mistake." He gulped another good swallow. "You are very cool, Rothwell. Very cool. She never guessed you had not followed her here."

Not yet she hadn't. He was counting on that visit to her cousins to distract her enough to keep her from thinking about the day's events closely.

"Longworth told her and his sisters that I removed the family money and brought the bank to the brink of ruin. That is how he explained his reversal in fortune to them. I gave my word I would not tell the ladies the truth."

"I trust you will make sure she does not pursue any truths that will reflect badly on this bank or me."

He gave the reassurances, not entirely sure he could deliver on them. He imagined Alexia learning through some casual conversation that bankers never commingled bank funds with their own accounts. It would be just like her to remember she had received a private draft today.

He turned the conversation to the reason he had come to this bank today. "Have you ascertained just which of the bank's patrons Benjamin Longworth defrauded?"

Darfield's face fell. "I have traced every case to its end and spent days in the records to see the signatures. I regret to say that it was as bad as we thought. Worse, actually."

"How much more do you need?"

"I do not think your solution is wise, Rothwell. Aside from the cost to you, my explanations regarding errors in records may not satisfy some of them. Nor do I care for so many members of polite society thinking that this bank cannot keep good records in the first place."

"Would you prefer that the world learn you had two criminals as partners? Would you prefer if the panic spreads to confidence in the government funds? When you ask for their signatures, all they will care about is that they have not lost a penny. Timothy continued to pay out the income, and now they will see their capital back. Most will not even understand what you are talking about." At least, he was counting on it working this way. "How much?"

Darfield sighed. He picked up his pen and scratched on a small piece of paper. He slid it across his desk.

Hayden read the sum. It closely matched the calculations he had made at night while his memory called up those pages of figures from Ben's hidden account. This time, finally, they had discovered all the victims.

"Regarding your wife's funds . . ." Darfield's expression finished the question. How were they to now sell funds that she no longer owned?

"I will tell her that as her husband I signed the documents to sell once you had them prepared."

"May I assume that, like other women, she lacks an understanding of finance and will not question your right to do so?"

"I will explain it to her. Do not concern yourself with this. She is the least of our worries."

"That gives me untold relief. It would be ironic, no, if this complicated solution came undone due to funds worth no more than four hundred pounds, and owned by your wife of all people?"

Damned ironic. Alexia might not be sophisticated regarding finances, but as a woman who had owned very little, she knew what was hers. Maintaining this final small deception might not be simple at all.

"Madam asked that her dinner be served in her chambers, sir." Falkner intoned the information as soon as Hayden entered the house the next evening.

He did not take it well. Her allusion to a long night together had distracted him all day. The naughty look in her eyes made him hard whenever he remembered it.

Now she had retired without seeing him at all, and she intended to go to Oxfordshire in the morning.

Falkner handed over a sealed note. Hayden opened it, expecting to read polite explanations of illness or some other excuse.

Written formally and in a good hand, the letter invited Lord Hayden Rothwell to join Lady Hayden, his Courtesan in Marriage, to a private dinner in her chambers. He could not believe she had actually put the latter title in writing.

"It appears I will not require the dining room either, Falkner."

"Very good, sir."

Hayden retired to his chambers. Nicholson was not there. A garment had been laid out, however. A note from Alexia rested on his midnight blue silk robe. *The party is an extremely informal one.*

Charmed by her little game, he stripped off his clothes and donned the robe. He spent some time trying to figure out how to hide a gift he had bought her and finally tucked it against his body, wedged where the belt bound his waist. He went looking to see what else she had devised.

Dinner had been laid on a table in her bedchamber. Alexia waited in a chair at another, smaller table draped in linens. Candlelight played over her face and deepened her eyes.

He might be undressed, but she was not. She wore a dinner dress that he had not seen before, one of a cool red hue and perfect fit that showed off her full breasts. Her little lures and directions had tantalized him, and seeing her so majestic in her beauty made his mouth go dry.

"The dress is lovely," he said. He gestured to his barely clothed body. "You have me at a disadvantage."

"I wanted to show it off. The first of my new wardrobe arrived today."

"It is beautiful." So much so that he was not sure he wanted other men to see her in it.

He gazed down at the other table and its array of covered platters and bowls. "No servants, I hope."

"I did not think any could be trusted by a courtesan in marriage to be discreet, so I ordered a meal that did not require service."

He was beyond caring what food lay beneath those covers. A different hunger had been burning in him all day. Her attempts to seduce him with this little play were adorable, and very effective.

He moved closer so he could see the dress better. Its silk fabric caught the light in watery highlights. It covered her more than her old garments, but it formed to her shape in a way that made it very sensual. Or perhaps it was his mind doing that. Or the way she looked at him with frank desire.

He leaned over to kiss her. "Do we have to eat dinner first?"

"I hope not." She rose and turned her back to him. "You will have to help me out of this, however."

He was happy to. There were a lot of hooks, whole rows of hidden bindings that needed attention. She flexed sinuously as his hands moved. Her head lolled slightly while he slowly freed her.

He took care not to ruin the dress after he removed it,

but laid it on a nearby bench. He then worked at the lacing of her stays. His body tightened more with each gentle release of her garments' restraints.

Soon she was in only chemise and stockings, as she had been on their wedding day. He did not want to watch her remove the rest this time, however. He slid the chemise down himself, unveiling her lithe back and narrow waist and the soft, round curves of her bottom.

She trembled visibly and looked over her shoulder. "I am supposed to be seducing you tonight."

"Trust me, you are." He turned her and sat her on the edge of the table. He took the chair and began rolling down one stocking. She appeared unbearably erotic sitting there naked and soft and pale, her breasts full and high. Her thighs were slightly parted, revealing the pink flesh now musky with her scent.

He burned hot and impatient just looking at her. He did not bother with the other stocking, but shifted her hips and spread her legs and used his tongue until her abandon left her weak.

He did not take her to completion, but she was crying for it when he stopped. She blinked hard and gazed with wild eyes while she drew a deep, composing breath. She still sat on the table in a scandalous pose, her arms propping her body from behind and her sex exposed to him.

She slid off the table and into his lap. She nestled her knees on either side of his hips and sat on his thighs. She kissed him, and her hands caressed his head and shoulders. They slid beneath the robe to his skin and began driving him mad.

Her hand hit the gift he had hidden. She stopped and

glanced at him in question, then removed it. She opened it, and her eyes widened when she saw the diamond parure within. A delightful giggle bubbled out of her throat.

He plucked out the necklace and clasped it around her neck. It glistened on her pale skin, catching the lights in her eyes, making little white flames above her breasts. She gazed down at it. "I think I will leave it on. It makes me feel very worldly and beautiful. Very bold too."

She was good to her word. Her little seduction became more aggressive. Her kisses and touch were designed to tantalize. She released the robe so he was as naked as she. She allowed his caresses, but she insisted on being the seducer. With increasingly desperate holds and kisses they entwined closer, but her hands moved low between them. There was nothing tentative in how she handled him this time. She had learned how to give pleasure and was merciless.

She broke away from his devouring kiss and looked down at what she did. Then she gazed in his eyes while her hand moved, watching her power. Her lips parted, and the tip of her tongue peeked between her teeth. His erection increased in an instant at that suggestive mouth, and his hunger turned ruthless.

She noticed. She frowned thoughtfully. He dipped his head to suck her breast to make sure she did not think too much.

"If this were not a game, if I were truly a courtesan in marriage, what would you want me to do when I seduced you?" Her words came raggedly between gasps as her cries stole her breath.

He was close to dying. He told her, hoping that it would not shock her into total retreat.

She watched her hands again, then disentangled herself. She dropped down in front of him so quickly it took a moment before he realized that she was going to do it. Just seeing her there, her shoulders near his knees and those diamonds flaming around her body, left his mind blank to everything except a desire so intense that an animal within bared its teeth.

Her kiss made him groan. She experimented, slowly becoming more confident. He barely noticed what she did, because the sensation sent him into a black velvet world where his arousal tightened and climbed while the pleasure increased and increased. It seemed he was there forever, barely holding on to one shred of control.

She rose and climbed on his lap again. He grabbed her close and lifted her hips. He brought her down on him so hard that they both shuddered with relief. Emboldened now, freed by her power, she rocked her body and held her breasts to his mouth and cried her pleasure into the air as they embraced each other in the ecstasy.

CHAPTER
TWENTY

~~~

Alexia gazed out her window at the city of Bristol. One could smell the sea, even though it was far down the channel. Some buildings along the street below even displayed the weathered wood caused by salt breezes. Beyond the rooftops, the very tips of ship masts could be spotted.

She had taken lodgings some distance from the docks. Her hotel sat on a street that inclined on a little rise, however, and she could glimpse the Avon River.

Her visit with Rose had been spent reassuring and cajoling in vain. Rose had not accepted the idea of Hayden's help. Her resentment of him did not require Timothy's presence to be sustained. Nor had Rose accepted the four hundred pounds easily. She had agreed to keep it for use only if she and Irene found themselves close to starving.

The arrival of Ben's trunks had not encouraged a happy mood either. They had dulled Rose's spirits, entombing Ben's memory as they did. Alexia had not encouraged her cousin to open the trunks and examine their contents. Perhaps someday Rose would. She would not find those love letters inside, however. Alexia had removed them.

Alexia now knew every word in each one of those letters. She had spent her carriage ride to Bristol reading them. The certainty with which this woman wrote further convinced her that Ben's entanglement had been a serious one. References to gifts indicated money had been sent or spent.

Reading the words had called up Ben's memory again, more vividly than she had seen it in weeks. Her heart twinged a little with the old poignancy and the newer pain. The letters had shattered her belief in his love that day in the attic, and a few of those shards cut her again.

Not very deeply, however. New memories had a way of crowding out the old now. Thinking about her last night with Hayden, remembering the erotic wonders and joyful play they had shared until dawn, salved any old hurts very quickly. She had astonished herself, and him too, she suspected. She had ridden down to Oxfordshire in a happy stupor and still had to corral her thoughts to the mission at hand.

She was glad she had been so bold as to read the letters. She had learned what she needed to know. Most of them had been signed the same way—*Lucy*. A few early ones, deep in the pile, had a more complete signature, however, and the name of the property from which she wrote.

Lucinda Morrison, Sunley Manor. Alexia now had a name and possibly the woman's location.

Her mind planned as she took in her view of Bristol.

How would she approach this woman? What should she say? She had been contemplating it for a day as she traveled here.

I am Benjamin Longworth's cousin, and I have come to return your letters. That would let Lucinda Morrison know that her visitor was aware of that love affair. It would be seen as a kindness, since Miss Morrison's letters might compromise her if she had married another man after Ben's death. It would also make Alexia's questions easier.

Then again, reference to Ben might close the door on her face at once.

She would know very soon which way it would go.

She checked her reticule. She buttoned her pelisse and pinned her hat. Steeling her resolve, she lifted the bundle of letters, now wrapped in cloth and ribbons like a present.

Sunley Manor was set back from the road three miles up the Avon River on the way to Bath. The lane approaching it appeared well tended.

Alexia saw the house after they crested a little hill. An old stone building, it displayed a newer wing at one end that greatly increased its already respectable size. Lucinda Morrison led a comfortable if isolated life out here in the country.

A carriage waiting in front suggested the presence of other guests. Alexia opened the trapdoor and told her coachman to stop. She peered at that carriage, debating what to do. She did not want to intrude when others were present. It would be better to do this on another day.

She was about to tell her coachman to turn around when the front door of the house opened and a woman stepped out. A man followed, wearing a high-crowned hat and carrying a walking stick. It appeared the guests were leaving.

A footman emerged as well, and Alexia realized the woman might not be a guest but instead Miss Morrison herself. She squinted to get a sense of what Lucinda looked like, if indeed this was she. She could make out blond hair beneath the richly plumed hat and a nice form encased in a dark carriage ensemble, but little else was distinct from this distance.

The carriage rolled down the lane. Her coachman began to move his equipage to the side. The lane was not broad back here, however. The other coachman saw the problem and stopped to allow Alexia's vehicle to approach the house where the lane widened.

A head poked out the window of Miss Morrison's carriage, and her escort assessed the situation. An odd reaction stirred in Alexia. She grabbed the window's edge and angled so she could see better. Her vision began to spin.

A voice sounded in the far distance, smothered by a roar in her head. Her carriage stopped almost side by side with Miss Morrison's. A man jumped out and ran the few yards to her. They stared at each other through her window.

His stunned expression cleared. Joy lit his face. He pulled open her carriage door. "It *is* you! I'll be damned. What a happy surprise, Alexia."

Black spots swam in her head, and she fainted right into Benjamin Longworth's arms.

———

She recoiled from the acrid smell and opened her eyes. Two faces peered down at her. The feminine one possessed a perfection of features and complexion that made time pause.

It was Benjamin's countenance that arrested her attention, however. He appeared relieved to see her awake. He was suddenly full of the smiles and bright spirit that marked his character. He did not reveal the slightest discomfort at the oddity of the discovery that had sent her careening into oblivion.

"She appears to be composing herself," the woman said. She placed a stopper on the vinaigrette and set it on a table.

"Yes, I am fine now. Thank you." Alexia pushed herself up and sat. The sofa that had held her was in a library. The shelves were old but the bindings fairly new, their leather and tooling gleaming expensively in rows of sedate luxury.

Her heart no longer tried to pound a hole in her the way it had in the carriage. She felt at her hair and garments, smoothing and assembling, while she composed something to say.

Benjamin waited patiently. One would think she had been invited for a visit and unaccountably taken ill. His beautiful blond companion displayed a bit more consternation.

"My apologies for acting so frail. It is not like me at all, as Benjamin can attest," she said. "However, when I saw my cousin—"

"You thought you were seeing a ghost," Ben finished,

patting her shoulder. "Understandable, Alexia. I was as shocked as you."

"I doubt that. *You* had no reason to believe *I* was dead, now, did you?" She looked at the woman. "Would you be Lucinda Morrison?"

She had not recovered enough to take satisfaction in their surprise that she knew the name.

"I came upon your name in some letters that Ben left when he—when he did not return and we thought him dead," she explained.

Ben's shock cleared and a new smile broke. "Ahh, the letters. Clever girl to realize what they meant."

"I had no idea what they meant. I found a name and address on a few and came here to return them. They should be in the carriage." Resentment was building fast, and she let Ben see it. "I never imagined I would find *you* here. How dare you allow me and your sisters to believe you were dead. Why did you not come home, or at least write? To look into a carriage window and see a man whom I believed long gone—" The memory of her shock sent her blood speeding again.

Lucinda Morrison caught Ben's eye. She maintained a calm expression, but her displeasure was palpable. Ben crossed his arms over his chest and calmly suffered the way two women glared at him.

"It would be best if I explained matters to my cousin privately," he said.

Lucinda Morrison's eyebrows arched high. She turned on her heel and aimed for the door. "Explain what you must."

After the door closed, Ben sat on the sofa. He turned

his body toward her and beamed another smile. "It is so good to see you, Alexia. I have missed you badly."

He hadn't changed a bit in the years apart. Still good-natured, still the happy traveler, he exuded the joy of life that made his presence intoxicating. Under these extreme circumstances, she found his innocent enthusiasm in bad taste.

"You knew where to find me if you missed me badly. I cannot say the same. Who is that woman to you, and why are you here? If you were rescued at sea, why did you not let us know?"

He reached over and tucked an errant strand of her mussed hair behind her ear. "It is a little complicated. I could not return. There was a very bad debt of honor to a man who would have ruined me. His demands had become impossible to meet. So . . . Well, if I died, the family would be free of that, and so would I."

She did not care for the familiarity of that subtle touch near her cheek and ear. Her head was clearing fast, and righteous anger eclipsed any relief in her heart. "You jumped off that ship, didn't you?"

He nodded. "We were close to land. I could see the lighthouse on Corsica. I swam."

"You could have perished! You could not judge the distance at night. You might have—"

"I knew it would work, and it did." He spoke lightly. All the possible dangers existed for others, not him. He had said something similar when leaving for Greece. *I will not be hurt. I know it.*

He had always been impulsive, and a little reckless, and too confident in fate's plans for him. She had never before wanted to hit him for it, however.

"Then you made your way back to England and allowed the world to think you had died," she said. "You came here. Why, Ben?"

He shrugged. "She is an old friend. The niece of one of Father's friends, actually. I thought that—"

"I read the letters, Benjamin."

His expression grew more sober. "Well, she had designs for a long time. But I—"

"I also know that you sent money to Bristol before you went to Greece."

Silence this time. Ben appeared totally serious for the first time in her life. Even when he used to kiss her, the affection had been full of smiles and laughs.

She would not think about that now. Except, with him here with her, so close and so real, his scent subtly tinged by the lemon-oil soap that he had always favored, it was hard not to. The memories wanted to deluge her and remained dammed only through concerted effort.

He looked to the closed door and cocked his head, as if listening for sounds behind it. "Are you recovered enough to walk? There is a little wilderness behind the house a ways. Let us take a turn if you are up to it."

"I would welcome some fresh air." She would also welcome the chance to speak with him far away from a beautiful woman who seemed far more worried by her intrusion than Ben was.

As soon as the trees obscured them from the view from the house, Ben took her hand. He raised it to his lips and pressed a kiss on it. "You cannot know how grateful I am that you arrived. How I wished I could write or contact you somehow and explain everything."

He mimicked Hayden's frequent gesture, kissing her hand like this. She extricated herself from his hold. "That you did not write to me is excusable. That you allowed your sisters and brother to believe you dead, that you permitted others to grieve, is not."

"Please understand that I dared not let it be known that I lived. You must trust me on this. I was in danger myself."

"Because of this debt?"

"The man I speak of demanded satisfaction, one way or another. Either I died or they would all be ruined with me. I did it for them. For all of you."

Maybe he did, in part. The ruin had come anyway, but not due to his actions or debts. That did not explain those letters, however. Or the money.

"Is Lucinda Morrison your wife?"

He sighed, and glanced in the direction of the house. "Yes."

"So you became entangled young and married secretly and came to her when you *died*."

"I married her after I came here to stay. How could you think that I was married when I—"

"I *read the letters,* Ben."

"*Her* letters. Her affections for me always exceeded mine for her, but when she agreed to help me, I was obligated to her. Also, I could hardly live here with her if we were not married." He leaned against a tree, rested his head against its bark, and closed his eyes. "It has been a devil's bargain, Alexia. Being dead is no fun. I can't go into town and can never return to London lest I be seen. I am not even known by my own name here. I have suggested we leave England and seek another country where we can mix with society, but she refuses. I am something of a prisoner of my circumstances."

She wanted to tell him he deserved it. He had made her, and also his sisters and even Timothy, suffer. If he had come home, Tim never would have been ruined and Rose would be happy and Irene would have had her season. If he had come home, everything would be normal and the way it was supposed to be and she—

She gazed at him. And she would have learned if he loved her or merely toyed with her. She would never have become Caroline's governess and Hen's companion, would never have been seduced by and married to Hayden Rothwell.

Hayden. She wished he were here. Looking at Benjamin, she missed Hayden terribly. It was an odd reaction, as if her heart feared the years with Ben dead had been a dream in which Hayden had merely appeared at the end.

No, not a dream. Real events had occurred, and real memories had formed. Events that had affected her and those she loved, and memories that stirred her even now as she looked at Ben.

"I am not alone in coming to Bristol," she said. "I think Timothy is in the town too."

His eyes snapped open. "Tim? Why?"

"He knows that you were sending money to Bristol." How long? How long had that money been sent? Jumping from that ship had not been an impulse at all if Ben was feathering his nest in this city. "He left your sisters, and Rose thinks he came looking for that money. He needs it badly, you see."

"Why? I left plenty, and there was the bank."

"He had to sell out his partnership when the bank faced failure during the January crisis. The debts he incurred to Darfield and others ruined him. They are living in Oxfordshire now, and Rose counts every penny and makes it do double work."

He pushed off the tree and walked deeper into the woods, as if wanting to put distance between himself and this news. She hurried after him, snagging her hem on a bush that she rushed past. She glanced down at the ruined cloth and thought how devastating that would have been mere months ago.

She caught him by the arm, stopping him. "You must help them. Even if you cannot let them know you are here, you must send them some money."

"How could the bank almost fail? It was solid a few years ago. More than solid, and Darfield would never allow the reserves to fall so low as to jeopardize his own fortune. No, Tim must have gambled or spent his way to ruin."

"It was the bank, I assure you. Hayden Rothwell abandoned it and removed all his family's accounts."

His brow furrowed. He stared at the ground. He shook his head. "Rothwell did this? He was my good friend and . . . I can't believe he did this to my family."

"Well, he did. And even if Tim had brought it on himself, your sisters should not suffer."

He linked her arm in his and coaxed her to stroll beside him. "Tell me everything, Alexia. Tell me exactly what happened and when. I am shocked by what you have told me about Rothwell." He laughed bitterly. "That bastard has an odd way of honoring his debts and friendships, it seems."

She swallowed hard. "Ben, the first thing I must tell you is this: I am now married to the man you insult as a bastard."

"Lady Hayden is staying with us, but she is not here now. She left in her carriage at noon and has not yet returned."

Mr. Alfred offered the information without hesitation once Hayden explained that the lady was his wife. Hayden turned and instructed his coachman to bring in his valises.

Mr. Alfred grimaced. "Lord Hayden, I regret to say that we do not have any vacant chambers. If we had known you intended to honor us with your patronage, of course we would have ensured—"

"I will use my wife's chamber, under the circumstances. I trust you gave her a comfortable one."

"One of our best."

"Then we will manage."

A servant took the valises. The coachman left to deal with the equipage. Hayden made his way up the stairs to Alexia's room.

It had not taken long to find the hotel Alexia used. He merely sought out the middling respectable ones in good neighborhoods. Alexia was too ingrained with practicality to stay at luxurious lodgings, and too much a lady to reside in a humble inn. All the same, the afternoon was waning before he lit upon Alfred's Hotel. He expected Alexia to return very soon.

While a hotel servant unpacked his garments, Hayden sat at the writing desk and jotted notes to several business associates in Bristol, requesting some information. He sent them off with his coachman, banished the servant from the room, and settled into a chair to wait for his disobedient wife.

He had not thought about her plans very much the day she left. She had made very sure he would not think about much of anything for a long while. The truth had only inched into his mind when her absence the next night had left him awake and hungry again. He then realized that practical, sensible Alexia had deliberately used her feminine wiles on him.

She had succeeded magnificently. The reason why had been obvious once he asked the question. She was not only going to Rose, as announced. She would make her journey to Bristol.

Night began to fall. A servant arrived with some food and to build up the fire and light the lamps. Hayden opened the window and gazed down on the darkening town. If she was searching for Timothy, she might find herself in unsavory areas. The coachman was with her, and she should be safe, but a touch of worry started to compromise the crisp annoyance that he had harbored all the way across England. Time began to tick past very slowly.

He had just convinced himself to go looking for her when the sounds of a carriage arrested his attention. He watched the familiar horses trot down the street and stop beneath his window.

A hotel servant hurried out to help with the carriage door. Alexia stepped down. She paused as the man said something to her. She tilted her head and looked up at the building's facade, to the window where he stood.

The golden light of the carriage lamp washed over her, muting her expression but not hiding it. He had anticipated resentment when she discovered he followed her. That or fear. Instead, her countenance expressed exhaustion. Her shoulders sagged. Her physical sigh said the husband waiting above was an unwelcome nuisance to be tolerated as best she could manage.

He moved away from the window. It took him a moment to conquer the hollow reaction that opened inside him. He had not expected her to be pleased by his pursuit, although a small, romantic fantasy had emerged in which she expressed so much delight in his arrival that he could not find the heart to scold. He knew better than to anticipate a joyful reunion, however, and knew a good row was the more likely result when he found her. That would have been preferable to what he had just seen. He did not like the visible evidence of just how indifferent she truly was.

He reassembled the self-possession that she had demolished with that long sigh. By the time the door latch moved, he had buried boyish anticipation where it would not make a fool of him.

She did not enter the chamber cowed or afraid. She merely walked in, closed the door, and began to unpin her hat.

"You followed me."

"I went down to Aylesbury Abbey to join you and

found you had departed. I knew where you must have gone."

She bent to check her hair in the looking glass propped on the dressing table. "You were not surprised, were you? You guessed while still in London, I think."

"I guessed."

She straightened and faced him. "It appears I am not a very effective seductress."

She was a superb seductress, but he'd be damned before he admitted what she did to him. "It took a few hours before I guessed."

He called up the words to the solid scold he intended to give her. He would not tolerate such disobedience. He could not allow her to travel about at will without informing him. He needed to know for her protection, but he also demanded to know as his right, etc. etc.

"You have every cause to be angry with me," she said, cornering his indignation before he had a chance to voice it. "I deliberately deceived you and took advantage of your attempts to avoid commands. I do not plan to make a habit of it, I want you to know. This one time, however, it was important to me to come here, and so I did it. I can only ask that you forgive me."

Checkmate. He had not even had a chance to make a move.

"You are very clever, Alexia. If I chastise you now, I am an unreasonable, hard man."

Her expression fell. Suddenly the fields of her eyes turned deep and dark. Her posture sagged much as it had outside. "You are correct, and it is not fair of me." She sounded distant. Distracted. "Nor do I have the strength to maintain the pose. Scold all you want,

Hayden. I am thinking it was a mistake for me to do this in any case."

He no longer wanted to scold. There would be no point anyway. In the years ahead, if she ever again thought it important to disobey him, she would.

"Did you find Timothy?" he asked.

She shook her head.

"I know a man here who should be able to direct me to the sorts of places where a young man flush with money might find diversion," he said. "I have written to him. I will find Longworth for you if he is in this city."

She half-emerged out of her daze. "That is very good of you."

"It would not do for you to harrow the gaming hells and bordellos, Alexia."

"I suppose not." She watched him intently now. So intently, so seriously, that she might have never seen him before.

Her outward calm hid a disturbing inner disquiet that trembled out of her. It affected the air and kept her miles away, even though she stood within reach. Far away and . . . sad.

"Where did you go today?" he asked.

"I dealt with the letters."

"Did you find that woman?"

She nodded.

The hollowness opened in him again. Anger tried to fill it. He clenched his teeth to control both reactions. She had spent the afternoon with Benjamin's lover. They had talked for hours. She was still there, her mind still with that woman. And with Ben. The day had all been about another man.

He walked to the window and gazed out so she would not see his reaction.

"Lucinda Morrison is very beautiful," she said. "Exquisitely so. I do not think there is a man alive who would not fall in love with her on sight."

"I would not."

"No, maybe not. That is too poetic, too illogical for you. You might want her on sight, and you might take her, but you would not fall in love with her."

He closed his eyes. She merely described the man she saw. The man that he was. So why did it sound like an insult? A year ago he would have nodded in agreement.

I fell in love with you, damn it. I wanted you on sight, I took you, and then I fell in love with YOU.

"What did Miss Morrison have to say?"

When she did not respond, he turned back to her. She stood, arms crossed over her chest, thinking hard. Her mind was miles away.

Her attention returned to the room, and to him. She unwound herself and came to him. "It was much as I thought and as the letters implied. There was a romantic entanglement, and he sent her some money."

Figures loomed in his head, of thousands of pounds going to Bristol. "How much?"

"I would like to speak of it later, if we could. Maybe tomorrow. There is much to tell you, but I do not want to do it now." She looked around the chamber, and her gaze lit on his personal articles. She finally noticed them, and their meaning surprised her. "You will be staying here with me? Using this chamber?"

"There were no others to be had."

"I am glad."

It was not the response he expected. It flattered him to a ridiculous extent, God help him.

She moved very close to him. The fields still stretched far and dark, the disquiet still trembled, but she was more herself now.

She placed her palm on his chest. "Can we talk later, Hayden? I only want you to kiss me now and take me to bed. I need you to, very much."

She did not have to ask twice.

CHAPTER
TWENTY-ONE

~

She clutched him to her body, tightly. She wrapped her body around his so he stayed near her, his breath entering her and his skin touching hers as much as possible.

She was so grateful he had followed her. So relieved. She needed him here, physical and real, reminding her that this was not a dream, not a memory, but her life now.

She had stayed too long with Benjamin. Talked too intimately. By the time their walk was over, her anger had receded and her heart had softened. For a brief while, too long, too dangerously long, the dam had broken and the old emotions had flowed. They were only poignant memories now, but she had been helpless to stop them.

Lucinda had understood her shock better than Ben had. She insisted Alexia remain for dinner. She had spoken of discretion regarding Ben and how no one else must know. She had wanted to send the coachman for Alexia's belongings and have Alexia visit at Sunley Manor.

Alexia did not want to stay at that house. She had resisted their efforts to convince her to do so. She could not think clearly while Ben smiled at her, could not escape the unreal cast of the entire day. They had delayed her departure past sundown, but she had finally taken her leave.

It all seemed like a peculiar, disquieting dream. She pressed her face against Hayden's arm and inhaled, hoping his scent would banish the confusion that waited like a gargoyle crouched on the edges of her passion. She urged him toward his completion, knowing she would not find her own. Too much of her mind raced elsewhere.

He tried to wait for her but finally could no longer. His power at the end eclipsed everything else. For a few perfect moments he filled her so totally that she had no separateness. She reclaimed the intensity of their passion where he was the only other person in the world.

There was peace then, and afterward for a while. She kept her eyes closed, holding on to it, pretending she had never left London and they were in her bed there.

He braced his weight on his forearms. A gentle touch skimmed her face. "What troubles you, Alexia? Tell me now."

She opened her eyes. He gazed down at her through strands of mussed hair. She wondered if his concern would turn to anger if she told him. Maybe the warmth would disappear behind the cool arrogance that so effectively masked the inner man.

"Did her beauty pain you, is that it? Do you assume he loved her more, now that you have seen her face? It does not always work that way. That kind of love is a shallow, brief emotion if there is no character to hold a man's interest."

She almost wept at his attempt to comfort her. He even broached the subject of her old love to do so. He thought it was childishly romantic to hold on to those memories, but now he tried to preserve them for her.

She did not deserve such kindness. And he deserved more honesty. He was her husband. She should not lie to him. She could not, even though Benjamin and Lucy had requested her silence. The thought of maintaining such a deception had saddened her when she learned who was waiting in this chamber.

She hesitated, painfully aware that she was making a choice between an old loyalty and a new one, between two men who had claims on her, each in his own way. Her heart whispered that there was no choice, not really. Hayden was her husband, and she wanted desperately to confide in him. Still, she could not escape the fear that she balanced on a precipice and any step would be ir-revocable.

"Hayden, it is not her face that distresses me, nor even his love for her," she said. "She does not live alone with his memory like I did. He is there with her, truly and physically. Ben is not dead as we believed. I saw him today and spoke to him."

He stared down, incredulous. As belief sank in, his expression darkened. His embrace tightened. "He can-not have you now. It is too late. You are my wife."

It was an odd thing to say on hearing that a dead friend actually lived. It was the last reaction she ex-pected.

"And she is his. He is married to her. Are you so

stunned that you cannot think straight? I said he is *alive*. He jumped off that ship, but not to his death. It was all planned, I am sure of it."

He moved off her and flipped onto his back by her side. His shock filled the air, darkly.

"That scoundrel," he muttered. "That bastard."

Ben had said the same thing about him. One good friendship would not survive this resurrection.

"Tell me all of it, Alexia."

She described their conversation but not the smiles and touches or the way he kissed her hand or walked close by. She explained the big debt and the ruin Ben had faced and his decision to fake his death to save his family. Hayden listened, not commenting even when she admitted she had told Ben about Timothy's fall in fortune and Hayden's own role in it.

"He wanted me to swear to tell no one what I had discovered, but I left without doing so," she said. "I wanted to think about that before I gave my word. His sisters should know he is alive, don't you think? It was very wrong of him to allow us all to grieve. I do not care why he did it or whom he protected, it was cruel all the same."

"He protected himself," he said. "Tell me about this property where he lives."

She described Sunley Manor. "They appeared comfortable. I told him he must find a way to send his sisters some money."

"Oh, I am sure he is comfortable. More than passing so." He turned on his side and cupped her chin in his hand. "You are not to return there. Not alone, at least, and not at all until I say."

"I told them that tomorrow—"

"No. I forbid it. Do not get willful on me, Alexia. Do not disobey this time. You will not return tomorrow."

She did not mind this command. She was not sure she wanted to return to Sunley Manor ever again. She was joyed Ben was alive, but she did not like how the day had confused and saddened her. The entire experience had left her stomach in knots.

He leaned over and gutted the lamp. She snuggled closer to him in the dark, relieved she had entrusted him with the secret, hoping she had done the right thing. "He is not happy. He called it a devil's bargain."

"That is a fitting name for such a scheme. Go to sleep now. Tomorrow I will find Timothy if he is in Bristol, and I will decide what to do about Benjamin."

She had begun to doze when a thought occurred to her. "Hayden, he said he is not known by his name here but by another one. Not Mr. Morrison either, I don't think. I do not know what name it is. I never asked."

"I think I know the name. I will be sure soon enough. I will know everything in a day or two."

She looked at his profile in the dark. She could tell his eyes were open. He had told her to sleep, but she wondered if he would.

She nestled in. His warmth comforted her. He would know what to do now. After all, he already had guessed Ben's new name. As she drifted into sleep, she vaguely wondered how.

The bloody rogue.

Hayden heaped silent insults on Benjamin Longworth while he stared into the night. He did not like being played for a fool, no matter what the reason, and Ben had been ruthless in doing so.

It had all been a feint. The melancholy. The feigned drunkenness. Had Ben guessed that Hayden would suspect suicide? Had that been part of the plan or a miscalculation?

The bastard. The *idiot*. He could have died trying to swim to shore. Of all the reckless, crazy things Ben had ever done, this had been the worst.

Only it had worked. He had escaped Suttonly's squeeze and been able to enjoy the fruits of his crimes. His mind's eye saw the dispersals from the Bank of England again. The ones to Bristol had begun long before those to Suttonly. This whole plan was an old one, then, started very early, probably when the forgeries first began. Ben might have intended all along to disappear. Suttonly had only made that move imperative.

Pennilot. That was the name on the Bristol account, and it was not an old debt of his father's that he repaid with that money. He pictured Benjamin grinning boyishly as he chose it, amused by his own cleverness. Pennilot. A lot of pennies. A man with a lot of pennies was worth a lot. Longworth. Knowing Ben, the whole plan, from the forgeries to hiding the money to jumping off that ship, had been one big adventure, a grand game in which one impulse followed another.

Except people had been grievously injured. Darfield and the victims of the forgeries. His own sisters and brother. And a dependent cousin who believed his lies of love.

He felt Alexia's breath on his shoulder and her warmth lining his body. He understood her mood tonight now. For the first time, they had not been alone in bed. Another had intruded. He had sensed the preoccupation that prevented her completion, the desperation of her embrace. Seeing Benjamin again had called forth the old love. It was not just a memory now.

He took comfort in the fact she had confided in him. She had not kept Ben's secret. She had told him as her husband and as Ben's friend. She slept peacefully now, as if her revelation settled everything. He doubted it did. Ben could not allow Alexia to return to London knowing what she knew.

She turned in her sleep. He moved behind her and formed his body along hers. He embraced her, careful not to wake her.

He did not know what lure Ben might hold out to her, but one thing was certain. She would not go to Sunley Manor alone again. It was a wonder they had allowed her to leave today.

He did not want to think Ben would harm Alexia, or any innocent person, but then, he would have never guessed Ben would commit the crime of utterance or steal a fortune. He would have never suspected Ben would let his sisters grieve over his death while he took his pleasure in Bristol. And this woman Ben had married might prove capable of worse than her husband.

A lot was at stake, after all. Right now in Sunley Manor, Benjamin was calculating just how much.

Alexia obeyed Hayden this time. She did not go to Sunley Manor the next day. She stayed at Alfred's Hotel while Hayden left to learn what he could about Timothy.

Morning waned and the sun rose high while she awaited his return. Hopefully Tim could be found before he wasted all the money from the Bank of England. No doubt he spent his days looking for secret accounts in Benjamin's name, but he might well be spending his nights in gaming hells.

Hayden had been very careful with her this morning. Careful and quiet but also firm in his commands. She was not to leave the hotel. She was not to travel to Sunley Manor. He told her coachman to refuse to take her, she suspected, just in case she chose to be willful again. She had not missed the lack of trust in the way he exercised his rights. She did not think it was her last disobedience that caused it.

He assumed she would want to see Ben again. He thought the memories held a power over her.

Did they? She tried to look beneath the shock and confusion and hear what her heart said about that. Bracing herself, she faced those memories squarely.

She could not deny that seeing Ben had freed the girl whom she kept imprisoned in her heart. A giggle had wanted to bubble through her too often yesterday. Ben could still evoke that in her, but it was a mere echo of a silly excitement from the past.

She looked over at the bed. There was nothing silly about what happened there. Nothing shallow about the power of that passion. Benjamin had tickled her heart like a light spring breeze. Hayden lured her essence into the deep mysteries of a hot summer night.

She closed her eyes and thought about her last night in London. She could not picture herself doing those things with Ben. Ben was all about laughs and kisses and flattery, not the soul-stirring unity that she experienced with Hayden. Hayden's inner man was a wonder to know and a mystery to be explored. She did not think Ben had any inner man at all.

She wished Hayden would return. She wanted him with her now, solid and real. She wanted him to soothe away all her distress and confusion as he had last night.

"Alexia."

She opened her eyes. A man stood just inside her room. It was not the man she wanted.

Benjamin smiled at her. Did she only imagine that his expression appeared cautious? It was hard to tell, because he wore a hat low on his brow. Its brim cast a shadow over his face.

"Mr. Alfred allowed you up here? Did he tell you which room was mine?"

He removed the hat. "I slipped up, and I saw you sitting by the window when I was down in the street. Please forgive me, but I had to see you. When you did not return to Sunley Manor, I decided to come to you."

"I thought you never came into town."

"Very rarely. A high collar and a low hat go far in hiding a passing face, however." He advanced on her. "Why did you not come back this morning as you promised?"

"I needed to think about my discovery. I wanted to recover from the shock of it before I spoke with you again."

"Is that what you were doing there, thinking and recovering? You appeared so serious."

"I am a rather serious person now. It was always in me, but circumstances have made it more significant."

He laughed lightly. "You were never so serious with me, darling."

"I was very serious. It may have been a game to you, but not to me."

His face fell. "A game? Is that what you think? I knew that I should have spoken more openly yesterday. I did not toy with you, Alexia. You stole my heart completely."

Not completely, but his declaration touched her anyway. Her pride liked hearing she had not been *too* stupid.

"I wish you did not come, Ben. It was unwise. Your wife will not be pleased."

"She knows I came. She is worried that you will betray me. She wants me to beg you not to do so."

"She worries a lot about a small thing. If your family knows you live, what harm is there? Your sisters and I can keep your secret. The man to whom you owed that debt will never find out."

"It is more complicated than that. I must ask you to trust me, darling. I cannot risk the world learning."

"And I cannot promise others will not learn. One has already." She glanced pointedly around the chamber.

Ben's gaze followed her direction to the man's brushes on the dressing table and the boots standing outside the wardrobe. His face flushed. "*He* is here? You never said that he had accompanied you."

Hayden walked in the door just then. "She did not know I was coming. I arrived last night."

Ben pivoted. They faced each other. Time inched forward.

"It is good to see you alive and well, old friend," Hayden finally said.

Ben tried one of his dazzling smiles. "There is an explanation."

Hayden sighed deeply. She doubted Ben noticed, but she did. His expression of forbearance revealed how this reunion pained him. He looked much as she had been feeling.

"Of course there is an explanation, Ben. However, there is no excuse." He walked over to Alexia, ignoring Ben for a moment. "I received the information I sought. I should locate him this afternoon." He raised his voice. "I am speaking of Timothy, Ben. You remember Timothy, don't you?"

"Of course I remember my brother."

"Why don't we seek him together, Ben? It will not take long. If you traveled this town's streets to visit another man's wife in secret, you can risk it to see that your brother is safe."

"Are you suggesting— See here, Rothwell, I will not allow you to insult her by insinuating—"

"I do not insult her at all. I merely impugn you." Hayden strode to the door. "Come now. We can argue as we go. Alexia, do not allow anyone in. Bar the door this time, even to servants."

"You were damned rude in there," Ben blustered as soon as he and Hayden reached the street.

"I found a man in a bedchamber with my wife. I have a right to be rude."

"She is my cousin."

"You were more than a cousin to her."

"If Alexia told you that she and I shared a *tendre,* she must have misunderstood my concern for her. You know how women can be, especially ones who have been left on the shelf. It is a damned shame when a man cannot visit his cousin without having scurrilous suspicions raised."

Ben's insistence that he had been tragically misunderstood took them all the way into Hayden's waiting carriage.

"Alexia is not a woman who would build dreams on nothing. Be glad I did not thrash you up there. Pray I do not now."

"That is a hell of a welcome back." He sank back on his cushions. He had the audacity to look hurt. "But I understand you are still too shocked to know your own joy." He beamed a smile and leaned over to clap a firm hand on Hayden's shoulder. "Damnation, but it is rum to see you. I am almost glad that Alexia confided in you, since it allows this reunion, even though I told her that I cannot let the whole world know."

"I am not the whole world. Just one man, and the last one you should fear knowing."

Ben smiled his way to indifference while he took inventory of the carriage appointments. He examined the upholstery, curtains, and woodwork so long he might be buying the equipage. It was the studied business of a man ill at ease.

"Where are we going?" he asked.

"To a tavern. This reunion deserves a good deal of drink, don't you think?"

"Like old times. I knew you would come around once you . . . well, once you got past—"

"Once I got past the urge to beat you bloody because you deceived me in the worst way? You let me think you died, and you allowed me to believe I left you to do so."

Ben rearranged his body on the bench, as if the carriage walls crowded him. "Is my brother going to meet us at the tavern?"

"I am fairly certain that we will find Timothy before the day is out."

The carriage stopped on a street of shops and businesses. Ben glanced out the window and his face flushed. They were in front of a tavern frequented by lawyers and tradesmen, the sort who would spend their days in the City if this were London. Across the street and up several doors was the entrance to Ketchum, Martin, and Cook, a county bank.

Hayden led the way out of the carriage and into the tavern. Finding a table next to the window, he positioned himself so he could see the street in front of the bank.

They called for ale, silently awaited its arrival, then sat facing each other over their pints. Ben looked over his shoulder at the facade of the bank only once, but every glance he sent Hayden contained growing caution.

"You have not said one word about your family's circumstances," Hayden said. "Alexia told you what happened, what I did, but you have expressed no anger and asked no questions."

"I was angry yesterday when she told me. I know how these things can go, however. Any crisis makes men worried, and this was a bad one. Over seventy banks have failed, after all. You had a responsibility to your family and decided the risks you saw were too great. I do not blame you. If my brother had proven a better banker, it might not have been necessary."

"That is damned understanding of you. I should have you talk to my wife and explain all that. She blames me most severely." He drank his ale while he checked the window's view again. "Of course, she does not know what really happened. The truth is that my family's money is still in that bank. Timothy told her a lie that I am bound by honor not to correct."

Ben looked relieved. "I told her Tim had most likely lost it all on gambling and such. I knew you would not destroy them like that. Not my family."

"Oh, I destroyed them. There is no question there. I sent them packing to Oxfordshire with little pride and less money. Oddly enough, it was intended as a kindness, as the lesser of two paths to ruin."

"I am sure you did your best." His tone communicated finality. *No need to explain, old friend. Whatever you did is fine with me.*

"Ben, I discovered that Timothy had committed utterance and embezzled money from bank patrons. His theft is why he is ruined. It was sell out and take on debt to reimburse his victims, or swing."

Ben's reaction would do a comic opera actor proud. "You shock me with this accusation against my brother. Utterance? Theft?"

"He was forging names on securities, selling them, keeping the money, and continuing to pay off the income."

"You have distressed me beyond composure. This is not my brother's character."

"He has the character for it, but it takes more than a lack of honesty to effect such a sophisticated swindle. The problem, and I should have seen it at once, is that while Tim could talk himself into stealing tens of thousands of pounds, he is not brilliant enough to figure out *how.* His character was up to it but not his mind."

Ben frowned, perhaps deciding if he should defend his brother's mental capabilities. "No doubt he read about a previous, similar embezzlement."

"It has only happened once before that is commonly known. I expect other banks may have found ways to compensate prior victims of similar crimes, all without the thief ever standing for judgment. No bank could survive the scandal if it became known."

"It doesn't sound like a complicated scheme. Tim could have devised the scheme on his own."

"But he didn't, did he? He learned it from you."

Ben went still. He gazed at his ale and no part of him moved, not even his fingertips resting on the glass.

"How much do you know?"

"Not that you were still alive, but most of the rest."

He sighed deeply. "The more I thought about what Alexia had told me, how you ruined them, the more I worried. All night my certainty grew that you had discovered it all. I knew you were not likely to make a move that would force the bank to fail. How did you find out?"

"Timothy made the mistake of forging my name and selling funds on which I was trustee."

"Damn." He slammed his fist on the table. "The *idiot."*

"Hell of a thing, isn't it? When the student does not learn the niceties from the master."

He received a snarling glare for that, but Ben could never remain angry long. "I suppose we should all thank you for not prosecuting him. Although . . ."

Although if he had, there would have been a run on the bank and it would have failed and closed. Maybe no one would have ever learned that the older Longworth brother had done the same thing. Should the earlier thefts come to light, they would have been blamed on the executed Timothy, not the dead Benjamin.

Ben rested back in his chair. His relaxation implied remaining on his guard had been an effort and he was happy to drop it. "The first time was a loan of sorts. An attempt to settle a debt honorably. I wanted to get out from under the last of my father's obligations. Unfortunately, it was a big one, to a financier of the worst kind. The little land left and the house in Oxfordshire had been pledged as surety, and he was going to take it in his impatience. So I looked for a way to pay it off fast and completely. I always intended to make them whole."

"Why didn't you?"

"One of the first discovered what I had done. He allowed me to reimburse him, but in order to do so I had to forge more names, sell more securities—well, by then I was in deep."

"That would be Keiller in York?"

"You do know most of it, don't you?"

"I found the account at the Bank of England. I saw the early dispersals to Keiller's bank account."

Ben stilled again. He did not glance back at the bank across the street, but his mind seemed to snap alert to the symbolism of their current location.

"I realized the danger then. Most of those funds sat there forever. Most were in trust. But there was always the chance someone would actually want to sell, after I had already done so. That would be awkward."

"That is how I learned you, not Timothy, had devised the scheme. Sir Matthew Rolland came to Darfield and wanted to sell."

"Sir Matthew? Who would have guessed. He rarely even came to town. Well, I knew that just such a situation could be my undoing."

"Is that how Suttonly learned the truth?"

Ben glared at him. "*Hell.* You did not let any of it go, did you? I hope that you confronted the bastard. He ruined everything. He kept bleeding me and bleeding me—it *amused* him to see me cornered, to see me sweat. Damnation, Hayden, for a smart man you have some bad judgments in your choice of friends. Suttonly is a bloody rogue."

Hayden smiled at the irony of Ben's indignation. It was a sad amusement, however. He would lose two old friends because of this sorry business and gain nothing at all.

That was not true. He had gained Alexia. But for this knot of crimes, he might have never come to know her. She more than balanced the accounts.

"I should never have gone near Suttonly's funds," Ben said. "It was careless. But it was such a damnably small amount. A thousand. A mere token, thrown in when you asked your friends to help me get established.

I assumed he would never remember it was even there. Nor did I dream that when I asked for time to produce the securities, he would send his solicitor to demand them immediately. I had no choice but to admit what I had done and offer to make him whole."

"He refused?"

"He knew one utterance was enough to send me to the gallows, no matter how small the amount. He could bleed me and there was nothing I could do to stop it."

Except die.

"I paid him fifteen times what I had taken, and he only demanded more. It seemed all I gained went to him. I was stealing just to satisfy him."

"Terrible."

"I know that tone." Anger crystallized his eyes. "Are you enjoying this? Approving of how that devil made my life hell? You think I deserved it, don't you? You are sitting there in that damned moral superiority paid for with Easterbrook money, thinking I was lucky to get bled only symbolically." He looked away in disgust. "Hell, the older you get, the more you are like your father."

It was an old goad, the one sure to get a reaction. Hayden barely controlled what it did to him. "Since I am his son, it is not surprising some of him is in me."

"More than some. More than in the others. *Some* of his sons escaped his legacy better than you ever will." Any attempts at hiding his frustration disappeared. "Why are we sitting here, in this tavern, at this table? What is your game? Are we waiting for a magistrate? Are you enough like him to do it? Hand me over in the name of justice and right?"

Hayden could not answer that. He had not decided that part yet.

His silence stunned Ben. "*Damnation,* man, are you really thinking of doing it? How can you? You *owe* me better. You would have been flayed alive in that farmhouse, and no one, *no one,* was willing to attempt to get you out. Except *me.* You like calculations, work that one out. What were the chances I would survive that day?"

Poor. At best one in five odds. But Ben's pistols were loaded and the Turks were busy enjoying their torture, and once a shot was fired, others had rushed to help too. Still—

It would have been a terrible death. Ignoble. The kind where the last conscious thought is horror and the last sound is one's own screams.

Ben leaned forward, pressing his advantage. "No other friend would have charged in that day."

"I accept that I owe you a debt of honor," he said. "I protected your brother because of it. I am protecting your name as well. There are limits, however, to what I will give you and what I will do in payment."

"You don't have to do anything except stay out of my way."

That was not true, but a movement across the street arrested Hayden's attention. A man with straw-colored hair beneath his high-crowned hat sauntered toward the entry of Ketchum, Martin, and Cook.

Ben stiffened as he recognized his brother. "What is he doing?"

"Looking for the money. He has been visiting all the banks in town. He must have guessed that the money sent to Bristol was not to repay one of your father's debts but to hide your treasure."

Ben watched his brother's progress with an expression of concern and indecision.

"He came to this bank first, because it is a corresponding bank to the Bank of England and would be easy for you to use while in London," Hayden said. "Of course, there was no account under the name Benjamin Longworth."

"So why is he returning?"

"He has realized you may have used a different name. He did not dally in London to examine that old account to see the dispersals, so he doesn't know the name. However, he revisited at least one bank already today, describing you, explaining the situation, providing the information on the London account. He is asking the banks to investigate those early drafts and where they went. He hopes to prove the account was yours, opened under an alias, and claim it as your heir." Hayden took a good drink of ale. "Unfortunately, it is an active account and one that Mr. Pennilot has used recently. If he convinces them you opened it under an alias, he unknowingly proves that you are not dead."

"Hell." Ben was out the door in an instant. Hayden followed.

Ben hurried across the street. He came up behind Timothy just as Tim was about to enter the bank.

Ben grabbed his brother's arm. Tim swung around, ready to fend off an assault.

They both froze. Timothy stuck his face close to Ben's, then reared back in shock. He shook the hand off his arm.

Another frozen moment passed while Ben said something. Hayden approached and saw Timothy's distorted expression as the implications of this resurrection sank in.

Just as Hayden was about to reach them, Timothy grabbed Ben's shoulder with his left hand. With his right fist, he landed a solid punch square on Benjamin's jaw.

CHAPTER
TWENTY-TWO

Dark had fallen by the time Hayden returned to Alexia.

"Did you find Timothy?" she asked.

"We found him. He has gone to Sunley Manor with Benjamin."

"I expect they have a lot to talk about."

"Yes, they have many things to discuss."

By the time he pulled Timothy off Benjamin, the most important one had been settled, however. The talk at Sunley Manor would be very practical now.

He had decided to let them deal with it alone. He preferred not to know what Ben would explain to his brother. Since Tim had been waylaid before entering the bank, no one might ever know that Benjamin Longworth and Harrison Pennilot were one and the same.

And Tim might never know that Mr. Pennilot had removed all that money from Ketchum, Martin, and Cook this morning.

Ben was going to bolt. He was sure of it. It would

resolve many things very neatly, but he could not shake a worry about it. Nor could he keep his mind from calculating all kinds of odds and probabilities and weighing whether he could afford to allow it to happen.

You owe me. Up to a point, yes. But not everything. There were limits to any debt.

Alexia went to the wardrobe and removed a shawl. "I am glad that you made Ben see Timothy. I have decided to tell Rose what we discovered here. It is only right. Perhaps Ben will agree to have her visit at Sunley Manor, so she can see him again too."

She might be chilled, but he was not. He removed his frock coat. "Ben's wife, Lucinda. While you visited yesterday, did you see a warm marriage?"

"I was an unexpected visitor, and the situation was hardly normal. He spoke of being a prisoner of his circumstances, but perhaps now that he can contact his family, he will not feel that so much."

She put more fuel on the fire. He watched her efficient movements. They were very elegant despite their practical purpose. The light from the fire illuminated her profile with a golden haze. Her eyes appeared a dark, royal purple.

"Do you want me to call for dinner? Or should we go below?" she asked.

"I am not hungry now. Are you?"

"I have been too unsettled to be hungry."

She hid it well, how unsettled she was. He sensed it in her, beneath her serene expression. Last night it had owned her, but perhaps she was accommodating the shock and all it meant.

Did she weigh it all as she brushed his coat and hung

it in the wardrobe? Was she thinking of Ben while she told him to sit and insisted on helping him remove his boots? He was glad she did not call for a hotel servant to tend to these domestic details. He did not want anyone else here with them tonight.

"He will not see his sisters. He is going to leave England, Alexia. Very soon."

She set the boots beside the wardrobe, closed its door, then rested her back against it.

"Did he tell you that?"

"No. However, I am sure he will." Ben had to leave now. He could not trust Hayden with his life. He had made the decision not to four years ago. The only question was whether he would go alone or take someone with him. Timothy, whose neck was also in danger? His wife, Lucinda?

Alexia?

"Why will he leave? Not because of an old debt, the way he says. What frightens him? He is very afraid, Hayden."

Her perception impressed him, but then it always had. She had a story that fit the facts she knew, but she saw more subterfuge than they warranted.

There was much he wanted to say to her. Not only about the knot of deceptions that began that day in the drawing room, but about things that caused other knots, in his heart and soul.

"You said on our wedding day that there was more to Timothy's ruin than I know. I would like to believe you would have explained it to me if you could."

"I have often cursed that I cannot."

She nodded thoughtfully. "I have had most of the day

to think about that, and about finding Benjamin, and these bank accounts that Timothy looks for. I have been thinking about you, Hayden, and the man that I now know you to be." She cocked her head. "You cannot tell me about my cousins, but you can tell me about yourself, can't you?"

"That depends on whether I know the answer. We don't always know ourselves well."

She laughed lightly. "How true. I am learning much about myself of late. My question is very simple. If you can answer it, I will know that some of what I concluded today is correct."

"Then ask it."

"Did you remove your family's money from Darfield and Longworth? Or was Mr. Darfield waiting for *you* that day that I visited him?"

He calculated what he could say and still honor his word of honor. "I removed Aunt Henrietta's trust."

She strolled across the chamber and sat in the chair by the writing table again. "I have done you a disservice in believing you wronged my cousins, haven't I?"

"Your trust in Timothy and your concern for your cousins were understandable. They are your family."

"But you are my husband."

The solid way she said it touched him. How strong would this new loyalty be if tested by an old one? He wished he were certain that duty would guide her, if nothing else did.

He could make sure there was no test. He had it in his power to ensure that Ben could never lure her, could not exploit her nostalgia, could not tug at the old memories and pull her away. He need only call for the justice of the peace and lay down information about Ben's crimes. No Longworth would get on any ship in the harbor then. And no appeals could be made to Alexia's long-held love.

She would hate him if he sent Ben and Tim to the gallows. He would still have her, but she would despise him. His father had held on to a wife through power and force. He had made every day of her life a punishment for loving another man. He hated his father for that. He hated even more that he now understood why it had happened, how pride and possession had brought it about.

It had never before occurred to him that it had been love, not cruelty, that caused that misery. The passion of a man for a woman who loved another could be dangerous. He was trying to control just how dangerous.

He went to the chair and knelt on one knee in front of her. He took her hand, so small and elegant, and pressed a kiss to its warmth. He closed his eyes and savored the sensation of her skin beneath his lips.

She stretched her fingers through his hair. "You are so pensive. Do you regret that he must leave so soon after you got him back?"

Do you? "It is not that. I was admiring how beautiful you are and noticing how your smallest movements are graceful."

She quirked a skeptical smile and ruffled his hair. The gesture dismissed what he had said.

"You do not believe me."

"I know I am not beautiful. It is sweet of you to flatter me, though."

"You are very beautiful. Just seeing you stirs me. Your beauty has left me helpless from the start, darling.

Reckless. It is more than pleasure that draws me. I am in love with you."

Surprise and disbelief shimmered over her face. The declaration made his heart too full, but he did not regret it. He needed her to know.

He did not wait for a response. He was not sure he wanted one. He caressed down her leg, lifted her skirts, and raised one of her legs to his knee. He slipped off her shoe and began rolling down her hose.

He pressed a kiss to the smooth white skin of the leg that he unveiled, then began on the other.

"You appear embarrassed, Alexia. I have undressed you before."

She smiled weakly. "That was different."

"How so? Because you accepted it as my courtesan in marriage before? Is it more embarrassing to be the wife I love?"

She blushed deeply. "Am I allowed to enjoy it if I am the wife you love?"

He laughed. He leaned over her, bracing an arm on the back of her chair. He kissed her and caressed under her skirts to the unbearable softness of her thigh. "If you do not enjoy it, I will be insulted."

Her hips shifted as his hand stroked her. "That may be the only insult I have failed to give you since we met."

"Then do not let what I said interfere now, my love. Do not feel an obligation to respond in kind either. Whatever you choose to call it, it was never just duty."

He released her dress hooks and stood her up so he could lower her garments. She blushed again as he slid off the last one and helped her step out of the pile at her feet. He admired her naked body, washed with the golden haze of the lamplight and fire. She was all soft and pale, like Correggio's Io, all gentle curves and totally feminine. She was so lovely it made him hurt.

He drew her to him and embraced her hips, his hands cupping her bottom. He pressed a kiss to her stomach, then laid his face on her skin. He lost himself in her scent and warmth.

Desire tensed through him. It arrived with a powerful force and ferocious impatience. He almost pulled her down on the floor to have her at once. To claim her the only way he knew how.

Instead, he stood and picked her up and carried her to the bed. He began stripping off his clothes. She knelt on the bed to help. She plucked at his cravat until it hung loose. With an impish smile, she carefully worked the buttons of his waistcoat.

He decided to let her. It meant he could use his hands for other things, like caressing her breasts. While she handled his garments, he handled her body, whisking the tight tips of her nipples until the pleasure made her balance unsteady. Her expression turned dreamy with erotic softness.

No one intruded this time. He did not know what the morning would bring, but she was completely with him now. He intended to love her so thoroughly, possess her so completely, that there was no room in her thoughts and soul for anything else tonight.

He began to unfasten his lower garments, but she returned his hands to her breast and reached for the buttons herself. "Do not stop. It is like heaven. I will do this for you."

He made it as heavenly as he could while she fumbled to release him. She pushed the garments down with sinuous caresses that had his control splitting apart.

He lifted her and stood her on the bed in front of him. He could touch all of her now, from her flushed expression of ecstasy to her feet. She looked down at him while he praised every inch of her with his hands, glossing her curves, saturating his memory with the sounds and signs of her abandon. The scent of her arousal perfumed the air. The slickness weeping onto her thighs said she was ready. Unsteady now, she parted her feet for better balance and held his shoulders.

He guided her head down so he could kiss her mouth, then tasted her skin down a path to her breasts. Her fingers gripped his shoulders harder as he flicked his tongue again and again over those sensitive tips. Her quiet moans entered his blood and made him harder and more determined to make her crazed.

So it surprised him when her body shifted away from his mouth and her own lips began blazing a path downward. Breath and warmth and moisture pressed at his neck and shoulders, then down his chest. She lowered her body until she knelt in front of him again. Her kisses continued their scorching, downward journey.

Roaring hunger crashed into romantic intentions. When her velvet palm encircled his cock and her other hand's fingers tortured its tip, the howling pleasure left room for no thoughts at all.

She looked down at the caresses she gave, then up at his face and the reaction she commanded. She was not blind to her power. She had recognized it the first night of their marriage.

Right now he was her slave. Desire's urge ruled every thought and sense, and he wanted her to use her mouth again so much it maddened him.

Her circling hand firmed, then slid up and down. Pleasure shuddered violently through his body.

"Is the wife you love allowed the same liberties as your courtesan in marriage?"

His mind sluggishly arranged what she said and what she meant. Women had some very odd ideas sometimes.

"Do you think I am such an idiot as to want you to be timid now?"

"I did not know. Men have some very odd ideas sometimes."

"Not this one. I'm close to begging the wife I love."

She smiled erotically. "We can't have that tonight. Another time, perhaps." Her hand moved again, obliterating his suspicions about that last sentence. Her head dipped. Teeth gently nipped. Lips softly kissed. Moist warmth encased him, and he was lost.

"Do not move." His voice drew her out of a sated daze. She had been as close to sleep as a body could be but still alert to his presence surrounding her. The sweet poignancy of their second loving still saturated her. There was no world outside this bed tonight.

He loved her. She doubted such a man lied about that. He was the kind who would be very sure before making such a declaration. He would examine the emotion this way and that, argue its validity, be skeptical of its truth. From what she could tell, he did not even believe in such things, so it must have been very odd to decide he was in love.

The words meant a lot to her, but the way she felt it in him tonight meant more. He had named a power that had been between them for some time. She was trying to decide if it was the right name, however.

He rose on one arm beside her. She lay on her stomach while he looked at her and caressed down her back and over her bottom.

The stirring began at once, those deep shivers that heralded the secret parts of her body coming alive. It did not take long for her arousal to grow and to demand more. Eventually the sensation and the need for completion would drive her to abandon and to an intensity that removed her from the world.

His hand beckoned her to go there now, to that state where she was reckless and wild and free. It slid over her nakedness in that masterful way he handled her. No other touch would affect her the same way.

She closed her eyes and just felt. Thinking was for tomorrow. When dawn came, she would know if the emotions of this night had been real. She would look at him away from the physical excitement, and she would know. The practical Miss Welbourne would never lie to herself about a man again.

She turned her head and looked up at him. Passion set his expression into that special sternness that made him too handsome to bear. It was the face of a man about to take what he wanted.

She glimpsed the palest gray light seeping beneath

the curtains. "Dawn comes." She did not remember so much time passing.

"Soon. Not yet."

His caresses created the most luscious stirring. It shimmered through her entire body. He splayed his hand over the hill of one buttock, and more concentrated arrows of arousal pricked at her. His fingertips slid along her crevice, and the erotic implications made her lift her hips.

His path aimed low, between her thighs. She parted her legs to accept it. He watched her body, her acceptance, *his* power. The way he watched made her feel small and vulnerable. He gently stroked the soft folds of flesh made incredibly sensitive tonight by his hands and mouth.

He dipped his head and kissed her shoulder. "I love you, Alexia," he whispered hoarsely. "I am very grateful that you married me."

Tears burned her eyes. She did not know why.

She thought he intended to possess her with the dominance he showed the night he found her crying in her bed at Hill Street. It surprised her when he lifted and turned her and laid her atop him. She rose up and took him inside her, and they joined in a beautiful rhythm of unity.

She could see him clearly the whole way. Silvery light bathed his face and body and revealed his expression of passion. Only now the warmth she glimpsed beneath his desire, the emotion that exposed the inner man, had a name.

Her heart trembled in response, then opened to accept all that he offered.

———

The notes were delivered while they ate breakfast in their chamber. Hayden knew they would be coming. He was waiting for them.

One was for him and one for Alexia. In his, Ben wrote briefly and without sentiment.

I must leave, of course. I cannot risk that you will stay the course forever, now that you know everything. Tim will come with me, since he is in danger just as I am. I ask you to allow my cousin to meet us at the dock, so I can give her some money for my sisters. We are sailing on the Tintern. *Tide is at eleven.*

He set the letter down and returned to his breakfast. Mr. Pennilot's money would sail on the *Tintern,* which meant someone else would pay off all those victims. Since he was that someone, being correct about the denouement of this opera did not make him smug.

Alexia's letter was longer. "You were correct," she said. "He is leaving England. I think that is rash."

"Well, he was always impulsive."

"He says he has some money for Rose. I guess there was an account here in Bristol after all. He was putting money away all those years, I think, and telling his family he was paying off their father's last debt. He let Rose go without a season so he could do this." Her mouth pursed with disapproval. "He has asked me to see them off. I will do so with some very strong words regarding his behavior."

"If he wants to say good-bye, he can come here."

"They are not at Sunley Manor this morning. There is no way to tell him to come here." She studied him, confused. "Are you forbidding me to go there and say good-bye?"

Was he? Should he?

He stood and walked to the window. In the distance, above the rooftops, he could see the masts of ships.

He was not accustomed to the fullness in his chest. The worst thing about love was that it lacked certainty, and perhaps permanence. It also made one weak, he was learning. Weak and sentimental and impractical and jealous and protective. It made one doubt what was real and question what was known. It complicated the hell out of life.

He turned back to her. She waited patiently for his answer. Would he forbid her to say good-bye to her two cousins? Would he be that callous?

"He is going to ask you to go with him, Alexia."

She unsuccessfully bit back a laugh. "You are becoming too dramatic. I know that love changes a man, but really, darling."

"I am very sure he will have bought you a passage and ask you to stay on that ship."

"He is married to one of the most beautiful women in England, and he knows I am married to you." She came over to him. Amusement brightened her eyes. "I am flattered that you think me worth such a scandalous proposal and that you care enough to be concerned. I am nothing to him now, however. I want to say good-bye all the same. And I want to get that money for Rose."

She was all confidence and certainty. That soothed

the lover's worry that wanted to make him foolish and severe.

He was not sure she would resist for his sake. Rather, the practical Miss Welbourne would never succumb to the blandishments of a man asking her to run away and live in adultery.

On the other hand, it would not be the practical Miss Welbourne whom Ben would lure but the young woman who had loved him and mourned him years ago.

He took her hand and pressed it to his lips. He gazed into violet fields that stretched for miles into the distance.

He would let her go to the docks. Not out of any obligation to Ben. He owed Ben much, but he did not owe the man his wife.

He would do it for Alexia, because he wanted her to have whatever would make her happy, God help him.

And he would allow it out of respect for his mother, who had been imprisoned in a practical marriage, apart from her first love.

But he would also do it for himself, so that maybe he would not become a man like his father, who turned bitter and hard from facing that unhappy wife and remembering the pain of her betrayal every day of his life.

It was not difficult to convince Hayden to allow her to go to the *Tintern*. He was not an unreasonable man. With both Ben and Tim abandoning their sisters most ignobly, she needed to obtain what money she could from them first.

She had not expected him to allow her to go alone,

however. She thought he would want to say good-bye to Ben too. Perhaps things had not gone well when they found Timothy yesterday. Maybe that old friendship had been destroyed by all the deceptions.

Her carriage brought her to the docks and where the *Tintern* laid anchor. High tide was due to crest soon in the sea channel downriver. She spied Ben on the deck, looking down at the bustle of a ship ready to get under way.

He saw her and waved his arm. He met her halfway up the gangway. "Come to our cabin and see Tim," he said. "I am very glad you came, Alexia."

"I look forward to seeing Timothy. I have something to say to him." She intended to scold them both soundly once they were in that cabin.

The cabin was larger than she expected. She noticed Timothy had lost no time getting ill again. He lounged on one of the beds, wearing all the signs of too much drink.

She noted the absence of any woman's baggage and the evidence Tim would share this cabin. "Where is Lucinda?"

"She never wanted to go abroad. She insisted on staying at Sunley Manor." Ben gave Tim a firm clasp on the shoulder. "Go get some air. Just do not fall overboard."

Tim thought that a great joke. Both brothers chuckled. Alexia did not think it was humorous at all.

Once they were alone, she spoke her mind. "Hayden said you would leave. Your sisters will have no protection if you do. No hope."

"They will not starve. Hayden will never allow that."

"They think he is the cause of their fall and will permit no help from him. At least give me the money you promised, so they are not destitute."

A little chagrined, he retrieved a fat stack of notes from a valise. "This is five thousand. They will also have use of the land and house in Oxford. It will be better than if Tim stayed, because his debts will flee with him."

She took the notes. It appeared Ben had not hidden so much after all. She began trying to stuff it all into her reticule.

"Alexia."

Ben's tone made her look up. He stood very near to her. He gazed at her warmly. He looked like the Ben of her memories, the happy, lighthearted young man who made her laugh.

"Alexia, I am not sorry that Lucy is staying behind. That was a mistake. She was a mistake. I wish I could go back in time and could follow my heart the way I wanted. I should have married you before I left for Greece and asked you to meet me after I was safe and free."

"Why didn't you?"

"This all began before my feelings for you became romantic. My course was set long before we first kissed."

"I hope to one day understand all that, Ben. The course I know of is not such a complicated one, but there is evidence that much more is involved. However, you did not marry me. You married her, and I worry now that you abandon her along with your sisters. Did you remove all the money from the Bristol bank? Do you leave her penniless?"

"Lucinda will never be penniless. She is shrewd and beautiful, and she will be buried dripping with jewels."

In other words, he had taken all the money.

"You are very good at explaining away your responsibilities, Ben. I never realized you had that tendency before, because you accepted me into your home when you did not need to."

"You were never a responsibility. Your company was always a pleasure. I have missed you horribly." He took her hand in both of his. His touch made her sad. "The ship will weigh anchor very soon. Great adventures await. Paris first, but perhaps America. Or sunny, exotic lands. We can make up for the years we lost. It will be great fun, and all the better if you are with me."

Surprise emptied her mind for a long count. Then one rational thought slid back in. *Hayden was right.*

"I am married. So are you."

"No one will know or care about that where we are going. We will be together forever, as we always wanted."

"Hayden will follow and kill you."

"He allowed you to come to the ship today, didn't he? He wants you to choose." He smiled a little smugly. "I saved his life, you see. In Greece. Those scars were the beginning of a terrible end if I had not saved him."

She removed her hand from his. She stepped away while she sorted what he said, hearing too much truth in it. Hayden had allowed her to come here, believing this would happen. He had not even come himself. He had decided not to fight to keep her.

No, that was not true. He had fought for her last night, in the way honor permitted him. He could not draw a sword or pistol on the man to whom he owed his life, but he had waged a little war all the same.

He had laid his pride at her feet to keep her.

Benjamin was right. If she chose to stay on this ship, Hayden would let her go. Not because he did not love her enough to fight for her. Because he loved her too much to imprison her.

"I booked a passage for you," Ben said. "Tim will move to another cabin."

He spoke as if it had been decided. Sounds outside indicated that soon the tide would decide for her if she did not disembark.

She pictured the life Ben described. Traveling and seeing the world. Free and reckless and laughing, laughing. She would never again be bound by calculations and deliberations and responsibilities. She would not have to be the practical Miss Welbourne. She might be a young girl again. Forever.

She looked at Ben. Only a girl could love such a man. No, not a man. A boy.

"I cannot."

"You can. There is no one to stop you."

"I *will* not." She walked to the door.

"Why? Because of his money? His brother's title?"

"No sensible woman can dismiss either of those qualities in a man. Nor could I ever repudiate my vows and duty. However, my reason is not nearly so practical or respectable. I love him, Benjamin. I love him so deeply that what you and I shared was a very shallow emotion in comparison. I would never leave him. I would never give up the chance to spend my life with him."

She opened the door. "Have a good life, Benjamin. Enjoy your adventures. Take care of Timothy, and please write on occasion this time."

They were already cranking up the gangway when she rushed onto the deck. She begged them to lower it again and stepped onto its wobbling planks so they would have to. Keeping her balance distracted her, but amid the noise of the docks she heard the thunder of hooves. As the cranking stopped, a coach clamored to a stop on the wharf. Hayden jumped out.

He strode toward the gangway. He saw her atop it and stopped.

She would never forget the relief she saw in his face then. His lips parted and his eyes blazed. It was the most romantic expression she had ever seen on a man in her life.

He strode up the planks and took her in his arms. Did she imagine that the sailors ceased their labor while he kissed her? Did the entire ship go silent?

He guided her back to solid ground.

The cranking began again. Gangway and anchor lifted. Bound together, they watched the ship slip from its place and the gap of water in front of it grow.

"You were correct," she said. "He asked me to run away with him. He had it all arranged."

His arm tightened around her. "Thank you for choosing to stay."

"It was the only practical and honorable choice, of course."

"Of course."

"Did you decide to come and make sure I understood that?"

"I knew you would see that part of it."

"Then what brought you here at a gallop?"

"I am not sure. Perhaps to beg." He shrugged. "Maybe to kill him."

"Then he is fortunate I was not swayed. How like Ben, to escape the price of his actions yet again." She patted her reticule. "Five thousand, for Rose. There is much more in his bags on that ship, isn't there?"

"A good deal more, I think."

"Hayden, he took that money from his bank, didn't he? He stole it."

She surprised him. He thought before answering. "Since you have guessed the worst, I will not break my word when I explain it all. Their sisters should not be told, however. Trust me, Irene and Rose do not want to know the truth."

Their. Timothy too, then. That was why Hayden came to the house that day. He had discovered Tim's theft.

"You did not have to let them leave," she said. "You could have called a magistrate."

"Yes, I could have done that."

But he hadn't. He had saved Tim's life with his silence, and now he had saved Ben's. He had not destroyed the Longworths. He had risked much to preserve his friend's family.

"When they stole that money, it was from people. Will they suffer?"

"They will all be made whole."

She guessed how. "Is it a lot of money?"

"A good deal of money, yes."

"Even for you?"

"Even for me, especially now that Timothy has run away."

"Then we will be practical for a few years, until you have dealt with it. We can stay on Hill Street, or a similar house, or even a smaller one. We can sell the diamonds if it will help. I love them, of course, but if it would make it easier, it would be better if we did that."

He laid his palm against her cheek. He appeared very serious, and stern in the best way. "The jewels are yours to keep, remember?"

Despite his set jaw, the inner man was so visible that her heart swelled. They stood on a public dock, but they were so close he might have been breathing into her after making love.

"If selling the jewels will help you, I would not mind at all, Hayden. You are more important to me than diamonds. I do not need gifts to know that you value me."

His jaw tightened. His eyes filmed. "There are many reasons I love you, Alexia. I look forward to telling you about each one. I am not accustomed to how you can move me with your honest faith and loyalty." He ran the backs of his fingertips along her jaw. "I do not want to speak of practical things now, however. Today, I only want to love you."

She felt herself blushing. It would take some time to grow accustomed to the frank way he spoke of being in love.

They walked toward his carriage but did not break

their embrace. Passersby raised eyebrows, but she did not care.

Faith and loyalty. They were virtues appropriate to a good wife. He had a right to know that she did not act only out of duty, however.

They stopped at his carriage. She looked out to the horizon and to the ship growing insignificant in the mist on the river.

"I did not stay because it was practical, or even because it was decent and honorable, Hayden. Those were not the reasons I gave Benjamin, nor the ones in my heart."

"Then why did you stay, Alexia?"

"I told him that I was in love with you." Saying the words made her shiver with exhilaration. "And I am in love with you. It was cowardly of me to wait for you to admit it first. I should have known my own heart better. I should have trusted what it said to me."

He embraced her again. He smiled so warmly that her heart flipped. "If you know it now, that is all that matters to me. I do not deserve your love, but I promise to treasure it as the beautiful gift it is."

His gaze held such tenderness that she could not contain the happiness glowing in her heart. Her whole being smiled. A giggle bubbled up and slipped out.

He touched her lips. "What a lovely, girlish, romantic sound."

"A girlish sound and excitement, but not a girlish love. I much prefer loving as a woman. It is much deeper. Much richer. Much more romantic, and I like that too. Different, however. Different enough that I did not know what to call the emotion that moved me so profoundly while I held you in my arms."

"I am relieved you love me, whether it calls forth the girl or the woman," he said. "It is nice to know I will not have to be a romantic fool alone."

She stretched up and kissed him. "Never alone, my love. We will be romantic fools together. Forever."

ABOUT
THE AUTHOR

MADELINE HUNTER's first novel was published in 2000. Since then she has seen thirteen historical romances and one novella published, and her books have been translated into five languages. She is a four-time RITA finalist and won the long historical RITA in 2003. Twelve of her books have been on the *USA Today* bestseller list, and she has also had titles on the *New York Times* extended list. Madeline has a Ph.D. in art history, which she teaches at an eastern university. She currently lives in Pennsylvania with her husband and two sons.

Read on for a sneak peek at

The

LESSONS

of

DESIRE

Coming Fall 2007

THE LESSONS OF DESIRE

On sale Fall 2007

CHAPTER ONE

Phaedra rose from her writing table in response to Signora Cirillo's call. If the woman wanted more money so soon—

A wonderful sight awaited her when she opened the door to her apartment. Signora Cirillo was not alone. Lord Elliot stood beside her.

Phaedra kept her composure even though she wanted to shout for joy. If he was here, it meant only one thing.

"Lord Elliot, please enter. *Grazie,* signora."

Signora Cirillo raised her eyebrows over her dark cat eyes at this dismissal. Phaedra shooed her away.

"You bring good news I hope, Lord Elliot," Phaedra said when they were alone.

"Your house arrest is over, Miss Blair. We have Captain Cornell of the Euryalus to thank. He spoke with Sansoni on our behalf."

"Thank God for the British navy." She ran to the window and threw open the shutters. The guard outside was gone. "I must take a turn along the bay this evening. I cannot believe—" She skipped back to Lord Elliot and embraced him. "I am so grateful to you."

He smiled kindly when she released him. He seemed to understand her excitement and forgive her exuberance. If his gaze had warmed just a little from her impulsive embrace, well, he was a man after all.

He appeared quite magnificent right now in his perfectly tailored, brown frock coat and high boots. His smile did much to soften the severity of the Rothwell face. Unlike his older brothers, Lord Elliot was reputed to smile often, and it appeared that was true.

He looked around her sitting room. His gaze lit upon her writing desk. "I have interrupted your letter, I fear."

"An interruption I most welcomed. I was writing to Alexia, and pouring out my story of woe, on the chance I could at least throw my letter down to you when you returned here."

"Why not complete the letter at once, and let her know all is well? I will take it to Cornell. He sails in two days for England, and will post it to London when he docks."

"What a splendid idea, if you will not think me rude to jot a few more lines."

"Not at all, Miss Blair. Not at all."

She sat down and quickly added a paragraph telling Alexia that all had been resolved happily, thanks to Alexia's new brother-in-law, Lord Elliot. She folded, addressed, and sealed the paper, and stood with it in her hand. Lord Elliot walked over and gently plucked it from her fingers. He tucked it into his frock coat, to bring to Captain Cornell.

He resumed his perusal of the sitting room and its views. "You came to the door yourself, Miss Blair. Where is your abigail?"

"I have no abigail, Lord Elliot. No servants. Not even in London."

"Is that due to another philosophical belief?"

"Rather it is a practical decision. An uncle left me a modest income, and I would rather spend it in other ways."

"How sensible. However, your lack of a servant is inconvenient."

"Not at all." She turned on her toes and the drapes of her black gauze garment and long hair fanned out. "A dress like this does not require a maid to truss me and my hair requires only a brush."

"I was not speaking of your dressing. I need to speak with you about this development, and with no maid in this apartment . . ."

He worried for her reputation should she be with a man alone. How charming.

"Lord Elliot, it is impossible for you to compromise me because I am above such stupid social rules. Besides, this is a business meeting of sorts, is it not? Our privacy is not only allowed in such situations, but also necessary." She doubted he would accept her reasoning, logical though it was. Men like him never did.

To her amazement, he capitulated immediately. "You are correct. Therefore we shall proceed. Will you not sit? This could take some time."

He appeared very serious all of a sudden. Serious and stern and . . . hard. His gesture toward the divan carried more command than his polite request implied. The temptation to remain standing nipped at her. She sat, but only because he had just procured her freedom.

He settled into a chair that faced her. He gave her a good look, as if sizing her up. He might have never seen her before and now tried to interpret the peculiar image she presented.

She could not shake the sense that, in a manner of

speaking, she had never seen him before either. There was none of his quiet amusement now, just a long, examining, invasive gaze that made her uneasy. A very feminine response rumbled deeply in her essence.

That was the damndest thing about handsome men. Their beauty left one at a disadvantage when they directed attention at you. This man was very handsome. He was also very masculine in most ways, and subtly so in the worst ones. Right now he seemed to be deliberately trying to unsettle her. He did not do it for carnal reasons, she was sure. Yet his aura projected that lure too, and her blood reacted to it.

Protecting, possessing, conquering— They were all facets of the same primitive instinct, weren't they? A man could not follow one inclination without arousing the others in himself, and a woman was easily vanquished if she did not take care. She wondered which ancient part of the male character motivated him now.

"Alexia did ask me to look in on you, Miss Blair. That was no lie. However, I had other reasons to seek you out and they must now be addressed."

"Since we only met once, at Alexia's wedding, and very briefly, I cannot imagine what your reasons might be."

"I think that you can."

Now he was annoying her. "I assure you I cannot."

His tone indicated that he found her annoying in turn. "Miss Blair, it has come to my attention that you are now a partner in Merris Langton's publishing house. That you inherited your father's interest in the business."

"That information has not been given out, Lord Elliot. With men assuming a woman cannot succeed in business, and with many believing it unnatural for a woman to even try, I chose to keep that quiet so prejudice would not affect the business itself."

"Do you intend to be active in it?"

"I will have a hand in choosing the titles published, but I expect Mr. Langton will continue to oversee the practical matters." Not that this was any of Lord Elliot's concern. "I would like to know who informed you of this. If my solicitor has been indiscreet—"

"Your solicitor is blameless." His attention left her for a spell, and his eyes assumed a brooding darkness. She had seen that in the past, ever so fleetingly. It hinted at the brilliant mind inside this elegant man about town, and the intellectual absorption that had led him to pen a celebrated historical tome before he turned twenty-three.

"Miss Blair, I regret that I bring you some bad news. Merris Langton passed away from his illness after you left London. He was buried a few days before I sailed myself."

She had feared Mr. Langton would not recover, but hearing of his death was surprising anyway. "That is bad news indeed, Lord Elliot. I thank you for informing me. I did not know him well, but a man's passing is always sad. I had counted on him helping me maintain that publishing house, but it appears I will be left to do it on my own."

"Is it all yours now?"

"My father founded the press and subsidized it all along. His share was his to bequeath, but Mr. Langton's became my father's if Mr. Langton died. So, yes, I do believe it is all mine now."

His distraction disappeared. The sternness returned. Coldly. "Prior to Langton's illness, he approached my brother. He spoke of your father's memoirs being published. He offered to omit several paragraphs in the manuscript that touched on my family, if a significant sum was paid to him."

"He did? That is terrible! I am shocked by this betrayal of my father's principles, and sincerely apologize for my partner."

She rose and began pacing, agitated by this dreadful revelation. Lord Elliot politely stood too, but she ignored him while she tried to take in the implications of Mr. Langton's foolish scheme. This might be all it took to bring that shaky press down.

She knew too well its precarious finances, and as a partner she was responsible for the unpaid debts. She had counted on her father's memoirs to pull them through, but if Mr. Langton had compromised the integrity of that publication, the world might dismiss the book entirely.

"This is all Harriette Wilson's fault," she said, her dismay edging into anger. "She set a disgraceful precedent in asking her lovers to pay to have their names removed from her book. I wrote and told her so, mind you. Harriette, I wrote, it is unethical to take money to expunge memoirs. It is just a pretty form of blackmail. She only thought of her empty purse, of course. Well, that is the result of the dependent life she chose and the foolish extravagance that she practiced." She strode more purposefully. "Mr. Langton no doubt approached others too. I cannot believe he would impugn the ethics of our publishing house in this way."

"Miss Blair, please spare me the theatrical outrage. My family was prepared to pay Langton. I sought you out to say that we will now gladly pay you instead."

Theatrical outrage? She paused her pacing and faced him squarely. "Lord Elliot, I hope that I misunderstand you. Are you suggesting that I would accept this money to edit the memoirs to your liking?"

"It is our hope that you will."

She advanced on him until she was close enough to see the thoughts reflected in his eyes. "Good heavens, you think that I knew Mr. Langton was doing this, don't you? You believe I was an accomplice to it."

He did not respond. He just looked back, visibly skeptical of her astonishment.

Furious about his assumptions, affronted by the insult, she turned away. "Lord Elliot, my father's memoirs are going to be published as soon as I return to England. Every sentence of them. It was his last wish, sent to me directly, and I would never pick and choose which of his words the world should read. I am sincerely grateful for your aid with Mr. Sansoni, but it would be best if we ended this conversation. If I had a servant I would have you shown out. As it is, you will have to find your own way."

To make her dismissal of him complete, she strode to her bedchamber and closed the door.

She had not collected herself before the door to her bedchamber reopened. Lord Elliot calmly followed her in and closed it behind him.

"My visit is not over, and our business is not completed, Miss Blair."

"How dare— This is my *bedchamber,* sir."

He crossed his arms and assumed that irritating, masculine pose of command. "Normally that might check me, but you are above stupid social rules, like the one that says I should not intrude here. Remember?"

She did not consider that particular social rule so stupid. It existed for a very good reason. A primitive one. This was her most private space, her sanctuary. She undressed and bathed and slept here. Every object symbolized activities that only a husband or lover should see.

The air began altering while he glanced at the wardrobe where her garments were stored and the dressing table that held her private items. His gaze swept over the bed slowly, then returned to her.

His thoughts were not as masked as he thought. She noted the subtle changes in his expression, the way the hardness he wore rearranged itself ever so slightly. A man could not be near a bed with a woman and not start wondering. It was just a curse of nature that they bore.

It irritated her that she wondered too. The manner in which he had just insulted her should provide the best armor against the intimacy threading through this chamber. The air grew heavy and full of a magnetic excitement that stirred her.

An image blinked in her mind, of Lord Elliot looking down at her, his face mere inches from hers, his dark hair mussed by reasons besides fashion and his desire completely unmasked. She saw his naked shoulders and felt the pressure of his body and the firm hold of his embrace on her skin. She felt . . .

She forced the image from her head, but acknowledgment flashed in his eyes. He knew her mind had wandered there, just as she knew his had.

He unfolded his arms, and she thought he might reach for her. She wondered if he would insult her further now by giving voice to what they were feeling. There were men who misunderstood her life and beliefs and proposed things in ignorance, but Lord Elliot was not stupid. If he attempted to act on the sensual awareness whispering between them, it would be deliberately and cruelly offensive.

He turned his attention from her, diluting the intimacy but not completely vanquishing it. Her pride was spared but her sexuality simmered with discontentment.

"Is the manuscript here?" he asked. "Did you bring it with you?"

"Of course not. Why would I do that?"

He eyed the wardrobe. "Do you swear? If not I will have to search for it."

"I swear, and don't you dare search. You have no right to be here at all."

"Actually, I do, but we will discuss that later."

What was that supposed to mean? "I left it in London, in a very secure place. It contains my father's memoirs, his last words. I would never be careless with it."

"Have you read it?"

"Of course."

"Then you know what he wrote about my family. I want you to tell me about that now. His exact words, as well as you can remember."

He was not requesting to know, but demanding. His dominating high-handedness was making her gratitude for his help dim fast.

"Lord Elliot, your family's name, and that of Easterbrook, is never mentioned in that manuscript."

That surprised him for an instant. His sternness cracked long enough for her to glimpse the amiable, helpful man who had first entered her apartment. It did not last. The brooding distraction took over and the sharp mind assessed what she had said.

"Miss Blair, Merris Langton approached my brother and described a specific accusation against my father. Is there anything in that manuscript that in your opinion could be interpreted as relating to my parents?"

She wished he had not phrased his question quite that way. She debated her answer. "There is one part that might be so interpreted, I suppose."

"Please describe it."

"I would rather not."

"I insist. You will tell me now."

His voice, his stance, and his expression said he would brook no argument. She had never before in her life been so pointedly ordered to do something by a man.

Perhaps it would be best if he and his family were warned, and could prepare for the scandal. The passage they discussed had been one of several in the memoirs to give her pause.

"My father describes a private dinner party several years before my mother died. They entertained a young diplomat just back from the Cape Colony. My father wanted to learn the true conditions there. This young man drank rather freely and turned morose. While in his cups he confided something regarding an event in a British regiment in the Cape."

The mention of the Cape Colony had garnered his attention too well. She inwardly grimaced. She had always hoped that rumor was untrue, but—

"Go on, Miss Blair."

"He said that while he was there, a British officer died. It was reported as from a fever, but in fact he had been shot. He was found dead after going out on patrol. There were suspicions regarding another officer who had accompanied him, but no evidence. Rather than impugn that other officer, a false cause of death was reported."

He masked his reaction very well now. She looked upon a face carved of stone. His silence turned terrible, quaking with the anger leaking out of him.

"Miss Blair, if you associated that man's story with my family, you must know the rumor about my father, and how he is said to have used his influence to have my mother's lover posted to the Cape Colony. A place where that lover died of fever."

She swallowed hard. "I may have heard something to that effect once."

"If you did, many did. Neither Langton nor you had any difficulty adding up the references and drawing a conclusion. If you publish that section, the insinuation will stand that my father paid another officer to kill my mother's lover. The lack of names in your father's memoirs will not spare my father's reputation, and he cannot defend himself from the grave."

"I am not convinced—"

"Damn it, that is exactly what will happen and you know it. I demand that you remove that portion of the memoirs."

"Lord Elliot, I am sympathetic to your distress. Truly, I am. However, my father charged me with seeing his memoirs published and it is my duty to do so. I have thought long and hard about this. If I remove every sentence that might be construed as dangerous or unflattering to this person or that, there will be little left."

He strode to her and looked down hard. "You will not publish this lie."

His determination was palpable. He did not require expressions of anger or verbal threats to emphasize the power he would use against her. It was just there, surrounding her, tinged by the sexual awareness that had never left this chamber, creating a mood that held all the edges of that dark instinct.

"If it is a lie, I will consider omitting it," she said. "If you can obtain proof that man died of fever, or if my parents' guest recants, in this one case I will do it. For Alexia, however, not for you or Easterbrook."

That checked him. "For Alexia? How convenient for you. Now you can retreat without giving me a victory."

He understood her rather too well. She did not care for the evidence of that.

He looked down much more kindly. Their closeness, born of his fury, became inappropriate suddenly. As his anger ebbed that other tension flowed again.

He did not retreat the way he should. The way her raised eyebrows demanded. Instead he lifted a strand of her red hair and looked at it while he gently wove it between his fingers.

"Did your father include the name of either of these men, Miss Blair? The young diplomat at the dinner party or the officer who was suspected?"

He was not touching her as such, but his toying with her hair claimed a familiarity that she should not allow. Their isolation in this bedchamber, even their confrontation, had demolished all protective formalities. The subtle tingling he created on her scalp was delicious, cajoling her to contemplate other physical excitements.

Conquering, possessing, protecting— She did not doubt that he was prepared to be ruthless and toy with more than hair if necessary. Nor was she confident she could defeat the challenge should it come.

"The young diplomat they invited to dinner was named Jonathan Merriweather."

He looked in her eyes, suspicious again. "I know of him. Merriweather is now an assistant to the British envoy here in Naples."

"Is he? How convenient for you. I had no idea."

"Didn't you?" His hand wound in her hair more firmly. The subtle play became controlling. "Did you journey here to speak to him, Miss Blair? Is that why you are in Naples? Do you intend to annotate those memoirs and fill in the names and facts that your father discreetly omitted? The book will sell all the better then and I daresay your press could use the income."

She purposefully took hold of the hair he held and pried off his fingers. Her indignation helped her ignore the sensation of his warm hand beneath hers, and the way his eyes reflected his awareness of her touch.

"I expect my father's memoirs to be popular without annotations, but I thank you for the suggestion. I am not here for that purpose, however."

That was a bald lie, but she felt no compunction about misleading this man. Her own interest in filling in the memoirs' gaps did not bear on his family. Her investigations concerned other portions, the ones that spoke of her mother.

"I am a mere tourist here, Lord Elliot. I have come to visit the excavations and ruins to the south. I need to prepare to leave this city at once and continue my journey as I originally planned. Therefore, I must ask you, once more, to leave."

He did not move immediately. Perhaps he believed that doing so would amount to giving quarter in whatever battle he thought they fought.

"Your tour will have to be delayed a few days more," he said. "I cannot allow you to go just yet."

She laughed. The man's presumptions had become ridiculous. "What you would allow is not of interest to me, sir."

"It is of essential interest to you. I warned that freeing you might entail conditions, and you promised to accommodate them."

She frowned. "You said nothing about conditions when you arrived."

"Your warm embrace distracted me."

She peered up at him distrustfully. "What are these conditions?"

He slowly looked down her flowing locks, which meant he looked down most of her body. She thought she detected a possessive interest, as if he had just received a gift and judged its value.

"Gentile Sansoni would only release you if you entered my custody," he said. "I had to accept total responsibility for you and promise to regulate your behavior."

Hot anger flared in her head. No wonder Lord Elliot was preening with arrogance and command all of a sudden today. "That is intolerable. I have never answered to a man. To do so would make my mother turn in her grave. I refuse to agree to this."

"Would you prefer to take your chances with Sansoni? It can be arranged."

The threat left her speechless.

Lord Elliot did not exactly laugh as he strode to the door, but he did not hide his amusement at her dilemma either.

"We will journey on to Pompeii together, Miss Blair, after I speak with Merriweather. Until then, you are not to leave these chambers without my escort. Oh, and there will be no Marsilios or Pietros visiting you either. I'll be damned if you will provoke more duels while you are under my authority. I swore an oath to control you, and I expect your cooperation and obedience."

Authority? Control? *Obedience?* She was so stunned that he was gone before she found the voice to curse him.